Praise for INHUMAN:

"Sexy, suspenseful, and utterly original, *Inhuman* is riveting from first to last page. This taut, unforgettable adventure is storytelling of the best sort, stealing your breath with its thrills and wonders and leaving you desperate for more." — Andrea Cremer, *New York Times* bestselling author of the Nightshade series

★ "Falls' first novel for teens is the nail-biting start of a new trilogy. . . . Readers will find themselves drawn into Lane's story through the author's consistent worldbuilding and striking turns of phrase. Lane is an appealing and credible protagonist." — *Kirkus Reviews*, starred review

"A quick favorite for any *Hunger Games* fan. In this realistic, futuristic, banished landscape, you'll fall in love with the characters and the plot." — *Romantic Times*

"The setting holds great promise, and its dangers are quite entertaining: from the dreaded chimpacabra and piranha-bats to people infected by lion, tiger, or fox DNA, there's lovely and bizarre imagery involved. A solid start." — *Publishers Weekly*

"The animal hybrids are sometimes intriguing and sometimes terrifying (like the half-bat half-piranha weevlings) but are always compelling. . . . This is a perfectly plotted, deliciously suspenseful journey through a lush, intriguing society in which nothing is quite as it seems." — *School Library Journal*

"Reminiscent of H.G. Wells's *The Island of Dr. Moreau* with a hint of Michael Crichton's *Jurassic Park*. The inhuman world that author Falls has shaped is both disturbing and fascinating. . . . This is recommended for readers looking for a thrilling, page-turning read." — *Voice of Youth Advocates*

Also by Kat Falls
UNDAUNTED
DARK LIFE
RIP TIDE

INHUMAN

KAT FALLS

SCHOLASTIC INC.

For my pride: Declan,
Vivienne, Connor, and Bob

Copyright © 2013 by Kat Falls

This book was originally published in hardcover by Scholastic Press in 2013.

All rights reserved. Published by Scholastic Inc., *Publishers since 1920.* SCHOLASTIC and associated logos are trademarks and/or registered trademarks of Scholastic Inc.

The publisher does not have any control over and does not assume any responsibility for author or third-party websites or their content.

No part of this publication may be reproduced, stored in a retrieval system, or transmitted in any form or by any means, electronic, mechanical, photocopying, recording, or otherwise, without written permission of the publisher. For information regarding permission, write to Scholastic Inc., Attention: Permissions Department, 557 Broadway, New York, NY 10012.

This book is a work of fiction. Names, characters, places, and incidents are either the product of the author's imagination or are used fictitiously, and any resemblance to actual persons, living or dead, business establishments, events, or locales is entirely coincidental.

ISBN 978-0-545-37101-8

12 11 10 9 8 7 6 5 4 3 2 1   15 16 17 18 19 20/0

Printed in the U.S.A.   40
First printing 2015

The text type was set in Sabon.
Book design by Christopher Stengel

· ONE ·

Now that I was actually on the roof of the skyscraper, I was having second thoughts. Maybe it was the spotlights sweeping the streets below, or the patrol planes flying in pairs along the top of the Titan wall, or maybe it was just my good sense reasserting itself. What we were about to do was not only stupid and dangerous, but also illegal, and in my sixteen years of life I'd made a point of avoiding activities that could be described with even one of those adjectives.

I paused halfway across the roof, letting the boys hurry ahead. "I'm suffocating." I tugged at the scrap of white vinyl — supposedly a vest, more like a corset — that I'd somehow let Anna talk me into wearing tonight. Without a shirt.

"Don't be such a slave to comfort." Anna pulled my hands away from the vest and gave me the once-over. Her short curls bobbed with her nod of approval. "Funny how a tight top can loosen a girl right up."

"I'm not sure loose is a good thing at thirty stories up." *Or ever, for that matter,* I thought.

"Now remember, I want it back, so don't go wild." Her dark eyes narrowed as she took in the rooftop gardens around us. "And no rolling in the dirt."

"Ew."

"Not even if Orlando asks nicely."

"Ew again. I told you: I am not into Orlando." Curiosity had propelled me up here, not the desire to roll around with either of the guys we'd come with — guys who were now fighting over the remote control for a toy hovercopter.

"It's my 'copter." Camden clutched the toy while warding Orlando off with an elbow.

"My roof." Orlando latched on to Camden's wrist. Anyone hearing them would think they were first graders, not seniors.

Music and laughter floated up from the penthouse below, and I wondered what part of tonight would upset Orlando's parents the most. That their son was having a party while they were out of town, or that he was on top of their building compromising national security? Probably the latter, though having so many people in their apartment — touching things, spreading germs — that would send a chill down any parent's spine.

Suddenly the boys' tussling sent them lurching toward the roof's edge. I gasped and Anna clapped her hand to her mouth. Just as fast, they reversed direction, still grunting and scuffling, completely oblivious to how close they'd come to falling. I exhaled slowly. As much as I loved animals — even the strays — I hated it when boys acted like animals. Out of control. Vying for dominace. Ugh.

"If you're not into Orlando, why are we up here?" Anna demanded.

"You know why." I swept a hand toward the wall that loomed like a mountain range, even though it was just across the street. "The Feral Zone."

She rolled her eyes.

"Yes!" Orlando wrested the remote control from Camden's grip and lifted his arm in triumph. "Let's get this baby in the air."

I split my long ponytail into two sections and yanked them apart, forcing the rubber band tight against my scalp. The tighter my hair was pulled back, the better my brain worked. Anna reluctantly followed me over to the roof's edge. I'd never been so close to the top of the Titan before and the sheer enormity of it loosened a flutter in my chest. The reparation wall, the quarantine line, the blight — all the names for the wall, even the bitter ones, were said with awe. Because the Titan wasn't just any wall. At seven hundred feet tall, it towered over downtown Davenport and stretched to infinity in either direction. The guards stationed along the top all had their guns and telescopes pointed east, toward the half of America that was lost to us — now known as the Feral Zone.

That's what really carbonated my blood: the thought that via toy hovercopter, I might finally get to see what was over there. When the wall went up eighteen years ago, that part of the country became as mysterious to us as Africa was to the rest of the world in the nineteenth century. The Feral Zone was our Dark Continent.

Anna, however, seemed immune to the zone's allure. She took one look at the gun turrets and scooted back, her dark skin ashen. "This is a very bad, very stupid idea."

"Worst-case scenario, I'm out a camera," I said lightly.

"Really?" She propped her fists on her hips. " 'Cause I'd say the worst-case scenario is we all get shot for crossing the quarantine line."

"We're not crossing. That is." Orlando pointed at the toy hovercopter in Camden's hands. "And it can't catch a virus. So technically, we're not breaking quarantine." His blond hair was as rumpled as his shirt. At least he wasn't in his bathrobe, which was what he usually wore during our virtual classes even though we were supposed to log on every morning at eight, fully dressed.

Camden tipped the mini hovercopter to check the camera that I'd attached to the underside. He gave a nod. "Let's do this before it gets too dark to see anything."

We probably wouldn't see anything anyway. The toy hovercopter had to fly over the wall and across the Mississippi River before it officially reached the Feral Zone. But I would be happy even with a distant shot — one that I could enlarge later.

I lifted my dial, which hung on a delicate chain around my neck. We all wore them. For our parents, the glowing discs were more than just phones. Our dials were their spy cameras. With a push of a button, a dad could see what his daughter was doing (and with whom) through her dial's screen, even if she didn't "take" the call — like that was ever an option.

With a tap, I activated the link between my dial and the camera. A second later, Camden's feet popped up on the dial's round screen. I pointed at him. "Action."

Camden lifted the hovercopter over his head. "Let 'er rip."

Orlando flicked a button on the remote, the rotor blades started whirling and the toy lifted out of Camden's hands.

The boys whooped and punched the air. Anna met my gaze with an arched brow.

I smiled. "Come on, you know you want to see what's over there."

"I know what's over there." She plucked a bottle of hand sanitizer from the back pocket of my jeans. "Rubble and disease."

"And mutants," Camden added without taking his eyes from the little hovercopter zooming toward the wall.

"There are no mutants." Anna squeezed a glob of gel into her palm. "Everyone over there is dead."

Orlando thumbed the remote, putting the hovercopter into a steeper trajectory. "If everyone's dead, why do we have guards patrolling the wall night and day?"

I looked up from my dial. "To keep the chimpacabras out."

"Don't even bring that crap up." Anna chucked the bottle of sanitizer back to me. "Because of you, I still sleep with the light on."

"Then maybe you shouldn't have begged me to tell you about them every time we had a sleepover," I said with a laugh.

Camden glanced over. "What's a chimpacabra?"

"Nothing. A monster my dad made up." Back when I'd believed his stories. Well, half believed. He'd started telling me fairy tales about a brave little girl and her adventures in the Feral Zone when I was eight, right after my mom died. She used to sing to me before bed. Stories were Dad's way of filling in the silence.

"A chimpacabra is a mole-monkey thing that has poison spit and lives underground over there." Anna pointed beyond the wall with a shudder. "It creeps out at night to steal kids from their beds. One bite and you're paralyzed and you can't even scream while it eats you alive."

I tore my gaze from my dial to stare at my best friend. "Um, Annapolis, chimpacabras aren't real. My dad made them up. Well . . ." I couldn't resist. "I mean, I think he did."

Anna circled a hand in front of her face. "See me not laughing."

At least Camden laughed.

"Here we go," Orlando crowed as the toy hovercopter sailed over the top of the Titan. "Fifty feet across and we're —" Loud popping cut off his words.

My dial cut to black and I looked toward the wall. "What happened?"

Along the far side of the ramparts, gun turrets swiveled toward the West, all taking aim at the sputtering hovercopter.

"Get down!" Camden dropped into a crouch as more shots rang out. Anna and I hunkered next to him, but Orlando took off for the door to the stairwell.

"It's okay," I whispered. "There's no way for them to know where the 'copter came from." Just then a spotlight swooped across the roof of the next building, scouring the shadows as it arced toward us. "Oh, crap. Run!"

Anna and I bolted with Camden at our heels. We dove through the door to the stairwell. Two minutes later, we slipped into the zoo that was Orlando's living room, acting like we'd been there all along.

Anna and Camden collapsed on the couch laughing. I couldn't — not with my heart still lodged in my throat. The loud music and press of bodies weren't helping. There had to be at least twenty-five kids inside the apartment, all face to face and breathing on each other. Some were even kissing. No, not just kissing. Old-fashioned kissing. Actually swapping spit. I couldn't dig out my hand sanitizer fast enough. Had they slept through every health class we'd ever taken, starting in kindergarten?

A pack of guys charged past me howling like wolves, carrying a laughing girl. "Not on the couch," Orlando shouted just as they tumbled the girl onto it, shoes and all.

Between the noise and Anna's vest doubling as a tourniquet, I couldn't even breathe my way into a zen state. I reached for the top snap, and then noticed Orlando watching me. We'd spent a lot of time online this week, planning our failed venture, but he'd thrown in a couple of cheesy compliments too. Now that we were together for real, I didn't want him getting the wrong idea. I left the vest snapped and plucked up my dial. With a touch, I deleted the brief recording of the wall — aka incriminating evidence — and then hit record and made a show of filming the party.

I wound my way through the crowd and onto the balcony to see what was happening on the wall. Nothing much. The guards were back in position. They must have found the broken toy and decided it wasn't worth investigating further. At least, I hoped that's what they'd decided.

For once I was grateful for the bars that enclosed high-rise balconies. Usually they made me feel like a caged bird, but tonight that cage was helping to keep me from the guards' view. Our parents liked to call the bars *trellises* and said that they'd been installed to support climbing vines. Who were they kidding? We knew the cages were yet another safety measure. Were kids really falling off balconies right and left before the plague? Doubtful. But there was no reasoning with a nation of trauma survivors.

"Sorry about your camera." Orlando joined me by the finely wrought bars.

"That's okay. It was an old one. I figured it —"

He angled in for a kiss, his mouth on mine before I could think to sidestep him. Now, with the bars at my back and him leaning into me, it was too late. No matter how gently I pushed him off or squirmed away, it would end up awkward and awful. I didn't want to hurt his feelings; I just didn't want him exhaling on my cheek or — suddenly his kiss turned wet as he tried to push his tongue into my mouth.

I wrenched my face aside, ducked under his arm, and stepped free.

"What's wrong?" he asked, sounding more confused than hurt.

I dragged a hand across my lips before facing him. "Sorry," I said, trying for a light tone. "Reality overload."

Orlando's brows drew together, creasing his pale skin. "But all week you —" A siren cut off his words. We stared wide-eyed at each other for a second and then whirled to peer through the balcony cage.

Anna skidded out of the apartment. "Are the line guards coming for us?"

"No way," Orlando said, though his voice quavered.

The siren screamed closer and then cut off abruptly. The flashing lights lit up the street below. They were not atop a fire truck or police car but a gray van, which meant only one thing. . . .

Orlando slumped against the bars in relief. "It's a biohaz wagon."

Six biohazard agents in white jumpsuits burst out of the van and pushed through the building's gate. Biohaz agents spent their time rounding up serious threats to public health, like contaminated meat and quarantine breakers. They wouldn't waste their time on a toy hovercopter. The line guards might; the jumpsuits, not a chance.

After a sidelong glance at me, Orlando clearly decided not to pick up the conversation where we'd left off. "Call me if they haul someone out," he said as he headed back into the apartment. "Their faces crack me up. They never see it coming."

Anna threw her hands up. "Well, there goes my night." At my blank look, she added, "My *parents*."

Right. Like the rest of the exodus generation, Anna's parents were massively overprotective. My dad was paranoid too, but he traveled a lot for work, so he couldn't keep me under constant surveillance. Instead, he signed me up for survival skills classes. As if knowing how to make a basket out of bark would keep me alive if there was another outbreak.

"The jumpsuits are probably after a fetch," I said, feeling a twitch of excitement. Almost no one fetched stuff anymore, even though plenty of people would pay top dollar to have a beloved item retrieved from the East. But these days you had to be desperate or demented to risk sneaking across the quarantine line. "Biohaz agents hunt down felons. Nobody you would have come in contact with."

"Are you using logic?" Anna demanded.

"Oh, right." I smiled. "Silly me."

She glared at the people gathering on the sidewalk. Many had taken out their dials to report the big event to friends or record the poor quarantine breaker's walk of shame.

"I may as well leave now," she grouched. "This is going to hit the Web before the jumpsuits even get the guy in the van."

And once his face got plastered across the news outlets, anyone who'd ever crossed his path would storm into an ER and demand a blood test. "I'll go too," I told her. "I need to get home and feed the gang."

She gave me a faint smile. "Your pets can go an hour without you. Stay. One of us should get to live a little."

A voice from inside the living room shouted, "Turn down the music! Someone's banging on the door."

They sure were. So loudly we could hear it out on the balcony. The music shut off abruptly.

"Hey, who said —" Orlando's shout was obliterated by the bang of the door opening, followed by a girl's scream.

"Don't move!" ordered a male voice.

Anna and I exchanged an alarmed look and rushed into the living room.

"I said, nobody move!" Agents in paper-thin jumpsuits and disposable face masks fanned out across the room. Only their eyes were visible. Not that we needed to see more to know that they meant business.

When Anna slipped an arm through mine, I shot her a sympathetic look. Knowing her parents, they weren't going to let her out of their apartment for the next year after this.

"It was just a toy hovercopter," Orlando said weakly. "We didn't —"

A jumpsuit stopped in front of him. "Is this your home?"

Orlando's nod was barely perceptible.

"We're here to collect Delaney Park McEvoy," the jumpsuit said. "Point her out."

My vision blurred into a single white smear at the end of a long tunnel. Delaney Park McEvoy — me. They'd come for *me*. But why? I'd never been anywhere. Biohaz squads rounded up line crossers and criminals, not a homebody who spent her Saturday nights editing shorts about the local animal shelter.

Anna's hold on my arm tightened like a blood pressure cuff. "That can't be right."

The squeeze should have jerked me into the moment but somehow I'd floated up to the ceiling. At least, that's how it felt — like I had an overhead view of everyone's reaction, could see them all backing away from me.

The jumpsuit pivoted to Anna. "Are you Delaney McEvoy?"

"No. Annapolis Brown."

"But you know her."

The threat of having to be identified snapped me back into my body. "Me." It came out as a croak. Swallowing, I tried again. "I'm Delaney." The jumpsuit slid his focus on to me, assessing. Was I going to be a problem? "Get your things." He ordered me forward with a curl of his gloved hand.

"Wait!" Anna cried. "You can't just haul her off without a reason."

Sensing trouble, the other agents closed in. "We have a reason," the main jumpsuit replied in a voice devoid of feeling. "Potential exposure."

I gasped. "To what?"

Why had I bothered to ask? Only one disease brought the jumpsuits out of their dungeon. Now I watched the man's mask move as his lips shaped the answer that I didn't really need.

"The Ferae Naturae virus."

Ferae Naturae: "of a wild nature." Supposedly it was a fitting name for the virus that had killed 40 percent of America's population, though some people said that it also described how Ferae affected the uninfected. Their natures turned quite wild when confronted with the virus's existence. Like now, I realized, seeing the growing anger in my classmates' expressions. I had just ruined their senior year of high school. Even if my blood test came back clean, there would be no more in-person get-togethers where a laugh could spray microscopic dots of saliva into someone else's eyes. The only contact they'd be allowed to have would be through their computer screens. We weren't alive nineteen years ago when the epidemic decimated the eastern half of the country, but we'd all grown up with the gruesome photos and footage — images that had to be flooding their minds now.

Backing off, Orlando swiped his arm across his mouth. "Crap, I kissed you!"

Yeah, suddenly they all seemed of a wild nature. So I didn't resist when the jumpsuit ushered me toward the door. I would much rather be poked and prodded in a quarantine center than ripped into bloody chunks by my classmates.

Anna took up my free hand, which surprised me. For all she knew, I could be contagious. "What are you doing?"

"Coming with you," she announced, her expression defiant.

The jumpsuit stopped short. "You're not. She's wanted for questioning and you're staying here." He faced the room. "You are all under house quarantine. No one comes or goes, except medical personnel."

Anna's grip on my hand tightened. I stared at our entwined fingers and swallowed against the rising ache in my throat.

Orlando shoved through the crowd. "How long are you going to keep us here?"

"Until you've all been tested and the results are in," the jumpsuit said in a flat tone. "Only a clear negative gets you out of here."

Swearing under his breath, Orlando snatched a bottle of vodka from his parents' liquor cabinet and took a gulp, but didn't swallow. Instead, he threw back his head and gargled the alcohol.

"Let go of her," the jumpsuit told Anna. "Now."

Reluctantly she released my hand.

Maybe Anna couldn't come with me, but she'd tried to. I wanted to wrap my arms around her and cry and thank her for being such a loyal friend. Actually, she'd gone beyond friendship — I should know.

Orlando angled closer, glaring at me. He gave the vodka in his mouth a last loud swish and then spat it on the floor, within an inch of my foot.

When we exited the elevator into the marble and glass lobby, the jumpsuit clamped a gloved hand onto my arm, as if I was going to try to make a break for it. The doorman practically dove out of the way as the biohaz agents propelled me through the glass door and onto the sidewalk. So many glowering faces. My stomach coiled in on itself. As soon as I was within five feet of them, the gawkers skittered back. Then they lifted their dials and my humiliation was complete. My vision blurred as I ducked my head.

A jumpsuit opened the back door of the van and thrust me forward. My knees locked. I couldn't climb inside the van. I didn't know these men.

"Move it," the jumpsuit growled.

I gritted my teeth and did as I was told. Clearly stranger-danger rules didn't apply to government agents.

Much of the van was crammed with high-tech equipment, all clicking and humming. I squeezed onto a metal bench. The agent clambered in, pulled the door closed, and settled on the bench across from me. Through the Plexiglas partition, I saw the other jumpsuit drop into the driver's seat.

"Give me your dial," the man ordered through his mask.

I wanted to use it to call our live-in housekeeper, Howard, and let him know what was happening, but I slipped the chain from around my neck and handed over my dial. The careless way the jumpsuit clicked through my screens made my face burn. Or maybe I was coming down with a fever. . . .

The first symptom of Ferae was a high fever — really high, as in usually lethal. I clenched my hand to keep from pressing my palm across my forehead to check my temperature. I didn't want the jumpsuit to think I was worried about my health. Because I wasn't. I did not have Ferae. I couldn't.

Dogs barked on my dial as the jumpsuit watched one of my shelter clips. "You're a real budding filmmaker, huh, Delaney?" he said after a moment.

Yes, ever since I learned that the fastest way to get people to care about neglected animals was to *show* them the animals. But what did that matter to this guy? "It's Lane."

He glanced up. "What?"

"I go by Lane." Only my dad called me by my full name, Delaney Park. It was where he met my mother — in Delaney Park, Indiana. People his age, they owned sentimental, which was why so many of them had named their kids after beloved places — places they knew they would never see again.

The jumpsuit set my dial aside. "Okay, *Lane*. What do you say we get down to business?" He dragged a metal box from under the bench and opened it on the floor between us. "Put out your arm."

I braced myself against the vehicle's sway. "Why?"

"So we can test your blood back at the lab. Don't you want to know if you've been infected?"

"How could I have gotten infected?"

"Spec sheet didn't say." He tossed a folded paper into my lap. It was a list of attributes and addresses — a summation of me. The addresses belonged to my friends, the animal shelter where I volunteered, two of my favorite coffee shops, and there were several more that I didn't recognize, which was just as well because I was already thoroughly creeped out. The description of me was the final insult: brown eyes, brown hair, average build. Why not just say average every-thing? Instead of smashing the paper into a ball and throwing it at him like I wanted, I handed it back without a word.

"Put out your arm," he repeated.

When I hesitated, he snagged me by the wrist and pulled my arm straight. He took a hypodermic needle from the box on the floor, and suddenly I was seized with the urge to bite his hand and free myself.

But I didn't.

I smothered the impulse; I'd never do something so dis-gusting. So feral. I relaxed my arm and looked away as he inserted the needle.

I figured that I should probably be thankful I wasn't marched into the quarantine center through the front door. Instead, when I was nudged out of the back of the van, I landed in what looked like an empty warehouse except for the stacked cots along the walls. I breathed against the pinch of Anna's vest and tightened my ponytail.

A new jumpsuit awaited us, her face mask firmly in place. A one-woman welcoming committee. Her spiky gray hair didn't move as she strode forward, tablet in hand. I saw my school photo on its screen.

"Delaney McEvoy?" The woman clearly knew she had the right girl, but she waited for my nod before continuing. "I'm Director Taryn Spurling. Head of Biohazard Defense." She turned to the jumpsuit who'd brought me. "Did you get a sample?"

He handed her the vial of my blood and my dial.

"Is someone going to tell my father I'm here?" My voice came out higher than normal.

Above her face mask, Director Spurling's laser-blue gaze sharpened. "You know where he is?"

"Visiting galleries in California. He's an art dealer."

She stiffened. "You're going to have to do better than that, Delaney. A lot better. You see, I've got all the evidence I need. I can issue the order anytime to have your father shot on sight."

Her words punched the air out of my lungs. "For what?"

"You're not going to help him by lying."

"But he *is* an art dealer," I said helplessly.

"Yes, of course." She spoke through a clenched jaw. "That's where the big money is. But my sources tell me that Ian McEvoy will retrieve *anything* if the price is right."

"Retrieve?" Understanding crawled out of the primordial mud of my mind, tiny and grasping. "You mean from the other side of the wall. . . ."

"Now that look almost works. You almost have me believing that you don't know" — Spurling leaned in until her face mask grazed my ear — "that your father is a fetch."

I recoiled. "No. That's not true."

Under that mask, the woman was smirking, I was sure of it. Well, Director Spurling was wrong. Dead wrong. My father was no fetch. He wore bifocals and was lactose intolerant. Him, scale the Titan wall and sneak into the Feral Zone? Not possible. But the word *fetch* had triggered my memory of the last fetch they'd arrested. He'd been executed by a firing squad in front of the Titan. As always, our online classes were cancelled so that we could do the patriotic thing and watch the event in real time. The worst moment wasn't when the bullets flung the man against the wall, as awful as that had been to see. It was earlier, when they'd forced a black hood over his head, making him face death in total darkness — alone. That seemed beyond cruel.

"Put her in a containment room." Director Spurling's thin voice dragged me back into the moment.

"You're keeping me here?" I began to sweat, which plastered the vinyl vest to my skin.

Spurling didn't spare me a glance, just headed for the door, tossing off a last order as she passed the jumpsuit. "Call me if she's still alive in the morning."

· TWO ·

I paced the cold, white box of a room. I'd been stuck in there for just over an hour and already I was losing it. It was too much like a hospital room. Too much like where my mother had spent her last days. But Director Spurling could lock me up for months if she felt like it. The Biohazard Defense Department had the authority to do whatever was deemed necessary to keep the nation safe.

What did it matter if they kept me in quarantine forever? I flopped onto the small, starchy bed. Even if I didn't have Ferae — and I absolutely, positively didn't — life as I knew it was over. A sneeze sent people running. A rumor of serious illness, even if it wasn't contagious, turned a person into a pariah. I'd learned that when my mother's cancer diagnosis set off a chain reaction of hysteria. Within days of her first chemo treatment, she was fired without notice. My father's gallery business dried up. But hardest to understand was the way our friends cut off all contact once they heard the news. I wasn't invited to a single birthday party or sleepover that year. Since our extended family had all died during the plague, in the end, as my mom grew sicker and sicker, it was just the three of us. Now we were a family of two, me and Dad.

The image of the last fetch — hooded and flailing as the

bullets hit — dropped into my mind. I buried my face in the pillow. The longer I stayed trapped in this room, the harder it was to convince myself that Director Spurling was full of crap. She had sounded certain in a way that usually came with proof. Plus, the more I considered our life, the more suspect it seemed. Dad's monthly business trips. The never-ending supply of valuable art. We didn't live extravagantly, but I had wondered if my dad's gallery was doing better than he let on. We had so much original art — paintings by Rothko, O'Keeffe, Lucian Freud, and more — hanging on our apartment walls. It was especially sketchy considering he'd had to declare bankruptcy after my mother died. Her hospital bills had created a gaping crater of debt and yet, within eight years, Dad had not only paid it all off, but also built up savings. Definitely sketchy.

"Your name is on everything in case something happens to me," he'd said once while giving me keys to several deposit boxes, all at different banks. At the time, I'd figured that *something* meant a terminal illness or car accident — not execution.

At least the biohaz agents hadn't arrested him. It was obvious Spurling didn't know where my father was and thought that I did. Probably because most parents didn't leave their kids with the housekeeper for a week every month with no way of contacting them. And I'd put it down as another one of Dad's quirks: He hated dials and refused to carry one. What if all along his real reason for not calling was that he'd been in a place where dials didn't work?

So, if my father wasn't in California and the biohaz agents didn't have him, where was he?

Please, please don't be in the Feral Zone.

If he was on the other side of the wall, he couldn't stay there forever . . . and not just because of the risk of infection. The only people living in the Feral Zone today were banished criminals. My art-loving father wouldn't last a week.

Footsteps clacked in the corridor outside my door. I sat up as the lock of my containment room clicked and the door opened. A woman with sharp features and spiky gray hair stepped in. Director Spurling, without a face mask, without a jumpsuit. It could mean only one thing. "You got my blood test back." I scrambled off the bed. "I'm fine."

"Would I be standing here if you were infected?"

A weight seemed to slip from my shoulders like a sodden coat. I hadn't even realized how worried I'd been. Some tiny part of me must have thought there was a chance that I'd been exposed. Probably the same part that was beginning to believe that my dad might be a fetch.

Spurling held out my dial. In her tightly cut black suit, computer tablet in hand, she was more than a little intimidating.

"Are you letting me go?" I slipped the dial's chain over my head.

"It's an option, but not one that will help your father."

"I don't know where he is. Really."

"I've been thinking, Delaney, that perhaps this situation can be salvaged. Follow me." Pivoting on her heel, Spurling strode away.

What else could I do? I followed. Though I couldn't help noticing that Director Spurling was moving suspiciously fast and that there were no other agents around. In fact, the halls were so empty they echoed. Every containment room we passed was empty too. Yes, it was late, but the whole scene felt wrong. "Where are we going?"

"We're problem solving."

"What does that mean?" I spotted a floating camera bot bobbing near the ceiling, but it didn't rotate as we walked past, meaning it wasn't recording us. Had Spurling turned off the security cameras? As director of biohaz she had the power to do anything she wanted. When she didn't answer my question, I slowed and put on my ice face. "I'd rather problem solve with my father's lawyer here."

Spurling turned so fast that I had to sidestep to keep from plowing into her. She thrust her computer tablet under my nose. "Don't get smart with me, Delaney. I have a whole file on you. I know about the orienteering and the self-defense classes. You think I can't guess why you take them?"

"Because my dad makes me." Other kids were forced to take piano lessons, but I had to suffer through night hikes in the park and memorize an attacker's five most vulnerable areas — eyes, ears, throat, shin, groin. Considering that our live-in housekeeper was an ex-Marine and our apartment building was tricked out like Fort Knox — as most were, in case of another plague — I didn't really need to know how to chop someone in the windpipe. Not that I was going to say this to Director Spurling, who looked like she'd chopped many a windpipe.

"Of course he makes you," she snapped. "You're his apprentice."

My surprise came out as a laugh, which I turned into a cough.

"He takes you out and times you running," she went on. "Why would he do that unless he's training you to be a fetch?"

I eased back a step. She was a little too invested in her theory. "Actually, I asked him to. I've been trying to break my —"

"Shut up."

I obeyed instantly since Spurling seemed on the verge of beating me to death with her computer tablet.

"I have been working on this investigation for five years, Delaney. Five years of trying to coerce rich scumbags into giving up their art supplier. They're like drug addicts, thinking only about their next fix. They'll clam up and lawyer up long before they'll tell you who their dealer is. But last year, I got a solid lead on your father. And finally, finally, I have the evidence against him and where is he? Poof, gone." She glared as if I had personally hidden him away. "I don't accept that. Not after all the effort I've put into getting Ian McEvoy right where I want him. Now walk."

Spurling pointed down the corridor, which ended at a massive steel door, made all the creepier by the bar across it, guaranteeing that it stayed shut. I focused on the bar in order to control the pricking sensation behind my eyes. If I dashed back the way we'd come, I could outrun this sadist in heels. But that wouldn't help my dad.

"If you're trying to make yourself cry, don't bother. I had my heart surgically removed when I took this job." She headed for the door. "Come on. Your father is going to need every minute."

I glanced up. What did that mean?

"I first got whiff of him," Spurling said, now sounding

positively conversational, "at a dinner party." She didn't slow her pace, so I was forced to catch up. "There I noticed a landscape by Ferdinand Hodler on the wall." She heaved aside the bolt. "It was an incredible moment. Not for the host, of course. He'd thought it was a safe-enough painting to hang in his dining room. Hodler is a fairly obscure Swiss artist. But I'm from Chicago." She glanced at me as if to check that I was paying attention. "And I'd seen that particular blue mountainscape many times . . . in the Art Institute."

"How is that an incredible moment?"

"Because it meant that some fetch had traveled all the way to Chicago and back — deep into the quarantine zone. No other fetch I've heard of will go that far, no matter how much a client offers."

Spurling pressed a key fob to a pad, which unlocked the door. As it slid open, a sigh of cold air prickled my skin. Lights flickered on to reveal metal stairs descending into darkness.

Seeing my hesitation, she said, "We're going under the wall," and started down the stairs. "So, I did a little digging," she said, continuing with her story without so much as a backward glance, "and found more valuable paintings here, in the West — paintings by Matisse, van Gogh, and Renoir — all from the Art Institute of Chicago and all on record as having been *left behind*."

As we rounded each bend in the stairwell, a new set of lights flickered on. The air smelled musty, and I felt like I was breathing in decades of old pain and fear. "What makes you think my father fetched them?"

"I don't think, I *know* he did."

I swallowed. Again the fate of the last fetch played like a viral clip in my mind. Another heavy steel door awaited us at the bottom of the stairs. Spurling swiped her fob across the pad. This door slid open with a hiss to reveal a darkness so cold and profound that dread swelled like a wave and crashed over me.

Spurling swept her hand toward the doorway. "After you."

I paused, unable to see anything in the darkness before me. I hoped that this wasn't a trick — that if I stepped into the room, Spurling wouldn't slam the door behind me, lock it, and leave me alone in the dark. Inhaling deeply, I stepped through the doorway and felt rewarded when the overhead lights snapped on to reveal an enormous white-tiled chamber. The air was stale, and dust coated the sparse furnishings: desks, chairs, and posts connected by chains to form a labyrinth of aisles.

"What is this place?" I eyed the two steel doors ten feet apart on the far wall. The doors were identical to the one we'd just come through. More camera bots floated like buoys inches from the high ceiling.

"It *was* a checkpoint chamber. One of ten entry points into the West." Director Spurling waved a hand at the door on the left. "The tunnel is just six hundred feet long, the width of the bottom of the wall, but with the security checks, it took days to reach this room. The people who didn't pass the medical tests were forced to return to the East through that door." Spurling pointed to the one on the right.

Shivering, I looked away, only to notice a beat-up leather satchel on the chair beside me.

"Recognize it?" Spurling asked in a silky tone.

I inhaled sharply and then wished I'd hidden my reaction — but she already knew the messenger bag was my dad's. This was her show, and I was just playing the part I'd been assigned.

Hefting the bag onto a desk, she dumped out the contents. Curiosity drew me closer. Some of the items could have belonged to anyone: a flashlight, rolled bandages, a bottle of iodine, matches, a map. But the bone-handled machete was unquestionably my dad's. And then there was the long rolled canvas stuffed into the side pocket. I didn't know what it was specifically, but I'd seen my father with others like it.

Spurling pulled the canvas free and unrolled it. "Personally, I've always thought Lautrec was gaudy and overrated." She turned the canvas toward me.

It showed a nightclub scene. The top hats and gowns, the garish face in the foreground, were all rendered with distinctive "heavy contouring" as my dad would say — unmistakably Toulouse-Lautrec. "It could be a copy." I knew how ridiculous that sounded the second the words were out of my mouth.

"I doubt Mack would risk his life for anything less than the original." Spurling rerolled the canvas.

I flinched. She'd used my dad's nickname like she was his friend. "If that's all you've got against him — his bag — then —"

In answer, Spurling activated her tablet and tapped the screen. The fluorescent lights dimmed overhead and the chamber filled with spectral light as the camera bots projected a holographic recording of the very room we were standing in. Tracing her finger across her tablet, Spurling made the camera bots circle the ceiling until the projected twin doors were aligned with the actual doors. I braced myself for what was to come, curling my hands into fists.

"For the past year, I was convinced that your father was bribing some line guard to smuggle him over the wall. That's how most fetches get east. But I couldn't find any evidence of it. And then I remembered the exodus tunnels."

The projected images were shadowy, though clear enough that I could see the door on the right slide open.

"After the West closed," Spurling went on, "the tunnels were backfilled with twenty feet of rubble. But if someone wants something badly enough . . ."

The chamber brightened as a flashlight beam appeared in the open door. It took me a second to realize that it was part of the recorded projection.

Spurling's expression turned smug. "When I had the cameras installed last week, I didn't expect such a fast payoff."

I watched with dismay as a ghostly version of my father stepped through the steel door, his messenger bag in one hand. I scooted out of the way as he walked past, and then I caught Spurling's faint amusement. When the ghostlike form of my dad was halfway across the chamber, a red light started flashing. Behind him, the door began to slide shut. My father whirled and raced for the tunnel, darting right through me. At the last second, he slipped sideways into the opening, but the messenger bag in his hand was too big and he dropped it just as the door closed.

Spurling frowned and froze the image. "He tripped the

motion sensor, which was supposed to lock down this chamber with him *in* it. That way he and I could have had a face-to-face chat. Instead, I have an overflowing case file, damning evidence, and a missing fetch. That wasn't the plan."

A knot of pain tightened in my gut. It tightened and tightened, hard and cold, until it was the only thing I felt. Why had she shown me this? My father was all I had and she knew it. "What do you want?"

She turned off the projection and the lights came back on. "I just told you," she said, tucking the tablet under her arm. "I want to talk to Mack privately, but at this point, that's not going to happen."

By "talk to" she meant "arrest." Why didn't she just say it?

Because she doesn't want to arrest him, I realized with icy clarity. *She wants something else.*

Spurling watched me without a word, as if willing me to piece it together.

I drew in a shuddering breath. So, what did she want? *To talk to Mack privately*, or so she'd said. But that wasn't really it. No, what Director Spurling specifically wanted was to talk to a fetch. One who had been all the way to Chicago and back . . . My heart rose in my chest. Maybe my dad's fate wasn't sealed after all. "You want him to fetch something for you. Something you left behind in Chicago."

"Aren't you the bright one?" Spurling took a cream-colored envelope from her suit pocket. "If Mack brings me what I want, I'll destroy the recording and his file. All the information he'll need is in here." She handed me the envelope.

I stiffened, seeing the catch. "I can't give it to him. I don't know where he is."

"Oh, but you do." She tipped her head toward the twin steel doors.

A heavy wave of cold moved through me. "You want me to go into the Feral Zone?"

"Of course not. You'd never make it across the river. Go as far as Arsenal Island."

My vision tunneled. Spurling, the envelope, the chamber, all slipped back as if to give me room to think. She was offering me the chance to save my dad. I didn't need to think. I'd do whatever it took — even cross the quarantine line.

Spurling watched me with sharp eyes. "You want to help your father, don't you?"

I nodded, not trusting my voice.

"Good." She began putting my dad's things back into the messenger bag, all except the rolled canvas and the map. "There's a doctor on Arsenal Island — Dr. Vincent Solis." She spread the map on the table and pointed to a rectangular island in the middle of the Mississippi River. "Dr. Solis will probably know where your father is. He has an ongoing deal with Mack."

"What kind of deal?"

Spurling gave me a thin smile. "I'm not at liberty to say. Just know that I have chosen to look the other way when it comes to Dr. Solis's activities . . . for now anyway."

The map had been printed pre-exodus — there was no symbol on it to indicate the Titan wall, which ran from the

Canadian border with its trenches and electrified fence to the Gulf of Mexico. Also, the map showed dozens of bridges crossing the Mississippi River when only one was still in existence. Known as "the last bridge," it crossed into the quarantine zone by way of Arsenal Island. Everybody knew that. Everybody also knew that the last bridge was heavily guarded.

"Isn't Arsenal Island a line patrol camp?"

"It is. Dr. Solis lives there with the guards. So, don't get caught," Spurling said as if it was no big deal. "If you do, don't expect me to intervene on your behalf. I'll deny everything. By the way, when you find Mack, tell him that he has five days to complete the fetch."

"Why only five days?"

"The patrol is shoring up the rubble along the east side of the wall. They start work on these tunnels Thursday morning." She flicked a hand at the two steel doors.

"Tell them not to!"

Spurling arched a penciled brow. "The line guards work for the Titan Corporation. They don't take orders from government officials, not even me."

"But what if it takes me five days to find him?"

"Arsenal Island is directly on the other side of the wall. It should take you ten minutes to get there. After that, either Dr. Solis knows where Mack is hiding or he doesn't. If he doesn't, do *not* go looking for your father. Just come back here and press the call button outside that door. I'll come get you."

"If I try but don't find my dad, will you still destroy the evidence against him?"

"Please. Why would I put myself at risk if I have nothing to show for it?"

"But —"

"The more time you waste now, the less Mack will have for the fetch."

Before my legs locked up entirely, I slung the deadweight of the messenger bag over my shoulder and picked up the map. I would find my father and give him the letter and then he'd do the fetch and everything would go back to normal. I could do this. I *would* do this. And I wasn't going to freak out about it . . . much.

I lifted my dial. "I need to call our housekeeper and tell him that I'm okay." Howard had to have heard from some parent that I'd been hauled off by biohaz agents. He was probably outside the quarantine center at this moment, trying to kick down the door.

"Howard was arrested hours ago." Spurling's tone was offhanded. "I have to say, for an old guy, he's a tough nut to crack."

"Crack?"

"He's being questioned about his knowledge of your father's illegal activities."

I stared at her, wanting to shout that Howard didn't know anything. But was that true? I wasn't sure of anything anymore.

"By the way," she went on, "we dropped off your pets at the local shelter. You have until the end of the week to claim them."

And I'd thought this woman couldn't make me hate her any more. "What if I can't?"

"Well, someone might adopt the one-eyed dog or the diabetic cat, but the rest? Even you have to admit they're a pretty sorry lot."

I drew a breath against the tightness in my chest. Director Spurling had just painted a bulls-eye on everyone and everything I loved. And if I didn't do what she wanted, she was going to start pulling the trigger. I cleared my throat. "I'd like to get going now, if that's okay."

"Of course." She led me across the room to the twin doors. "I knew you were the right girl for the job, Delaney," she said, and pressed her fob to the pad on the wall.

The door on the right rolled open and I found myself staring into a gaping darkness. Feeling close to heart failure, I stepped into the tunnel.

"One last thing," she said. "I'm sure you've heard that the Ferae virus isn't as lethal as it was nineteen years ago."

I nodded, though I wasn't planning on testing it out.

"Then you've probably also heard that instead of dying, when people get infected now, they mutate."

A cold feeling crept along my neck. "Those are just stories."

"No, actually, they're not. So be careful."

Every muscle in my body went rigid. "What? Are you saying there are *mutants* over there?"

"On the far side of the river, yes. Stick to the island and you should be fine. Good luck, Delaney." Spurling pressed the lock pad again and the door slid shut behind me.

· THREE ·

The instant the enormous door closed, darkness engulfed me, sending me into a frenzy to get the flashlight out of the messenger bag. I switched it on but didn't feel any calmer.

Mutate how? I wanted to scream through the steel. The rumors I'd heard were never clear on that point. The only consistent part was that criminals who were banished to the Feral Zone ended up deformed somehow. But who believed stories that were whispered at slumber parties?

I couldn't catch my breath, and it wasn't because of the stupid too-tight vest this time. I leaned back against the cold metal door and aimed the flashlight down the tunnel. The beam pushed the shadows back only a few feet and the air tasted of mold and decay.

Enough. I had to get moving. If I didn't find my dad, if he didn't complete the fetch, Spurling wouldn't destroy the evidence against him. I forced myself to start walking, though seeing nothing but darkness ahead was plucking at my last nerve. With each step I took, I felt like I wasn't traveling forward but back through time, and when I reached the end of the tunnel, I'd emerge into the most horrific event in American history. I aimed the flashlight's beam at walls covered in graffiti — names, prayers, and notes from people who had been sent back into the Feral Zone. I lifted my dial. There was no phone signal, of course — not under tons of concrete. Still, I tapped the screen and let the dial hang from my neck, where it would record whatever I passed.

My footsteps echoed off the concrete floor and ceiling, which would alert anyone or anything up ahead that I was coming. Shaking off that unhelpful thought, I moved on and came to an open suitcase with clothing spilling out. In the beam of the flashlight, I saw more suitcases and bags scattered ahead, along with random possessions: a bottle of Scotch, the Bible, a child's tin robot. And then more ominous items: a handgun and gas mask that stopped me in my tracks. Talk about a reality overload.

What was I doing here? No matter what Spurling wanted to tell herself, I hadn't been trained as an apprentice fetch. I wasn't prepared to venture into the Feral Zone. Or anywhere, really. My dad had hired Howard to be my bodyguard as much as our housekeeper.

The weight of the wall pressed down on me. The tons of ugly concrete had been so hastily piled, who knew if it was structurally sound? Everything about the plague had been hasty. The speed with which the virus overtook the eastern seaboard. How quickly the rest of the world cut us off. The hurried mass exodus to the West. And the erection of first a fence and then the wall, courtesy of the Titan Corporation. Titan had been required to build the wall in reparation for creating the Ferae virus. A just punishment. Or so I'd thought until now as I stood beneath the result.

I hurried on, humming to distract myself, but then heard the sound echoing off the tunnel walls. I fell silent. The last thing I wanted was to attract something's attention. I picked up my pace and didn't stop again until I stepped into a cavernous room like the one I'd just left. A checkpoint chamber. My flashlight beam swept the dusty air. Across the room, a sloping rock pile blocked off the passageway. I hurried toward it, only to trip halfway. The flashlight flew from my grip as I landed on something stiff and dry. Crawling over it, I snatched up the flashlight and looked to see what I'd fallen over. My chest compressed, forcing the air from my lungs and a scream from my throat. Dozens of dried-up corpses lay scattered across the floor. Worse, some were in pieces. Shriveled limbs were flung every which way like hunks of beef jerky.

I scrambled back so far that my shoulders banged into the wall. I stayed huddled there, heart pounding, until I was certain that if I got to my feet, I wouldn't bolt back the way I'd come. Mummified corpses couldn't hurt me. They had to have been lying here since the exodus ended seventeen years ago. These were people who'd been denied entry into the West — probably because they'd been infected.

I shoved my flashlight under one arm and pulled out my hand sanitizer. According to my tenth grade biology teacher, you couldn't catch Ferae from dirt or grime, which this chamber was crusted with, or a corpse, even if the person had died from Ferae. Just the same, I squeezed sanitizing gel into my shaking hands. Ferae was like rabies, passed on by the bite of an infected mammal . . . humans included. That's why people said we could never reclaim the East — because there would always be animals that carried the disease, and we had no vaccine for Ferae and no cure.

That didn't matter though, because I wasn't going to get infected with Ferae. I flicked the flashlight forward and made a wide semicircle past the corpses, while facts about the early days of the plague crowded my mind. How the infected became aggressively psychotic — like rabies times ten — and would go in search of people to bite: doctors who were trying to help them, friends, even family. The military had been forced to firebomb a lot of the eastern cities to stop infected people and animals from spreading the virus.

The rubble was stacked up to the ceiling. After a moment of scanning my flashlight across the sloping mess, I spotted a gap at the top where fresh air drifted in. My nerves jumped: What if an infected person had wiggled through that hole and had been inside the tunnel with me all along? I whirled, my flashlight beam whipping around the chamber. Nothing. But now my heart was beating triple-time and sweat slicked my palms — not so good for rock climbing. But then, neither were high-heeled ankle boots.

To even have a shot at making it to the top, I'd need to use both hands. I set my dial on glow — enough to see by — and left it recording. Why not document my first glimpse of the East? After one last scan of the chamber, I turned off the flashlight and stuffed it into the messenger bag. I reached for a large chunk of broken cement for leverage, only to recoil from the slimy feel of it. Water had trickled in through the hole along with the air. The whole rock spill was a slippery mess. Heart still on overdrive, I started up the treacherous mound, backsliding every few feet. While I climbed, I kept my eyes pinned to the gap in the rubble above, just in case something crawled in.

Finally I reached the hole, a long burrow with a lighter shade of dark at the end. It was so narrow, I couldn't believe that my father had managed to get through it. But he had. And so would I. I took off the bag, pushed it into the space ahead of me, and with a deep breath I wiggled in.

A glimmer of moonlight beckoned me forward as I crawled across the jagged rocks that lined the burrow. No, wrong word. This felt less like a bunny warren and more like I'd been buried alive. My hands and forearms were bruised, scraped, and cut by the time I reached the end, grateful to peer out and breathe the warm night air. I could hear the sound of rushing water and even see Arsenal Island, smack in the middle of the Mississippi River, the last stop before the Feral Zone.

The island glowed as though it generated its own sunshine via giant floodlights. In contrast, the bridge leading to the island was just a looming shadow over the water. The only illuminated area on my side of the river was the black-topped landing pad next to the bridge's entry gate. A spotlight swept across the jeeps and hovercopters parked to one side, and onto the rocky hill that led down to the river. When the spotlight arced back to zip along the base of the wall, I ducked into the hole again like a skittish rabbit.

Once the spotlight passed, I crept out onto the top of a bulldozed mountain of debris made up of earth, bricks, and chunks of cement mixed with broken glass, pipes, and roof shingles. A tetanus infection just waiting to happen. I perched on the rubble of what used to be the east side of Davenport. At the bottom, the bricks and cement chunks spilled onto a muddy patrol road, which meant that line guards could drive by in one of their open-topped jeeps at any moment.

I waited for the spotlight to move onto the hill again and picked my way down the wreckage, stepping as lightly as I could. Even so, rocks spilled down behind me. When I finally stepped onto the unpaved road, I found a length of pipe and jammed it into the foot of the rubble pile as a marker. Okay, orienteering, not a complete waste of time.

I paused to look back at the wall, so massive that it blocked out most of the night sky. A small thrill wound through me at seeing the Titan from this side — in person no less, not via toy hovercopter. Was it really just hours ago that I'd stood on Orlando's roof hoping for a glimpse of the East? It felt like days ago, and yet I was still squeezed into Anna's vest.

Her *white* vest, which in the moonlight may as well have been phosphorescent.

"I can't believe I let you talk me into wearing this," I muttered and undid my ponytail so that my hair fell down my back in dark waves. My hair was thick and long but it didn't hide the vest completely. "And I know you said don't get it dirty, but . . . sorry." I scooped up a handful of mud. Ew. How many germs were cupped in my palm? I couldn't think about it. I smeared the mud over the exposed parts of the vest — grimacing the whole time — and then wiped my hands on my jeans and rubbed them down with more hand sanitizer.

Now what? I knew where I was supposed to go — Arsenal Island — but I didn't dare just start walking. I slung off my messenger bag, unzipped it, and went through its contents more carefully than I had under Spurling's watchful eye. The flashlight, the bandages, the iodine, the matches, the map, the machete — I didn't even want to consider what I might need that for — and finally, a silver badge embossed with the words *Line Patrol.* I stuffed it all back into the bag except for the badge. What had Dad used this for? A single badge wouldn't get him past a sentry. I flipped the badge over but there was nothing written on the back, just stiff black plastic.

Something glimmered in my peripheral view. I glanced across the road. A greenish glow had appeared on the ground at the base of a tree. I grabbed the messenger bag and jogged closer. The tree was leafless, dead. The crater next to it suggested an explosion. I reached out to touch the trunk, and my fingertips came back dusted with soot.

The skeleton tree, black as night.

This burnt hunk of wood was exactly how I'd pictured the skeleton tree in my dad's stories. Maybe this blackened tree marked the start of a path as well. I'd just have to keep away from the harpy eggs. . . .

All right, now I was getting loopy. Though it did make sense that my dad's stories would come to mind now. When I was little, I always asked him to tell them when I was scared of the dark, or sad — two emotions I was definitely feeling right now.

In the time that I'd been standing there, the greenish light on the ground had grown brighter. I crouched. A fist-sized rock was nestled among the tree roots and glowing like a firefly. I reached for it, but then some glimmer of a memory made me snatch back my hand.

Of course this glow-in-the-dark rock wasn't an exploding harpy egg from my dad's stories. But what if it was something just as lethal? Like maybe a land mine? The rocky hill between here and the riverbank was probably covered with them. I backed onto the road. How weird that I may have just avoided death because of a coincidence: that real-life land mines and imaginary harpy eggs both cast a green glow.

My knees locked as realization dropped on me like a cartoon anvil. It was not a coincidence. The exploding eggs in my father's stories were land mines. The burnt tree before me was the skeleton tree, black as night.

As the spotlight arced my way once more, I hurried back to the rubble pile and hunkered by a piece of a marble column. My mind spun. Why had my dad woven details from his life as a fetch into bedtime stories? Was Director Spurling right? Was he training me to be a fetch without telling me?

Not a chance. He'd never willingly let me do something this dangerous.

Whatever his motive, I wasn't taking another step until I thought this through. Maybe there was a reason that his stories always began the same way. *In a very tall tower, next to a very tall mountain, there lived a little girl who longed to have an adventure. One day when she was walking along the base of the mountain, she discovered a cavern that was so long and deep, it took her through the mountain to the other side.*

When she stepped out of the cavern, she saw a river that was wide and wild. She also saw that across the river there was a magical forest just waiting to be explored. As she was about to make her way down to the riverbank, she heard a cry for help. Turning back, she saw that a sheep had gotten caught in an immense bramble bush at the foot of the mountain. Because the little girl had a kind heart, she helped the sheep free itself from the thorny brambles. This turned out to be a good thing, because the grateful sheep revealed that there was a secret way to get down to the riverbank. The sheep sat down on a boulder and, while using its own wool to knit a sweater, it told the little girl that she must look for the skeleton tree, black as night, which marked the start of the path. If she strayed from that path, she might step on a harpy egg. They looked just like rocks, the sheep warned, except for their faint green glow. If you so much as nudged a harpy egg, it would burst into flames.

The little girl followed the sheep's instructions to the letter and made it safely down to the riverbank, only to discover that an army of silver robots guarded the only bridge across the river.

Up to this point in the story, the only detail my dad ever changed was the type of animal caught in the bramble bush. The animal's warning about the path to the riverbank was always the same — look for the skeleton tree and watch out for the harpy eggs. But once the girl made it down to the riverbank safely, her methods for getting past the killer robots varied. Sometimes she'd seek out the wizard who lived with the robots and spent his days devising magic potions. . . .

Wait. A wizard surrounded by silver guys. Silver, as in light gray uniforms, maybe?

Okay, Dad, got it. Dr. Solis and the line guards. Wow, that wasn't even subtle.

I got to my feet. I didn't need to take the story any further because I didn't need to know all the ways that the little girl made it across the bridge and into the magical forest. I wasn't going anywhere near the magical forest, aka the Feral Zone, even if that was where the little girl met the boy who lived all alone in a castle. He was wild and uncivilized and would say the rudest things imaginable, which, of course, delighted me when I was younger. Out of all of my dad's characters, the wild boy was my favorite. But tonight, there would be no wild boy, no bridge crossing, and no magic forest for me. All I had to do was talk to the wizard. Dr. Solis, who was surrounded by killer robots. With Uzis. No problem.

I studied the rocky hill that lay between the road and the riverbank. I didn't see any other green glowing spots on the slope below, but they were there for sure. If I couldn't see the land mines, how was I supposed to avoid them? Too bad there were no talking animals around to give me advice. I crept closer and suddenly the land mine by the blackened tree lit up again. Had I activated it by moving?

No. The land mines wouldn't glow in warning when you got close or quarantine breakers like me would just avoid them, making the mines pointless. However, the guards who set the mines would want to know where not to step. . . .

I held out the patrol badge as far as I could without leaving the road. Not only did the glow by the tree intensify, but also, farther down the embankment, other rocks began to glow.

Thanks, Dad.

I zigzagged my way down the steep hill, steering clear of demolition wreckage, trees, and glowing harpy eggs. I headed for the landing pad next to the gated bridge. Of course, I still didn't know how I was going to get across the bridge or find Dr. Solis once I was in the patrol camp. For some reason I'd pictured a patrol camp as a few rows of tents — an image that had nothing to do with reality. How did the word *camp* apply to what looked like a medieval town, complete with limestone buildings and a clock tower? But that was most definitely the line patrol camp. The rows of barracks on the south end of the island was one giveaway, the high chain link fence topped with razor wire another. And then there were the spotlights and watchtowers.

How was I supposed to snoop around such a brightly lit and highly guarded island?

Pounding footsteps sent me darting behind a tree. When I dared to peer out, I saw a man throw open the gate, leap off the end of the bridge, and bound down the gravel slope to the riverbank. He took cover in the shadows as three more people burst through the gate and ran onto the landing strip. They paused under a floodlight to scan the area. With their crew cuts and military fatigues — gray on gray camouflage to match the wall — they had to be line guards. Also known as killer robots. After a moment of whispering, they fanned out.

I didn't dare hope that the fugitive hiding in the shadows below was my father. Though who else would be running from line guards? If that was my dad down there, he'd make a break for the tunnel at some point. I'd have my answer then. In the meantime, I was staying put.

The man stumbled along the dark riverbank and dropped behind a rubble pile, the remains of some demolished building.

When he appeared on the other side of the rubble and started up the steep hill, hope rose in my chest.

No way. My father, here, now. That would be too lucky.

The three guards exchanged hand signals that didn't take military training to figure out, and then two skidded down the gravel slope by the bridge. The tallest one jogged across the landing pad and disappeared behind a patch of scrubby bushes — gun in hand.

I had to see the fugitive's face. I spotted him crouching behind a rock outcropping halfway up the slope. Below him, the two guards swept the riverbank with flashlights. The bushes off to my left rustled. The third guard was closing in fast. I tucked the badge into the front of my vest and scurried along the ridgeline until I was directly above the fugitive, which meant closer to the lit-up landing pad. Not good. I crouched in the shadows and waited for the man to do something — to make a run up the hill. But the seconds ticked by and he remained as still as an animal caught in the glare of headlights. The guards below gave up on the riverbank and turned their high-powered flashlights onto the hill, inching their way up. I couldn't wait any longer. Scooting a little ways down the slope, I whispered, "Hey."

The fugitive didn't move.

"Hey," I said a little louder.

He whipped around at the noise and rose, but his face remained shadowed. Just as I considered creeping down farther, I caught a flash of his eyes in the moonlight — yellow and bestial — and knew then, beyond all doubt, the man was not my father.

I wasn't even sure he was human.

· FOUR ·

Fast-rising panic surged through me as I stared at the fugitive man crouched on the hill below. His yellow eyes glowed with hostility and I'd swear he was growling. Horrified, I shoved back, kicking earth to get away, but he lunged up the hill after me. I heaved my bag at him, hitting him squarely in the face. He stumbled back.

Turning, I scrambled up the steep slope, only to feel a steely grip clamp around my ankle. I cried out and clawed at the weeds, trying to get a handhold, but still the terrifying man dragged me to him. As I kicked at his hand, a hornet blew past my ear, its wings brushing my skin. The man released me with a roar. He slapped at his arm, which had somehow sprouted a dart. When he tore it out, another dart punctured his neck.

I crabbed backward up the hill, only to get hooked from behind and hauled to my feet. I whirled to run and slammed in to a wall of a boy. His badge and dog tag dangled against his chest, inches from my nose. A line guard.

He dragged me aside with a "Shh" and raised his gun. Mouth tight, he took aim, but before he could pull the trigger, the maniac on the slope toppled over. The guard exhaled slowly, and then turned a cold look on me, made even colder by the color of his irises — pale gray, the exact shade of the wall. "What are you doing over here?" he demanded.

I couldn't speak. My brain had blown a circuit back at yellow eyes. *Yellow.*

"Who gave you permission to cross the —" The guard's words cut off as his gaze swept over me. "Oh . . . got it. You're one of the captain's friends."

I nodded dumbly. He could assume whatever he wanted as long as he let go of my arm so that I could put some serious distance between me and the groaning, yellow-eyed man.

"Stay here," the guard ordered. "There's no reason for them to see you." He tipped his head toward the bottom of the hill, indicating the other two line guards, and then he lowered his voice. "They resent the brass enough as it is."

He said it like he wasn't one of them, though he sure looked like any other line guard — hair buzzed, expression brutal.

"Do not try to walk back without me. Understand?" He slid the dart gun into a thigh holster. "You'll just get blown to pieces."

Right, land mines. Nice scare tactic, jerk. I nodded again.

"Cruz," a voice yelled from the riverbank. "Did you find Bangor?"

"I tranqed him. He's down," the guard at my side shouted back.

I jumped at the sound. I needed to get a grip, and fast.

"I'll be right back," the guard named Cruz whispered, then he picked his way down the slope.

One hippopotamus, two hippopotamus . . . With the patrol badge in hand, I dashed up the hill, watching for the telltale glow of the mines. On the rise, I paused, gasping, and ducked behind the same bush as before. Wait there so he could come back and arrest me? Yeah, right.

But Guardsman Cruz wasn't going to forget about me. As soon as he got yellow-eyes under control, he'd be back. Some fetch I was! Spurling had warned me about the line guards. So had my dad — only he'd called them killer robots. Yet I'd managed to get nabbed within twenty minutes of coming east. And to top it off, I'd left my dad's messenger bag on the hill next to the maniac. How stupid could I be? Very, obviously.

The other two guards hiked up the slope. With their backs to the bridge and the gate unguarded, this was my shot. *Move,* I told myself. *Now!* My legs didn't obey.

"Over here," Cruz called to the other two. He ran a hand over his bristling dark hair.

The flashlight beams bounced across the hill until they landed on the writhing maniac on the ground and set his drool glistening. Cruz glanced up the hill even though there was no way he could see much in the darkness. Still, I stayed down and turned off my dial. As much as I wanted to keep recording, I couldn't risk someone spotting the tiny red light that indicated my dial was on.

When the other guards got close, Cruz asked, "How did he get infected?"

"How should I know?" said the stocky guard with biceps as thick as his thighs. "I was on gate duty and Bangor shows up." He flung a hand toward the crumpled man. "Says the captain wants me. So, I go, right? I'm maybe twenty feet down the path and I hear the bolt slide open. I look back and

Bangor's yanking on the gate. That's when I yelled for backup."

The gate. Right. I redirected my attention to the bridge's dark silhouette and crept several bushes closer to the landing strip. The hill wasn't as steep here. Staying low, I dashed down the slope to the nearest jeep and crouched.

"Okay, he's out," I heard Cruz say as I snuck along the row of vehicles. When I reached the last one, I stole another look at the guards. Their eyes were locked on the man on the ground, now deathly still.

"He was on river patrol today," said the third guard, whose blond crew cut looked like baby chick down. "They found a raft on the west bank. Maybe Bangor found the owner."

"More like the owner found him," said the stocky guard.

"Hey, maybe it's not —" The blond guy shifted uncomfortably. "Maybe Bangor just cracked from the stress."

Cruz dropped to a knee and touched the tranquilized man's forehead. "Maybe." Even from fifty feet away, I could hear the lack of conviction in his husky voice. "Take him to the infirmary."

"Why? He's turning," the stocky guard said, his voice rising.

"Because the doctor is going to want to know what bit him."

"We know what," the guard snapped. "A feral."

"Yeah, but which strain?" Cruz shot a glance up the hill — probably trying to check on me.

"Who cares?"

"Are you trying to find a cure?" Cruz got to his feet,

which gave him the height advantage. "No? Then shut up and get him to Dr. Solis."

Dr. Solis, the very person I was supposed to find. And maybe now that wouldn't be such an impossible task. I could follow these guards right to him.

The blond guard stepped away, hands up. "He might bite."

I twitched, remembering a line from a documentary about the outbreak: *Ferae killed half the nation, one bite at a time.*

"So what?" Cruz asked. "Even if he has Ferae, it won't get into his salivary glands for a while."

"Did you read that in one of your science books?" the stocky guard sneered.

"Fine." Cruz unclipped something from his belt and tossed it to the blond guard. "If you're so worried, muzzle him."

"I'm not putting my hand near his mouth." He tossed the leather strap to the stocky guy. "You do it."

That one didn't even bother to catch it; he just let the strap bounce off his chest and fall to the ground. "Not a chance."

"Oh, for — He's unconscious." Guardsman Cruz sounded like he was at the end of his patience.

I had to get out of there before he realized that I wasn't waiting for him to come arrest me. At least he hadn't told the other two about me.

"If you're so freaking sure, *you* muzzle him," the stocky guard said.

Cruz dropped his dog tag and badge down his shirt and scooped up the piece of leather. "Move." The other two had several years on him and yet they jumped out of the way as he bent over the tranquilized man.

With the guards' attention wholly on their task, I slipped through the gate, which they'd left ajar. Rock music drifted out of the darkness upriver. I pressed against an iron support beam and peeked back at the trio on the slope. Cruz stepped aside as the other two guards slung the maniac's arms over their shoulders and lifted him. If they were following his instructions, they'd take the infected man to Dr. Solis. All I had to do was keep to the shadows and trail them.

Layers of rust stuck to my palms as I peeled away from the beam. Ugh. But there was no time to whip out the hand sanitizer. I sprinted for the gate at the far end of the bridge, not trusting the soft wood beneath my feet — it felt rotten — but at least it muffled my footsteps.

Lights appeared from around the bend and the music grew louder as a patrol barge cruised downriver. Onboard, patrolmen aimed spotlights at the banks. I pressed against another support beam, trying to make myself invisible, only to hear a clank as the guards lugged the unconscious man through the gate. Cruz wasn't with them — probably because he was searching for me on the ridge. How long would it take him to realize that I wasn't there?

I stayed plastered to the iron beam. If I dashed through the gate now, the approaching guards might see me. But I couldn't stay here. They'd be on top of me in a minute. Jumping was definitely out. The river looked not just fast, but schizo. With all the cross currents, I'd get swept under in a heartbeat.

Peering down through the planks of wood, I watched the patrol boat cruise under the bridge. When a guard tilted up his light, I jerked back from the gap. The guards behind me dragged the unconscious man to the railing as the boat emerged on the other side. "Hey," the stocky guard yelled down.

"What are you slack-offs doing up there?" a voice shouted back.

Go go go! I dashed for the gate — left open and swaying in the night breeze.

"Nothing good," he called down. "Tell you when you're back in camp."

I slipped through the gate and into the shadows beyond. Six rows of barracks lined up before me, with several buildings per row. That was housing for a whole lot of guards, and who knew, there might even be more. The bridge I'd crossed was located at the southwest tip of the island and Arsenal was a very big island. Luckily, the bridge faced the backside of the barracks. The six-story clock tower read one o'clock and yet spotlights blazed throughout the camp. A security measure? I dashed into the narrow alley between two barracks and made my way to the front of the building. I peered around the corner, only to have my heart plow to a stop.

There were line guards everywhere.

Young men and women, all in gray fatigues, stood in distinct groups in a courtyard that was bound on all sides by barracks. Under glaring arc lights, the guards slammed their guns around in some sort of rhythmic line dance. Or maybe this was what they called a drill. I edged back into

the shadows, but couldn't tear my gaze from their synco-
pated movements and implacable faces. If they marched en
masse in my direction, I had no doubt that they'd mow me
down without noticing and pound my body to a bloody pulp
under their boots.

Watching them, it was hard to believe the fact that before
the plague, the line patrol was a private security force for
indoor theme parks. These guards were all too young to
have worked for Titan back then, when the company was
known for its elaborate labyrinths that were acres wide and
fifty stories high. Clearly the guards' training now involved
more than helping people through a maze.

I ran back down the alley to watch for the guards who
were going to take the yellow-eyed man to the infirmary. I
crouched by the back corner so that my vest would disappear against the building's cement foundation. My heart
thudded, keeping time with the relentless stomping from the
courtyard. How was I going to make it to the infirmary in
a white vest — muddy or not — without one of the robots
noticing?

Behind me came the clatter of boots on wood as the two
guards dragged the infected man through the gate. "Don't
lock it yet. Cruz is coming," the stocky guard called to a
young woman who veered toward them.

She stopped midstride. "Why's Bangor muzzled?" she
asked sharply. "Oh no, is he infected?"

"Shhh," the two guards hissed in unison.

A head popped out of a far window. "Someone got bit?"

That was all it took. Within a minute the news had
spread and guards rolled in from all directions to circle the

men hauling Bangor, bombarding them with questions. Luckily none charged down the alley I was hunkered in.

As the glum little parade headed down a walking path, I slumped back against the building. I couldn't follow them to the infirmary — not with a crowd of anxious guards on their heels. I'd have to hang back and —

"I told you to wait for me," said an irritated voice.

I looked over to see Cruz, the dark-haired guard from the hill, striding toward me. I got to my feet. Could I outrun him? Not a chance. As tall as he was, there was nothing awkward about him: He'd bootcamped his body into fighting condition. Plus, there was the dart gun issue. . . . I decided to stay put and hope that he didn't know every guard on Arsenal Island.

He closed the distance between us, stopping less than a foot away — closer than I was comfortable with for several reasons, starting with his size and ending with his not-messing-around-here expression. He held out my father's messenger bag. "Yours?"

I might as well claim it. He already knew that I'd been on the riverbank. "Thanks." I reached for it, but he didn't let go of the strap.

"The pilot should have walked you in from the landing pad," he said reprovingly. "Make sure to tell Captain Hyrax so that it doesn't happen again."

Not knowing what to say, I nodded stiffly.

"Relax," he said, releasing my bag. "I'm not going to arrest you. What the captain calls R&R is his business, but you can't go wandering around camp. Can you find your way to the officers' quarters?"

"Uh . . ." I'd happily jump onboard whatever he had assumed was my reason for being here, if only I could figure out what it was.

"Fine, come on." He gestured me forward, looking less than pleased. "I'll take you to him." When I didn't budge, he frowned. "If someone sees you on base and reports it, Captain Hyrax will lose his post. That won't break my heart, but you'll be down a client."

I gasped. "You think I'm a . . ." I fumbled past my shock and offense to find the word. "An escort."

"My mistake," he said dryly. "Since obviously you're a . . ." He lifted a hand, at a loss.

"Guard," I said, and then added, "I'm off duty."

His brows rose. Clearly he'd need convincing, but I didn't have time to answer questions. Every second I stood here was wasting time that my father might need on the back end. "Look, I was just —"

A screech cut through the night, a sound like nothing I'd ever heard. I spun, looking for the source. That screech — it had sounded almost human. Almost.

"Okay," Cruz said. "One, no guard, male or female, has hair past their ears."

Before I could gather my wits to come up with a reply, another tortured scream straightened out my nerve endings.

"And two, we're way past reacting to that."

How could anyone get past reacting to *that*?

His expression hardened. "Now, why don't you tell me what you're really doing here, Miss?"

· FIVE ·

Guardsman Cruz had shifted into stone-cold line guard mode — every inch of him, every synapse. Probably something the patrol hammered into the guards during training: how to seem simultaneously decent and reasonable yet capable of sudden violence. It was chilling. Even if my nerves weren't stretched to snapping point, which they were, I wasn't going to try spinning another lie. Not only did I not have the practice, I'd be worse under duress. And with his steely gaze pinned on me, Guardsman Cruz was laying on some serious duress.

"I can't tell you," I said, choking out the words.

A muscle ticked along his jaw as he studied me. "What's your name," he said finally. Grammatically, it was a question, but it sure didn't sound like one.

"Lane."

"Just Lane?"

"Delaney Park." Not a lie, though I was hoping that he'd think Park was my last name.

"You crossed the quarantine line, Lane. Maybe you noticed it — that three-thousand-mile-long wall back there. Your being here is a capital offense and I am two seconds from arresting you, which is exactly how long you have to tell me what you're doing here."

"Okay, all right. I'm looking for Ian McEvoy."

Shock leapt into Cruz's expression. Clearly he recognized the name. "I was hoping Dr. Solis could tell me where he is," I finished.

"He can't." If Guardsman Cruz could have crammed his answer down my throat, he would have.

"How do you know?"

"Because I report to Dr. Solis." Cruz ground out the words. "I spend every day in his lab, doing whatever he needs me to because he's trying to cure Ferae. You know what he's not doing? Associating with a known fetch."

"That's not what Director Spurling says."

"Who?"

"The head of Biohazard Defense." I tried not to sound smug. Smug would not go over well with this guy.

Cruz shot a look over his shoulder and then snagged my wrist and pulled me deeper into the shadows between the barracks. "They caught Mack, didn't they?" His tone was low, hard, and not even a little sympathetic. "What did he tell them about Dr. Solis?"

"Nothing! Ow," I said pointedly, raising my arm. He released my wrist and I took a moment to gather my adrenaline-soaked thoughts. Spurling would have a fit if she knew that I was confiding in a line guard, but I couldn't see another way forward. "Director Spurling doesn't *have* my dad, just evidence against him."

He sucked in a sharp breath. "Mack is your father?"

"Yes. And she already knew about his deal with your boss. Will you please take me to him now?"

"No," he said in a tone that closed the discussion as definitively as the Titan wall had closed off the West. "Go back to Director Spurling," he said, practically spitting her name, "and tell her that the doctor doesn't know Ian McEvoy. Has never even heard of him."

"She's not going to buy that. Anyway, she's not looking to arrest anyone. She has a job for my dad."

His eyes widened. "A fetch?"

"Yes. If he brings her back what she wants, she'll destroy his file."

Cruz scrubbed a hand over his jaw. Hopefully, he was reassessing the situation. He turned that considering gaze on to me. "And this director sent you here — to Arsenal Island — to tell Mack about this deal?"

When I nodded, he frowned. "How old are you? Sixteen?"

"Seventeen." Close enough. My birthday was coming up — in three months, anyway.

"What your dad does, fetching, it's a felony. But that doesn't give an official the right to send a kid over here where you could get infected or killed or worse."

I bristled. "There's something worse than being killed?"

"How about being eaten alive?" he asked casually.

All right, yes, that was worse, but *kid* was simmering in my gut. "You know, having my dad's file erased would be good for Dr. Solis too. 'Cause if they put my dad on trial, it'll come out that —"

"I can fill in the rest. Thanks." Despite his cool tone,

Guardsman Cruz didn't look mad. He tipped his head up to the sky and let out a slow breath.

Wait — was he really considering not following orders?

"What's your name?" I asked quickly. "Your first name." I didn't want to talk to a killer robot anymore. I wanted him to be a person.

His expression relaxed a fraction. "Everson."

"Where's that?"

"It *was* a town in Pennsylvania where my mother grew up."

He had a mother? Wow. Guardsman Cruz was becoming more human by the second.

"Stay here," he said, nudging me aside. "As in *really* stay this time."

I blocked his path. "Where are you going?"

"To get you some clothes. No guard would be caught in that getup on Arsenal." He nodded at my vest. "Not even if she's off duty."

"It isn't mine. My friend —"

"Do something about your hair." He pushed past me, clearly not interested in why I was dressed like the stepdaughter of a stripper.

I slumped against the barracks wall. Everson, Pennsylvania. It sounded like a nice town, but was the boy nice?

Please. He was a line guard. Nice didn't apply.

The killer robot returned with a pile of clothes, combat boots, and a gray cap. I tensed, waiting for more guards to appear. When no one marched around the corner, I relaxed a little. He hadn't reported me. For now.

Everson held out the bundle. "I got them from the women's barracks, so feel guilty. Some guard is going to —"

"From a clean pile?"

"Does it matter?"

It did to me. But based on the press of Everson's lips, I dropped the issue. "Where can I change?"

"Here."

"Uh, no. I — can't."

"And I'm not taking you anywhere dressed like that. So either change or cross back over the bridge."

Another nonchoice. His eyebrows — straight and dark over his eyes — gave him a stern look, which made me reluctant to push my luck. I'd just have to change fast. "Are you going to turn around?"

He shifted his gaze to the basketball court — like that would be enough to put me at ease. What did he think I'd do? Clobber him when his back was to me?

Gritting my teeth, I kicked off my ankle boots and got the snaps on the vest undone, but that was as far as I could make myself go. As humiliating as the vest was, I didn't want to change into someone else's dirty laundry in front of a line guard while standing outside in an alley where anyone might waltz by.

"What's taking so long?" Everson asked.

He looked over. Good thing I hadn't flung off the vest. "Can you *please* turn around? I promise not to make a run for it."

"So you say."

"You don't trust me?"

"I don't want you doing something stupid."

Nice. "Well, how about trusting that I'm smart enough to realize that you know your way around here and I don't. So, if I were to run, I'm guessing you would catch me."

"Good guess," he agreed.

"And considering you're as big as a cow, I'd probably end up dirty and hurt. Two things I hate. So, believe me, I'm not going to run."

He eyed me like a pop quiz that he hadn't studied for, but then gave me his back — ramrod straight, of course. I felt a little better. I still had to get undressed outdoors, but it was reassuring to know that logic worked over here.

"Cow?" he asked, sounding put out.

"Bull. Whatever. Big." I gave the shirt a sniff. It wasn't too bad, so I pulled the stretchy neoprene over my head. Between the shirt's high neck and the three-quarter sleeves, it would keep me a lot warmer than Anna's vest had.

"Ready," I said, once I'd gotten everything on, including the boots. I transferred the bottle of hand sanitizer and guard badge from my jeans to a side pocket on the camo pants.

Everson tugged my cap low over my eyes. "You're lucky I'm the one who found you. Any other guard would have hauled you off to Captain Hyrax."

I tensed. "Why didn't you?"

"I didn't drink the Kool-Aid. Come on, let's go."

I wasn't sure what he meant and I didn't care. Just so long as he didn't turn me in. "One minute." I tried to roll up Anna's vest but the vinyl was too stiff. It didn't fold well either and was not fitting easily into the messenger bag.

"You're not planning on following in your father's foot-steps, are you?"

I wasn't, but that didn't mean I wanted some line guard pointing out my shortcomings as an amateur fetch. I shot him a dirty look.

"Just asking," he said.

Was that amusement in his voice? He tugged the vest out of my hands and snatched up my white boots. "Hey," I hissed as he stalked off. "I have to give those back."

Stepping from between the barracks, he tossed the things into the first trash can he passed. I frowned but didn't try to fish them back out. As grateful as I was for his help, Guardsman Cruz was starting to rub me the wrong way. Were all line guards so bossy? I tucked my ponytail under the cap and joined him.

"You'll pass."

Darn right, I'd pass. I could do the whole ramrod posture, perfectly-made-bed robot thing. Okay, maybe not the marching and the push-ups . . .

"Good job on the boot size," I said, but he just waved me forward. Whatever. I wasn't here to make friends. Still, I was pleased that everything fit. I even felt a little tougher dressed in military pants and a carbon-gray top. Now I could slip through the shadows like a real fetch instead of shining like a beacon of westerness in white vinyl.

We didn't take the trail the guards with Bangor had hurried down. Instead, Everson guided me alongside the fence that enclosed the island. A high-pitched yammering echoed from the far bank of the river. Everson didn't seem to hear it. I paused to peer through the chain link into the darkness beyond, but could see nothing.

"Don't touch the fence," he warned.

"Is it electrified?"

"Yeah. It's set to stun-lethal. Meaning, touch it once, the shock will knock you flat. Touch it again, your heart stops."

When the yammering started up again, he jerked his chin toward the sound. "Feral."

I looked, but I couldn't even make out the river, let alone the east bank. "You mean an infected animal?"

Everson cocked his head, listening. "Human, I think. One that's too mutated to talk."

My gut twisted. Mutated. So the rumors were true. "Is Bangor going to mutate?" Everson nodded. "Okay," I said, though it absolutely wasn't. "But why was he acting crazy?"

"Right now he's just fevered. Bangor's body is trying to kill the virus with heat, but it's not working, so his body keeps upping his temperature."

"Why were his eyes yellow?"

"Because even if he lives through the fever, Bangor is still grupped." Everson glanced back at me. "Genetically corrupted."

Ahead of us, a pool of light illuminated a massive gate made of chain link and corrugated steel, topped with canti-levered spikes wrapped in razor wire. As if that wasn't intimidation enough, a guard booth was stationed beside it. Everson pointed past the gate. "We're at the bridge."

"The *last* bridge?" I peered through the fence and could make out its skeletal silhouette against the river.

"The one and only."

Despite all the spotlights aimed at the gate, the bridge itself was disappointingly dark. Probably another security measure. Still, when Everson wasn't looking, I pushed record and aimed my dial toward it. It was a famous landmark, after all.

"Listen," he whispered.

I'd heard it too. A child's voice saying, "Please help us." The guard didn't stir in his sentry station, even though he had to have heard the child as well. Everson slipped behind the guard booth. I followed and saw a little girl in a filthy T-shirt clinging to the chain link on the bridge side. Clearly the gate itself wasn't electrified. A man in a blood-soaked shirt and torn pants lay in a wagon beside her, his limbs draped over the edges. At Everson's approach, the girl looked up with eyes a nice, normal shade of brown. If she wasn't infected, where had she come from?

"Please help him." The girl pushed a snarl of black hair behind her ear. She had to be ten at most.

Everson peered through the fence at the unconscious man. "Was he mauled?"

Mauled. The word wound up my spine and clung there.

"My mom turned. She went — She was about to . . ." Shuddering, the girl looked down at the man in the wagon.

His face was tipped away from us, which was probably a good thing since the sight of his chest and right leg made me light-headed. I couldn't tell stripped shirt from stripped flesh. Only the faint wheeze of his breathing revealed that he was alive.

"Get away from the gate, you stupid grunts!" shouted an angry voice. I turned to see a ruddy-faced guard step from the booth. His gaze skipped over me and onto Everson. "You," he spat. "What a surprise."

Ignoring him, Everson crouched so that he was at eye level with the little girl. "What's your name?" he asked in a voice so low and gentle that I couldn't help but stare. Where was this guy when I was back on the hill? Or standing in my underwear between the barracks? Moments that wouldn't have been nearly so nerve-wracking if he'd used that tone with me.

"Jia," the girl said, still clinging to the chain link.

"Did your mother bite him, Jia?" Everson nodded to the unconscious man with blood pooling by his outstretched leg. The girl gave a pained shrug. "Where is your mom now?" Rising, Everson looked past her into the darkness beyond.

Jia took up the man's hand. "He shot her. . . ." She said it so softly I wasn't sure that I'd heard her right. "To save me."

The ruddy-faced guard stalked toward us. "I told you, no one here is going to help you," he snapped at her. "So, take off. And take him with you." He pointed his gun at the mauled man.

"I'll test them." Everson turned on the guard. "If they're clean, you're going to open the gate."

The two glared at each other. Then, surprisingly, the guard retreated. "Sure, let them in. What do I care?" he snarled before slamming back into the booth. "Let them *all* in, big man."

Guess I wasn't the only one who thought Everson was bossy.

"I need to get some things so I can test your blood," Everson told Jia. "And his."

"But he needs help now," she cried.

"I can't touch him yet. But I'll be back with a couple of

medics who've had a lot more training than me. If he's not infected, they'll help him. I promise."

As we hurried toward a large building, there was so much I wanted to know — like did uninfected people live in the Feral Zone? But I was too worried about the little girl to think straight. "If Jia's mother is dead, where will she go? Who's going to take care of her?"

"If she tests clean, I'll take her to the orphan camp," Everson said. "It's on the other end of the island."

Orphan camp. That didn't sound too awful. It had to be better than living with a mother who attacked people. "How could Jia's mother have mauled that man?" I asked from behind him.

"Later."

But as another series of screeches erupted from beyond the fence, I caught up with Everson. "What is happening to these people?"

He sighed, relenting, but didn't slow his pace. "You know Ferae is a bootloader virus, right?"

"I don't even know what that means."

"It means Ferae carries foreign DNA. Animal DNA, to be exact. So do other viruses — swine flu, avian. The difference is that Ferae dumps its load into the infected person's system. It's called viral transduction. And when that happens, the person is epically grupped."

"Because he'll mutate . . . but *how*?" The screech from across the river trailed off. A chill skittered through me and I stopped short. "They become animals."

"Not all the way." Everson faced me, his expression grim. "They're still *part* human. . . ."

SIX

The moment I set foot in the dimly lit infirmary, memories of my mother threatened to shut me down. The building had clearly not been designed to be an infirmary — doors with frosted windows lined the hall, making it seem more like an old office building — and yet the antiseptic smell gave away its current function. The smell also brought back the desperation I'd felt the day they'd checked my mother into the hospital, knowing it was for the last time — that she'd never come home again.

Everson led the way through the echoing corridor, and I kept my face ducked until we stepped into a dark office. When he flipped on the light, I glanced at him and was caught by surprise. He was younger than I'd thought — only a year or so older than me. And despite the cropped hair, military fatigues, and the fact that he stood a head taller than me, he wasn't nearly as intimidating as before. Probably because he wasn't trying to be.

I tore my gaze from him and wiped my sweaty palms on my pants. The office was a mess. Crumpled food wrappers and blue inhalers littered the floor. All the cupboards were flung open and a mini refrigerator sat precariously on a stack of storage bins. Had biohaz agents come here and tossed Dr. Solis's office because of his association with my father?

"He's probably in the lab," Everson said as he pulled a couple of latex gloves from a box. Since he didn't seem the least bit alarmed, I figured the doctor must leave his office like this all the time.

"What kind of doctor is Dr. Solis?"

"A virologist," Everson said, pocketing the gloves. "A long time ago he worked for the CDC."

"What's the CDC?" I scooped a midnight-blue inhaler off the floor.

"The Centers for Disease Control. It was a government agency that got cut before the plague."

"What did they do?"

"Prevent plagues . . ." He loaded on the irony.

I snorted. Every history lesson about the early part of this century seemed to end with a *ba-dum-bum-ching*. I shook the inhaler by my ear but there was no slosh. At one point it had contained a sleeping spray called Lull, which I was somewhat familiar with. It had been prescribed to my father back when he'd had hernia surgery. After just one night, he'd thrown the inhaler away because the Lull had knocked him out cold for twelve hours straight.

Everson's dark brows drew together when he saw what I was holding. "The doctor has trouble sleeping."

He must — since the trash can contained enough inhalers to conk out a herd of stampeding elephants.

Everson strode to the desk and picked up an inhaler lying there. "He's been on call since dawn, so he'll be dying to sleep." He met my gaze as he pocketed the Lull. "If he takes a hit before you two talk, you may as well ask the wall about your dad. I'll tell him you're here, then I'm going to try to convince a couple of medics to come back to the gate with me." He headed for the door, snagging a white box off a shelf on his way. At the door, he paused. "Don't touch anything."

I stiffened. Did I look like a thief?

"I didn't mean — There are eighteen strains of Ferae in there." He pointed at the mini fridge. "You don't want to infect yourself — that's all I meant."

"Oh." No, I definitely did not want to infect myself. In fact, I was going to sit down and keep my hands in my lap until Dr. Solis showed up. Maybe I'd even keep my breathing to a minimum. I did a slow turn in place, trying to decide what spot looked the least germy. Would it be rude to move the doctor's paperwork? I eyed the stack of files on the chair next to me. A corner of a photo stuck out from the pile. I stared at it. Moving the stack — questionable. Riffling through it — definitely rude. And yet I reached for the photo, gently pulled it free of the pile . . . and then nearly swallowed a lung.

I flipped the photo over before the image gave me brain damage, but of course, within a second I had to take another peek. The picture was of a person's open mouth with a scattering of oozing sores where teeth should have been. In some of the gaps, new teeth were growing in — triangular, serrated, and definitely not human.

My conscience pinged but I couldn't stop myself; I sifted through the stack and found a manila folder labeled "Stage Two: Physical Mutation." Inside were more photos of human body parts gone very, very wrong. Two curling yellow horns that poked through someone's dark hair. A child's fingers that ended in claws. A man's forearm sprouting patches of spotted fur.

"Not an attractive bunch, are they?" asked a voice behind me.

I spun as a man with graying hair closed the office door — Dr. Solis, judging by his white lab coat. He was so willowy that a child could have pushed him over. He smiled. "I don't suppose they show you pictures like that in your science classes."

"No, never." I slid the photos back into the folder, despite feeling a pressing need to flip through the rest of the pile. Actually, what I really wanted was to swipe a few and smuggle them into the West to show Anna. I needed someone to shriek with.

"I'm Vincent Solis," he said. "And you are Delaney. It's good to finally meet you, even if the circumstances aren't the best." He saw my surprise and added, "Everson says you're looking for Mack."

Yes, I was, but the mutated body parts had hijacked my thoughts. "Can you cure them?" I pointed to the file with the photos.

"No." Sighing, he settled into the chair behind the desk. "I can't even develop an effective vaccine until I have samples of all the different strains. So far the most I've come up with is an inhibitor that slows the rate of the mutation. It's not much, but they're clamoring for it over there." He waved airily toward what I guessed was the East. "Every month, your father takes a crate of it to a group of infected people living in an old quarantine compound. They tell him about any changes they've noticed or if they're experiencing side effects. It's not an ideal way to conduct research, but until the law changes, I don't dare go myself."

"Why not?" It was okay for my father to risk infection and arrest, but not him?

"Titan pays for all of this" — he swept a shaky hand at the room and the corridor beyond — "in the hopes that I'll find a way to immunize the line guards. They don't care about those who are already infected. The CEO, Ilsa Prejean, has made it quite clear that if I ever cross the river to collect data, she'll cut my funding. You see, the corporation that gets paid to enforce the quarantine can't afford to employ a quarantine breaker. That's why I'm so grateful to your father. I couldn't have gotten this far without him."

"Do you know where he is now?"

"Mack cut through camp last night. Stopped by just long enough to tell me that biohaz agents were right behind him. They weren't. Not that I saw anyway." Dr. Solis began patting down his lab coat until he found a blue inhaler in a pocket.

"Where did he go?"

Dr. Solis shook the inhaler, frowned, and tossed it aside. "To Moline, the quarantine compound I mentioned. Mack has friends there."

My mouth went dry. He'd gone back into the Feral Zone where mutants with claws and horns went around mauling people? Inhibitor or not, that sounded suicidal. "What if one of them bites him?"

"I don't believe any have progressed to stage three of the disease."

"What?"

"I'm sorry. You're worried about your father and I'm talking like a virologist."

"No, it's okay. I want to know."

With a nod, Dr. Solis leaned forward, bracing his forearms on the desk. "There are three stages to Ferae. The first presents with a high fever within one to ten hours after infection. Once the virus is established, the fever ends and the patient regains his faculties. After that, the virus begins a slow takeover of the body and the patient starts to manifest physical signs of infection." He gestured toward the file of photographs. "Anatomical deformities. Stage two can last anywhere from weeks to years. It all depends on the patient's health, genetics, access to antiviral medication. . . . Many factors." He sighed and rubbed his eyes. "The third and final stage of Ferae is insanity. The virus invades the brain, at which point the patient becomes animalistic and highly aggressive."

"Oh." And I'd thought his photos were gruesome. What was playing in my mind now, however, combined those images with sounds and actions to terrifying effect.

"Incubation, mutation, psychosis — those are the stages." Dr. Solis rose and moved unsteadily toward the bookcase. "We used to compare Ferae to rabies. Now we know the better model is syphilis, which has a symptomatic stage that can last decades before dementia finally sets in."

After a moment of scrounging through boxes on the shelves, he found an inhaler and gave it a dreamy smile.

"Anyway, Mack tells me that in the past year, no one in Moline has progressed to the final stage. I'd like to think it's because of the inhibitor he's been taking them, but who knows?" Squeezing the inhaler, the doctor sucked in the Lull and, surprisingly, he seemed to straighten up. Guess the drug didn't work very well on him. "You needn't worry, Delaney. Your father will lie low for a while and then come back to check that the coast is clear, which it is."

"It isn't," I said, feeling a throb in my temples. "The bio-hazard agents *are* after him. They recorded him breaking quarantine."

Dr. Solis's gaze sharpened despite the Lull in his system.

"Have you seen the recording?" he asked. "You know for a fact that it exists?"

I nodded. "Where is Moline?" What I really wanted to know was just how far my father had ventured into the Feral Zone. Stuffing the cap into my back pocket, I took out my dad's map and spread it across the desk. "Show me?"

Why was I bothering with this? Spurling's orders were to come right back if I couldn't find my dad. Still, I watched as Dr. Solis pointed to a spot on the map — a city, which had been circled in dark ink.

"It's directly across the river," he said. "Just off the northeastern tip of the island. There used to be a bridge there, back in the day, but not now."

I touched the tiny line that was the last and only bridge across the Mississippi. Like the bridge that I'd crossed to get from the west bank onto Arsenal, the last bridge to the Feral Zone was on the south end of the island. "How big is Arsenal?"

"A thousand acres."

"I mean from end to end."

"A little over three miles." He sank into the chair behind his desk. "Are they threatening execution?"

"Yes," I said softly.

The doctor dragged his hand down his face. "Mack knew that it might come to this — that something could happen, making it impossible for him to return west."

"Why didn't he warn me about that possibility or tell me that he's a fetch or mention anything about any of this *ever*?" It came out harsher than I'd intended.

"If it helps, Mack goes around that issue all the time. It always comes down to the lie detector test."

"What?"

"The one they'll give you if he's caught. They're very good now, those tests. Accurate ninety-nine percent of the time. A person's body gives him away with the tiniest release of chemicals. If that test revealed that you knew your father was crossing the quarantine line, you'd be condemned as a traitor and executed alongside him."

"Oh." The vision I had of my dad being shot by a firing squad . . . He must have had a similar one of me — one that had played in his mind for years. For the first time since the jumpsuits had hauled me out of Orlando's party, I felt my guts unknot a bit. Now my father's silence made sense. If I only could talk to him and tell him about Director Spurling's offer, then he could put aside that worry.

"How can I get a message to him?" I asked Dr. Solis.

"You can't. All we can do is wait for Mack to come out of hiding."

"Wait?" I didn't have time for that. Correction, my dad didn't.

"You're welcome to stay, like Everson, like me," the doctor murmured. "Stay because of a parent."

What was he talking about?

"Like you, I'm here for my father."

Dr. Solis looked old enough to be my grandfather. Could his father even be alive? "Is he living in the Feral Zone?"

"No, no, he died many years ago. He was a doctor too." Dr. Solis sank lower in his chair. "He left Cuba the year he finished medical school. He had to go; to stay meant death. But for the rest of his life, my father thought about his countrymen — the *cubanos* who hadn't gotten out. They didn't fare so well. So when the exodus came, I couldn't cut and run. I'd taken on the burden of his guilt."

"What did your father have to feel guilty about? You said he would have died if he'd stayed in Cuba."

"Yes, he *had* to go, just like those who left during the exodus. Fleeing death is perfectly reasonable." He gave me a wry smile. "Reason has its advantages. Unfortunately, it doesn't do much for insomnia. Or heartbreak . . ." His voice faded as his chin sank onto his chest. The Lull had finally kicked in. I hoped that sleep would bring him some relief from his exhaustion and sadness, even if only temporarily.

I picked up the map and traced the circle around Moline. If I were to cross the last bridge — a very big if — I would then have to walk three miles up the riverbank to reach Moline. Three miles in the Feral Zone . . .

I folded up the map and returned it to my dad's bag.

What was three miles? Nothing. If the road was flat, I could jog it in under an hour.

Suddenly a howl, long and pained, cut through the corridor. I swung around to stare at the closed door, heart jumping in my chest. Did I want to know what that was? No, I did not. But if I planned to cross the river — and I realized I did — I should know what I was in for. I snatched up the messenger bag, pulled the cap over my hair, and slipped out of Dr. Solis's office.

I followed the keening sound down the hall to a door, open just a crack. Inside, the infected guard, Bangor — red faced and sweating — struggled against the leather straps that bound him to a bed. In the far corner, a guard hunkered in a chair, his hands over his ears, his body turned toward the window like he wanted to dive through it. I didn't blame him. Bangor seemed to be having a seizure, with his throat muscles bulging and eyes rolling. What if he bit off his tongue? They should have left the muzzle on. He let out another savage howl, followed by a jumble of sounds — almost words — that sent me backing down the hall.

Voices around the next corner were heading my way. I darted into a dark room marked "Supplies." I made a quick scan of the rows of metal shelves and then returned to the door. But as I peeked into the hall, hands grabbed me from behind and twisted my arm up my back.

"Crappy reflexes for a guard," a harsh voice whispered in my ear.

· SEVEN ·

Contorting, I tried to see my attacker, but he forced me to face the wall. I swallowed my scream. Better to contend with one man than bring a whole slew of guards down on my head. I stopped struggling as well. Whoever this guy was, he wasn't going to let me go until he wanted to. Begging wouldn't help — that much I remembered from self-defense class.

"I'm not going to report you," I said in the calmest voice I could muster.

He *tsk*ed. "That was too easy. Most guards don't promise that until after I've tied them up."

The scornful way he said "guards" meant that he wasn't one. Figuring I had nothing to lose, I said, "I'm not a guard."

"Right," he scoffed. "You just dress like one?" His breath warmed the side of my neck as he leaned closer. "And smell like — Hey, how come you smell like a meadow?"

"Get off me!" I shoved my elbow back, hitting what felt like ribs.

Spinning me around, he pulled the cap from my head. "You're *not* a guard." He smacked the wall beside me and the lights snapped on, bright and blinding.

As my eyes adjusted, the first thing that struck me was his lack of a shirt. Since line guards did not waltz around showing off an acre of sun-kissed skin, he clearly didn't belong here any more than I did. I raised my gaze and lost my breath.

Hopefully he'd put my open-mouthed silence down to having startled me. Then again, with that face, he had to be used to gawkers. Sculpted lips, aquamarine eyes — an artist could put a sword in his hand and paint him as the archangel Michael. Fierce and beautiful.

"Feral got your tongue?" he asked.

Yes — if being from the Feral Zone meant that he was a feral. Wait, *was* he? He didn't seem to have any claws or stripes or hooves or —

"Breathe, rabbit. I'll only hurt you if you do something stupid."

I cleared my throat. "Define *stupid*."

When his lips pulled back, I flinched, only to realize that I'd amused him. "Have you been locked in a tower your whole life?" he asked. "There's not a mark on you."

Was he making fun of me? Probably, since he had to be around my age and yet was showing some serious wear and tear: Scars crosshatched his ribs and arms. Another edged his left eye. A few were the results of crude stitches, but the rest . . . claw marks? Scratches? Who cared?! I snatched my cap from his fingers.

"You know it's illegal to impersonate a guard," he said.

"Like you're going to report me." I didn't know where to look. I wasn't used to talking to half-naked boys.

"That goes both ways." His mouth held the hint of a smile, but then he strolled away, lithe and unself-conscious, his pants riding dangerously low on his hips. They'd been slashed off below the knees — probably by the same knife that had done the hack job on his light brown hair. He crouched by a dirty green knapsack on the floor, stuffed to overflowing. After trying several times to zip it up, he resorted to dumping out some of the contents. I angled closer and saw pill packs, syringes, moldable casts, and sterilized packets of silica gel.

My anger flared. Having worked in a rescue shelter I knew just how valuable those supplies were. "You can't steal from an infirmary!"

"Maybe *you* can't." He zipped up his knapsack and rose. "I've got it down to an art."

He stood within a foot of me — close enough that I could smell the river on him — and looked me over, slow and deliberate. As much as I wanted to retreat, I smothered the impulse. Running from a stray dog just triggered it to give chase. And this guy was all street dog — definitely stray. "How did you get across the bridge?" I asked.

"Trade secret." He swung the knapsack onto his back and headed for the door.

"Wait, are you going back to the Feral Zone?"

"What's it to you?"

"Can I follow you?"

He swung around, surprised. "No, you can't follow me."

"I won't get in your way."

"Looking at you gets in my way."

I wrinkled my nose. He was making no sense at all. But I had a feeling I knew how to speak his language. "I'll pay you to take me to Moline."

His eyes narrowed with interest. "Pay me how?"

"How much do you want?"

"How much of *what*?"

Was he being dense on purpose or along with those scars had he taken a few too many blows to the head? "How much money do you want for escorting me to Moline?"

"Money?" His grin softened the precise angles of his face. "That's good. Silky, the only thing I can do with paper money is burn it or wipe my —"

"Got it," I said quickly. "You don't need money."

"What've you got to barter?"

I pulled off my father's bag and peered inside. "A flashlight, matches —"

"How about a sleeping bag?" he interrupted.

I slumped. Of course, something like a sleeping bag would be valuable in his world. "No."

"Perfect. Share mine tonight and I'll take you to Moline in the morning. Deal?"

My lips parted, but words failed me. He wasn't serious. He couldn't be. "You're a pig!"

"Absolutely not." He extended his arms as if offering himself up for inspection. "I am one hundred percent human."

"That's debatable," said a voice from the doorway.

I turned to see Everson with a gun in his hand. With relief I took a step toward him, only to be jerked backward, hard. A tan forearm stretched across my ribs. The guy's naked chest was pressed against my back. With a cry, I tried to pry his arm off, but then a cool line touched my throat. His knife.

Everson's alarm froze me into place. "Rafe, right?" His too-calm tone amped up my panic another notch. It was the pitch I used when trying to soothe a snarling stray. "Let's talk about this."

"Jerk, right?" Rafe said, sounding sociable, though his arm tightened across me. "Shut up and get in the closet." He tilted his head toward a door on the far wall.

Everson might have been taller and broader, but I had no doubt about which of them was more dangerous.

"Let the girl go first."

"Why?" Rafe asked. "What's she to you?"

Everson glared at him. "Let her go." He set his gun on the floor and held up his hands. "And you can walk out of here. I won't stop you."

"Heck of a deal. Here's my counter. . . ." The pressure of the knife against my throat vanished.

Releasing my breath, I started to pull away when a flash of pain seared across my forearm.

"You son of a —" Everson beat a fast path into the closet. Once he was inside, Rafe dragged me over as well. Stumbling, I stared at the blood beading up on my arm.

He'd cut me. With a knife. Who did that?

He flung me against Everson, sending us both sprawling against the shelves at the back of the closet. "She's all yours," he said, and slammed the door shut.

Everson leapt up and grabbed the knob just as there was a loud scrape from the other side. The knob turned futilely in his fist. Crouching, I peered under the door and saw two legs of what must have been a leaning chair propped under the knob.

"Have fun, you two," Rafe mocked, and his footsteps faded away.

· EIGHT ·

In the dim glow from my dial, Everson did a quick search of the shelves and tossed me a gauze pad. "Press it to your cut. It'll slow the bleeding."

I gingerly did as he said and was rewarded with a throb of pain. Trapped and bleeding. Just when I didn't have a minute to spare. "Who was that scumbag?"

Everson ran his hands over the wall on either side of the door. "A thief who's turned Arsenal into his own personal Quickie-mart." He gave up patting down the wall and crouched beside me. "The light switch must be outside the closet." He nodded to my arm. "Show me."

I lifted the bloody wad of gauze and bit back a cry. That savage had sliced a nasty three-inch cut into my arm. What passed for civilized over here? Not eating your neighbor?

"Could be worse." Everson snagged a bottle of hydrogen peroxide from a shelf.

"That's comforting," I grouched. At least my tetanus vaccination was up to date.

"You could've gotten knifed in the gut, like the cook's assistant. His mistake? Walking into the pantry while Rafe was cleaning it out last month."

Okay, yes, that was worse. But I still wasn't happy about having an open wound this close to the Feral Zone.

"Can your dial go brighter?" He ripped open a new gauze pad.

I lifted my dial, remembering only then that it had been recording the whole time. This was going to make a heck of a movie — if I survived to edit it. With a tap of my finger, I made the screen glow with emerald light — not as bright as a flashlight, but enough to see by.

Everson crouched next to me where I was sitting against the door — all the other walls were lined with shelves. He gently took my forearm and tilted it. I winced as he poured peroxide over the cut and watched as he neatly wiped away the excess froth with gauze. His movements were steady and efficient as he bent over my arm to bandage it, I'd always thought crew cuts were ugly — still did — but I was tempted to brush my palm over his hair just to see how it felt. Soft or bristly?

He sat back and caught me staring. I tugged my arm away and pretended to try to activate the dial's call function.

"It won't work as a phone," he said, standing to reshelve the supplies. "The patrol jams the signal. We're not allowed to have dials or cameras — nothing that can record. Actually, I should confiscate that." He walked toward me, and I clutched the dial protectively. "But lucky for you, I'm only a guard on the outside." He stepped over me to get to the door.

"What are you on the inside?" I asked.

He started pounding, trying to attract someone's attention. Guess I wasn't going to get an answer.

After a while with no results, he gave up. "I brought Jia

here so the medics could work on the guy. I left her asleep in one of the empty beds." He shoved a hand through his hair. "I need to get her to the orphan camp before someone finds her and sends her back across the bridge."

"Is she okay? Not . . . grupped?"

He sank down beside me, his shoulder brushing mine. "She tested clean. So did the man, according to the medic. But it might be too late for him. He lost a lot of blood."

And here I'd been feeling resentful about the passing time. Yes, every hour mattered if my dad was going to escape execution, but for the man who'd been mauled, minutes meant the difference between life and death. The air in the closet suddenly tasted stale.

I tugged down my sleeve to cover the bandage, even though I was starting to feel sweaty. "How come we know nothing about what's going on over here?"

"Titan makes sure of it." He leaned back, one leg outstretched, not seeming to care that we were trapped in a cramped closet together. "All of our communication is monitored — radio calls, letters. And those are just to other bases. We're not allowed to talk to civilians while we're stationed east of the wall." He glanced at me, a hint of a smile on his lips. "So, I'm incurring some serious infractions right now."

Was he flirting with me? Not a chance. Robots didn't flirt. "What about when you go home? What's to stop you from talking then?"

"Our mission is categorized critical-sensitive. If a guard reveals anything about what he did or saw over here, he'll be court-martialed."

Sitting with our shoulders and legs touching felt strange. Awkward. Maybe line guards got used to living up close and personal on the base, but I sure wasn't used to it. I rarely brushed against anyone other than my dad and Howard. If I slid over, would Everson notice? Would he care?

I rubbed my damp palms on my pants, but stayed put. Why risk offending the only line guard on my side? "How come no one noticed the mutated humans running around before the wall went up?"

"It didn't start happening until a few years after the wall was finished. During the first wave, if you caught Ferae, you went psychotic and died within days. We're seeing more of the nonlethal strain now because when the host survives, he goes on to infect more people."

"Okay." I crossed my legs and twisted to face him. "But why's the patrol keeping that secret? So what if we know that people don't die from Ferae anymore, that they . . . mutate?" I choked on the word.

"It's not just the patrol. People in the government know, but they contracted Titan to secure the quarantine line, so they're following Titan's protocol."

"And they're all keeping quiet about the ferals because . . . ?" I pressed.

"Think about how fast the exodus happened. A lot of people left without being able to get ahold of family members in other cities and states. By now, they're assumed long dead. If people start to think there's a chance their relatives are still alive, they'll want to go looking for them. They'll try like crazy to get past the wall and make it impossible to keep the quarantine line secure." Everson shot me a look. "When you're worried about someone you love, you don't care about anyone else's health — sometimes not even your own."

Ouch.

I sat back against the door to avoid his gaze. He had a point, but as soon as we got out of this closet, I was going to cross the last bridge. I'd just have to deal with the guilt . . . and the ferals. Suddenly something Everson had said in the office came back to me. "If Dr. Solis has eighteen strains of Ferae, does that mean people can mutate into eighteen different kinds of animals?"

"Fifty. You can only get infected once, but there are fifty strains of Ferae, each carrying the DNA of a different animal. Until Dr. Solis has a sample of all of them, he can't even begin to develop a vaccine."

"If he doesn't have them all, how does he know there are fifty strains out there?"

Everson looked at his long fingers, which dangled off his knee. "You know where the virus came from, right?"

I nodded. I knew our country's history. "Titan created it in a lab. They were going to add cool animal hybrids to the mazes in their theme parks." I couldn't help sounding excited about it — it did sound fun — but Everson slanted a cranky look at me. "And then some fringe group bombed Titan's labs," I went on, "and the infected animals escaped. In reparation, Titan built the wall."

"The wall was a PR move," he scoffed.

"I still don't get how Dr. Solis knows there are fifty strains."

"When the plague began, Titan's CEO, Isla Prejean, made Titan's research available to the scientific community. She was hoping that someone could find a way to stop the spread of infection. That's how we know there are fifty strains." Everson's jaw tightened. "If we're ever going to reclaim the eastern half of our country, we need a vaccine. Better yet, a cure. And we're never going to develop either if someone doesn't go deeper into the Feral Zone and find people infected with the strains that we're missing."

"Then what? You'd bring those people here?"

"No. All Dr. Solis needs is a sample of their blood."

My brows rose. "Good luck collecting that."

"It's dangerous, yeah. But I'd go. I volunteered."

"The patrol won't let you?"

"The brass won't even consider it. They say our job is to secure the quarantine line, not cross it."

"Why doesn't the president send in the army?" Even before I finished asking it, I knew the answer. "Because our military is a joke." Anyone who wanted to enlist these days usually chose to work for a private security force, like the line patrol. Not only did corporate militias pay better, they also had state-of-the-art weapons, equipment, and training centers.

"The national armed forces aren't a joke," Everson said sternly. "Every branch lost more than half their people during the outbreak because they were stationed in hot zones, trying to contain the spread of infection."

And clearly he admired them for it. "Are you sure you're not a guard on the inside?"

A flash of something dark crossed his features and he glanced away.

"Sorry," I said quickly. "Why did you join the line patrol instead of the army?"

He tipped his head back against the door and stayed silent for a moment. Just as I thought he wasn't going to answer, he spoke, his voice low and rough. "You know how everyone says their parents are overprotective?"

"Yes, because they *are*."

"Okay, take that paranoia, multiply it by a thousand, and you have my mother. She lives in terror of catching Ferae. My father died in the first wave of the plague and she never got over it. When I was growing up, she wouldn't let me go anywhere or do anything with anyone."

"Join the club."

"No, I mean literally." He turned to me, his expression serious. "She has blowers set up in every room. Plastic sheeting over all the windows and doors. She works from home, so the only people she sees are her employees, who have no choice but to put up with her insane rules. Even my tutors had to change into sanitized clothes before they could come near me."

"Tutors, as in teachers you met with in person?"

He nodded stiffly. "When I was seven, I tried to sneak out. That's when my mother told me that I was born with an autoimmune deficiency and that if I ever left home, I'd die."

I struggled to understand. His mother had lied to him about having a birth defect just to keep him at home? "But it's not true?"

"Obviously." He gestured to the air around us.

"Whoa." And I'd thought I had it bad. Suddenly my dad's obsession with survival skills and self-defense seemed almost sane. "That's . . . um, pretty messed up."

"Yeah." He rubbed his forehead like he'd downed a slushy too fast.

"When did you find out that you're fine?"

"A year ago," he said, dropping his hand. "I left home that day and joined the patrol. I'd read that there was a doctor on Arsenal working on a cure, so I got myself assigned here. I'd rather fight Ferae head on than spend my life hiding from it."

"I didn't know line guards got to choose their assignments."

"I'm not your average guard," he said offhandedly. "For one thing, I've completed all of the undergrad science courseware and passed the exam."

"Undergrad as in college?"

"Yes." At my incredulous look, he shrugged. "I was locked inside for years. What else was I going to do?"

It was possible. Now that school was held online, you could move at your own pace, fast or slow. Even I'd skipped a grade. I sighed inwardly. So what if Everson was smart? He was also a guard who was supposed to keep the quarantine line secure. He was not about to help me find a way to get across the river, which was all that mattered right now.

He nudged my knee. "You're handling all this really well. That or" — he shifted to see my face — "you're great at hiding your feelings."

"Showing them doesn't change anything." You just ended up looking pathetic, like when I'd called my supposed friends after my mom died, begging them to play with me, sobbing on the view screen when they'd refused. Dad and I moved to Davenport a year later, and I never saw any of them again, but I still cringed thinking about it.

Everson waited for me to say more, but I just shrugged. What else was there to say? Of course I was wrung out with worry for my dad and scared sick just thinking about crossing the bridge, but I could handle it — would handle it — because seeing my dad get executed . . . That I couldn't handle.

"So," Everson said after a moment. "What does that director want fetched? Must be important if she's willing to risk her career to cut a deal with Mack."

"I don't know." I couldn't believe I hadn't opened Director Spurling's letter to my dad. I pulled the messenger bag across the floor and took out the envelope. I held it flat on my open palm. It was wrong to open other people's letters.

Everson plucked the envelope from my hand and tore it open unceremoniously. So much for holding it in the steam of a teakettle so I could open it without having to admit it later. I pulled my ponytail tight as he unfolded the letter, written on heavy cream-colored paper that matched the envelope.

"Dear Mack," he read aloud. "I'm told that's what your clients call you, and that's how you should think of me, as a client — only I won't be paying your exorbitant fee in money. There is something I left behind in Chicago that I want very badly. If you can find it and bring it to me, I will erase the recording I have of you entering the checkpoint chamber and delete the files I've been amassing for the past several years on you and your clients.

"If you do complete the fetch, rest assured it will be your last. I know that your wife's cancer bankrupted you, but surely you have enough now to live on until you find honest work in your field. If you value your life and your freedom, you will never again after this fetch cross the quarantine line. Say good-bye to the East, Mack, for good, for your own sake and for your daughter's."

Everson held the letter between us and pointed to what Spurling had written at the bottom of the page. An address in Chicago and "Arabella Spurling, age 6. Brown hair, blue eyes. Any photo in good condition."

Arabella Spurling. She must have been Director Spurling's daughter. I actually felt a little bad for her for a moment, until I remembered that she was the reason my dad was on the run in the Feral Zone.

Everson let the letter drop to the floor. "What kind of person sends a clueless girl into the most dangerous situation possible for a photo?" There was as much venom in his voice as in a bucket of chimpacabra spit.

I knew it was a rhetorical question, but I thought about it anyway. What kind of person did such a thing? A desperate one. I wondered if her memories of her daughter had begun to fade. I could still remember what my mother had looked like, because I had file upon file of digital video of our family. I could still see her face and hear her voice any time I wanted to. Except for right now, of course.

What I couldn't do was feel her arms around me or her kiss at the edge of my hairline. I could still remember how she smelled — like honey, somehow — but there might be a day when I couldn't conjure that up. If that ever happened, I could imagine feeling quite desperate.

I picked up Spurling's letter. Wait. What had Everson just called me?

"I am not clueless," I said, sitting up straighter against the door. "In fact, my dad has been telling me about the Feral Zone for years."

"But he never mentioned the grupped ferals who live there?"

"He did. He just didn't call them grupped ferals." They were the were-beasts, mongrels, and manimals from his bedtime stories. Only now I knew that they weren't fiction. Dad had been describing his day at the office, which happened to be in a forbidden quarantine zone. "And yes, okay, he may have sugarcoated things a bit. But it doesn't matter because no one forced me to come here. And even after being attacked by an infected guy and seeing a man bleeding to death in a wagon because he'd been *mauled* and finding those horrible photos of mutated body parts, I'm still glad I —"

I couldn't breathe.

I put my head down and tried to take in air, but my lungs grew stiffer by the second. And then the gasping started and I heard myself suffocating.

Everson held something up to my face, commanding, "Inhale."

A prickly scent blasted up my nose and into my brain where it switched on strings of fairy lights at the back of my

eyeballs. Choking, I shoved his hand away. "What was —"
Then I saw the dark-blue inhaler in his palm and my bones
melted.

"It's Lull," he explained. "I didn't press long enough to
put you out. It'll just calm you down." He tucked the inhaler
into the front pocket of my pants. "If you're still anxious,
take another hit."

Another hit? I fell back against the door.

"Okaaay . . . ," Everson said, surprised.

The air around me turned into gelatin as I dripped down
the wall.

"Actually," he said. "Let's keep it at one."

Sure. Whatever. The door lolled against my back. My
cheek dipped onto my shoulder. I tried to straighten up, but
had lost my sense of up. Much easier to let gravity do the
figuring so I let it pull me down. My head landed on something that wasn't the floor. Not too soft, not too hard. "Just
right," I murmured.

"Oh crap," said a voice, warm on my ear. "I'm sorry. I
didn't know you'd be so sensitive."

"S'okay." Rolling to my side, I snuggled down for the
night. My fingers curled into the sheet and pulled it to my
chin. "I like the scary ones," I assured him. And I did. I also
liked it when he stayed until I fell asleep. I reached up and
cupped his cheek, firm and warm. "You need to shave," I
murmured, tracing a finger down his sideburn, and then
wondered why that would make my father gasp.

· NINE ·

I couldn't place what was wrong with the scream. The note. The pitch. Something was off. The person screamed again, which dragged me into consciousness. He didn't sound scared. . . . I rolled onto my back, listening to the drawn out howl.

"It's Bangor," said a voice so close I flinched.

Sitting up, I searched the darkness. As my eyes adjusted, my memories came flooding back. I was still in the supply-room closet. Twisting, I found Everson seated behind me. My gaze narrowed on his lap. "Did I —"

"I'm sorry about the Lull. I didn't mean —"

"How long was I out?"

Everson rose, avoiding my gaze. "A couple of hours. I'm not sure. I fell asleep too. Look, I didn't —" He sighed and rubbed the back of his neck. "Sorry."

A couple of hours — that was all? The muddy flow of my thoughts felt like the result of a weeklong coma.

A gunshot rang out, startling us both, followed by another scream — agonized this time. Everson dropped his face into his palm. When boots sprinted into the supply room beyond the door, I rose on usteady legs.

The chair wedged under the knob was flung aside with a crash and the closet door opened.

The infected guard, Bangor, stood before us, wavering on his feet, though his yellow-eyed gaze seemed sharp enough as it settled on me. When he lunged, Everson shoved me back and grabbed Bangor by the shoulders, holding him at arm's length.

Where were the other guards?

I had to help Everson. I snagged the tranq gun from his thigh holster. Who knew if the safety was on or if the thing was even loaded? Still, I aimed it at the yellow-eyed guard.

"Lane, don't" Everson said.

What? I stepped aside to see his face, but his gaze was locked onto Bangor.

"Help me, Ev." The man clutched at Everson's shirt. "Don't let them put me out there. I'm okay. The fever's broken. I'm going to be okay. Tell Dr. Solis he can try anything on me. Just let me stay here."

The guards arrived then, and Bangor bellowed as they dragged him backward out of the closet doorway. A guard knocked Bangor's hands off of Everson so that the others could force him to the floor. Everson took the tranq gun from me, reholstered it, and stepped out of the closet. I stayed as far back as possible and pulled on my cap.

"You shot him?" Everson stared down at the scuffling men.

I followed his gaze and found the hole in the thigh of Bangor's pants, the growing aura of blood around it.

"What were we supposed to do? He ran." The tremor in the guard's voice matched the one in my stomach. His gaze flicked to me and then back to Everson. "What are you two doing in there?"

"We were locked in." Everson pointed at the chair Bangor had flung aside. "Rafe."

Another guard shot to his feet and looked around the supply room. "Is he still here?"

"Long gone."

"I hate that guy," the guard muttered, rubbing his side as if he'd just taken a punch.

Bangor wept as the guards set to work binding his wrists and ankles with leather straps. I edged into the doorway of the closet. No one seemed to be paying me any attention at this point. Not with a crying, bleeding man on the floor. "Where are they taking him?"

Something dark flickered in Everson's expression. "He's infected. He can't stay in camp — patrol rule."

Once Bangor was trussed, a guard put on latex gloves and gingerly wrapped a hospital gown around Bangor's thigh. He began to struggle, trying to get away, but there were too many of them. "I'm okay now. I'm not going to infect anyone. Just leave me here and let the doctor study me."

Without a word, the guards hefted him up and carried him from the room.

Everson went back into the supply closet and threw some things in a cloth drawstring bag. Then he took off after the guards, skirting the puddled blood on the floor. I snatched up my dad's messenger bag and followed. If they were going to force Bangor into the Feral Zone, they'd have to open the gate. This could be my chance to cross the bridge. But did I really want to?

I caught up with Everson at the infirmary's entrance where he stood, blocking the guards from going through the doors. "At least let the doctor take the bullet out of his leg," he said to them.

"Listen to him, guys, please. Just take me to Dr. Solis. And I've got to call my wife. You know she's pregnant. Let me call her. I've got to call her!"

The glass door opened behind Everson. "Move aside, Cruz."

Everson glanced over his shoulder, took in the balding, middle-aged man, and stepped out of the way. From the insignia on his jacket, I guessed that he was an officer or something.

The guards carrying Bangor pushed past Everson, who followed right behind.

"Captain Hyrax, sir, if he's going to have a chance of surviving in the zone, he can't go in with an open wound."

"I hear Solis is whiffed out," the captain said, sounding disdainful. "Two guards tried to wake him. I'm not keeping an infected man around while we wait for the good doctor to rejoin the conscious." Under the floodlights, the captain's face seemed abnormally pale. Only his eyes burned dark.

"Then let me take the bullet out," Everson offered. "You know I can."

"So you get your hands wet with infected blood?" he snapped. "That's sure to go over with corporate." With a jerk of his chin, he ordered the guards to take off with Bangor.

"At least let me give him some supplies. Hold up!" Everson hurried after the guards, the white cloth sack in hand. I ran after him, hoping the captain didn't notice me. Was I supposed to salute or something?

"There are some bandages in here and some hydrogen peroxide," Everson said, bending to look into Bangor's yellow eyes. "If the bullet is close to the surface, try to pull it out with the surgical tweezers I put in there. Get to the quarantine compound in Moline if you can. You know where it is?"

Bangor turned his head away, and Everson tucked the bag down his shirt.

Captain Hyrax watched this coldly. "Cruz, if you want to protect the population, you gotta stop seeing the people. There's a greater good at stake here."

I couldn't believe that they were going to force a sick, wounded man into the Feral Zone. Everson followed them, his fists clenched, while I trailed behind like a zombie until they reached the bridge. There was no one on the other side of the gate now, and as far as I could tell, the bridge was empty. I could barely make out its eerie silhouette through the cold morning fog.

As the huge gate rolled open, the captain stepped in front of Bangor, who had begun to sob. "Please let me talk to my wife. Our baby is due next month. I need to tell her —"

"I'm sorry about this, son," the captain said. "Truly, I am. But you'll have to find another way to live now. I'll see that your compensation check gets to your wife."

He moved aside and nodded to the guards, who then cut Bangor's bindings and heaved him through the open gate. I clapped a hand over my mouth to keep from screaming at them. I'd never seen anything so deliberately cruel in my life.

Bangor hit the bridge hard and lay there, moaning. Here was my chance, and yet I didn't move. I couldn't just step over Bangor, who looked like he'd gone crazy again, rolling side to side and howling his despair to the sky. The sound made me want to claw out my ears. Then without warning, Bangor shot to his feet and threw himself at the diminishing gap in the mechanized gate, but as hard as he yanked, he couldn't stop it from clanging shut. Skin glistening, he leapt onto the gate. He had a bullet in his thigh, his pants were soaked with blood, and yet he started climbing the fence effortlessly.

"Get down, Bangor," Captain Hyrax yelled, pushing back his jacket to draw a gun from his shoulder holster.

I shoved my hands into my pockets and my fingers brushed the Lull inhaler that Everson had tucked there the night before. Great. If things got any uglier, I could always knock myself out.

"Let me tranq him, Captain," Everson said, lifting the dart gun. "He'll wake up calmer. Maybe then he can handle this."

"Get back, Cruz," the captain snapped. "Last warning!" he shouted to Bangor and took aim. But Bangor didn't see the gun. His yellow gaze was fixed on the top of the gate. He reached the jutting metal blades strung with barbed wire and, as if he were immune to pain, he gripped the wire and swung away from the gate, trying to get enough momentum to flip over the angled blades.

"No!" Everson yelled at the same instant a shot rang out.

Bangor hung from the wire for a second as red bloomed across his shirt, and then his fingers uncurled, and he dropped onto the bridge with a thud and lay without movement.

The guards who had been carrying him went to the gate and peered out at Bangor's prone form.

"He's dead?" Captain Hyrax asked as he jammed his gun back into the holster.

"He looks dead, sir," a guard called back.

"Open the gate," the captain ordered. "Get his body." He looked over at Everson. "When they're coming at you, you kill them. Period."

Going by Everson's clenched hands, he wasn't on board with the coming-at-you-kill tactic. "I will never kill a man in cold blood," he said under his breath. "Never."

The gate rolled aside once more, and an icy feeling washed over me. It was as if they were collecting my father's body after his execution. The guards spilled onto the bridge and surrounded the lifeless man.

"Take it to the incinerator," the captain told them. "Burn it and send the ashes to his family."

Fate was offering me one last chance. I started toward the open gate but a hand clamped onto my arm. "Don't even think about it," Everson hissed in my ear. "You want to end up infected?"

I struggled in his grip as he dragged me back. No one paid attention to us. The surrounding guards were watching the men carry Bangor's body through the gate. I tried to dig in my heels but Everson was like the outgoing tide, an impassive force dragging me off. Fighting him wouldn't get me free — not even if I struck one of his five vulnerable areas. He was too big and too well trained. But I had another way to stop him. I pulled the inhaler from my pocket and squeezed a wet cloud of Lull into his face. Everson reeled back, releasing me as he gagged.

"I'm sorry." I lifted the strap of the messenger bag over my head so that it crossed my body.

He blinked at me, uncomprehending, and then crumpled to the ground. I paused over him. He looked so much younger asleep — spiky lashes against flushed cheeks. Sweeter, too, with the crease between his brows smoothed out. I wanted to look longer, linger even, but the creak of the gate snapped up my gaze. I sprinted for the narrow opening, barreling past the guards carrying Bangor's body.

Someone yelled, "Whataya doing?" as I squeezed through just before the gate clanged into place. I skipped over the smear of blood and dashed across the bridge.

"Who is that?" the captain demanded.

I reached the fog bank at the far end and glanced back to see several guards clutching the chain link. "You'll die over there!" one called.

I really hoped not. I turned and stepped into the fog. All that waited for me in the West was loneliness and the possibility of seeing my father executed. Given that, I'd rather take my chances in the Feral Zone.

· TEN ·

The bridge ended at a blockade of stacked sandbags, sheet metal, and scaffolding. I slipped through a narrow opening and stepped into a windswept meadow. A few rusting tanks jutted above the waist-high prairie grass. I paused, listening for the sound of boots crossing the bridge, but heard only the breeze in the surrounding trees, many of which were showing fall color.

On the eastern horizon, pink and purple gave way to orange. I took out my father's map and traced my finger along Route 92, which ran parallel to the river all the way to Moline. If I stuck to the road, I should run right into the compound. Easy . . . provided I could find the road. According to the weather-beaten sign in front of the blockade, I was at Twenty-Fourth Street, which fed onto Route 92, but I didn't see anything that qualified as a street. I took another step into the misty meadow and realized that the meadow *was* the street. The prairie grass had broken the asphalt into a huge jigsaw puzzle with wildflowers providing sprinkles of color.

I set out along the shattered road, scanning the trees to my right — the woods of my father's bedtime stories. With most of humanity hiding beyond the wall, Mother Nature had reclaimed this area with a vengeance. I decided to jog.

At the crest of a hill, I came to the turn off for Route 92, although the sign bore other words as well, added in spray paint. "All who bear the mark of the beast will drink the wine of God's wrath."

What a comforting thought to share with infected people. Although, really, was this graffiti any less brutal than building a giant wall? I paused to look back at the monolith that overwhelmed the entire landscape. Then, with a bounce, I jogged onto Route 92.

The two-lane highway wasn't nearly as overgrown as the smaller street, and it was easy enough to follow the islands of asphalt within the waist-high scrub. I quickened my pace, wondering how many of my father's stories were true. The piranha-bats? He had to have made those up, right? I glanced at the sky, grateful that the night was retreating, and pushed on. My breathing was steady. I could keep up this pace all the way to Moline, no problem. But could I find the old quarantine compound? And what if my dad wasn't there?

I mentally mashed the question to pulp. I could only handle one worry at a time. Right now, all I had to do was follow the broken asphalt and ignore the eerie fluttering of leaves. I'd never been so alone in my life. I couldn't even see Arsenal Island anymore because the highway had veered inland. At least I could still hear the rush of the river over my pounding feet. And a thumping off to my right . . . I stumbled to a stop.

What went thump in the woods? Lots of things. Branches and . . . those thumps hadn't sounded like falling branches. A roar cut through my thoughts, and my legs almost gave way. That didn't sound like any forest animal I knew — or wanted to know. It sounded like a jungle cat. Spinning toward the woods along the riverbank, I looked for a place to hide.

"Easy there, whiskers!" a male voice commanded. A voice that held no trace of panic.

My curiosity got the better of me. I slipped through the dew-soaked bushes toward the voice as quietly as I could, getting my arms as damp as my pants and shoes. On the other side of a half-fallen tree, something rustled. I put my fingertips on the moss-covered trunk to steady myself and rolled onto my toes. A young man in a white thermal shirt was crouching in the ferns. His light brown hair fell around his face, hiding his expression, but whatever he was doing, he was wholly absorbed in it. Stretching to stand *en pointe*, I tried to see what lay at his feet. A dirty green knapsack! My eyes swept back to the guy with skin as tan as his pants and sun-streaked hair and I gasped. It was the jerk who'd locked me in the supply closet. Rafe.

I froze, certain that if I so much as released a breath he'd turn and see me, but I didn't back away either. What was he up to? His knapsack was fastened to a pack frame now, with a shotgun bungee-corded to the back. He bypassed the gun and rose with a crowbar in hand, and I knew I wasn't going to like what came next.

Rafe rounded a large bush, and the roar of an enraged beast split the air. I heaved myself over the fallen tree to peer around the bush, only to be brought up short by the sight before me. What I'd thought was a forest was really just an overgrown median strip. Beyond it, another endless stretch of broken asphalt. Rafe stood at the edge of the road, and beside him, hanging upside down from the crossbar of a highway sign, was a . . .

Tiger!

He'd trapped a tiger! The animal thrashed under the highway sign, its head several feet above the asphalt, ankles ensnared, its vivid orange-and-black stripes writhing. The tiger slashed at Rafe, who was circling it with calm precision. For all the emotion he displayed he could have been calculating a tricky jump across a stream.

Blood soaked the tiger's fur where the snare was cutting into its flesh. If left dangling much longer, the animal would lose the use of its hind legs . . . legs that were encased in black nylon pants. That wasn't possible. I crept closer — close enough to see that the tiger was indeed wearing pants. When Rafe lifted the crowbar and took a practice swing at the creature's head, my stomach turned inside out.

"I'm not wasting a bullet on you," he snarled.

"Don't!" I rushed from my hiding place. Either Rafe didn't hear me or didn't care. He slammed the crowbar into the tiger-man's skull, wreaking a scream that was followed by a roar of torment.

Sprinting, I closed the distance, not stopping until I was at Rafe's back. My first glimpse of a feral up close took away my breath. Okay, so he had fur and a tail — he was still human. A terrified, injured, thrashing human. When Rafe lifted the bar again, I darted forward. "Stop!" But I was too late. The crowbar cracked into the tiger-man's head again and his arms dropped and hung limply. I grabbed Rafe's wrist and tried to drag him back. "You're killing him!"

He shook off my grip. "Get out of here."

"But that's a person!"

"That's a grupped-up man-eater."

I looked past him at the limp tiger-man. Fine orange fur striped with black covered his chest and arms. His face, though upside down, seemed tigery too. My nerves jerked taut. He wasn't unconscious like I'd thought — he was watching me through slitted eyes. "How do you know he's a man-eater?" I asked.

"He's infected with *tiger*," Rafe said as if that were proof enough. Lifting the crowbar, he prepared to swing again. "Adios, cat chow."

"But what if you're wrong?" I darted between him and the upside-down man. "What if he hasn't done anything?"

"There will be one less feral in the world, which is fine with me."

"*You're* the feral!" I shoved him so hard that he stumbled back, tripped over a chunk of asphalt, and hit the ground. "You can't murder someone because he's sick. Sick people have rights. They have families who love them and aren't ready to lose them just because you're scared of a virus."

Rafe didn't answer. In fact, he didn't move at all.

I bolted forward, dropping to my knees, and touched his face. He was out cold! But he'd landed on a patch of prairie grass.

I slipped my hand under his neck to feel the ground, and went numb. A jagged rock jutted out of the dirt right under Rafe's head. "Oh no, no, no, no . . ." What had I done? I rolled him onto his side and touched his hair. "I'm sorry." At least there was no blood.

What was happening to me? He was the second boy I'd knocked out today.

Something squeaked and I twisted to see the tiger-man swinging back and forth in the air, turning his body into a pendulum, even though the movement had to be making the wire cut deeper into his ankles. He was reaching for the steel post on the right, claws extended from his fingertips.

He was going to escape from the snare!

Just because I didn't want Rafe murdering him in cold blood didn't mean I wanted to be here when the tiger-man got loose. Would he come after Rafe for trying to kill him? I shook Rafe's shoulder. "Wake up," I whispered in his ear. "We've got to get out of here." I slapped his gorgeous face, too softly at first, and then harder. *That's for cutting my arm*, I thought. He moaned but didn't wake. I lifted his limp arm and dragged him across the gravel and weeds to the bush at the edge of the median strip.

I stepped back to catch my breath and saw the tiger-man swing toward the steel post again and snag it this time. He then pulled himself up the pole, hand over hand, until he could reach the crossbar. Hooking his knees over the bar like a trapeze artist, he swung himself up to sit on it. Without his body weight pulling the snare tight, he was able to loosen the wire and slip it over his feet.

Was that my cue to run? No. I couldn't just leave Rafe lying here, not when it was my fault that he was unconscious. I hurried back to the road for the crowbar, but then hesitated to pick it up. Would the tiger-man see me as a threat and feel compelled to attack? My mind ran in circles, which meant I froze — exactly what my self-defense instructor had said never to do. Great. Now I had her voice in my head, telling me to get out of my head, and I still wasn't moving.

The tiger-man flipped backward off the highway sign's crossbar and landed on his feet. Right — cat.

Despite being upright, he seemed unsteady. Blood streamed from his wide, flat nose into the black scruff that framed his face like a beard. He had the slightest deformation of his upper lip, like the split lip of a cat. All I could do was gape as he pulled a handkerchief from a pocket of his pants and wiped the blood from his face. His bare feet made no sound as he padded through the weeds toward me, staring with auburn eyes as if unable to believe I was real. The feeling was mutual, though my disbelief made me shiver. He seemed more curious than menacing . . . which didn't mean he wouldn't kill me. My cat, Gulliver, would bat a cricket around for twenty minutes before making his final pounce. Cats liked to play with their food.

Whatever the tiger-man was planning, I couldn't tear my eyes from him. He was a fairy-tale creature come to life. Rings glinted on his fingers and diamonds sparkled in his ears. He was heavily muscled, with pale orange skin and luxuriant fur covering his chest and arms. The pictures I'd seen in Dr. Solis's office had made it seem like the Ferae virus deformed its victims, but this man's appearance was more alluring than horrifying.

"Your kindness astounds me."

He could talk! My stomach flipped over in excitement, but then the truth hit me. I was standing face-to-face with an infected person. People woke up screaming just from dreaming about this. I edged back and brought in a slow breath. "Are you, um, okay?"

"I will be, because of you."

His voice was low and rumbling and his pronunciation odd, maybe because of the curving split in his upper lip. Or maybe because his ivory fangs — top and bottom — were so long and thick they didn't fit neatly into his mouth. Still, I was *conversing* with a tiger-man. When had I taken a hard left out of reality and into a bedtime story?

The man cleared his throat. "I am Chorda," he said formally. "And I can't thank you enough."

He seemed to have forgotten about Rafe, which was a good thing. I was also relieved that he didn't extend his hand, because chances were I couldn't have gotten myself to shake it. "I'm Lane."

Chorda's gaze lingered on my face and then skimmed down me. "You're not from here," he said, as if trying to work out the puzzle that was me. "No one here is so . . . human."

Rafe had said he was 100 percent human. So were the little girl at the gate and the wounded man, so there were humans living in the Feral Zone. "You mean *humane*?"

"Yes, humane." His coppery eyes glowed as if he'd just come across a beautiful stone. "No one here has such a *humane* heart."

"I'm from the West."

He chuffed in surprise. "Someone pushed you out of a plane? I don't believe it."

A laugh rose in my throat, but I stifled it. "No, I'm not a criminal." Well, at least I hadn't been until I snuck across the quarantine line.

"Then what are you doing here, Lane, risking your humanity?"

That sounded so much worse than just risking my health. Suddenly Chorda's eyes narrowed and his lips pulled back. He was looking past me. I turned to see Rafe striding out from behind the bush with the shotgun in his hand.

When I turned back, Chorda was streaking across the road, heading for the trees beyond, faster than I'd ever seen anybody move. Rafe took aim, cursed, and then sprinted after him. I decided I had better not be there when he returned. *He* being the human.

I ran back to the median strip, dashed through the overgrown brush, breaking spiderwebs with my face, and snatched up my messenger bag. When branches crashed to my right, I choked back my scream and sprinted onto the other side of the highway.

Farther up the road, Rafe pushed through the trees, carrying the pack and still gripping the gun. Spotting me, he dropped his pack and rushed toward me. I took off for the river. My only hope was to swim back to Arsenal Island.

With my heart hammering in my ears, I didn't hear the water until I was right on top of it. I skittered to a stop at the edge of the bluff — too high for diving and too sheer to climb down. I thought Rafe must be right behind me by now, but when I whipped around, I didn't see him anywhere. He wasn't in the clearing in either direction. I scanned the tree line along the median strip — nothing. The sky was empty and blue with the start of the day. Where could he have gone?

I took a tentative step back toward the weed-choked

road. He must have been lying in wait somewhere, belly to the ground like a snake. I slipped the bag from my shoulder and drew out my dad's machete. Now I was a match for him. So long as I discounted things like height, weight, slabs of muscle, and killing experience. I stepped onto the broken asphalt. The last of the fog had burned away but the landscape still had a desolate feel.

"This is what I get for trying to keep you from becoming meat," a voice said. My heart jerked. His voice seemed to rise from the ground itself. "Man, my head hurts!"

I crept forward, watching the thigh-high scrub for movement.

"You might want to watch your step."

I froze in place. Just ahead of me, half-hidden within a thatch of weeds, was a hole. Not a round manhole, but a long jagged gap where the asphalt had recently caved in. Probably under Rafe's weight, since pebbles were still spilling in. With my feet planted so firmly they could have grown roots, I leaned forward and spotted him in the darkness below. His eyes had the shine of a wild animal cornered in its den . . . a situation in which only an idiot extended her hand.

"Sure took you long enough to come over for a look." I heard the faint disdain in his tone, as if I was stupid for being cautious. Well, I wasn't nervous now. Not with him stuck twenty feet underground. Even an Olympic high jumper wouldn't be able to pull himself out. I tested the ground and then knelt for a better look. Rafe was standing in the middle of some sort of underground cavern. The only light came from the crevice that he'd fallen through, but as far as I could tell, the walls were dirt — impossible to scale. Releasing my breath, I sat back on my heels.

"I could use a little help here," he said without bothering to hide his irritation.

I got to my feet. "You can rot down there. Call it karma."

"You think you're scared now? Of me? Wait till that thing comes back."

I peered back into the crevice. "He's not a thing!"

"What do you call a beast that tears out people's hearts?"

My mouth dropped open. "Hearts?"

"He probably eats them, but who knows? Maybe he's got a collection going."

His words had me scanning the tree line and breathing so hard, I couldn't hear anything else. No. I couldn't let this scam artist get to me. I gritted my teeth until the muscles in my jaw crackled. If the tiger-man — Chorda — had wanted to hurt me, he could have. Instead, he'd thanked me politely and introduced himself. The only feral thing around here was down in that hole.

"The rogue just got started in Moline," Rafe went on, "which is why no one will be using this road anytime soon. Except you. And you sure caught its attention. You should know that once a feral has your scent, it can track you anywhere."

"Will you please be quiet?"

His smile was a flash of white in the darkness below. "That was the most polite 'shut up' I've ever heard."

I was tempted to kick dirt down on him. "I'm glad the tiger-man got himself free. You were going to murder him."

"I was going to put him down. You can't murder an animal. Now how 'bout you get me out of here?"

I stalked away from the fissure.

"Oh, that's good. You'll help a slobbering beast but not another human. Hypocrite!" he shouted after me.

Hypocrite I could live with. But helping him out of that hole would make me a fool. I didn't get far, though, before I tripped over something and went sprawling face-first into the scrub. It was his stupid knapsack. He'd probably left it there on purpose to trip me up. His shotgun lay a few feet away. Good to know it wasn't with him.

Getting to my knees, I shoved my machete into my messenger bag. *Let's see who you really are, thief.* The pack frame was loaded with a rolled army blanket and the weatherproof knapsack, which I unzipped without a single pang of guilt. The medicine that he'd stolen from the infirmary sat on top of the jumble along with vacuum-packed food pouches bearing the line patrol logo. The nonedibles included a crank flashlight, a water bottle, balled-up shirts, and a bunch of weapons. Okay, technically the ax wasn't a weapon, but after what I'd just witnessed, it counted.

I sat back, thirsty and uncomfortably damp in my dew-soaked pants. After sniffing the water bottle, I risked a sip. It was time to start walking again. I had to get to Moline and find my father. It was okay to leave the thief in the pit. He was dangerous. And I had a cut to prove it.

"Get me out of here and I'll take you to Moline like you wanted," Rafe called up, making me spill water on my shirt. "There's a rope in my bag."

He was trying out a new tone. Friendlier. Just how stupid

did he think I was? Still, I shoved aside his clothes and silver food pouches until I found a long, coiled rope made of some kind of high-tech fiber. Lightweight and strong. Great. Now there'd be no telling myself later that I couldn't have helped him even if I'd wanted to.

Rope in hand, I returned to the gap. Rafe sat on the dirt floor below, eating blackberries off a branch. Where had that come from?

He glanced up. "We both knew you weren't going to leave me down here."

He made it sound as if being a Good Samaritan was a flaw. I dropped the rope by my feet, which at least got him to stand up again. "Why do you have so many weapons?"

"I'm a hunter."

"Killing sick people, that's your job?" I asked acidly. "Who pays for that?"

"Any town with a feral problem. Right now, it's Moline."

"A feral problem?"

"All ferals are dangerous. Unless you're looking to get bitten, you steer clear of them and mostly they'll steer clear of you. But sometimes a feral goes rogue, the way bears and mountain lions do. Meaning, it starts hunting humans."

"Why?" I glanced over my shoulder at the woods.

"It could be old or hurt and we're easy prey. Or maybe it's got a grudge against people. Or sometimes, a feral just gets a taste for human meat."

His eyes glinted in the shadows. He'd savored that last part — *a taste for human meat* — like a storyteller warming to his task. At ten, I would have shrieked at that line, pulled my blanket over my head, and then begged my dad to say it again. Now, I just stretched and cracked my spine. "So, how will the good people of Moline pay you?"

"You don't believe me."

"Does anyone ever?"

His eyes narrowed. "Fine. It's your heart." He tossed aside the blackberry branch. "The mayor of Moline is offering one hundred meals to the hunter who bags the feral. Cooked fresh or in bulk. I get that squared away and I'm good for the whole winter."

"And you just kill these rogue ferals in cold blood? You don't even try to relocate them?"

His brows shot up, his expression incredulous. "Even I won't sell a lie that stupid, not even to save my own skin." He headed for an opening in the wall that I hadn't noticed. It looked like a tunnel carved into the dirt. If there was a way out, why had he waited until now to use it?

I knelt to see him step over something lying on the cavern floor and then caught a gleam of open eyes. "Is that an animal?"

"Lynx," he said without looking back. "Paralyzed. Want to relocate it?"

"Did it get hurt when it fell?"

He paused by the tunnel opening, which came up to his shoulder. "It didn't drop in with me. It was already here, like them." He gestured toward the far wall.

I had to lean in farther, precariously so, to see the pile of fur. More animals — raccoons, rabbits, and even a wolf — some twitching, some still as death, but all with open eyes. "What's wrong with them?"

"Chimpacabra bite."

The way he said it, he could have been talking about hot sauce, and yet my nerves jerked taut. "Chimpacabras aren't real!" The scoff came out tinged with horror, which ruined its effect.

Ignoring me, Rafe ducked to peer into the hole. A chimpacabra hole. I wanted to laugh, but my memory was too busy fact-checking my father's stories against what lay below. A chimpacabra larder, which he'd described as being like a mole's larder, only instead of paralyzing earthworms and bugs with venomous saliva like moles did, chimpacabras stocked up on bigger prey.

"At least toss me a light," Rafe called over his shoulder.

Returning to his knapsack, I dug out the flashlight. By the time I got back to the crevice and chucked it to him, I knew I couldn't leave him down there — not if chimpacabras were real. "All right. I'll get you out of there." I picked up the rope. "But I want your word that you'll take me to Moline."

He strolled into the shaft of sunshine to gaze up at me. "Cross my heart."

Looking down at him with his tangled hair and gleaming eyes, mistrust bubbled up inside me again. Before I totally lost my nerve, I dropped one end of the rope into the hole. He caught it midair with cobra-strike speed.

"Now what?" My voice came out raspy. "Should I wrap my end around a tree for leverage or —" My question became a scream as the ground under me crumbled and fell away.

· ELEVEN ·

Every part of me rang with pain until I tried to take a breath and turned it into a siren's wail. I rolled onto my back. How many bones had I broken — all of them? In two places each?

"Might want to move it," said a nonchalant voice. "I bet the chimpacabra felt that. It'll probably be here soon to see what dropped in for dinner."

That unglued my eyelids. I blinked into the sunlight pouring in from high above. I'd more than tripled the size of the gap. Sitting up sent pain shooting through my limbs, and a groan escaped me. Well, at least I could breathe again, which meant no punctured or collapsed lungs. Rafe stood nearby, re-coiling the rope, stone-faced. From this angle, he seemed bigger than I remembered. Was he angry that I hadn't gotten him out?

"You'd be feeling worse," he said, slinging the rope over his shoulder, "if you hadn't dropped right into its nest."

I scrambled to my feet to see that yes, I'd landed on some sort of horror-movie prop pile. Furs of all sorts lay clumped together, surrounded by branches, but they weren't the problem. It was the dung and claws and animal faces still attached to the pelts that had me fumbling through my pockets for my bottle of hand sanitizer. I oversqueezed and ended up with a mound of gel in my palm, which I rubbed up my arms and onto my neck and face, but even then I didn't feel clean.

"You missed a spot." Rafe said, gesturing to my ear.

He could snicker himself to death for all I cared. I pocketed the bottle without offering him any. "I can't believe chimpacabras are real." Anna was going to have a heart attack when I told her. "What about weevlings, are they real?"

"Too real, like most mongrels."

"*Mongrel* as in a dog?"

He shook his head and I groaned, seeing the gleam in his eyes. He liked scaring me. So what? Let him. I was going to find out about everything that I might have to face out there. "Okay, I give. What's a mongrel?"

"An animal-animal hybrid. Like a wolf juiced with cobra DNA. Or a hyboar."

"Hyena-boar," I said, remembering them only too well from the stories. Nasty, carnivorous creatures with razor-sharp tusks.

"How'd you know that?" Rafe looked disappointed.

Guess I'd deprived him of giving a good, gruesome description of them. "Are there a lot of mongrels in the Feral Zone?"

"Yep. And right when you think you've seen every combination possible, they mate and you get offspring mash-ups with three species in them. It's disgusting." He headed for the tunnel, but then paused by the mouth. "Just so we're clear, the deal's off."

I hurried after him. "Do you know where that tunnel goes?"

"Nope." He unholstered a serrated knife and pointed to the wide swath of sunshine. "You wait there."

"What?!"

"When I get out, I'll drop the rope and pull you up."

"No way. I'm going with you."

"You'll be fine in here where it's bright. In the tunnel, you'll just flip out and bring the chimpa running — and then probably try to stop me from killing it."

"A chimpacabra is not the same thing as a sick *person*." The words snapped out of me too hot. I felt exposed, like I'd leaned over too far and given him a good look down my shirt. In a calmer voice, I said, "I was going to do the decent thing and get you out of here."

"Some would say you took advantage of the situation, bargaining with me."

Prickly heat crept up my neck. "I'm sorry. That was wrong of me. I shouldn't have —"

His laugh cut me off. "Silky, the smartest thing you did up there was cut a deal. But the odds are still better for both of us if you wait here."

My insides ached, and not from my fall. "Please, let me come with you. I'll do whatever you say."

"Whatever I say?" he scoffed, but then he waved me over. "Fine, but keep up. When the tunnels branch off, I'm not yelling back to tell you which one I took."

I nodded. As he ducked to enter the hole, I glanced over my shoulder to see if my messenger bag had fallen in too, but I didn't see it. "Hey," I whispered, already breaking my resolution not to be an annoying silky, whatever that was. "Can I carry the flashlight?"

"No. You won't put it to good use. Down here, it's a weapon."

"Because chimpacabras have really sensitive eyes."

He paused to look back at me, surprised, and then just pushed up the cropped leg of his pants, took a knife from an ankle sheath, and handed it to me. The blade wasn't even metal, but fiberglass. Doubting its effectiveness, I touched the point.

"Sharp enough?" he asked blandly.

Blood welled from the prick. I clamped my mouth shut, curled my fingers into a fist, and joined him in the tunnel. The dank, dark smell of the earth enveloped me.

"If you see a gob of slime on the wall, don't touch it," he said and started forward.

Good thing he told me, because, of course, touching slime would be my natural inclination. Why not warn me not to eat it?

If he was impressed by how well I kept up, he didn't let on. I had two things going for me: I was a runner, and I didn't need to crouch nearly as much as he did to keep from scraping the tunnel's ceiling. What I had going against me was that everything my father had ever said about chimpacabras was now replaying in my mind. Part mole, part chimpanzee, all nasty — especially the nugget that my dad had thrown in about them crawling out of their warrens at night to steal human babies from cribs. When I was older, I figured that my father had swiped that detail from a little-known fact about chimpanzees: They really did eat human babies if given the opportunity.

At least the tunnel finally seemed to be sloping upward —

because I could not get out of this nightmare fast enough. We spilled into a chamber like the one we'd just come from. But then the flashlight revealed walls that were pocked with more tunnels. This wasn't another larder; it was a hub. Rafe paused before each opening and inhaled deeply — probably checking for fresh air. After making a full circle, he shrugged.

"What if none of them lead to the surface?" I whispered.

"One does. Blackberry bushes don't grow underground."

I remembered the branch he'd been holding. "You're saying the chimpacabra went outside and got the branch."

"Not much gets past you, huh?"

Could he cut me a break? It wasn't like I spent my free time exploring chimpacabra warrens. "Okay, Marco Polo, which tunnel is it?"

"Crapshoot." He pushed the flashlight into my hands. "So, let's split up."

An icy finger traced down my spine. "Like you'll come back for me if you find the way out."

He tested his lighter, flicking it on and off several times. "I wouldn't leave you down here."

"Yes, you —"

"*Whatever I say?*" he reminded me pointedly and then nodded toward a hole. "You take that one."

I crossed my arms. No way was I crawling down a dark tunnel alone. He glanced over, took in my expression, and unslung the rope.

Stupid! Why couldn't I just follow orders? I jerked up the fiberglass knife to ward him off.

His brows rose. "Is something wrong?"

"What are you doing?"

"Giving you peace of mind. Lift your arms."

He didn't seem mad, at least not enough to tie me up and toss me down a hole just to be rid of me. I lifted my arms a little. After sheathing his knife, he wound an end of the rope around my waist and tucked it in. "That's it?" I asked.

"You want me to tie you up more?" He didn't smirk but I sensed his amusement.

"I meant," I whispered through gritted teeth, "what's this going to do? You didn't knot it."

"We're not mountain climbing."

Maybe not, but I knotted my end anyway and pulled it extra tight. He rolled his eyes and tied the other end of the rope around his waist. "If either of us finds a way out, a tug will bring the other."

"What if I run into the chimpacabra?"

"Tug, but it'll probably attack before I get to you. The bad news, there's no cure for chimpa venom. The good, it's not strong enough to paralyze a human completely. So, if the thing's about to bite, give it your leg. If it nips you any higher, your throat will freeze up and you'll die of thirst."

Okay, then, leg it was. Shivering, I wondered if the doctors in the West had a cure for chimpacabra spit. Sure, they did — considering that I was the only person in the West who'd even heard about chimpacabras and until now, I'd thought they were imaginary.

Rafe traded knives with me, taking the small one for himself. "On the bright side, you can't catch Ferae from a chimpa." He gestured to the hole.

I stalled. "Why can't you catch Ferae from a chimpacabra?"

"'Cause they're like tenth-generation hybrid. Mongrel parents pass on their messed-up DNA, but not the virus, and the offspring have a natural immunity. Lucky them, right? Now, in you go."

Seeing no difference between the tunnels, I stepped into the one he'd indicated, and he entered the next over. Fifty feet of rope lay on the floor of the connecting room. We could each go twenty-five feet before the slack ran out. It hadn't sounded like much when Rafe said it. But now that I was alone in a tunnel, surrounded by damp earth and facing only darkness, twenty-five feet was a lot farther in than I wanted to go — especially since this tunnel was much narrower than the one we'd been in before. And yet, I crept forward like a hunchback with both the flashlight and knife raised. Equally effective weapons, according to my father's stories.

I slunk along the narrow dirt passage, wishing my dad were here now. He'd have never made me go alone. I'd bet Everson would have insisted we stick together as well. I felt a sudden welling of warmth for the tall line guard with the serious demeanor. He was exactly the kind of person you wanted by your side in this type of situation. Not that this situation was common enough to be a type.

My tunnel ended abruptly and I was in another scraped-out chamber. I flashed my light around to see bones littering the dirt floor. Even more disturbing — the dead coyote at my feet. And was that a felox next to it? I directed my beam on the shuddering red fur and remembered my father telling me about the half fox, half cat creatures. My heart broke for it, trapped here, waiting to be eaten alive. But there was nothing I could do if there was no cure for the venom.

A movement in the corner caught my eye and I directed the flashlight toward it. This creature was on its feet, its yellow-furred back to me. It stood as tall as a small child. Maybe, like a human, it was too big to be fully paralyzed by a chimpacabra's bite. But in the split second that I considered it, the creature flicked around, a rabbit carcass cradled in its taloned hands. An icy wave of understanding crashed over me. It hadn't been bitten by a chimpacabra. . . .

It *was* a chimpacabra! Real. In the flesh. And hissing! When I lifted the light to see its face, I glimpsed a flash of maggot-white eyes, but then the creature threw back its head and howled with rage. My muscles melted, leaving me barely able to stand. Flinging aside the dead rabbit, the creature bolted for the far side of the cave. From there, it peered at me with an apish face as yellow as old parchment. I eased back into the tunnel while keeping my gaze pinned on the creature's blood-smeared mouth. When it sprang forward, I whipped the flashlight into its eyes again. The creature let loose an ear-piercing screech and ricocheted back. With the flashlight aimed behind me, I ran.

Holding the knife between my teeth, I yanked the rope, but it came too easily; there was too much slack. It would take forever to get to a level of tension that Rafe would feel. I dropped it and took the knife in hand again as I ran. The chimpacabra scrabbled after me, just beyond the reach of the flashlight beam, and with every turn in the tunnel I heard it make up ground.

"Rafe!" I screamed. Dashing through the hub room, I darted down the tunnel he'd taken. Every time I swerved the flashlight too far to one side, the chimpacabra lunged forward only to fall back as I straightened the beam. Rafe's tunnel was so much twistier. Navigating it without looking was next to impossible, but I didn't dare take my eyes from the creature, which was one pounce away. I ran past the other end of the rope, lying in the dirt. It took me a moment to register what that meant.

Rafe had untied himself and abandoned me!

Another bend in the tunnel and daylight blasted me as I ran into a dirt wall. A dead end, the bottom of a hole. The only way out was up. Roots lined the shaft, looking tough and thick enough to cling to. The chimpacabra couldn't come out of the tunnel after me because of the sunlight, but that didn't stop it from reaching around the bend and making a swipe for me. I pressed into the earthen wall and sucked in my gut as the four-inch-long talons narrowly missed my stomach.

I jammed the knife through a belt loop, shoved the flashlight in my pants pocket, and began to climb. Digging my feet into the soil, I created toeholds. Grabbing root after root, I pulled myself up. But long before I reached the hole at the top, I ran out of roots.

"Help! Please, someone —" The rope around my waist jerked taut, cutting off my cry. I tightened my hold on the roots but the tug from below turned into a steady pull, and I started slipping inch by inch as the chimpacabra dragged me toward the darkness.

· TWELVE ·

My feet slipped from their toeholds, leaving me kicking at empty air. I couldn't spare a hand to untie the rope; I'd fall before I could get the knot undone. The roots I clung to loosened under the pressure, sending dirt raining down on my head. Then the downward pull turned into violent yanks, and I screamed as my hands slid the length of the roots.

Just as the ends slipped through my fingers, a hand snagged my wrist. I looked up to see Rafe leaning into the hole, holding me in a viselike grip. As I twisted in midair, I grabbed his wrist with my other hand. But as hard as he tried to haul me up, the creature below was trying to drag me down in a game of tug-of-war that was going to tear my arms out of their sockets.

Suddenly Rafe slammed me against the wall of the tunnel. When a gunshot blasted next to my ear, I nearly lost my grip. I looked up to see the shotgun in his free hand. The pressure from below lessened for a heartbeat and he jerked me up another foot, but then the drag was back.

"Use your knife!" he shouted. "Let go with one hand and cut the rope."

But I couldn't get my fingers to uncurl from his wrist and couldn't think where I'd put the knife. My belt loop. Rafe took aim again and shot past me. I forced myself to release my death grip on him and fumbled for the blade, nicking my hand in the process. I wiggled the knife free. Between the twisting and swinging I couldn't see what I was doing. I felt for the rope and then pushed the tip of the blade under it and sawed. The snap was instant. The rope whipped from around my body and fell into the darkness. Rafe hauled me out and onto the ground where I spasmed in a fit of panting and moaning.

"This . . . this . . . did not just happen." I covered my head with my arms. "It didn't. It didn't. It couldn't." Almost eaten by a chimpacabra. And all because . . . I sat up. "You took off the rope!"

"Yeah," he said, sounding completely unrepentant. "I couldn't reach the end of the tunnel with it on."

"You weren't going to come back for me."

"I heard the chimpa scream," he said defensively. "If you'd been bit, there was nothing I could do. And if it hadn't gotten you yet, your chances were better if I came back with more than a knife."

I didn't love his answer, but how could I complain? I was in one piece, not paralyzed, and my throat still worked. I wiped my hands on my pants, leaving long smears of sweaty dirt.

"You okay?"

I shot a look at him, but his concern seemed genuine enough, so I nodded and got to my feet. In the sunlight, I was once again aware that his face was a heart-stopping combo of hard planes and a lush mouth. "Thanks for pulling me out," I muttered.

"You're lucky." He holstered his gun and took a coil of wire from his knapsack. "You didn't even get a scar to remember this one by."

"This one?"

"Lesson. You know" — he pointed to a mottled line along his collarbone — "don't lower your weapon until you're sure the mongrel is dead." He turned the back of his fist toward me to reveal another scar. "Don't put a wet rock in the fire; it'll explode."

"Learn a lesson, get a scar?" I asked, brows raised. "You mean like this one I'll have on my arm?" I pulled up my ripped sleeve, revealing Everson's bandage. "Thanks, but I'd rather stay dumb."

"Not dumb. Inexperienced." He glanced at the bandage without even a murmur of apology. Then he went back to measuring a length from the coil and trimming it with wire cutters. "Want to know why we call the line guards silkies? Because of their skin. They come east with skin as lived-in as a newborn's, like yours. And then there's your boyfriend; he's got to be the silkiest of the whole bunch." He strode to the nearest light post, carrying his pack.

"He's not my —" Stop. Who cared what this creep thought? "If you saw what most men in the West are like, you wouldn't think Everson was so silky."

"Uh huh," Rafe said, disbelieving. "I was on Arsenal the day that stiff arrived. New recruits normally get dropped out of 'copters into the river. It's part of their training. But not him. He flew over the wall in a sleek little two-seater plane."

"Whatever. So, exactly what am I supposed to have learned from all this? Don't fall down chimpacabra holes?"

"That's worth knowing, but no. Try: You don't belong in the Feral Zone. You're too tame. So hurry back over the bridge and beg them to open the gate." As he spoke he looped the cable over the neck of the post, and created a snare at the end.

If exasperation was a ledge, he'd just nudged me off. "I'm not tame."

He snorted. "Right. You're petted and pampered and fed on demand. All you're missing is a jeweled collar. . . . Actually, that would look hot."

As insulting as it was to be compared to a lapdog, Rafe wasn't completely wrong. I didn't belong here. And now that I knew chimpacabras were real and had come close to being one's lunch, I couldn't imagine taking another step alone. "I know I didn't get you out of the hole, but would you please walk with me? It's only a couple of miles."

He crouched to hide the snare in the tall grass. "If going alone scares you, you shouldn't have come alone. I'm working."

"You can't take off one hour?"

"No." Rising, he faced me, his expression intent — fierce, even. All the easiness about him had vanished to reveal what he truly was: a ruthless hunter set on a kill. "The feral I'm after, it doesn't stay in one place for very long. Usually it starts a killing spree by taking victims that no one misses right away, so that by the time people realize there's a predator in the area, it's too late, and the feral has moved on."

"You think it's about to take off again."

He nodded. "I've been tracking this rogue for two years. It lies low for months between sprees and there's no knowing where it'll show up next. So, this is it, my chance. Because I *will* be the one who kills it."

"I see." And I did. As soon as my dad completed the fetch, we'd go back to our side of the wall, and worrying about being eaten would seem as distant and fictional as a bedtime story. But to the people who lived in the Feral Zone, it didn't get any more real.

"So, you're going back to Arsenal now, right?" he said.

"No. You do what you have to, and so will I." I spotted my dad's bag in the grass beside the fissure.

Rafe frowned, brows knit, but he didn't ask me what was so important in Moline. He probably felt like he'd wasted enough time on the tame girl from the West. Treading carefully, I made my way over to the messenger bag. The last thing I needed was to fall into another hole.

"Do you at least have a weapon?" Rafe asked.

I scooped up my bag. "A knife."

He grimaced as if I'd offered him a glue-stick smoothie. "To do any damage with a knife, you have to get in close. Is that what you want?" he asked. "To get within a foot of a feral or some convict that got booted over the wall?"

No, I most certainly did not.

He waved me south. "Go back to Arsenal."

"I'm going to Moline."

"Suit yourself." He started to walk away but then swung back. "Only if you're going on the road, don't act like prey and don't go around being helpful."

Right. What a terrible flaw — being helpful.

When I turned to head north, he snagged my sleeve. "I'm just saying, be smart. If you see a freak caught in a trap, walk away."

"What if the freak is stuck in a chimpacabra hole? Should I walk away then?"

"Yeah," he said, sounding dead serious. He released his hold on my shirt. "As fast as you can, without looking back."

I slid my dad's machete out of the messenger bag. "I'll be fine." At least I hoped so.

Rafe straightened, eyeing the machete. "That's not a knife. . . ."

I dropped my bag and stepped back, blade up. Weapons had to be valuable over here. Revealing my father's machete was probably the same as waving around a wad of cash in a bad neighborhood. Rafe's gaze shifted to my leather bag. "There's nothing in it that would interest you," I said, toughening my tone.

A smile pulled at his lips. "How would you know what interests me?"

I pointed the machete at him. "You said you had work to do. Why don't you get going?"

He grinned outright. "You're trying to *relocate* me. Just so you know, it's useless. Predators always come back."

"Is that what you are?" I demanded. "A predator?"

"I'll tell you what I'm not, silky, and that's a pack mule." He pointed to my messenger bag. "Grab it and let's go."

"Go where?"

He zipped up his knapsack. "You wanted me to take you

to Moline, right? Well, quit burning daylight." He strolled past me, gear in hand, and headed north — toward Moline.

I shook off my surprise, snatched up my bag, and raced to join him. I wasn't putting the machete away anytime soon, however. "What changed your mind?"

"I didn't want to get cut."

"Right. You were trembling in fear," I scoffed. "You knew I wouldn't do anything."

"Sure about that? The Feral Zone has a way of bringing out the animal in people."

I should drop the issue. Now I didn't have to make the trek alone, and as far as escorts went, having a hunter along was about as good as it got. Still . . . "Seriously, why did you change your mind? Just tell me."

"'Cause Mack wouldn't want his daughter wandering around the Feral Zone alone."

I stumbled to a stop. "What?"

"In fact," he paused, eyeing me, "I know that he doesn't want you here at all. Ever. So why *are* you here? Is Mack in trouble?"

"How — how do you know my dad?"

"He's a popular guy over here."

"Okay . . . but how do you know who I am?"

He raised a brow as if the answer was obvious. He gestured to the machete. "That's Mack's and so's the bag. Doesn't take a genius IQ to guess that you're his daughter. We don't get a lot of silkies popping over. Especially one as clean and shiny as you." He swept his hand, indicating me from head to toe. "It's like you just broke your seal and slipped out of your plastic wrap."

"Why does everything you say sound obscene?"

"You look like a doll that's never been played with. That's all I'm saying. I can't help it if you have a dirty mind."

"I don't have —"

"I answered the question, Delaney. Now, spill it. What's going on?"

"Lane," I corrected. I couldn't think of a reason not to tell him. It wasn't like he could march up to the line patrol and turn my dad in for being a fetch — not when he was wanted for stabbing someone. "You know it's illegal for people in the West to come over here, right? Unless you're a line guard."

"Kind of figured that went along with the giant wall."

"Well, if someone does get caught coming over here or if there's evidence proving —"

"He's executed by firing squad. Are you saying they have something on Mack?"

I nodded. "But he can fix it if he does a fetch for an official."

"Nice to know that people are the same no matter which side of the wall they're from." Rafe's smile was bitter. "Okay, let's go. If Mack is in Moline, I know where he'll be."

He set off down the road, moving at such a quick pace that I had to race-walk to keep up with him. Between breaths, I gave him the details of Director Spurling's offer. When I mentioned where my dad had to go for the fetch, Rafe made a face. "What?" I asked. "Are there a lot of ferals in Chicago?"

"Yeah, but I hear the humans are worse."

"Keep your eyes open," Rafe said as we entered the outskirts of Moline. "There are mongrels all over the place." He gestured to the empty buildings that lined the shattered street. Several doors bore remnants of yellow quarantine tape. "And I guarantee they're sniffing us out right now, trying to decide if we're easy pickings."

I scanned the trees and other plants that poked through window frames and spilled out of gutters. In some cases, woody vines and ivy cloaked entire houses, obliterating them from view. It was as if the buildings themselves had gone feral. When we came to a whole block of scorched rubble, I asked, "Was Moline firebombed during the epidemic?"

"Nope. Gas leaks did it," Rafe said cheerfully. "Least that's what I've heard. Houses are always blowing up because of the paint and chemicals stored in them."

I glanced in the broken window of a store as we passed. The darkness inside seemed to shift and writhe. I veered toward the other side of the street where dead leaves swirled past rusting cars and an overturned school bus.

"Don't get so close to the cars," Rafe warned. "Things nest in them."

I snapped back to the center of the road. "What about the feral people? Where do they live?"

"They're around and they'll bite if you get close. Other than that, they're as dangerous as the animal they're infected with. For example, a guy infected with tiger — *very dangerous*."

"He's still part human," I pointed out.

"So?"

"So humans can control their impulses."

He cocked a brow at me. "What humans have you been hanging around with?"

I knew I should let it go, but for the tiger-man's sake I didn't. "His name is Chorda and he didn't act dangerous. He was very polite and —"

"Polite how?" Rafe demanded, stopping short.

"He thanked me and introduced himself."

"And you understood him?"

"Perfectly."

Rafe frowned. "He didn't say anything to me."

"Maybe because you were hitting him with a crowbar!"

"So what?" Rafe started walking again. "There've been other ferals that could talk."

Well, that didn't sound defensive at all. I caught up with him. "Are you saying most ferals can't talk?"

"How should I know? I don't go around chatting them up."

I hooked his elbow and got him to face me. "You're mad because you know I was right to stop you."

"Yeah, I'll toss and turn all night, crying over that grupped-up beast." He snorted, amused at his own joke, and then pulled free of my hold to jog up the nearest stoop. "We're here."

"Where?" It looked like every other five-story building we'd passed.

"We're making a quick stop."

"No, I have to find my dad as soon as possible."

"Okay, follow the road until you hit a wall of cars. The compound's inside." He pointed at the top floor of the building. "I'll be up there in case you change your mind."

Despite how much I hated giving in to the smug jerk and despite the tick-tick-ticking in my brain, I said, "Fine. I'm coming."

He didn't even glance back as he headed in. "Figured as much."

Dirt and rubble covered the ancient lobby floor, black mold climbed the walls, and the elevator door opened onto an echoing darkness. What were we doing puttering around in a crumbling firetrap?

Many of the doors to the apartments stood open, revealing rooms littered with furniture, books, clothing, and other personal possessions. During the exodus, people brought only what they could carry, since they had to go through the checkpoint on foot. Everything else got left behind.

A coyote stood inside one doorway, watching us climb the stairs. Rafe barely gave it a glance. I, however, kept my eyes on the coyote until we reached the top floor. I don't know what I expected it to do, but I wasn't taking any chances. It was a wild animal after all.

Rafe stopped at the first door on the landing, turned the knob, and entered. No knock. No "anybody home?" Was that typical in the Feral Zone? Probably. If he was anything to go by, civilized behavior was a thing of the past. I followed him in. The apartment was vintage, with high ceilings, but the floors were practically buckling from the weight of all the furniture. Jewelry was piled on every surface, and we were standing ankle deep in cash. The old kind — pre-exodus — which was worthless in the West.

"Great," Rafe muttered. "Another nutjob who thinks the quarantine will end in his lifetime. Dream on, pal."

We moved through the front hall into the main room where a girl, barely a teenager, sat in the open window. In her green gown and gold necklaces, with her dark hair falling to her waist, she looked every inch the fairy-tale princess . . . until she threw a jelly jar at us. "Get out of here!" She smeared her sticky, red fingers on her dress and then jiggled her wrist until something dropped from her sleeve into her palm. A switchblade! Snapping open the blade, the girl sprang at us, only to be brought up short by the chain around her waist.

I followed the winding chain with my eyes from the padlock at the girl's hip to the other side of the room where it wrapped around a defunct radiator. Was she feral? I scuttled back. Why else would she be chained up? Although Rafe didn't seem too concerned as he strolled past her. Nor did he seem fazed that the girl had her switchblade pointed directly at him. "I'm looking for Alva Soto. Is that you?" he asked as he opened a closet door.

"What are you, a thief?"

"Nope." He brushed his hand over the colorful gowns and fur coats hanging in the closet.

"You look like a thief."

"Yeah? Usually I get astronaut." He double-checked the furs with a rough shake.

"If you're looking for my papa, he's out."

He glanced back at her. "I'm here to talk to Alva. That you?"

Pursing her lips, the girl turned her glare on me. I was tempted to apologize for busting in and for the way Rafe was pawing through her things.

"Alva, yes . . . no . . . ?" he prompted, but the girl just glared at him. "Come on, Lane." He turned for the door. "Guess we have the wrong crappy building."

"Wait!" the girl screeched before he'd even gone a step. "I'm Alva."

I tensed, expecting him to laugh at Alva's quick about-face, but his expression was placid as he turned, like this situation was no big deal. "Glad we got that settled."

"Who left you like this?" The words blurted out of me. I couldn't believe how blasé they were both being. "Who chained you up?"

"Who do you think, smart girl?"

My mouth dropped open. She was locked up, in need of help, and yet she was giving us attitude? Alva swished the chain, knocking over a dozen empty jelly jars on the coffee table. "I'm not talking unless you get this off me."

"All right. Where's the key?" Rafe asked.

"You've got a gun. Shoot it off." She lifted the padlock.

"What happens when the bullet rebounds and hits you?"

Alva frowned, considering it.

"Your dad has the key?" Rafe guessed.

She nodded. "He doesn't want me to go outside. He's scared I'll disappear like my sister." There was irritation in her voice, nothing more, which made the whole scene worse.

"You know ferals can climb stairs, right?" Rafe said. "So can mongrels and scumbags. Anything could have walked through that door and found you."

"You think I asked for this? Lecture my papa, not me." Alva closed the switchblade and tucked it back into her sleeve. "He's going crazy," she grumbled.

"We noticed." Rafe waved at the piled jewelry that made the place look like a dragon's lair.

"What's that got to do with anything? He's crazy because Fabiola is gone."

"So why are you still living outside the compound?"

She shrugged. "Papa thinks people in town will steal our savings."

I really hoped she wasn't referring to the obsolete electronics stacked in the corners.

"If it were powdered milk or potato flakes, maybe. But this crap?" Rafe snorted.

The girl didn't reply, just traced her fingers over the knife in her sleeve. He shouldn't make her feel bad about her father. I nudged him. "Can you do something about that chain?"

Sighing, he pulled a couple of thin tools from his back pocket, swept a stack of pre-exodus money off the coffee table, and sat. When Alva moved to stand in front of him, he studied the padlock. "So, how long has your sister been missing?" he asked without looking up.

Alva inhaled sharply. "That's why you're here, isn't it?" Her hands flew to her throat. "Because of Fabiola. Someone found her. She's dead!"

"No," he said quickly. "I mean, I don't know. I just came for information."

The tension left Alva's body and she slumped. "Is the feral back? That's what Papa heard. That it ripped up a farmer."

"Nobody knows for sure what killed him. Lots of things have claws." Rafe went to work on the lock. "Is there any chance your sister just ran away?"

"If she was going to take off, she would've told me."

"Does she have a boyfriend?" He jiggled the slender tool and the padlock popped open.

"We're not allowed to date." The chain snaked from around Alva's waist and clattered to the floor, but she didn't move, just fingered her many necklaces. "Papa worries. He told us to carry a blade at all times. A lot of good it did her," Alva said, sounding as if all the fight had been stamped out of her. "The feral is back."

Rafe got to his feet. "Did you see something?"

"No, but when we were outside, Fabiola felt it. She *knew*." Alva drew in a ragged breath. "And I told her she was crazy."

"Knew what?" I asked.

"That she was being hunted."

· THIRTEEN ·

"You were checking to see if Alva knew something about her sister that their father didn't," I guessed when we were outside again.

"Yeah." Rafe exhaled slowly. "Too bad she didn't run off with a boyfriend. Means the feral probably did get her."

The buildings slouched closer together as we walked north, and yet the street seemed rural because of all the creeping, climbing vegetation that was slowly tearing down everything man-made.

He pointed down the road a ways to a wall of crushed cars, stacked like bricks. "Welcome to the Moline compound," he said. "When we get inside, stick close."

I bristled. "I'm not totally helpless you know. I've taken self-defense classes and kickboxing and —"

"Yeah, 'cause Mack made you."

I stopped in surprise, but Rafe walked on. "He worries that you're too nice," he said over his shoulder.

"I'm not too nice!"

Rafe held up his hands. "Getting no argument from me."

"Oh, I'm supposed to be more like you? A selfish jerk?" I jogged to catch up. "Stealing from infirmaries, throwing people in closets when they get in the way? Cutting them!"

He shot me an amused look. "You might try it sometime."

I shook my head, suddenly feeling sick.

"What?" he asked, catching my expression. "You've been the good girl your whole —"

"No. Not when I was little. Just the opposite." The words felt like broken glass in my mouth. "I was so . . . so awful. I wore my mom out."

His brow furrowed. "Your mother died of cancer."

"The doctor said she had a year to live, but she died two months later — because of me."

"Says who?" Rafe scoffed.

"The home health nurse." I rubbed by eyes — like that would erase her red, sweaty face from my mind.

"She told you that?"

"She said I was an unmanageable little beast and that I'd send my mom to an even earlier grave." I caught my breath. I hadn't thought about that horrible nurse in years and I didn't want to now. "Can we go find my dad now?"

I strode toward the car wall, only to realize that Rafe had known how my mother had died. I slowed my pace. "What else did my father tell you? Why would he talk to you at all?"

"Get a mug of moonshine in Mack and he won't shut up."

"That's not true. He's very private and he almost never drinks."

Rafe shrugged. "So he cuts loose over here."

Or maybe I didn't know my father at all.

We'd reached the wall of crushed cars, but my legs felt so unstable I couldn't take another step. A scorching sensation rolled over my skin. I cast about for somewhere to sit.

Rafe's aqua eyes widened. "What are you doing?"

"Leave me alone." I sank onto a car bumper that barely jutted out of the wall. I put my hands over my face.

"Oh no," Rafe scolded. "We are not stopping out here in the open. Come on, let's get inside the compound. Then you can cry all you want."

"I'm not crying," I snapped. Though I wanted to. What else had my father lied to me about?

Rafe unslung his pack and dropped it at his feet with a sigh. "I guess Mack wasn't exaggerating. You are as tough as a declawed kitten."

"Stop talking."

"Whoa, you dropped the *please*. That's progress."

When I didn't look up, Rafe settled by me on the bumper. "Want to know what else he said?" Rafe put his lips near my ear. "That with the right guy, you'd turn wild."

I shoved him hard. He was laughing before he even hit the ground. I shot to my feet and glared at him. "You're disgusting."

Grinning, he rose and dusted off his pants. "Got you up."

I hated him in that moment. He was obscene and obnoxious, but he'd also escorted me to Moline as promised. If I found my father inside the compound, then he'd helped me save my dad's life. "Thank you for bringing me," I ground out.

"Don't thank me yet." He strode toward a break in the car wall. "You're not past the gate." Cupping his hands around his mouth, he yelled, "Hey, Sid, open up!"

I peered through the bars of the gate at the compound beyond. Like everywhere else, invasive vines and stray plants had reclaimed the town center, but I was starting to get used to the lush ruins. Even starting to see the beauty in them.

"Sid, get your porky self out here!" Rafe shouted.

Inside the compound, a short, pudgy man appeared in the doorway of a ramshackle building across the street. "What are you doing back so soon?"

"What's it to you?" Rafe replied. "Unlock the gate." He stepped in front of me as Sid hurried over with a jangling key ring, but Sid had already spotted me.

"Who's she?" he demanded.

"Aren't you full of questions?" Rafe said, still blocking me from view.

"That's how I earn my keep, you know," I heard Sid huff.

"Open the gate, or I'll kick your guts into sausage."

With a grunt, Sid unlocked the chain and pushed the gate just wide enough for us to slip through. "I'm not supposed to let strangers in without checking them out first." Rafe rolled his eyes but Sid's back was turned as he relocked the gate. "It's a big responsibility, you know, keeping this compound safe. It all rests on me."

From the back, Sid was an oily little guy in a stained undershirt and suspenders. I waited for him to turn so that I could assure him that I wasn't a threat, but when he finally did, I jerked back with a gasp. Tusks curled out of his mouth and ended in sharp points on either side of his piggy snout.

"You got a problem?" he squealed, thrusting out his chin, ready to charge.

Laughter erupted behind me. "She's seen a guy infected with tiger." Rafe nudged me aside. "I don't know why you'd freak her out."

"I'm so sorry," I sputtered. "I didn't mean to —"

"Mayor's holding a compound meeting," Sid told Rafe, while turning his back on me. "In the station, as soon as Jared's memorial service finishes up." He shot me one last indignant look before trotting back across the street with his giant key ring jangling.

"I thought you silkies were big on manners."

I turned on Rafe, who was still grinning. "Why didn't you warn me?"

"About?"

"That he's . . ." I lowered my voice. "A feral."

"Sid's not a feral. He's just an eyesore."

"But . . . his feet, his nose — they weren't human."

"Wait till you see his tail. Actually, you won't get to. He's pretty self-conscious about it, with good reason."

"Why is he *inside* the gate? I thought this pile of cars was supposed to keep the ferals out."

"Learn that from your knight in shining armor?"

"Who?" I asked and then realized he was talking about Everson. "Just answer the question."

"Your line guard might call everyone who has Ferae a feral, but over here, we have distinctions. Our lives depend on it."

"What distinctions?" We entered the town square, which was bounded on one side by the Mississippi River. A path of boards, laid over mud, led past the buildings toward the rushing brown water. Tattered store awnings flapped in the wind, giving the place a desolate air. Or maybe I was getting that feeling because other than a few vendors standing by carts loaded with vegetables, the square was empty.

"Everyone must be at the service," Rafe said, nodding toward the church. "We'll wait in the station." He pointed at the largest building on the square, a red brick box with several three-blade wind-power rotors spinning lazily on the roof. Strangely, a dozen bathtubs were mounted on top of the station as well. The tubs' drainpipes ran down the wall and into four enormous tanks on the ground.

I wanted to ask more about Sid but was distracted by a woman pushing a tarp-covered shopping cart across the square. Slouching along, she cast her head from side to side in a weird manner that made the hairs on my arms stand up. She seemed off in a way that I couldn't pinpoint. But off didn't even begin to describe the vegetable vendor she stopped to talk to. He was covered in pale gray *fur*. "Distinctions," I prompted. "How do you know who's feral?"

Rafe followed my gaze to the vendor. "Is he drooling?"

"No." If anything, the man seemed perfectly nice as he bundled up carrots for the old lady.

"Growling? Chasing his tail?"

"Ferals do that?"

"Ferals are *feral*. They've got animal brain."

I remembered Dr. Solis saying it took a while for the virus to take over the infected person's brain. "When will he get animal brain?" I made a discreet head tip toward the furry vendor.

Rafe shrugged. "No way to know. Some people beast out fast — usually if they're infected with some kind of reptile. But most people stay sane for years, like Sid. We call them —"

"Manimals!"

"If you knew, why'd you ask?"

"I didn't know I knew." So, my dad's stories were true, right down to the details. I'd loved the manimals he'd described, with their distinct personalities, often squabbling, sometimes eccentric, but almost always friendly. They walked upright and would offer the little girl help or advice when she got lost in the magical forest.

And that's what Chorda was! A manimal, not a feral. He could talk; he was sane. I had been right to stop Rafe from killing him, even if Rafe didn't want to admit it.

"Sid has Ferae," Rafe went on, "and he's mutating, but he's not feral. . . . Not yet."

"But he will be someday for sure?"

"They all think they can beat it, that their human side will stay dominant, but the beast always wins. Sooner or later, every one of them turns into a slobbering animal."

His words gave me the sick feeling of free-falling. "That's — that's awful."

"For them," he said coldly. "What you need to know is that they can turn without warning. One minute you're out scavenging together, the next, she's leaping for your throat."

"She?"

"Or he." Rafe glanced away. "No one's immune. Which is why most compounds have a sundown law. Manimals can visit during the day to trade or see their families, but they have to be out by sundown. Moline is the only place I've seen that lets them live inside the compound along with the humans. It's stupid, taking that kind of risk when everyone knows manimals are walking, talking time bombs."

"Nobody asked you," growled a voice behind us. I turned to see a manimal whose oversized teeth protruded from his elongated face, while his hair seemed to grow naturally into a mohawk. I tried not to recoil, but couldn't completely hide my alarm at the horse-man's distorted features. So far, these people were nothing like the charming creatures I'd imagined whenever my father added a lemur-man or a camel-girl to a story. Nor were they alluring like Chorda.

"Was I talking to you, Trots?" Rafe snapped back. "Go eat some hay."

I steered him toward the station. "You don't have to be rude."

As Rafe and I passed the church, a woman came out, looking sunburnt and tough despite her flowered dress. She wiped at her eyes and then propped open the double doors. The sound of organ music drifted out. I paused in the street and saw mourners inside in their somber best. I hadn't really heard organ music since my mother's memorial service. Of course, then it was just piped into the room where my dad and I sat alone with the casket, listening to something by Bach — Mom loved Bach. That day, each chord had hit me so hard, I thought they would pound me right through the floor.

My mom had had lots of friends and though I didn't forgive them for staying away when she was sick, I had still expected to see them at her service. It was their last chance to see her and say good-bye.

"Where is everybody?" I'd asked my dad.

"Doesn't matter," he'd said softly, gathering me onto his lap. "We're here and we're her family."

People and manimals started filing out of the church in groups of two and three, squinting in the light. Like Rafe, they all wore weapons, mostly guns and knives, as well as strange combinations of clothing. Several had loaded on the jewelry like Alva, and many wore hats. I squirmed at the sight of the humans and manimals so close together. I wasn't about to tell Rafe, but I did understand his reaction at a gut level. I didn't want to get too close to infected people even if they weren't technically feral yet. At least I made an effort to hide my discomfort, unlike him.

The manimals were not only walking side by side with humans, but also hand in hand or with their arms around each other, which weirded me out even more. Then again it had been a funeral, and they were all clearly feeling the loss. A sobbing woman passed us, buoyed along by a man so huge and hairy, he could only have been infected by bear. Two young children held the clawed hands of a man with vertical stripes of dark fur over his eyes and gray hair sprouting thickly from his ears. Badger maybe?

"Who was it?" I asked Rafe quietly as we joined the flow of people and manimals headed for the station. "The first victim?"

"Yeah, Jared. He had farm duty," he said. "The shift had ended, but he wanted to finish the patch he was working on, so he was out there alone. When he didn't come back that night, his wife and Sid went looking for him. He'd made it halfway home. He couldn't make it the rest of the way, what with being ripped open and all."

I felt the color in my face drain away.

Rafe waved me forward. "The place will fill up fast.

Usually it's just hacks hanging out at this time of day." At my questioning look, he added, "Path hackers."

"English, please."

"Someone you hire to get you from compound to compound safely. They know the best routes and will hack up any ferals along the way. You don't want to travel without one." He stopped next to a low stone wall and dropped his pack onto it. "Mack spends a lot of time in there." He unzipped the knapsack and pulled his filthy shirt over his head. "It's a good place to pick up information about what's happening in the zone." He began pawing through his bag. "Anyway, stick close. Most of them aren't worth the dirt they're caked in. Except me, of course." He shot me a sly smile.

Why was it that every time I saw him bare chested my mind went to art? When we'd first met, I'd thought of an archangel, and now, Rafe reminded me of Michelangelo's David. All he needed was a rock in one overlarge hand and a slingshot flung over his shoulder. Even his stance was like the statue's, slung back and yet poised for action. When I was little, I'd spent way too much time staring at a photo of David in one of my father's art books. "A High Renaissance interpretation of the idealized male form," the caption had read, and I'd agreed wholeheartedly. David had been my first celebrity crush. I was definitely an art dealer's daughter.

Rafe groaned. "You know Mack is around here somewhere."

"I hope so."

"Then have a heart and don't look at me like that." He pulled a clean thermal shirt over his head — light blue this time. "I don't want to take this test." He swept a hand at my body. "I'll fail."

My face caught fire. "I wasn't looking at —" I gave up and hurried over to the door. A part of me was flattered that such a gorgeous boy found me tempting, but a bigger part wondered why Rafe had suddenly developed morals. This was the guy who'd invited me to share his sleeping bag five minutes after meeting me, and yet now that he knew who my father was, he didn't want me staring at him. Not that I had been.

An answer popped into my mind. One that I didn't like, but now I couldn't unthink it.

Rafe hefted on his pack frame and joined me by the door.

"How old are you?" I asked in a rasp of a voice.

"Seventeen, eighteen. I was born right after the wall went up."

His answer didn't dispel the ugly thought in my head. "Tell me again how you know my dad?"

"Mack used to take me on fetches." Rafe pulled open the door to the station and waved me in.

I stayed put. "What are you telling me?"

"That I was his lookout."

"Why *you*?"

"I don't know, ask him."

"I'm asking you. So, why don't you just come out and say it?"

Rafe released the door, letting it close. "What are we talking about?"

I dug my nails into my palms, letting the pain brace me for his answer. "Is he your father?"

· FOURTEEN ·

Rafe's smile returned. "Nope. I'm not your brother, Lane. I know that's got to be a disappointment." He paused, considering it. "Or maybe not. Now you can throw yourself at me. Just not when Mack's around, okay? He's not my dad, but he *is* the guy who busted me out of an orphan camp when I was ten."

Rafe's answer should have relieved me, but it made me feel even heavier. My dad had taken Rafe on fetches — a kid not even related to him — and yet he'd never told me anything about this part of his life. Yes, Dr. Solis had explained about my father's fear that I'd have to take a lie detector test. But the good doctor had also been right when he'd said that sometimes a reasonable explanation wasn't comforting.

"Now what's wrong?" Rafe asked.

"All that time my dad left me alone, he was here with you." My words came out choked.

Rafe wrinkled his nose. "Ugh. You're making me sound like the other woman. I've been on my own for years now, not waiting around for Mack to show up."

"But you did when you were younger? Wait for him to show up so you two could go off and have fun?"

"Fun? Yeah, that's life in the Feral Zone. One big septic tank o' fun. We yuk it up —"

"Please, stop talking." I swallowed against the ache in my throat.

"I don't know what's got you so worked up. Mack loves you more than anything. You've got to know that much."

"I don't know anything anymore."

"Okay, if you want to be all tragic, go ahead. Stay here and kick rocks. Me, I'm going in to find Mack . . . because I'm the good kid." He hauled open the door.

What I really wanted to kick was him. But I shoved past him and entered the station. Of *course* I was questioning everything now, trying to fit pieces together. I wasn't going to apologize for it either. Last night, my reality had been turned upside down and shaken beyond recognition. I just wished that my insides didn't feel so bruised and broken.

What had been a train station before the exodus was now a marketplace and dining hall. Along the perimeter, food stalls displayed the offerings of the day: plates of grilled meat and glasses of foamy beer. Carcasses hung from iron support beams — turkeys, geese, and chickens — yet the place didn't reek of blood. The smell was more reminiscent of a summer barbeque. The center area was taken up with various tables and chairs, everything from wooden picnic benches to elegant dining room sets — probably plundered from abandoned homes.

Despite the dirt and debris tracked across the inlaid floor and the somber reason for holding the town meeting, the station didn't have the desperate or unhappy feel that I'd expected. These people were living in the Feral Zone, and yet as they found seats, they exchanged greetings and words of reassurance with those around them. There was even a sprinkling of laughter as children chased one another, some of whom were manimals. Still, there was a worn, scuffed quality to the adults' faces. Clearly life within a quarantine compound wasn't one big campout with sing-alongs and s'mores.

Rafe paused by a food counter piled with smoked meats to survey the area. I looked around too, searching the crowd for the familiar head of wavy dark hair, the wire-rimmed glasses, my heart accelerating with the anticipation of seeing my father's face. How surprised would he be to see me here? Would he be mad at me? Considering the trouble he was in, me coming to the Feral Zone had to be the least of his worries.

"Hey, Rafe, did you kill it?" a young voice asked.

I turned to see two boys sitting on the other side of the meat counter. They wore baseball caps pulled low, yet not low enough to cover the faint green speckles that ran from their temples to circle their eyes, which made them look moldy. Their vertical pupils were even more disturbing.

Rafe frowned slightly, a pucker between his brows.

"It's Andrew Lehrer, remember?" said the boy.

"And Avi," said the other. "You did a job for our grandma last month."

"No, I didn't kill the rogue yet," Rafe said in a flat voice and returned to surveying the crowd. "Mack here?" he asked without glancing back.

"Haven't seen him." The boys took me in with curious eyes.

"Thanks," I murmured to them and hurried to catch up with Rafe, who'd strode off. "You know, you could be nicer when you talk to them. . . . Manimals."

"Why? So they think we're friends?"

"Would that be so awful?"

He shot me a look and leaned against a massive pillar. Then he nodded toward the center staircase. Halfway up the stairs, a middle-aged woman, dark-skinned and curvy, stood alone, looking out at the crowd. Her riot of curls and high cheekbones gave her an exotic look, which was saying something, considering she was dressed like a lumberjack in jeans and a plaid shirt.

"That's the mayor," Rafe whispered. "Hagen."

With a bartender's apron wrapped around her hips, Hagen wasn't the western vision of a mayor, but her demeanor was serious enough. "Okay, people," she said loudly, "I'll get right to it." The room grew impressively silent. "Every one of us is torn up about losing Jared, but none more than his family. I know that Ruby and her sons can count on all of us to pick up their work shifts as they navigate their grief."

People and manimals at the tables nodded, while I continued to scan the crowd for my father. He should have been easy enough to spot in this odd assembly, but I didn't see him anywhere.

"When we found Jared," Hagen continued, "the circumstances suggested a feral that's gone rogue — probably the one that was preying on people in this area two years ago."

A cry went up from the crowd and hovered over the room like a storm cloud. Hagen lifted a hand, and the voices faded. "I'm sure you've all heard by now how Jared died. . . ."

I nudged Rafe. "I don't think my —"

Rafe put a finger to his lips.

Fine. I'd go look in the back of the station by the food stalls. Maybe my dad was —

"And I'll confirm it," Hagen continued. "His heart was ripped out."

I stopped short with a gasp. Ripped — how was that even possible? When Rafe told me about the rogue, I thought he was just trying to freak me out. What was I doing in a place where people got their hearts ripped out?

"And now a teenage girl has gone missing a mile south of here," Hagen went on. "I don't want anyone else disappearing, so I've allocated compound resources to offer a reward to the person who brings in the rogue. And thankfully, we have a bunch of hunters and hacks willing to try." She gestured to a small group of people in the back corner. No surprise that from where I stood they looked like the sketchiest clump of humanity I'd ever seen. I needed to get out of this place ASAP. But my dad wasn't in the crowd as far as I could tell.

When questions swelled in the room like a roaring wave, the mayor clapped her hands. "One at a time! Leonard, spit it out." Hagen pointed at a man seated in front.

"Are we going to be stuck inside the compound again? We were holed up for weeks last time," Leonard said. "We couldn't trade or hunt. If it's going to be like that —"

"It'll be worse," Rafe said loudly. I slid another foot away from him as the townsfolk twisted in their seats to see who'd spoken.

Leonard scowled at him. "That thing snatched anyone

who set foot in the woods and if we were lucky — *if* — we'd find a heap of bloody clothes days later. How much worse can it get?"

"Two years ago, the feral skimmed the edges of the compounds, grabbing people who were outside the fence. It's bolder now." Rafe's voice easily filled the echoing space.

"How much bolder?" Hagen asked, clearly dreading the answer.

"For the past year it has been going into compounds after dark and dragging people from their beds."

Gasps and cries rippled through the room and I didn't blame the crowd one bit. I was verging on hyperventilation myself over that image.

Hagen rubbed a hand over her eyes. "And you have no idea what it is?"

"Nope. Only that it's strong. A couple of months ago, it hauled a 250-pound man over the Peoria fence." Rafe's gaze settled on me. "I do know there's a guy infected with tiger in the area. I can't *prove* it's him, but that's where I'm placing my bet."

"Tiger!" The word cut through the crowd, followed by a horrified silence.

I glared at Rafe. How dare he bring up Chorda when he knew that the tiger-man wasn't feral based on what I'd told him? Now those hunters would shoot Chorda on sight — no questions asked — because Rafe had just declared it open season on tigers.

"And here's what else I know," Rafe went on. "This feral has hit five other compounds — enough that I've picked up on a pattern.

"This rogue doesn't have a pattern," scoffed a greasy hunter in the back. "No one knows where it'll hit next."

Rafe looked unfazed. "True, but once this feral shows up in an area, it does have a routine."

"And what's that?" Hagen asked.

"It'll stick around for about a week, kill one person a day, and then disappear for a couple of months. I don't know where it goes when it's lying low, but that's its pattern. And here's what you all *really* need to know: This feral isn't taking whatever dirtbag crosses its path anymore. It's gotten much pickier about its prey. Now it'll stalk the person it wants, waiting for its chance to pounce."

I wondered if Alva Soto had confirmed that for him when she'd said that her sister had sensed something hunting her.

"That's a load of crap." The greasy hunter sneered. "Ferals don't plan — rogue or not. They eat, they sleep, and some howl at the moon. They're *animals*."

A low grumble of protest came from the manimals in the station. One gave an agitated flick of his hand, rejecting the statement, while I shuddered at the sight of his long black claws.

"*Animals* also hunt and they have preferences when it comes to prey." Rafe folded his arms over his chest. "But I'm willing to consider another theory. Maybe it isn't totally feral. Maybe it's a manimal — evil as all get out, but still thinking straight."

I frowned. He was throwing that out there so that he didn't have to admit he was wrong about Chorda.

"Why a manimal?" A large man got to his feet. A layer of gray filmy skin hung from his cheeks, half peeled away.

Considering his whiskers and downward pointing tusks, he was probably infected with walrus. "It could just as easily be fully human. Serial killers were around long before us."

"The victims' chests were ripped open with claws" — Rafe waggled his fingers — "not fingernails."

"Rogue, alien, demented nun . . . I don't care what it is," Hagen said loudly. "I just want its head in a Hefty bag. *Comprende*, people?"

"Excuse me." A young woman stood, her eyes on Rafe as she nervously fingered the knife tucked into her belt. Pockmarked and wiry, she could have passed for a boy. "You said the feral is choosing its victims. Who is it choosing?"

"Two years ago, it stuck to the bottom of the food chain, mostly picking off drifters. Now it only goes for respectable people. That's a broad range, I know, but it *is* selecting its victims. Every person who went missing this year told someone that they felt like they were being watched the day before. So if you have that sense, come find me."

"So, the feral's already picked its next victim?" the greasy hunter scoffed. "Well, heck, I guess that means the rest of us can kick back and relax."

"You can, Tox," Rafe retorted. "Like I said, it's only snatching decent people."

The hunter started to reply but Hagen cut him off. "Okay, everyone, here's what that means," she shouted to be heard above the frightened chatter. "Mandatory curfew. No ifs, ands, or buts. The gate doesn't open for anybody after sunset. Anyone out at night will be considered a threat. Manimals, that goes double for you."

"Why double for us?" the walrus-man huffed.

Hagen held up her hands. "That's it, meeting's over."

"Come on, Ed," said the normal-looking woman beside the walrus-man. "Leave it alone." She tugged at him until he followed her, glowering over his shoulder at the mayor. When he caught me staring at him, I looked away quickly.

"If Mr. Walrus is smart, he'll leave town," Rafe said, watching the couple go.

"Why? Is the rogue killing manimals too?" My voice caught on the word *manimals*, but I got it out. Maybe someday it would even sound like a real word.

"No. But when the humans start looking for someone to blame," he said, gesturing to the departing crowd, "it won't be one of their own."

"Won't they blame the rogue feral?"

"Sure, until somebody says that it's punishing the compound because of something someone did. That's when the tar and feathers get dragged out."

"You've seen that happen?"

He nodded and took another long look around the room. "Mack's not here."

My heart slammed against my ribs. "Where else could he be?"

"Hagen will know if he's in the compound." Rafe pulled out a chair at an empty table. "Sit."

"I'm not a dog."

"Do you want to be? I'm sure the mastiff there would be happy to get a mouthful of you."

The jowly man at a nearby table looked up from his meal and glared at Rafe. I wished the floor would split open and swallow me, but I settled for whispering, "Sorry," before slipping into the chair and ducking my head to inspect my silverware for spots. Why did I have to be stuck in a new place with the rudest person alive? How were we going to get answers about my dad if he went around insulting everyone? I looked up to find him grinning at me.

"I've never seen anyone turn that red," he said, sitting beside me. "Including the baboon dude back there." He pointed over my shoulder — as if I was going to turn around. He smirked. "You know you want to look."

"Shut up," I muttered.

Rafe grinned. "Sure you don't want to stick a 'please' on the end?"

"Okay, pretty boy," Hagen said, joining us, "what are you doing back so soon?"

"I got a bunch of traps set and hung up poisoned meat. But then something came up."

"You mean *someone*?" She sounded annoyed, though the gaze she turned on to me was friendly enough. "Where are you from, hon?"

"The West," Rafe replied for me.

Hagen laughed. "And I just got back from swimming in the California surf."

I felt a weird twinge of pride, knowing that I no longer looked like a silky from the West.

"She's Mack's daughter."

There was something in the way Rafe said it that told me that this was significant information for this woman.

Hagen's face twitched, and she pushed her chair back

abruptly from the table. She saw me watching her and said, "It's not that it isn't good to meet you, Delaney Park."

Did everyone in the Feral Zone know about me?

"The problem is that your being here means Mack is in trouble."

"How did you know?"

"She's your dad's —" Rafe started.

"— good friend," Hagen finished.

I'd have to have been an idiot not to catch that subtext. However, I decided to ignore it. If my father had a girlfriend over here, that was one secret I didn't mind him keeping. "It's nice to meet you."

The crease in Hagen's forehead deepened. "Mack came by here to tell me that biohaz agents were probably looking for him. He took off again last night to see if he could bribe a line guard to fly him over the wall. He was planning to clear out of Davenport." She studied my face. Her eyes were a beautiful amber color. "So how did you get dragged into this mess, little girl?"

"She's supposed to give Mack a letter," Rafe said, "and then she's going back to her side of the wall to eat bonbons and paint her toenails."

Any other time, his barb would have set my teeth on edge, but now I didn't care. I slumped back in my chair, feeling as if I'd given too much blood. I had crossed the last bridge, broken quarantine, hoping to find my dad in time. And now I knew without a doubt that I'd failed.

· FIFTEEN ·

I rose abruptly as if the floor had pitched me upward. My dad didn't know he had to do a fetch for Director Spurling, didn't know that his life depended on it. Maybe there was still time to find him. How far could he have gone? Rafe gripped my arm. I stared at his fingers, tan lines against the white of my forearm. Why was he holding me so tightly?

"What are you doing?" he asked.

"Going back to Arsenal," I said.

"What exactly is going on?" Hagen demanded. "How did biohaz find out he'd come east?"

"They've got a recording of Mack in the exodus tunnel," Rafe explained. "Now he's got to grease a big wheel or they'll turn him into target practice."

"Oh no," she whispered.

Rafe tugged me back into my seat. "Rushing off hot-headed isn't going to help Mack."

"You're right," I said, pulling my ponytail tighter. "If he's going to try bribing a line guard, he'll probably go through Dr. Solis, and Dr. Solis will tell him that I'm here."

"Oh, that's good," Hagen said with relief. "Now all you have to do is wait for him to come looking for you."

"But what if he doesn't go to Dr. Solis?" They were friends. Maybe my dad wouldn't want to implicate him. "Or even if he does go, what if the doctor is so whiffed out on Lull that he can't tell my father he saw me?"

"That's a lot of *ifs* that you can't do anything about," Rafe said and turned to Hagen. "What's on the grill today?"

He couldn't be serious. He wasn't going to eat at a time like this. . . . Even Hagen looked put out until Rafe pulled a wadded-up shirt from his knapsack and unrolled it to reveal a bottle of viscous pink liquid. "Amoxicillin. That should be worth at least two meals."

Hagen rose and slipped the bottle into her apron pocket. "We've got the usual, chicken and fish for the noninfected."

"Is that how most people pay?" I asked. "With medicine?"

"If you live in the compound, you don't pay, as long as you're signed up for work duty. It's the hacks who have to trade for food," Hagen said.

"Ammunition, matches, weapons, booze," Rafe said. "They'll get you everything you need. Like a plate of Hagen's grilled chicken, which is what I need." He pointed at me. "You?"

The thought of food made me ill, and the mastiff-man at the next table wasn't helping as he wolfed down a hunk of bloody steak and then licked his lips with his black tongue. "I don't eat meat."

"No one eats mammals," Hagen said. "Well, unless you're already infected, then it doesn't matter if the animal had the disease before it got turned into a hamburger. The rest of us won't take that chance."

"Can you catch Ferae from eating an infected animal?" I asked.

She shrugged. "Who's going to put it to the test? Since we know for sure that birds and fish can't get Ferae, that's what we grill up."

"I don't eat birds and fish either."

Rafe exchanged a look with Hagen. "Are you sure you're Mack's daughter?"

How many times had my dad made that same joke while devouring a drumstick? "Do you have oatmeal?" I asked.

"Sure, but it'll taste old to you."

"That's okay." My brain was dangerously close to clicking into "thrash mode" — where anything and everything that made me feel crappy flashed through my mind at once. Until this moment I'd really thought that I would find my dad in time and he'd do the fetch. Now I didn't know what to do.

As soon as Hagen headed off, I pulled out Spurling's instructions and my hand sanitizer.

Rafe plucked the paper from my fingers. "Is this the job?"

I nodded and tried to squeeze gel into my palm, but the bottle was empty. "Great," I muttered, tossing it onto the table. "Guess I'll be getting dirty."

Rafe glanced up from the letter. "You can wash your hands in the river." He hooked a thumb at the back door.

I managed to stifle my *ew*. "There's bacteria in the river. And parasites."

"And fish pee. So what? The only germ that matters is the one that turns you into a slobbering animal. And that you can't catch from a river." He dropped the letter on the table. "All this for a photo?" he said with disgust. "Her kid died nineteen years ago. When is she going to get over it?"

Never. And if my dad couldn't come home, I wouldn't get over it either. He had to come home. But if he didn't know about Spurling's offer, how was that going to happen?

"I have to do the fetch for him," I said quietly.

"Right." Rafe chuckled and then saw my face. "Wrong! You'd get infected or killed."

"I won't," I said firmly, though the words *infected or killed* did give me a mental shiver. "I'll manage."

Rafe groaned. "Fine. All right. I'll go to Chicago."

"You'll do the fetch?" I wasn't sure whether to be suspicious or hug him. "Why?"

"Mack saved me from the orphan camp. I owe him. Okay?"

"Okay." I was too grateful to pull apart my tangled feelings about my father's secret life. A life in which Rafe had played a major role. My gratitude slipped a notch. "But I'm going with you."

"Not happening," he said firmly. I opened my mouth to protest but he held up a hand and said, "I know that Mack would rather face a firing squad than risk his pretty princess getting Ferae."

I smacked his shoulder, but Rafe didn't so much as wince. Still, it was satisfying. "Call me that again and I will mess you up," I added for good measure.

"Okay, that's hilarious, but it doesn't change the fact that Mack wouldn't want you going into the zone for him."

"I'm already in it."

"Please. This is the cradle of civilization. The quarantine compounds around here are actually on the map. But head east and who knows what you'll find. Those compounds have been isolated for eighteen years — enough time to go native. And they *have*. There are cults and cannibals that come in more flavors of scary than you want to sample."

Cannibals? He was exaggerating for effect. He had to be.

Crossing his arms, Rafe tipped back in his chair. "Remember the chimpacabra?"

I shuddered, remembering it too well. It would be a miracle if I ever got a good night's sleep again.

"Well, there are mongrels out there a lot more dangerous than a chimpa, and then there's the feral that's ripping out people's —"

"Okay, all right." I put up my hands to ward off any more nightmare fuel. "I get it. I'll stay here."

"Glad that's settled," he said as Hagen plopped a whole spit-roasted chicken in front of him. "Is Mack's bike still in the garage?" he asked her.

"Yep." She set a steaming bowl of oatmeal in front of me. "If you take it, it comes back in the same condition."

"Bike as in motorcycle?" I asked.

"Bike as in bicycle." Rafe ripped off a chicken leg. "Ferals don't hear you coming, you can carry it over rubble, and you don't have to feed it."

"Why not take a car?"

Rafe snorted. "Why not a hovercopter? We can fill the tank with magic fairy dust and wish ourselves there."

Got it. All the gas in the East had probably been siphoned out of the stations long ago. "How long will it take you to bike to Chicago?"

"Eighteen hours."

"What? Why so long?"

"It's one hundred seventy miles from here," Hagen explained. "Over broken road."

"But I have to get back to the tunnel by Thursday, before the line patrol fills it in with rubble."

Rafe dropped the chicken leg onto his plate. "Guess I'm getting this to go."

"Bring the bike around," Hagen said, picking up the plate. "I'll wrap this and meet you in front." She headed off.

"So, can you get to Chicago and back in time?" I asked as he rose.

He zipped up his knapsack and slung the whole pack onto his back. "We'll find out." His tone wasn't reassuring. He left through the station's back door — after shoving a bear-man out of his way. Even if I could keep up with him on a bike, and that was unlikely, I was just as happy not to go. I'd seen enough of the Feral Zone and had my fill of adventure. Staying here was a much saner plan.

Hagen returned with a child's old lunchbox, into which she packed the chicken. "Don't worry. He'll do the fetch and wear himself out to get back in time. There's nothing he wouldn't do for Mack."

"Because my dad got him out of an orphan camp?"

"Yes, after Mack saw how bad it was. The guards treat the kids like slave labor."

My skin prickled. Everson had said he'd take the little girl, Jia, to an orphan camp. Were they all awful?

"Mack felt responsible because he was the one who put Rafe there," Hagen added.

"Why?" I asked.

"On one of his fetches, Mack found Rafe living like a wild child out in the woods. Half-starved and alone."

"What happened to his parents?"

Hagen pursed her lips as if considering how much to tell me.

"They were killed by a feral, weren't they?" I guessed. That would explain why Rafe hated infected people.

She sighed, relenting. "I don't know what happened to his parents. He was raised by his sister. But you've got the right idea. When her husband got infected, the three of them moved out of the compound where they were living. Not Moline. They were squatting in some abandoned house, making the best of it, and then one day, the guy turned and killed Rafe's sister right in front of him. He was eight."

I clapped a hand to my mouth. Eight?! No wonder he'd made a career out of killing ferals.

Hagen angled a finger at me. "Don't tell him I told you. He hates anyone feeling sorry for him."

I nodded, though it would be hard not to look at him differently. How could anyone help but feel sorry for him after hearing that story?

"You want something to drink?" she asked. "There's no coffee, but we have tea."

"What I really want is more information." If I was stuck in Moline, at least I was going to learn as much about the

East as I could — especially about my father's life here. "Is my dad coming over just to fetch art and make money, or is it more than that? Dr. Solis said he brings medicine over here, to the compound."

"The money's a part of it, don't kid yourself." Hagen settled in the chair next to me. "But yeah, Mack brings medicine that we wouldn't get any other way. It slows down the virus." She gestured to the man infected with mastiff and another with froggy eyes who now sat on opposite sides of a checkerboard. They wore blue jeans and sweaters that were too small for them — probably scavenged from abandoned stores. The mastiff picked up a mug, his claws clicking on the ceramic handle, and tipped it to his muzzle. His black tongue lapped as he swallowed and hot chocolate dribbled onto his shirt, which he dabbed at self-consciously.

"Keeps them from mutating as fast," Hagen went on. "But they have to keep taking it. Every month."

A man approached the table. "Hagen, if you're going to set a curfew, you should issue a shoot-to-kill order along with it. Post people on roofs. Anything out on the street tonight gets a gut full of bullets. That'll solve our feral problem real quick."

"The way the military gunned down people during the plague?" Hagen snapped. "Great idea, Nestor. Let's bring back anarchy. It worked so well last time."

"Forget the plague. Remember two years ago? Do you want to lose eight more people — full-blooded humans?"

"What I'm not going to do is resort to tactics that end in tragedy — always." Hagen's voice took on a steely edge. "Thanks for your input, but I got this one."

"I hope so. Because a lot of people have been saying it's time to hold another election." He moved off.

Hagen massaged her temples. "This is going to get ugly before it gets better. I don't see a way around it."

"The rogue killed eight people two years ago?"

Hagen nodded. "We only found three bodies. But the other five people were never seen again, and those are just the ones we know about. No one notices a missing drifter, and there are a lot of those in the Feral Zone."

"Does my dad know that there's a man-eating feral on the loose?"

"He heard the talk last night before he took off. I wouldn't worry about him. Your dad deals with worse every time he goes into Chicago. He says the people in that city have gone truly insane." She leaned back with a sigh. "Actually what's more surprising is that the rest of us haven't."

"Why didn't you leave during the exodus?"

"You say that like it was my choice. The plague hit so fast — there were a million people diagnosed with a new, unnamed virus in one day."

I imagined something like that happening now, in the West, and it staggered me.

"Of course," Hagen went on, "all those people managed to go feral and bite someone before anyone knew what was going on. And animals were getting it too. By the third day, public transportation was shut down and the interstate roads were all closed to try to stop it from spreading any farther. But the hospitals were overflowing — there were just too many new cases — so infected people ran through the streets, and the police began gunning them down. The rest of us didn't dare leave our homes for fear of getting bitten or shot. We barricaded our doors and watched the news as city after city was overtaken with feral people and animals, not to mention corpses, because back then most people died within days."

I nodded. This part had been on the history sites.

"The exodus across the Mississippi began, and those of us stuck in the East stayed put, waiting for the government to get the situation under control, which they promised to do. But they never even tried."

"What do you mean? They did get it under control. That's when they set up the immigration checkpoints, to make sure the survivors would be safe."

Hagen smiled at me grimly and shook her head. "I finally ventured out, and made my way here." She cocked her head toward the river. "They'd already put up an electric fence on the western bank. Within a year, the wall replaced it. I've never seen anything that huge constructed so fast."

"But did you cross to Arsenal and go to a checkpoint? They were still letting people in after the wall went up."

"Only if you had a guaranteed contact over there who could give you a place to stay and help you find a job. They said they didn't want refugees living on the streets."

"What? No. You just had to be an American citizen and —"

"'Not pose a health risk to the general population.' On paper, it looked like you just had to test clean for Ferae. But that phrase was twisted to suit the gatekeepers. And it suited them to keep a lot of people out."

My hands had balled into fists on the table. How could the government have abandoned all these people? "I just can't believe it," I said.

"Sorry, honey." Hagen chuckled. She reached out and patted one of my hands. "It's true. I should know, I lived —" A long, loud squeal cut her off. We turned to see Sid running through the front door. "Mayor!" he shouted.

She sighed. "It's always something. Come over here and spit it out, Sid."

"Line patrol," Sid wheezed. As others turned to listen, the place fell silent, except for Sid's hooves tappity-tapping across the marble floor. "They're here!"

"What?" Hagen strode over to meet him with me close on her heels.

"They have assault rifles!" Sid said. "When I wouldn't open the gate, they shot off the lock and drove in. Drove! They wouldn't answer my questions. And they nabbed Rafe."

"Rafe?" I echoed.

"Yeah. Out on the square." Sid dabbed his brow with a dirty handkerchief. "He gave them a good run, but they got him."

I turned to Hagen. "I thought line guards weren't allowed to cross the bridge."

"They aren't," she said, her jaw tight.

I still couldn't fathom it. "They broke quarantine just to come after Rafe?"

"No, missy." Sid cast his piggy eyes on me. "They came for you."

SIXTEEN

Sid smirked at me, but Hagen snapped, "The line patrol just arrested the one guy who knows something about the feral that's terrorizing this compound. Exactly how is that funny?"

Sid wiped the amusement from his porcine face. "They came in asking if I'd seen a girl with long brown hair, wearing clothes like theirs." He pointed at my camouflage pants.

An engine roared in the square. Those still inside the station crowded at the window for a look.

"Lane!" Rafe's voice didn't sound upset. If anything his tone carried a hint of triumph. "Come on out!"

Hagen and I hurried to the door, but when she threw it open, I hung back. "What if they've come to arrest me for breaking quarantine? The whole patrol saw me cross the bridge."

"People have done a lot worse on Arsenal Island and escaped across the bridge, but no guards ever came after them," Hagen assured me. "Seems to me that someone high up is bending the law for you. Someone with a whole lot of clout — like that big wheel you mentioned."

Not a chance. Spurling wouldn't risk her reputation for me. She'd said as much to my face.

"Come on, Lane," Rafe shouted. "They just want to talk to you. Everything's okay."

Brows raised, Hagen held open the door. Still, I hesitated. Rafe had gotten me out of the chimpacabra warren alive, escorted me to Moline, and offered to do the fetch on my father's behalf. Discounting the supply closet incident and his prejudice against manimals, he deserved my trust. So why was I feeling so wary?

"Would you get your butt out here?" he hollered.

Inhaling deeply, I took the machete from my bag and stepped outside to find Rafe lounging in the back of an open-top jeep. Two line guards stood beside the vehicle, dressed in carbon-gray body armor. They had their assault rifles drawn and at the ready. The pimple-faced, pale-skinned male guard gaped at the furry vendor, while the young black woman scanned the square, her gaze always coming back to Rafe. They seemed very jumpy, considering the fact that other than the vendor, there weren't any manimals on the square.

"What is that thing?" I heard the male guard mutter under his breath.

Rafe, on the other hand, seemed completely relaxed, as if it were a day at the park. He waved me over and introduced the guards as Fairfax and Bear Lake. "She goes by Bearly, as in barely able to resist me," he added, giving her a smile but getting no reaction from her. Her mouth was drawn down at the corners. "This is Lane," he added. Neither guard so much as glanced my way. They were distracted, watching for the ambush they apparently expected.

Rafe rose in the back of the jeep, which required dragging a handcuff up the vehicle's steel-tube frame. The other cuff was on his wrist. "She's all yours," he called to someone behind me.

I spun to see Everson by the door. How had I walked past six-foot-plus of stone-faced line guard and not noticed him?

"Hey," Everson said. His eyes ran over me, catching with surprise on the machete in my hand. I could feel my face flush. I wondered how messed up I looked compared to the last time we'd seen each other. After all, since then, I'd met a tiger-man and barely escaped a chimpacabra. My fatigues were caked with dirt. My face had to be too. I squashed the impulse to smooth my hair.

"I'm sorry about the Lull," I said.

He smiled faintly. "You owed me. Are you okay?"

I nodded and shifted, unsure of what to say. I'd forgotten how deep his voice was. "Please don't arrest me. I know I shouldn't have come, but —"

"Arrest you?" he interrupted, coming toward me, his gun pointed at the ground. "Lane, I came to help you."

My heart picked up tempo. There was nothing he could do, but still, he was the first person to offer without sounding resentful.

"Quit acting noble," Rafe said from the back of the jeep. "You're just here 'cause she's hot."

In any other situation, I would have warmed to hear that adjective applied to me, but out of his mouth, it was just a way to slam Everson, who shot Rafe a death threat of a look. Rafe just chuckled.

"I don't understand." I touched Everson's arm and he returned his gaze to me. "How did you get permission to come here?"

"Blackmail," he said like it was no big deal.

"What?"

"You gave me the idea," he said, lowering his voice. "I told Captain Hyrax that if he didn't approve me for an immediate reconnaissance mission to Moline, I'd be forced to file a report about the unauthorized 'friends' he has flown over the wall."

Everson's determination to help me was flattering and dashing and kind, but still my stomach dropped. "The captain will make your life awful after this."

"I'm not worried," he said. And for some reason, he wasn't. I could feel the excitement coming off him in waves. At least somebody was happy to be here. "Did you give Mack the letter?" he asked.

I felt my brief pleasure at seeing him drain away. "My dad isn't here."

"Okay, you got her," Fairfax called to Everson. "Let's get out of here before that pig thing comes back." He glanced around the square and shuddered, which sent a flash of anger through me.

As if I had the right to judge him. I was horrified too when I first laid eyes on Sid. "It's okay. Sid's not feral. None of them are." Fairfax didn't seem to hear me — or else he didn't think I was a reliable source.

"Aren't you all forgetting something?" Rafe jangled his handcuff. "I held up my end."

I gasped as I realized what he meant. "You lying scumbag." I strode to the jeep. "'Come on out. Everything's okay?' You got me outside in exchange for your freedom."

"I did it for you," he said without a drop of irony. "You'll be safer on Arsenal."

Everson joined me by the jeep. "She'll be safer away from you."

"Whatever you want to tell yourself, silky, but we had a deal."

"Like the deal where you were going to let her go if I put down my gun?"

"That wasn't a deal," Rafe protested.

"Okay," Everson agreed. "I'm just reneging then."

"No way! You can't. You're the good guy."

"I'm in your territory," Everson said dryly. "I figured I'd play by your rules."

"Come on!" Rafe dropped back into the seat.

"Cruz, dump her in the jeep, and —" Fairfax jerked up his rifle and aimed it at the station. Bearly did the same, and I turned to see a horde of compound residents — human and manimal — pushing out the door, their weapons drawn. Hagen led them onto the square with Sid at her elbow.

"Don't come any closer!" Fairfax shouted.

I swore I could taste the adrenaline radiating off all three guards. "It's okay, they're not feral," I said again.

Everson's storm-cloud eyes were practically flashing heat lightning. "Look at them," he whispered, sounding agitated. "There are so many. They're so mutated." He glanced back at Rafe. "How long have they been living like this?"

Rolling his eyes, Rafe cupped his free hand to his mouth. "Hey, Sid, Ace here wants to know how long you've been a pig thing."

Sid scowled. "Let me think. . . . Oh yeah, screw you, that's how long."

Rafe sent Everson an *I tried* shrug. "Being a freak makes him touchy."

"What kind of sicko place is this?" Fairfax asked, his voice edged with hysteria.

"You came to us," Hagen said coldly. "Broke through our gate, so if we make you uncomfortable, maybe it's time for you to go."

Fairfax didn't seem to have heard her. He jabbed Rafe's arm with his rifle. "What are those people doing standing so close to grupped-up ferals?"

"Well, they're married." Rafe nodded at the walrus-man and his wife. "And those two" — he pointed at a grizzly-man holding hands with a young woman — "they've been shacking up for a while now. She has a thing for furries. The hairier the better, right, Alice?" he called over.

"I hope the rogue rips out your heart, Rafe," she retorted. "Oh wait, you don't have one."

"Huh." He sat back. "Don't know why *she's* touchy."

"Won't she get infected?" I asked.

He shrugged. "As long as she doesn't kiss him on the mouth or let him bite her, she'll probably be okay. Well, till he goes feral. Then all bets are off."

"Enough," Bearly said. "Let's go." She climbed into the driver's seat and revved the engine.

Hagen moved toward the jeep while taking her gun from

its holster. "Rafe stays." She cocked her head and the crowd surged forward to surround the jeep.

Rafe put a hand over his heart. "I'm touched."

"Ev, get in the jeep," Bearly hissed. "Now."

But Everson couldn't take his eyes off the manimals. "Record them, will you?" he whispered to me. "Every angle you can get. Dr. Solis will learn a lot more from seeing their mutations than from hearing Mack describe them."

As I hit my dial's record button, a man with a scaled face and a pointed snout flicked out his long, thin tongue. "Who're you calling mutated?"

"You're infected with armadillo!" Everson's hands trembled as he holstered his gun and shifted the shoulder strap of a box labeled "med kit" so that it was in front of him. "I need a sample of your blood."

Now it was the manimal who looked stunned. "What the heck for, ya weirdo?" He backed away from Everson.

"In case you haven't noticed, Ev," Bearly said in a low, lethal tone, "this situation is verging on unstable."

Everson ignored her. "Your blood will bring us closer to developing a vaccine for Ferae, maybe even a cure," he told the armadillo-man while taking a syringe and rubber-topped vial from the med kit.

The crowd erupted in excited chatter. Several voices rose over the rest, lobbing questions at Everson. The sudden shouting electrified all three guards. Everson edged back, Bearly popped the jeep into park and lifted her gun, while Fairfax totally lost it. He jumped onto the back of the jeep, waving his assault rifle. "The first freak that bleeds near me is getting a snout full of lead, and I am not kidding. In fact, move one inch closer and I will shoot your hairy freaking freak faces off."

The buzz of the crowd turned hostile and they clustered more tightly around the jeep.

A muscle contracted in Everson's jaw; however, he dropped the vial and syringe back into the med kit and snapped it shut. "All right, we'll go." He beckoned to me. "Come on, Lane."

"Not until you free Rafe," I said, even though I had no intention of leaving with the guards. "The compound needs him right now." And I needed him uncuffed.

"You bet they do," Rafe chimed in.

Everson stiffened in surprise. "You're defending him after what he did?" His hand brushed my forearm. "He cut you."

"He also saved my life."

Fairfax was still on top of the jeep, brandishing his gun. "We're taking the skag in. The captain promised fat bonus checks to the guards who catch him."

"But you came here to get me," I said.

"*He* did." Bearly jerked her chin at Everson. "We're here to make sure he gets back to camp in one piece."

"Why?" Rafe asked. "What's so special about him?"

Everson frowned and led me away from the jeep until we were out of earshot. "I'm working on another way to help your dad. One that won't get you infected or killed."

A small tendril of hope uncurled inside of me. I wanted to rely on him, but that was a dangerous desire. Everson didn't understand the scale of the problem — couldn't — because he hadn't witnessed Director Spurling's determination to get what she wanted. "Unless you have another way right now, I can't take that chance."

"What?" He sounded astonished. Guess most people didn't reject his help. "But I — How does staying here help Mack?"

"Rafe said he'd get the photograph for me."

"You believe that?" Everson scoffed. "After he just gave you up to save himself?"

Did I believe it? I looked at Rafe. . . . Well, no. And considering the way my notion of reality kept shattering and reforming with each new piece of information, I didn't expect to trust anybody anytime soon. Still, one truth hadn't budged — if my father was going to escape execution, someone had to fetch Spurling's photo.

"I don't even want to think about what that lowlife has planned for you," Everson growled.

"What are you two whispering about?" Rafe yelled. It seemed the standoff between the crowd and the guards was beginning to make even him nervous.

"I know he's not the most trustworthy person on the planet, but he's willing to do the fetch for my dad."

"Forget the fetch." Everson paused, his wide shoulders shifting. "My mother has clout . . . political clout. Let me see what she can do for Mack. There are better — smarter — ways to help your dad. Ways that don't require a machete," he added, gesturing to the weapon in my hand.

He was offering me a real solution. The inside of my skull filled with floating dots, and my legs started to tingle. Everson seemed so confident and capable in his Kevlar body armor. He could take me away from this dangerous place of snuffling, shuffling manimals and bring my father home safely as well. But did his mother really have the clout to help my dad? And even if she did, why would she? She didn't know me or my father. What if Everson couldn't persuade her to help us? As good as his intentions were, I couldn't risk it.

"Cruz, stop jawing and let's get out of this slum hole." Fairfax hopped off the back of the jeep.

I shoved the machete into my messenger bag. Everson was right about one thing, though. Blindly trusting Rafe was stupid.

"Slum hole, huh?" a voice rasped.

I looked back at the jeep. The armadillo-man had resurfaced at the front of the crowd. He flicked his tongue at Fairfax, coming within an inch of his nose. Bellowing with disgust, the guard jerked up his gun and took aim. "You want to be put down, animal?"

"Fairfax, stand down!" Everson shouted.

A sick feeling bloomed in my stomach. The guards were here because of me and now it was looking more likely they weren't going to make it back to Arsenal unscathed.

"We're leaving, okay?" Everson told Fairfax and started toward him. Over his shoulder, he said, "Come on, Lane. No one here can help you."

"You're right." I shouldn't have kidded myself for even a second that I could put my dad's life in someone else's hands, sit back, and hope for the best. "I have help myself, and I'll need your jeep."

Everson stopped short, his momentum rocking him up on his toes. "What?"

I headed for him. "It's the only way I can get to Chicago and back in time," I said, trying to sound reasonable.

He stared down at me. "I'm not lending you our jeep."

"You've got walkie-talkies. Call for another one."

"No," he said firmly, every inch the line guard again. "You're out of options, Lane. Just come with us."

I was getting really tired of people telling me that I was out of options. Spurling, Rafe, and Everson. Especially because it wasn't true. I had another option: I could *take* the jeep.

But how? The guards had guns and I had . . . manimals. I turned to the crowd. "Excuse me, everyone. Hi. My name is Delaney Park McEvoy."

"What are you doing?" Everson hissed.

"McEvoy?" the walrus-man asked. "Are you Mack's kid?"

"Yes, I am. I came here because he's in trouble. Big trouble. As in, his life is on the line. If I want to save him, I have to do a fetch." I pointed at the jeep. "And this is the only way I can get it done in time."

That was all it took. I didn't need to mention that if something happened to my dad, he wouldn't be bringing them medicine anymore. I didn't even need to tell them how they could help me. They knew. Before Fairfax understood what was happening, the walrus-man had locked him in a clinch, and the mastiff-man had ripped the gun from his grip. The others surged forward and stripped Bearly and Everson of their weapons the instant I'd finished speaking.

Everson flushed with anger. "Are you crazy?"

"No. Desperate." I opened my palm and a squirrely looking girl handed me Everson's handgun, which was heavier than I'd expected.

Rafe whistled with appreciation. "Guess you are Mack's daughter after all."

Hagen clapped. "Nice."

"Not anymore," I said firmly. The weight of the gun intimidated me. I didn't know where to put it, and I had no idea how to load or shoot. But Rafe would know, and by the time we got to Chicago, so would I.

SEVENTEEN

I faced Bearly, who looked none too happy to be surrounded by Moline townsfolk. "I need the key to Rafe's handcuffs."

Scowling, she dug in her pocket. "Cruz pulled every string there is to come here and get you. This is how you thank him?" She dropped a key into my palm and moved away from the jeep.

"Hey, Bear Lake, I want my gun back," Rafe said.

She held up her hands. "One of those things took it off me."

"Which of you hairballs has my shotgun?" Rafe asked the crowd. "Hand it over now." When no one offered it up, he scowled.

"All right, people, mission accomplished," Hagen called out. "Give 'em some breathing room. Ed, put him down!"

The walrus-man released Fairfax from his viselike hug. The guard crumpled to his knees, wheezing for breath.

"Sid, please open the gate," I said. With a nod, he trotted off. "Sorry," I told the guards, without meeting Everson's eyes. I didn't feel good about leaving them here unarmed. "You can call the base as soon as we're out of Moline."

"What do you mean *we*?" Rafe demanded. "You're not going."

"There's been a change of plan." I tossed my messenger bag onto the backseat next to him. "I'm the fetch. You're the hack."

"Forget it," he growled.

"I had a feeling you'd be like that." I climbed behind the wheel. "And that's why you're staying cuffed until we're out of the compound."

Hagen looked worried. "Mack is not going to like this."

"Yeah, and guess who he'll blame?" Rafe glared at me in the rearview mirror.

I didn't care who my dad blamed as long as he escaped the firing squad. "I'll tell him that I forced you to take me along."

Rafe waved off my promise. "If I don't knock you out the first chance I get and haul you back to Arsenal, Mack's not going to want to hear it."

"Thanks for the heads up." I put the jeep in reverse. "Now I'll keep you cuffed all the way to Chicago."

"That better be a joke," he warned.

With a shrug, I steered the jeep into a three-point turn. "Guess I don't have such a humane heart after all."

"What?"

I glanced into the mirror to see Rafe's brow furrow. "Nothing. It was just something Chorda said."

"The grupped tiger-guy said something" — his voice turned hard — "about your heart. . . ."

Leave it to him to mistake civilized conversation for murderous intent. He wasn't going to let a little thing like logic change his mind. So why waste my breath arguing that Chorda was not the rogue? I had bigger worries. Now that I had the jeep pointed toward the open gate, I shifted into drive, only to catch movement out of the corner of my eye. Everson shoved past the walrus-man, dashed for the jeep, and dropped into the passenger seat.

I lifted my foot off the gas. "What are you doing?"

"Coming with you," he said.

Bearly hustled over. "Ev, get out. Our orders were to go as far as Moline."

"I'm done following orders."

"You're going rogue?" she gasped.

"Can we not use that term?" Rafe asked from the backseat.

"Don't be stupid, Ev!" Bearly gripped the edge of the jeep's windshield. "Not for some unruly girl."

Unruly. I kind of liked it.

"Think the patrol will ever let me cross the bridge again after this screw up?" Everson asked her. "Not a chance. If I'm going to get the blood samples Dr. Solis needs, it has to be now."

She scowled. "Well if you're going, then I have to."

"Why do you have to babysit him?" Rafe asked her.

"She doesn't." Everson stepped on my foot, forcing me to floor the gas pedal.

"Yes, I — Hey!" Bearly shouted as the jeep launched forward. "Stop!"

But it was too late. With my foot trapped under Everson's, all I could do was steer toward the gate, leaving Bearly in a cloud of dust.

Sid waved as we sped through. "Sayonara!" He held up a shotgun and then banged the gate closed behind us.

"That pig has my gun!" Rafe jerked on the handcuff. "Unlock me."

I shoved at Everson as we pulled onto the broken road. "Get off." Good thing I was wearing steel-toed boots.

"When I get back, I'm going to tenderize some pork!" Rafe shouted at Sid.

When Everson lifted his foot off mine, I slammed on the brakes. "I don't know what you think you're going to get out of this, because I'm not stopping along the way so you can hunt for forty different strains of the virus."

"We're only missing thirty-two," he said calmly.

"You should go back to Arsenal with the others."

"Look, I'll get whatever blood samples I can." He popped the portable GPS unit out of the dashboard. "And if we can't stop, I'll keep track of where the infected people are." He clicked a button on the side of the device, and a red dot appeared on the screen. "If I have specific locations, it'll be easier to make a case for coming back."

I turned in my seat to face Rafe. "Tell him how dangerous it is in the Feral Zone. Tell him about the rogue ferals and chimpacabras."

"Actually, I think it's a good idea to bring hunky and his fancy compass."

Everson made a face. "Don't call me that."

"You said he was the silkiest of the bunch," I reminded him.

"Who cares? Look at him." Rafe flicked his free hand toward Everson. "The guy's a Sasquatch. He'll make good backup."

"We don't need backup," I said.

"Really?" Rafe scoffed. " 'Cause I'm thinking the feral has picked its next victim. You. And we have one gun between us. So if you won't let this stiff take you back to Arsenal —"

"No," I snapped. "And I'm not staying put in Moline either."

He leveled a hard look at me. "And I'm not taking chances with Mack's daughter."

"What's that mean?" Everson asked. "The feral has picked its next victim?"

"It means you could get hurt."

"Wow," Rafe said, oozing sympathy. "Guess all your guard training doesn't impress her."

"That's not what I meant." Why did Rafe have to turn everything into an insult?

"Look, unless he skipped boot camp — You didn't, did you?"

"I ranked highest in my class in every skill set," Everson ground out.

Rafe turned to me. "See? The silky can use a gun and compass. If something happens to me, he'll get you back to Arsenal. Right?"

Everson frowned. "Of course."

"Okay. Discussion over." Rafe jangled his cuff. "Now how 'bout unlocking me?"

I tossed him the key and looked at the two of them — one clean-cut and controlled, the other a lewd, crude scam artist. What could possibly go wrong? "Promise you won't fight."

"I'm not going to arrest him, if that's what you're worried about," Everson said.

"That's not what she's worried about." Rafe dropped the handcuffs onto the floor, leaned back in his seat, and propped his booted feet by my headrest. "She's worried we're going to fight over her."

I shoved Rafe's feet off the seat. "I am not. That's not what I was saying."

I really hoped Everson didn't believe that. I glanced over and caught his grin, which was big and broad — like him. Well, he could choke on it. Yes, the idea of two boys fighting over me was hysterical, but he could've at least tried to hide his amusement. I flopped back into my seat and stomped on the gas. "Forget it. You two can kill each other for all I care."

They both cracked up. So glad they could share a laugh over a joke, except that I hadn't made one. I narrowed my gaze on the weedy road and turned the wheel sharply, sending them spilling toward the jeep's open sides. Their amusement vanished as they scrambled for handholds.

"Pothole," I said with a shrug and got a couple of disgruntled looks in return, which had me smiling. *Should be an interesting trip.*

We sped past ravaged, desolate towns and overturned cars, all of them either scorched or rusting. But each time I started to feel hollow over the devastation, around the next bend I'd spot deer in a pasture, grazing like small herds of horses. There was wildlife everywhere, and above, the sky was blue, with high puffs of clouds.

Even though the land itself was as flat as a book, the road was so broken up, I felt like I was riding a bucking bronco. Still, Everson and I twisted in our seats, eyes wide, trying to take everything in.

Rafe had long since given up his carefree attitude and turned into an old lady, complaining about how fast I was going and how bumpy the ride was. At first I'd taken it personally, since I considered myself to be a conscientious driver, but then Everson asked Rafe if he'd ever ridden in a moving vehicle before. To my shock, Rafe hadn't. Now he sat in the backseat, looking very green. Had he been anyone else, I might have felt sorry for him.

I made a sudden swerve off the road and heard Rafe gag as the jeep bumped down the embankment. I hadn't had a choice. Smashed, burned-out vehicles clogged the highway in a miles-long collision dating back to the exodus. I had seen plenty of recordings of that time and been required to watch documentaries about it for school ad nauseam. But as horrifying as those recorded images were, passing miles of wreckage and glimpsing charred skeletons still belted into their seats gave me a sense of what it had really been like during the exodus. How people's desperation to escape the plague had messed with their judgment.

After we'd driven along the shoulder for nearly an hour, Rafe said, "Got to make a stop. Pull in there."

I didn't want to slow down, let alone take a break, but I thought maybe he had to pee. Rafe directed me onto what once had been a golf course, according to a sign. The links were gone, replaced by deep ditches as far as I could see, and another weather-beaten sign, which read "Quarantine Cremation Site."

As soon as I touched the brake, Rafe hopped out and strode through the waist-high grass toward one of the ditches.

If this was a cremation site, then these were graves, I realized with a start.

Everson pulled off his Kevlar body armor shirt and refastened his gun holster over his T-shirt. "I'm taking this back," he said, scooping his gun from off the seat between us.

"Look." I pointed to the ditch on our right. "It's still smoking."

As Everson and I climbed out to take a look, I saw Rafe snap a wildflower from its stem and toss it into the open grave. His lips were moving, but from where I stood, I couldn't hear what he was saying. As Everson and I approached the smoking crater, I had a sudden, creeping sense that we weren't alone. I paused to scan the tree line beyond the open graves, but saw nothing within the red-gold foliage — human or otherwise. Ahead of me, Everson let out a long breath, and I hurried to join him.

Blackened bones and ash filled the pit, with burnt skulls topping the heap. My self-control splintered. "Why are they burning bodies?"

"They can't bury an infected corpse," Everson said grimly. "An animal might dig it up."

I wondered who Rafe was paying his respects to. Everson followed my gaze. "Here's what I don't get — that guy is only out for himself, so how did you get him to agree to do the fetch for you?"

"Not for me. For my dad. He got Rafe out of an orphan camp."

"Yeah, the one on Arsenal," Everson said. At my look of surprise he added, "That's why all the career guards know him . . . and hate him."

"They don't hate me," Rafe said, coming up beside us. "I'm fun."

"Fun? You stabbed the cook's assistant." Everson snapped. "The guy lost two feet of intestine."

Rafe shrugged. "He was coming at me with a butcher knife."

I stepped between them. "You said you wouldn't fight." I waved Everson toward the driver's seat, figuring it would keep him distracted, and I climbed into the passenger seat. Rafe gave the open grave a last look, swung into the back of the jeep, and wiggled the rolled blanket out of his pack frame.

"Your sister?" I asked softly.

Rafe stiffened. "What do you know about my sister?"

Shoot. I'd forgotten that I wasn't supposed to mention it. "Hagen just said . . ."

"What?" he pressed.

I swallowed. Why had I brought up his sister? "That her husband went feral and killed her." *Right in front of you . . .*

Everson glanced over in surprise.

"No, he didn't." Rafe stretched out on the backseat, using the blanket roll as a pillow. "He felt it coming on and took off before he could hurt us. But then we didn't go back to the compound like we should have. We kept living in the Feral Zone because my sister couldn't bring herself to leave with him still out there."

"What happened?" Everson started up the jeep.

I braced myself, knowing this story was going to leave a bruise.

"He came back. Because that's what ferals do." Rafe gave me a pointed look. "He knew her scent, and what used to be love got twisted up in his animal brain and mistaken for hunger. He came back and he tore out her throat."

I clapped a hand to my mouth as my mind reeled, trying to reject that mental picture even as it formed. And he'd lived through it firsthand. How could he function with a memory like that? I'd never leave my house again, never even go near a window, knowing what might be outside.

Rafe caught my expression. "It's ancient history. I'm fine." He draped an arm over his eyes. "Maybe if I saw it I'd be screwed up, but I stayed under the bed, looking out for my own hide. It's a talent of mine."

"You were a little kid," I protested.

"I've seen kids make a difference in a fight with a feral. I didn't even try." Rafe's tone was nonchalant. Too nonchalant.

I wanted to spill into the back seat and hug the memory right out of him, but I remembered Hagen's warning. Rafe didn't want my pity. So I stayed up front and ached for the little boy who'd heard his sister die, even if he hadn't witnessed it.

Everson cleared his throat. "Who was in the grave?"

"Hagen's daughter," Rafe replied. "Delilah."

I wasn't sure I could bear another devastating story, but Everson was clearly in research mode. "Did a feral bite her?" he asked.

"Her dog. The mangiest-looking mutt you ever saw. When it started shedding, she didn't think anything of it. Had no idea the stupid animal had gotten itself infected."

Everson glanced back at him. "Which strain?"

"How should I know?" Rafe sat up, looking annoyed. "All her hair fell out. Does that tell you something? After that, she went feral fast and got driven out of the compound."

A chill settled into my muscles, into my bones, and slowed my pulse. "What happened to her?"

Rafe studied me as if deciding whether to answer. Finally he said, "Hagen sent me after her."

"To bring her back?"

"To put her down."

Everson's gaze jumped to the rearview mirror. "She sent you to kill her daughter?"

"You better get off that high horse, silky, before it throws you," Rafe snapped. "It's what Delilah wanted. She made Hagen promise to do it, but when the time came, Hagen couldn't. I did them both a favor."

Again I wanted to reach for him, but I wrapped my arms around myself instead. "How awful for you."

He snorted. "I don't cry over dead grups," he said roughly. "Not even one who used to be a friend." He leaned back and closed his eyes, ending the conversation.

Everson sent me a sidelong glance. He wasn't buying Rafe's blasé act either.

I wondered if Rafe had been in love with Delilah . . . and felt my guts twist. Whoa. What was that? I couldn't possibly be jealous of a dead girl on account of a boy I didn't even like. This place was making me crazy, and I hadn't even been bitten.

After another hour, we drove into what once might have been a quaint little town of one-story shops, but now was a debris-littered wasteland with crumbling buildings. Power lines draped what was left of the street and Everson had to swerve to avoid a snarl of downed wires. The jeep scraped along the jagged curb until, with a bang, its right front tire dropped into an open storm sewer. Despite having four-wheel drive, the jeep was completely and utterly stuck.

The three of us climbed out to survey the situation. "And this would be why we ride bikes," Rafe said and then his expression turned wary. "How far east did we get?" He turned in place, eyeing the town. "I can't keep track of the miles, going so fast."

"Fast?" Everson mocked, and popped out the portable GPS. "We're sixty miles outside of Moline."

With over a hundred left to go before we reached Chicago. "We need to find a car jack." I looked for a garage among the empty shops that lined the street. "There." I pointed to a filthy gas station sign at the end of downtown.

Rafe frowned at the sky. "We do not want to be on this stretch of road after dark."

"Why not?" Everson asked as he took a flashlight from a compartment under the seat.

"Tell us after we get the jeep unstuck." I took off toward the gas station with the guys right behind me. Unfortunately, the station was attached to a convenience store, not a garage. A rusted pickup truck sat in the parking lot. Behind the squat building, the land seemed to drop off.

The guys checked inside the store and I crossed the parking lot, which ended at the edge of a steep hill. A lake lay in the valley below with woods on the far side. I took a deep breath, letting the smell of pine and the rustle of cattails fill up my senses. Dusk was almost upon us and we still had miles to go and yet I didn't feel like a girl with an impossible task ahead of her. Instead, my body and mind were humming as if the oxygen on this side of the wall were laced with caffeine.

The door to the abandoned store squeaked open. "I'll check the pickup truck," Everson said.

I was about to turn around when movement drew my attention to the bottom of the hill. Two large dogs were tussling in the reeds. One gave a low-pitched growl, which sounded like the noise my dogs made when we played tug-of-war. I had a creeping feeling, however, that these dogs weren't fighting over a dish towel. I eased back slowly to keep them from noticing me.

"What's with all the blood?" I heard Everson ask. The dogs below heard him too. Their heads snapped around and their growls deepened.

Oh crap! I spun back onto the asphalt, looking for Everson, who had the gun. He and Rafe stood frozen in place with their eyes locked onto something beyond the rusting pickup truck.

"Dogs!" I hissed, hurrying toward them.

"We know," Rafe whispered and held up a hand.

I stopped just short of Everson, who was several feet behind Rafe. On the other side of the pickup, four mutts were brutalizing a bloody carcass.

The other two dogs scrabbled over the rise and started barking.

"Great," Rafe muttered as the rest of the pack lifted their blood-soaked muzzles and glared at us. He glared back and I could have sworn that he was growling as well.

Everson took aim and fired. The shot ricocheted off the metal of the truck and hit the asphalt next to the biggest dog — a black mutt. The pack scattered.

Rafe spun around, eyes blazing. "You said you could shoot."

Everson lowered the gun. "I wasn't trying to hit it." At Rafe's incredulous look, he added, "What? I was supposed to open fire on all of them?"

"Yeah, Ace, that's the idea."

Everson rolled his eyes. "They're gone and we're only down one bullet." He jammed the gun back into its holster.

"Were the dogs feral?" I asked, crossing my arms to stop them from trembling. "As in *feral* feral?"

"They wouldn't have run if they were." Rafe nudged a bloody bone with the toe of his boot.

"What was it?" I asked.

"Turkey."

Everson leaned against the bed of the pickup. "You can tell that from a bone?"

"No. From that." Rafe pointed to a chewed-up turkey head by Everson's foot.

Everson scooted back, only to slip on gristle and land in a puddle of coagulated blood. With a yell of disgust, he shot to his feet and tried to wipe off his blood-coated hands with the hem of his shirt. He caught the glimmer in Rafe's eyes. "You think it's funny?"

"It's a little funny."

My mind reeled with the potential dangers. This situation could have been scripted for a freshman health class. "It's not funny at all! What if he has an open cut? What if the turkey had Ferae?"

"Birds can't get it," Rafe said.

I knew that, but still . . . "There's no running water over here. How is he supposed to wash off?"

"He could try using that." Rafe pointed past me to the lake.

Everson and I skidded down the hill to the water's edge where he washed his hands, but his blood-spattered clothes posed a bigger problem.

"Take them off," I said.

Rafe sauntered down the hill. "You were just waiting for the chance to say that."

"Shut up." Everson tossed him the holstered gun and pulled off his shirt to reveal washboard abs.

I hadn't been waiting for the chance to see him shirtless, but maybe I should have been. I cleared my throat so my voice didn't come out squeaky. "We can find him new clothes. That's easy, right?" I dragged my gaze away from Everson's perfect chest to look at Rafe, but he was staring at the sky. I glanced up to see what had put the crease in his brow — the setting sun.

"We're done traveling," he said abruptly. "We need to find a place to hole up for the night." Then he seemed to remember Everson. "Oh crap. You're gonna bring them right to us." With two hands, he shoved Everson backward into the lake.

"Bring what to us?" I asked.

Everson came up spitting mad, but Rafe pushed him down again, getting himself soaked as well. "Get the blood out of your clothes!" His tone made it clear this was no joke. Everson rubbed his pants down under the water.

"That'll have to do. Come on," Rafe hissed, waving him out. "See that?" He pointed at a small cottage on the other side of the lake. "That's where we're sleeping tonight."

"Why not pick one in town?" I asked, gesturing up the hill to the road. "Those are closer."

"Because that one is boarded up."

He was right. Big wood shutters covered the cottage's windows as if someone had closed up the place for the winter.

Holding his shirt in one fist, Everson slogged onto the bank. At that moment, a faint rattling sound started up, as if dried seedpods were shimmying in a breeze. But the lake's surface was still, and the cattails on the bank around us remained ramrod straight.

"What's that sound?" I asked.

Rafe froze, listening, and his expression darkened. "A whole lot of nothing good. Go." We took off, cutting through the tall reeds along the lake's edge with Rafe leading the way.

As the sun sank toward the horizon, the lengthening shadows seemed to turn up the volume on the odd sound. Less of a rattle now and more like the hard, dry clicking of a hundred bead curtains being swept aside. The houses on the ridge seemed to quiver with the noise. I sloshed through the marsh and tramped over fallen logs, trying to match Rafe's fast pace. But the clicking intensified to the point where I swore I could feel the sound waves bouncing off my skin. I glanced back. Up on the ridge, black smoke billowed out of a church spire.

I stumbled to a stop and turned to watch. "It's on fire. . . ."

"What is?" Everson paused beside me.

"Everything."

Smaller wafts of black smoke rose from the houses, pouring from upper-story windows and holes in the roofs. High in the darkening sky, the undulating columns melded together to become one rippling, shifting mass. And suddenly, I knew — remembered — what I was seeing. "That's not smoke. . . ."

"Don't stop!" Rafe yelled, but when he followed our hypnotized gazes, he froze midstride. "Oh, come on!" He swiped a fist at the growing black cyclone. "What is this, their spawning season?"

Everson shouted to be heard above the frenzied clicking. "Are they bats?"

I clamped my hands over my ears. "Weevlings." The word alone triggered mental epilepsy, but making it worse was my father's description of how the creatures would descend upon a cow like a smothering black shroud, only to fly off a moment later, leaving nothing but a skeleton. "Piranha-bats."

Rafe shook off the trance first. "Go, go, go!" But it was too late. Moving with gang intelligence, the weevlings zoomed in our direction. "Scratch that, hit the ground!"

A musky smell pressed down on us two seconds before the clicking mass descended.

· EIGHTEEN ·

I dropped my bag and burrowed into the tall reeds between the guys. We dragged the stalks closed above us as the torrent of weevlings passed overhead. I couldn't breathe, wouldn't move. I might as well have been drowning. My muscles quivered from terror and lack of oxygen, but then Everson entwined his fingers with mine. The warmth and strength of his grip calmed me, and I took in small amounts of air until the weevling funnel swept over the lake and crested the trees.

"Go," Rafe whispered. "Keep low and run."

In the failing light we sped for the two-story wooden cottage. A piercing howl tore out of the woods and I shuddered, knowing that the weevlings had descended upon some poor creature. The howl came again followed by agonized yowling and then finally — thankfully — silence.

We clattered onto the porch and Rafe motioned for me and Everson to stay put. No problem. Rafe approached the door. As he pulled out his tools for the lock, I scanned the sky for the black cloud. I'd left the messenger bag somewhere in the reeds by the lake but I wasn't going back for it. Everson was still clutching his wet shirt.

There was a creak behind us, followed by Rafe's "Okay."

As I hurried past him through the now-open door, the light from outside caught the glimmer of spiderwebs. I stopped in my tracks.

"Give me a hand with this." Rafe swatted the webs aside without so much as a flinch and pointed at a couch with rotting upholstery. "We don't want anything bursting in on us while we sleep," he said and got no argument from us. Together, we propped the couch against the front door and then Rafe dug into his knapsack for a flashlight. "Don't open any door that might go to the attic," he said. "In case you missed it, that's where weevlings like to roost."

"If fish don't get Ferae, how can weevlings be part piranha?" I asked.

"Because they're bats that have been infected with fish DNA, not the other way round," Everson said.

"This area is the only stretch that I've come across them," Rafe said. "But I've never seen a swarm that big. If they keep breeding like that, they'll be everywhere before too long. And won't that be fun?"

Musical notes suddenly banged behind us. We whirled to see an old piano. Rafe grinned at our alarm. "Mice. What, don't you have them in the West? Or were they stopped at the wall like the other vermin? Tuck your cuffs into your socks when you sleep. Keeps them from crawling up your pants."

"What if they bite?" I searched the shadows for infected mice.

"Mice don't get Ferae. . . ." Rafe said. "No rodents do. Same with squirrels and rabbits."

"Why not?"

"I don't know. Ask the geek."

Everson shrugged. "They're resistant to rabies too." His pants were still dripping with lake water and he was bare chested.

I shivered, thinking again of the puddle of blood that he'd landed in. "We should find you some clean clothes." I plucked Rafe's flashlight from his hand and headed for the staircase with Everson beside me.

"If he gets grabby, give a shout," Rafe called after us.

Everson shot an annoyed glance over his shoulder. "She doesn't have to worry about that."

"Why not?" Rafe asked. "You don't think she's pretty?"

"No, I — Shut up."

Rafe's laugh followed us up the stairs.

A tingle ran down my back. Rafe had been trying to bug Everson — I knew that — but the way he'd said it . . . it had almost sounded as if Rafe thought I was pretty. And Everson had nearly admitted it too.

It doesn't matter, I reminded myself. As soon as I did the fetch, I'd never see either of them again. Anyway, pretty was relative. Life was hard on this side of the wall and people here looked older than their years. Of course I seemed like a clean, shiny doll to Rafe. And Everson? He'd been locked up in his mother's house until he joined the patrol. The only girls he knew marched around in military fatigues. So, there was no reason for me to be feeling giddy right now. Or flattered. None at all.

The majority of the towels in the hall closet were piles of fluff, shredded from generations of mice nesting in them.

Luckily, a couple on the top shelf were usable. Everson stood in a kids' room, complete with bunk beds, rubbing down his chest and arms like he wanted to scrape off a layer of skin. I didn't blame him. Anyone who'd grown up in the West post-exodus had been schooled on how to avoid disease. Coming in contact with blood — huge no-no. Okay, so it was bird blood. But what if Rafe was wrong about the dogs? If even one of them had Ferae, then there could be infected saliva mixed in with the turkey's blood.

"I'll do your back," I said, taking the towel from him. He might miss a spot, and besides, the task would keep me from thinking about how close we'd come to being eaten alive. Which brought it to a total of two close calls for me today.

What was I doing in the Feral Zone? I didn't belong here. I should be back home debating between doing homework or going to a movie with Anna, whom I suddenly missed so much my insides hurt. If I didn't make it home, Anna would never know what happened to me; I seriously doubted that Director Spurling would fill her in.

"Thanks."

Everson's voice startled me. He started to turn but I put a hand to his shoulder, stopping him. As I inhaled, trying to calm myself, I studied the wall of his back before me — his muscles and sinew were in perfect rippling condition, not shredded by weevlings, and his skin, faintly tanned and smooth, was wholly intact. Not a cut or scratch on him. Nowhere the virus could have entered his bloodstream. I heard him inhale sharply, almost a gasp, and realized that I'd dropped the towel and was tracing my fingertips across his back. Lifting my hand was like prying a magnet from metal. I wanted to touch his skin, to run my palms over every silky inch of it. But I gave myself a mental shake and folded my arms across my body. "You don't have any cuts."

"Are you okay?" he asked, his voice hoarse as he turned.

He was standing just inches from me, half dressed. If I'd found his back appealing with those perfectly delineated muscles, his chest was even more tempting to touch. Heat rushed to my face. I scooted back and tightened my pony-tail. "I'm fine," I said, and headed for the closet. "Let's find you something to wear while your pants dry."

I flung open the closet doors, grateful to have something else to focus on. Finding clothes to fit him wasn't going to be easy.

"This will work." He pulled a blanket from the bot-tom bunk.

A sudden banging in the next room made me jump. "It's Rafe," Everson explained. "He came upstairs with an ax a few minutes ago."

Following the noise, I found Rafe in the master bedroom chopping up a chest. He'd taken out the clothes and left them on the floor. Squatting, I nudged through the pile with Rafe's flashlight. I wasn't going to risk sticking my hand into any rodent nests, even if they didn't get Ferae. The clothes, all sweaters and T-shirts, had belonged to a petite woman. I scooped up a black tank top and gave it a sniff. The scent of cedar filled my nose, which was about as good as it got when it came to old clothes.

I threw the tank over my shoulder and checked out the

queen-sized bed. Dusty but sturdy. I panned the flashlight across the water-stained, buckling ceiling and hoped the roof didn't collapse while we slept. "Want me to start a fire?" I asked.

Rafe paused to consider me. "You know how?"

I shot him an evil look and bent to collect the wood that he'd chopped. "I *am* Mack's daughter."

Downstairs, I found matches on the mantel and got a fire going in the fireplace without any problem at all. The flickering light pushed back the shadows in the living room. I moved closer, drawn by the warmth of the flames and the rich smell of wood smoke. After a few minutes, Everson came down, carrying his wet clothes. He'd found some baggy gym shorts to put on and had the blanket draped over his shoulders. When he was done hanging his clothes on a chair near the fire, I thought he'd join me on the floor, but no, he headed for a dust-covered desk.

"Before you forget," he said over his shoulder, "tell me which strains of Ferae were in Moline."

Right. The missing strains — the whole reason he'd come. And it *was* an admirable reason, I reminded myself. "You want me to name the different types of manimals that live there?" I asked, twisting to face him.

He stopped rifling through the desk drawers and glanced back at me. "Manimals?"

"A person with Ferae who hasn't reached stage three," I said, remembering Dr. Solis's description of the stages of the disease — incubation, mutation, and psychosis.

"That's smart, making distinctions." With a pad of yellowing paper and a pencil in hand, he swung the chair around, ready to work. "I want to start a list of the strains we've come across so far."

"Sure," I said and then described every manimal I'd seen, starting with Sid. When I'd exhausted my memory, Everson cozied up to the desk and began listing the possibilities for the unknown strains based on the details I'd given him.

The fire had warmed me up enough that I ducked into a closet and exchanged my muddy line guard shirt for the black tank. Back in the living room, Everson was wholly absorbed in his task and Rafe was nowhere to be seen. I entered the dining area, which was connected to the main room, and panned the flashlight over the photographs that crowded the walls. Generations of a family, from sepia pictures of immigrant grandparents to colorful shots of a family piled together on the porch steps of this very cottage. Father, mother, three kids. Happy.

Another photo showed the same family members knee-deep in the lake, laughing, their arms entwined. My vision started tunneling. What were the chances that they were all still alive today and together?

Miniscule.

I flipped through the dust-covered mail piled on the dining room table — mostly bills — and then unfolded a yellowed newspaper dated eighteen years ago. The headline: "Containment Fails." I scanned the article, reading the quotes from the top scientists of the time. "The transgenic virus was accidentally released into the ecosystem and has wreaked havoc within the human and animal populations." And, "We have been brought low by genetic contamination and yet we never saw it coming. We worried about chemical and nuclear pollution, which turned out to be insignificant by comparison, even though one brought on global warming and the other resulted in waste so toxic it stays lethal for thousands of years."

On the next page was a photo of Ilsa Prejean promising that her corporation's manufacturing facilities, which had built Titan's enormous indoor labyrinths, would now put their efforts toward constructing a quarantine wall. She looked absolutely wrecked in the photo and no wonder: The caption underneath read "Mother of the Plague." An awful label, and also ironic — Ms. Prejean was clearly pregnant in the photo. It was hard to believe that she'd once been as beloved as Walt Disney. My dad said the Titan labyrinth parks were incredible and that he'd spent way too many weekends in his youth trying to work his way from the fiftieth floor down to the first. He said that often he'd happen upon a beautiful or fascinating room within the maze and end up spending the whole day in it.

I'd never been to a Titan labyrinth park. The company closed their theme parks in the West to focus their efforts on building and maintaining the quarantine line. And all the parks in the East had been long since abandoned.

I set aside the newspaper and glanced up to find Everson turned in his seat, watching me. He ducked his face to consult the yellow pad in his hands. "I have a question. . . ." He flipped a page and then another, and finally looked up with a sigh. "I can't remember what it was."

"Well, we'll be here all night," I said lightly.

"Yeah, about that . . . Thanks. I wouldn't be here at all if it weren't for you."

I stiffened. "I didn't force you to come. Just the opposite. I told you to go back to Arsenal."

"That wasn't sarcasm," he said, smiling. He leaned back against the desk and propped himself on an elbow. "I've wanted to see the Feral Zone for I don't know how long, but it always seemed like this impossible thing. Like something I'd do *someday* . . . maybe. But you? You just showed up on Arsenal and did it — crossed the bridge. And knocked out anyone who tried to stop you," he added ruefully, though throughout the rest of it, his expression seemed . . . admiring?

That couldn't be right. He was not only a line guard, but *the* line guard who'd disapproved of me putting my dad's well-being over the rest of the country's.

"Same thing in Moline," he went on. "I was excited to get that far — to finally see stage two ferals up close — and I wouldn't have gone any farther if you hadn't hijacked our jeep and" — he swept his hand forward — "blazed the way."

He was different in the Feral Zone. Warmer, more relaxed. Or maybe this side of him only came out when his guard fatigues came off. Whatever the reason, I liked this new version of him. "So . . . you're thanking me for being a bad influence?" I asked with amusement.

"The worst," he agreed with a straight face, though his eyes held a smile. He then turned his chair back to the desk and his attention to the list.

"You're welcome," I said, hoping I didn't come off breathless. Though that's I how I felt — like my chest had been pumped full of bubbles. And all because Everson had made me sound bold in his take on the events. In reality, I'd been stymied and scared. But why let facts get in the way of a good feeling?

I pushed through the swinging door into the kitchen to see what I could scrounge up foodwise. The cabinets held dishes and glasses that were neat but dusty. The sliding doors on the opposite wall probably hid the pantry — the most likely place to find preserved food. As I crossed the kitchen, my flashlight beam glinted off cans stacked on the floor beside a long board. I plucked one up. Peaches.

I rifled through the drawers and found what I guessed was a can opener, though I'd never used such an old-fashioned tool in my life. I even figured out how to operate it without having to ask for help. The peaches didn't look spoiled. I picked up a fork and speared a chunk. It smelled like heaven and tasted even better.

On my second bite, I considered the cans on the floor and the board beside to them. A pantry shelf maybe? But why would someone remove it? With the can of peaches in hand, I slid open the pantry door. Yahtzee! Shelves lined with dry goods filled the shallow space. Boxes, jars, cans . . . a sealed tin of baking mix looked especially promising.

I stepped back to check out the bottom shelf, but it was missing. In its place lay a small, hairy creature in stained overalls. He was curled on his side with his back to me, shivering. His silver fur gleamed in the flashlight's beam.

I stumbled back with a gasp, right into the pile of cans, sending them every which way. The noise startled the little manimal into action. He leapt to his feet, only to slam into the shelves above. Cans and boxes tumbled across the floor. A bag landed on his head and burst open with a poof of white.

The flour-covered creature tore past me. His hunched body and long arms looked powerful, though he only came up to my chest. When he flew through the swinging door into the dining room, I sagged against the counter. His body was simian — like the chimpacabra — but his frantic escape had come off as pathetic, not scary. Not that I was taking any chances. I waited for the boys to show up, which they did in under a minute. Everson slammed through the swinging door with a "What happened?" just as Rafe clattered down the back stairs, ax in hand.

I exhaled slowly. "We've got company."

NINETEEN

Finding the ape-person was easy enough. He was crouched in a corner of the living room with his back to us. Where he wasn't streaked with flour, his fur appeared to be a fuzzy silver gray. With his forehead pressed into the wall, the little guy seemed to think that we couldn't see him, and that made him a lot less scary to me.

Rafe made a face. "What is *that* doing in here?"

"He was hiding in the pantry," I explained.

Everson panned his flashlight down the manimal. When the beam got to the overalls, Everson's brow furrowed. "What is it?"

"He's human," I whispered. Everson looked unconvinced, which I got. Even though the manimal was barely four feet tall, he was as barrel-chested as an ape. But I was sure that he had human DNA as well. "Hey," I called softly. "We won't hurt you."

The little manimal covered his head with his arms.

I gestured to Rafe to put the ax away, but he just tucked it behind his back. I still had the can of peaches in my hand, which gave me an idea. Moving closer, I set the can on the floor with a thunk so that the manimal would know it was there.

"You're wasting food on him?" Rafe demanded.

"Shh!" I took a step back.

At first the manimal didn't move, but curiosity must have gotten the better of him because he peeked under one arm to see what I'd left. "Go ahead," I coaxed. "They're peaches. You'll like them."

He looked from me back to the open can and slowly inched around until he was facing me. He crept forward, not quite on all fours, but leaning heavily on his knuckles. He sniffed the can, bent, and dipped in his tongue. That was all it took. He snatched up the peaches, quickly turned away from me, and drained the can. Once he'd licked out every drop, he looked back at us.

"What's your name?" Everson asked.

Instead of replying, he crept toward me, his eyes averted.

"Hi," I said. He crouched swiftly, his back to my legs — near me, but not touching. A show of trust?

Rafe rolled his eyes.

"My name . . ." a husky little voice said. I froze and looked down at the manimal's fuzzy head. He kept his face lowered as if that made talking easier. ". . . is Cosmo." His words came out oddly and strained, but intelligible. He swallowed and tried again. "My name — is — Cosmo."

Moving cautiously, I circled to face him. "My name is Lane." I crouched and gently offered him my hand. "Lane."

Slowly, he extended one long finger. He poked my hand and then snatched his own away.

Well, it was a start.

"You . . . think I am — I'm" — he patted his head hard with both hands — "an animal."

"'Cause you are," Rafe said.

"I don't." I smiled when he parted his elbows to steal a glance at me. His eyes were a beautiful sky blue and his face was smooth and pale, but mostly he resembled a small ape. "Are you still hungry?"

He dropped his hands to look at me.

Rafe started to protest, and Everson elbowed him in the ribs. Rafe scowled, but he closed his mouth.

"Let's go see what else is in the pantry." This time when I held out my hand, Cosmo slipped his long fingers into mine.

"He's not staying here tonight," Rafe snapped. "He could turn while we're sleeping."

I ignored him and led Cosmo from the living room. Behind us, Everson said, "What's your problem? Shove a dresser in front of your door if you're scared."

"If a feral wants in, a dresser won't stop it." Rafe's voice turned bitter. "They're hopped up on adrenaline. But you wouldn't know about that, would you, silky? This is just a field trip for you."

"Yeah, trying to help get a cure for the virus that wiped out half of America, that's a field trip."

I let the kitchen door swing shut, blocking out their argument.

We ate by candlelight at the dining room table, feasting on peach pancakes that I'd cooked using an iron skillet over a tin can filled with embers from the fire.

"How do you know how to do this?" Everson asked, sounding impressed.

"Bush skills." Seeing his confusion, I added, "My dad made me take all these crazy survivalist classes."

"What do you mean crazy? Survival skills are important," Rafe scolded. "Knowing how to find shelter and clean water, that can mean the difference between life and death."

"Not in the West," I told him. "They were a waste of time."

He scowled. "Mack lived through the plague. He's trying to prepare you in case there's another outbreak and things get ugly again. You should thank him."

"So what's the plan for tomorrow?" Everson asked Rafe, obviously trying to change the subject.

"Get the photo and get out."

Everson studied him. "Have you ever been to Chicago?"

"Yeah, lots of times. I haven't been inside the compound, but that's only the downtown area."

"Is Director Spurling's house in the downtown area?" I asked.

"No," Rafe said. "Just north of it. But we'll have plenty of other problems to worry about. Mack says the area is crawling with guys in leather aprons."

"Handlers," Cosmo said softly.

The three of us looked at him.

"How do you know what they're called?" Rafe demanded.

"I was born in the king's castle."

"In Chicago?" Everson asked.

When Cosmo nodded, Rafe frowned. "Why didn't you tell us?"

"Because we didn't ask him." I touched Cosmo's arm.

The pale gray fuzz was softer than chick down. "You lived in a castle with a king?"

"In the basement," he said. "Then the handlers said I was too big to stay in my mom's pen, so they moved me to the farm. I took care of the chickens," he said proudly. "I brought eggs to my mom in the kitchen every day."

"Why'd you leave Chicago?" Everson asked.

"You can't guess?" Rafe reached for the canteen. "They kicked him out when he got infected."

"Ignore him," I told Cosmo. "He's awful to everyone."

"Not if they're human." Rafe tipped back his head to drink, but the canteen was dry. I'd used the water to make the pancakes, which I now realized might not have been such a good idea.

Cosmo pulled a ratty dish towel from the front pocket of his overalls and scrunched it up under his chin. "That wasn't why," he said softly. "Mom was making a cake and I licked the spoon. A handler saw. He took me to Omar."

"Who's Omar?" Everson asked.

"The head handler."

"And this Omar made you leave Chicago just for licking a spoon?" The thought made my insides churn.

Cosmo shook his head. "Omar said I was a dirty animal. He put me in the . . . zoo." He choked out the word as if it were the ninth ring of hell. "With the scary people."

Everson leaned forward in his seat. "What scary people?"

"Ferals," Rafe said, and Cosmo nodded.

"How did you get out?" I asked.

"Mom stole the master key from Omar. She snuck me outside the fence and told me to run away as far as I could."

"Heck of a plan." Rafe tipped back in his chair. "Come on, was it really so bad in the zoo? You had a roof over your head. They fed you. . . ."

"Shut up," I said, and seriously considered kicking his chair over.

"What, I can't ask an honest question? He can handle it."

Cosmo bobbed his head. "I'm okay."

"You've got food and a fire. That's better than okay," Rafe told him, making a circle with his index finger and thumb. "You're A-okay."

"Cosmo," Everson said, a crease in his brow. "How old are you?"

"Eight," he said into his scrap of a security blanket.

I wished I had heard him wrong. "Eight years old?"

Even Rafe looked shocked. He thunked his chair legs down. "Why didn't your mom leave with you?"

"She said the queen would send the handlers after her, but nobody would look for me."

Rafe frowned as if he didn't quite believe that answer. Did he think Cosmo's mother didn't go with him because he was infected? What kind of mother would do that? Then again, what kind of people would put an eight-year-old in a zoo?

"Who's the king?" Everson asked.

Cosmo lowered his brow, obviously confused by the question. "The king."

Rafe shot Everson an irritated look. "What do you care?"

"I want to know how Chicago ended up with a king," Everson snapped back.

"I can tell you," Rafe said. "The guy was military — the

person left in charge of the compound when everyone headed west. He had the guns, the men, and total authority. After ten or fifteen years went by and no word from the West, he gave himself a promotion."

"Is that a fact or a guess?" I asked.

"A guess based on the dozen other compounds I've visited, which is more than most people in the zone. Some places set up fair-square governments. Like Moline, where people have a say in how things get done. But plenty of other compounds let the person with the most guns take over. The guy in Chicago just gave himself a fancy title to go with the job."

Everson turned to Cosmo. "Is he right?"

The little manimal shrugged.

"Of course I'm right." Rafe got to his feet. "I can figure stuff out without checking my compass. Like the fact the fire is going out." He headed upstairs with the ax.

Somewhere in the night, a beast lifted its voice to greet the moon — too guttural to be a wolf. I got to my feet. "Guess we can leave the pans and dirty plates in the sink." We could leave it all on the table for that matter. We'd be gone in the morning and there was no one else around. Still, Everson and I stacked the plates and took them into the kitchen. Old habits died hard. Cosmo stuffed his dish towel down the front of his overalls and followed with the glasses.

Everson watched the little guy concentrating as he placed them on the counter. "How long have you been like this, Cosmo?"

"Always." Cosmo headed back into the dining room.

"One of his parents must have been infected," Everson mused.

That made me think of something that Rafe had said earlier. I pushed through the swinging kitchen door. Rafe came down the front stairs with an armload of wood — pieces of a chair maybe.

"Were you born with animal DNA?" I asked Cosmo as he carefully lifted the last two glasses.

He looked up with his big blue eyes. "I was supposed to have white fur."

"What?"

"It was supposed to be like my mom's, but I came out wrong."

"Did your mom say that?" I asked, trying to keep my anger from showing.

"No, the queen."

Rafe dropped the wood on the floor. "What did she expect? You're an ape-boy. Why would you have white fur?"

I glared at him as he tossed a chair leg onto the fire and sent up a shower of sparks.

"My mom isn't an ape," Cosmo said, looking cross. "She's part arctic fox."

"Oh, that's why your hair is so light," I said, stroking his silvery head. And now that I was looking for it, I could see a smidge of fox in his features.

"Is your father the ape?" Everson asked.

Cosmo shrugged self-consciously. I guess he didn't know who or what his dad was. I turned to Rafe. "If the parents have Ferae, then the offspring are immune, right? They can't be infected, and they can't infect anyone."

Rafe gave me a disgruntled look but he nodded.

"So Cosmo won't go feral, right?" I pressed. "It's fine if he sleeps inside the cottage with us." I didn't wait for Rafe to answer. I turned to Cosmo and smiled. "Why don't you go pick out which bed you want?"

He eyed Rafe warily and pointed to the kitchen. "I sleep in there."

"You don't have to," I said. "We're here if a feral breaks in."

"Have you ever slept in a bed, Cosmo?" Everson asked.

Cosmo dropped the glasses he'd been holding and ran back into the kitchen, shaking his head as he went.

"Nice going. You hurt his feelings," Rafe said with a smirk.

I started for the kitchen but Everson strode past me and disappeared through the swinging door.

"What are you doing?" I asked as Rafe slung a couple of canteens over his shoulder.

"Going to the lake," he said, as if it were obvious. "We need water." He caught my look of horror. "I'll boil it."

"No, the weevlings! And the rogue feral?"

He gestured to the ax he'd tucked into his belt. "Not my first road trip."

He shouldn't be the one to go; I'd used up the water. "Can't we get it in the morning?"

"It'll take me ten minutes." He shoved the couch aside enough to crack open the door. "Then I'll check the garage for a jack." He paused in the doorway. "Unless you want to go skinny-dipping. I'd risk being out at night for that."

"Funny," I said.

"What? You don't know how to swim?" he teased.

"Not in an unchlorinated lake in the Feral Zone at night, I don't."

"You don't know what you're missing." He slipped outside. "Come out if you change your mind," he said and pulled the door closed behind him.

Without a second thought, I settled next to the fireplace and tossed on another chair leg. A surge of smoke warmed my face and I smothered a cough against my arm. Everson came in with the blanket around his shoulders. He shrugged it off and joined me on the floor, looking grouchy.

"How's Cosmo?" I asked.

"Curled up in the pantry. He says only 'people' get to sleep in beds."

"He's a person," I protested.

"Apparently not in Chicago." Everson snagged his gray shirt from the back of the chair where it had been drying and pulled it on.

With him so close, I suddenly felt as dirty and drab as an old dish towel. I hadn't washed my face since yesterday. I should have done it when we were by the — No. What a stupid thought — washing my face while Everson rinsed the blood out of his pants. My father was missing, I was camping in the Feral Zone, and suddenly I wanted to clean up in case this boy glanced over? Considering how intently he was watching the fire, that wasn't going to happen anytime soon. Anyway, being grubby was a good thing. I was officially a fetch now. A profession that required going unnoticed — especially by line guards. Even the ones with nice hands.

"You're staring." He looked over — not out-and-out smiling, but clearly in an improved mood.

My stomach dropped. "I was thinking . . ." I struggled to come up with an excuse. "That they're probably worried about you back on Arsenal."

He shrugged. "Let 'em worry."

"So, no girlfriend then, waiting back at camp . . . worrying." As soon as the words left my mouth, I wanted to throw myself into the fire. I *had* wondered, but what was the point of humiliating myself? I was here to do a fetch, not fall for some boy.

If Everson thought I was pathetic, he didn't let on. "Nope." He leaned back to prop himself up on his elbows, legs outstretched. "Guards don't do it for me," he said finally.

"Got something against camo?"

"No. It looks good on the right person." He shot me a smile, which warmed me right down to my toes.

When he didn't say anything more, I asked, "Is it because you're not a guard on the inside?"

"Yeah," he admitted. "Line guards have one job: Keep the virus out of the West. We're trained to think of ourselves as the first line of defense. The wall is the second. And the ferals? They're 'the enemy who have the potential to infect and/or kill every man, woman, and child in America.'"

"Sick people aren't the enemy," I protested.

"The patrol doesn't call them sick because then you might feel sorry for them. And when you spot one on a raft, trying to cross the river, you'd hesitate instead of shooting him in the head like you're supposed to. There's no gray area for line guards. Empathy just messes them up. Which is why the captain says: To protect the population, you have to stop seeing the people." Everson sat up again, looking like he'd just swallowed vinegar. "I don't ever want to stop seeing the people. But I can't say that to another guard."

Everything about this boy was so right — from his compassion to his soft lips. It was almost enough to make me forget that kissing spread germs. "What you're doing — coming here, searching for the strains that Dr. Solis needs — it's really noble."

Everson frowned. "It's not. It's what the line patrol should be doing. The Titan Corporation started this. They should fix it, not just put up a wall." His shoulders drew together, like he was keeping something vast trapped inside of him. "Know why Ilsa Prejean hired scientists to find a way to create chimeras in the first place? Because she wanted a Minotaur for her maze." He practically spit the words.

His bile wasn't unusual. Titan's CEO had gone from being the most loved woman in America — universally admired for her incredible imagination — to the most hated. Even now, nineteen years later, people were still sending her death threats. "I read that she's a total recluse now, terrified to leave her penthouse, and that she looks like Howard Hughes. Scary, unkempt."

"She doesn't look like Howard Hughes," Everson said, his eyes on the fire.

"How do you know?"

He took a breath and turned to me. "Ilsa Prejean is my mother."

TWENTY

I stared at Everson. He may as well have said that he was the crown prince of fairyland. Or demonland, according to my dad, who hated the Titan Corporation as much as he hated cancer.

"And there it is." Everson nodded at my expression. "Man, do I love getting that look."

He was the baby born during the construction of the wall. The baby whose birth had turned a lot of people into savages. They'd plotted — publically — to infect him with Ferae so that Ilsa Prejean would know what it was like to lose a child. No wonder she was paranoid about his health. I swallowed against the tightness in my throat. "Why is your last name Cruz?"

"It was my dad's name."

An itchy, rashy feeling erupted across my skin. Ilsa Prejean's hubris had destroyed the world, and yet she was richer than ever — richer than 99 percent of the country. Her company, Titan, had single-handedly brought down America, but had gone on to become one of the most powerful corporations in history. And Everson would inherit it all.

"Why are you here?" I asked hoarsely. "On this side of the wall?"

"Isn't it obvious?"

"Not to me." There had been so many clues. The captain refusing to risk Everson's health when he'd wanted to take the bullet out of Bangor's leg. Bearly and Fairfax being assigned to look out for him. Even Rafe had noticed that Everson was treated differently. I should have figured it out back in the supply closet. He'd certainly dropped enough hints. I managed to get my feet beneath me and stood.

"Wait, Lane." He tried to take my hand but I stepped away.

"That's why the others all do what you say."

"No one does what I say," he said irritably. "I'm a guard. Lowest of the low. I went through boot camp like everyone else. I sleep in the barracks and eat the same crap food. I don't get special treatment."

"You got flown over the wall in a two-seater plane," I said.

His eyebrows lifted. "How do you know that?"

"Your mother owns the line patrol. You weren't assigned to work with Dr. Solis because you're good at science. She arranged it."

"She arranged it because I didn't give her a choice." He got to his feet. "Everything I told you was true. I did finish the college courseware. That's how I found out who she was and what she'd done — in an online biology lecture. Something my tutors failed to mention."

"When you blackmailed the captain, all you did was threaten to tell your mother about him, didn't you?"

"Yes, and it worked. I'm here, collecting information that'll get us one step closer to a cure."

"I thought you were risking arrest," I said, "but you can go back anytime you want."

"What does that matter?"

It mattered because he could break the law — cross the quarantine line — and no one would ever threaten to execute him. "This *is* just a field trip for you. This is Rafe's life...." I didn't know what my point was. I just felt stupid — really stupid — and ... what? Betrayed?

"Last I checked, you grew up safe and sound in the West too," he said tightly.

"Not in a germ-free penthouse, surrounded by tutors and bodyguards."

"Actually, it was in one of the old Titan labyrinths and it was a great time, let me tell you."

"Don't." I backed away from him. "Don't try to make me feel sorry for you. Cosmo was locked in a zoo."

"Is that my fault?"

"It's your mother's."

He flinched like I'd hauled off and hit him, and then looked away. "Tell me something I don't know."

I took a breath. I used to think people were over the top in their hatred for Ilsa Prejean. Especially my father. But now that I'd met Cosmo and spent time in this ruined world ...

"I get it," I said softly. "You're here to try to make up for what she did. But I'm going to bed now because ..." I lifted and dropped my hand. "Just because." I couldn't explain my sudden overwhelming sadness and exhaustion. I just knew that if I didn't go upstairs right now, I'd end up on the floor, curled in a ball.

I heard Rafe come through the front door as I climbed the stairs. "Hey, where are you going?" he called.

I didn't glance back. "To bed."

"What'd you do?" he asked Everson accusingly.

"I was born," Everson replied, sounding tired.

I shouldn't have hurt him, but I ached too much to go back down now. I just wanted to be alone. I crawled onto the queen bed. Let the guys fight over the top bunk. Finally, in the dark, I let loose my tears. I cried for the children like Cosmo, trying to survive on their own in the Feral Zone. And for the "scary people" living in cages in a zoo. People who had been human and had lost everything — families and lives, and finally their minds — to a virus that shouldn't exist.

My father should have been doing more than bringing crates of medicine to Moline. He should have pushed farther into the zone and come more often. And he should have told me about this place so that I could have been helping too.

The bats swarmed around me, but I couldn't get away because I was chained to a radiator in the middle of a meadow. And then there was my green silk gown that was so tight fitting, I couldn't move my legs to take even a step. But suddenly I remembered the switchblade hidden in my sleeve. Nudging it out, I tried to slash at the bats but there were too many. They tore at my gown with sharp teeth and claws and dive-bombed my chest. Screaming, I tried to stab them but only ended up cutting myself as the swarming creatures tore my flesh off in strips.

I lurched awake with a cry, my hands pressed over my heart as I tried to keep my skin in place. Slowly, my senses kicked in and I began to separate fact from fantasy. *Just a nightmare*, I told myself, *that's all*. A dream couldn't hurt me.

"Lane, are you all right?" Everson asked from the doorway.

Wearily, I nodded and rolled to my side. I didn't want to talk about it. Or anything else. The nightmare had left me feeling raw and vulnerable, and now embarrassment was kicking in. And the bed smelled like mice, even though I'd changed the sheets and blanket. Or maybe the whole room reeked of rodents. I could hear them too. Small rustlings in the box springs. I sat up, jammed my pants into my socks, and curled up under the blanket. The mattress dipped as Everson sat down next to me and propped a pillow behind him.

I scrunched myself into a ball and pressed my face to the cool sheet. What was he doing? I'd been wretched to him. But when he slid his arm under me, I was too surprised to protest.

"Come here." His voice was heavy and rich.

I rolled to face him. "I'm sorry I was so mean about your mother," I whispered.

"I've heard meaner." A shaft of moonlight streamed through the shuttered window and fell across his face. He didn't look mad at all. "Bad dream?"

"Awful."

"Put your head down," he coaxed.

I'd never laid this close to a boy before — let alone in a bed. This was a bad idea. "Just for a minute," he said.

He smelled like smoke from the fireplace — a cozy, comforting smell. It would be nice to let someone else keep an eye on the window. I let my head sink onto his shoulder and heard the soft cadence of his heart.

I'll just lie here for a minute, I told myself and closed my eyes. *Only a minute.*

I was dreaming again — but this dream was of a very different sort. In some part of my mind, I was aware that the morning had broken, but I wasn't ready to open my eyes and get up. I felt cozy and safe with my Great Dane stretched out on the bed beside me. My eyes tore open. That wasn't my dog's warm body so close to mine. It was *Everson's*. Thank goodness, he was still asleep; his steady breathing told me so.

Blades of sunlight streamed in through cracks in the shutters. Without moving, I tried to remember how we'd ended up this way. Nothing had happened last night; I was sure of it. I was still in my clothes and Everson was touching me only lightly, his hand on my hip. But somehow I felt different. I smiled. Almost laughed. Maybe it was just the high of realizing I was *alive*. I hadn't gotten paralyzed by a chimpacabra or eaten by weevlings. I was on my way to Chicago; I would do the fetch and my father would be fine. Or maybe this buzzing feeling inside of me was from something else entirely. All I knew was that I wanted to snuggle back into Everson and savor it. The thought sent ripples of heat through me. Actually, what I really wanted was to turn in his arms and kiss him. But I wanted him to stay asleep while I did it. Was that asking for too much?

Yes, I told myself firmly. Kissing a sleeping boy would be

crossing the line, and I'd done more than enough line crossing these past few days. I sighed and lay still, enjoying the
way his breath tickled the back of my neck — until the
sounds of someone moving downstairs startled me right out
of the bed. The last thing I wanted was to give Rafe anything else to tease me about. He was already obnoxious
enough about Everson. With real ammunition, Rafe would
humiliate me. So, before the boy on the bed so much as
cracked an eyelid, I bolted from the room.

The wide pine planks of the living room floor creaked as I
crossed them to peer through the sliver of space between the
shutters into the backyard. Outside, red and gold leaves dap-
pled the ground. I used to love mornings like this, cold and
sunny. I put my fingers on the chilled window, overcome
with a memory of my father. I was six, and we'd been having
a picnic in a freshly mowed public park. That grass smell
was in the air, and my dad had tossed me up into it. Flinging
me to the sky and laughing as he caught me with both hands.
I remembered screaming with joy at each drop — the scari-
est moments. Now I avoided that breathless, out-of-control
feeling. When had that started?

I found Cosmo in the kitchen sharpening a knife, which
sent a crawly feeling up the back of my neck. Rafe entered
and dropped other sharp objects on the counter — a screw-
driver, a nail file, a letter opener. "Sleep well?" he asked me.

His expression was bland but I didn't miss the insinua-
tion in his voice. "Nothing happened."

"Course not," he said with a smirk. "Two silkies
together . . . Kinda hard to get any friction going."

I rolled my eyes but wasn't going to get drawn into that topic. "Not that I care what you do," Rafe went on as he lazed against the counter. "You being who you are, I have taken myself out of this triangle."

"What triangle?"

"Come on. One girl, two guys. Oh, he's so smart and strong," Rafe said in a falsetto while pressing his clasped hands to his cheek. "But *he's* so hot. Anguish, anguish."

I crossed my arms. "And which one of those is you?"

"Yeah, you're right. I fit both. Point is, crush on the stiff all you want. Doesn't concern me." He held out his hand and Cosmo offered up the knife he'd been working on. "Though you do know Mack hates line guards, right?" Rafe swiped the knife along the back of his wrist. "He thinks they're evil drones."

"Killer robots, actually," I corrected.

"Same thing." The blade shaved off a patch of the golden hair on Rafe's arm with the precision of a razor. "Not bad," he pronounced and then glanced at me. "Don't worry. I won't tell on you."

"There's nothing to tell." I headed for the stack of canned fruit.

"Uh huh." He tucked the knife into his ankle sheath, which had been empty ever since the line guards arrested him in Moline. "When you're done with those," he told Cosmo with a nod at the pile, "put 'em in my knapsack."

I stopped sorting through the cans. "Why are you bossing him around?"

"He likes it." Rafe turned to Cosmo. "You're fine, right?"

Cosmo bobbed his head enthusiastically. "A-okay."

"See?" Rafe said to me. "He wants to make himself useful. Because he knows that if he doesn't" — Rafe sent him a pointed look — "he can't come with us."

"He's *not* coming," I burst out, only to see the little manimal's face crumple. "Cosmo, you told me that the king locks manimals in cages. Why would you want to chance getting caught again?"

His lower lip curled out. "I want to see my mom."

"He wants to see his mom," Rafe repeated, in case I didn't feel bad enough already.

"What's in it for you?" I asked him. "You're not doing this to be nice."

"He'll come in handy. He's strong."

"He's *eight*."

"Nothing's going to happen to him." Rafe tuned to Cosmo. "Show her."

Cosmo curled back his lips and bared his teeth. He reminded me of a puppy, playing tough.

"Scary, huh?" Rafe said and then hunkered near Cosmo like a coach. "Now, gimme some ugly." Cosmo hunched and lowered his brows. "Growl." Cosmo did and Rafe stood triumphantly. "Would you look at that? That is the best get-back face I have ever seen. Do that when we're in Chicago and no one's gonna mess with us." He pointed at me. "Lemme see your get-back face."

"I don't have one," I said and selected a can of pineapple chunks.

"Everyone should have one. What if you need to scare off some freak?" he scolded. "You use your get-back face. You gotta work on it. Perfect it."

"I'll get on that." I headed for the table. "He's *not* coming with us," I whispered as I passed Rafe.

While I devoured the pineapple chunks, I practiced holding the letter opener like a weapon. What I really wanted was my dad's machete, but it was in my messenger bag, which I'd left by the lake.

Rafe made a face at my lame attempt at a jab. "Didn't Mack show you how to use a knife?"

"Yeah, for self-defense," I admitted. "But I never practiced."

Rafe settled on the counter with a can of Dinty Moore beef stew. "He tried to teach me manners," he said, then poured the stew into his mouth straight out of the can.

"How much time did my dad spend with you when he was here?"

Rafe wiped his chin on his sleeve with an exaggerated groan. "Are we doing the sibling rivalry thing again? 'Cause you win. Every category, every time."

"I just don't get why he didn't tell me he was a fetch. I mean, I *understand* it logically. But it feels like he lied to me."

"He did. So what?"

"So what?" I snapped. Cosmo glanced from Rafe to me, looking nervous.

"He didn't want you worrying about him." Rafe chucked the empty can into the sink. "He wants you to be happy and safe. And that's a *good* thing, having someone look out for you like that."

How was I supposed to be happy or safe if something happened to my dad? "I'm going out to the lake," I said abruptly. There was no explaining anything to this boy.

"I'll come with you."

I needed to pee. As much as I hated the idea of being outside alone, the thought of Rafe hearing me urinate was worse. "No." I pulled on my borrowed boots but didn't tie them. "I want privacy."

Rafe looked like he was about to argue but then he shrugged. "Yell if you see anything with teeth."

The morning echoed with woodpeckers' knocking and the love songs of frogs. Stomping through milkweed and patches of black-eyed Susans, I made my way to the reeds where hopefully I couldn't be seen from the porch. Nearby a gaggle of geese were preening their feathers in the sun. They were huge birds and made me a little nervous — which was pathetic. I'd come face-to-face with a chimpacabra and piranha-bats, and now I was scared of a few geese? They didn't even have teeth, so I had no excuse to yell for Rafe. Not that I would have.

My boots and pants were soaked with dew by the time I reached a dense patch of cattails near the water's edge. After taking care of my most pressing need, I pushed through the stalks topped with fluffy seed heads and found a rocky patch of shore where I could hunker and wash my hands. The lake was sparkling, clear, and excruciatingly cold. I lifted my dial and got some shots of the lake and autumn colors.

I tucked my dial into my shirt, kicked off my boots, rolled up my pants, and waded in. The chill bordered on painful, but it was exactly the kind of jump-start I'd been hoping for. Now I just needed to find my dad's messenger bag. I pivoted to scan the bank behind me, only to have my guts turn to liquid.

The dogs from last night were back.

They slunk through the reeds, spreading out along the bank. They might be half-starved, but they were huge and, worse, smart enough to stay silent as they surrounded their prey — me. I inhaled sharply, preparing to scream for Rafe to bring the gun when the pack leader stopped short and pricked up his ears. The black mutt lifted his snout to the wind and then dropped into a crouch with a whine.

I couldn't believe what I was seeing. The enormous dog began to back off. With its hackles raised, the mutt glared past me to the woods on the other side of the lake. A low growl rose from its throat. Underbrush crunched somewhere behind me. I was desperate to turn and see what the dog was sensing, but I couldn't take my eyes from the rest of the pack. One of them might still crash into the shallow water and leap for my throat. But no, they all crept back as they too sniffed the air. Whatever was prowling through the trees had the whole pack cowering. And if these dogs were terrified, I knew I'd better run too. The lead dog gave a sharp bark that ended in a yelp, and then as one, the pack reeled about and raced up the hill out of sight.

"You looked like you could use some help," a deep voice purred.

I whirled to see Chorda, the tiger-man, step out of the woods.

· TWENTY-ONE ·

Chorda didn't seem surprised to come across me so far from Moline. Had he followed us?

Rafe would tell me to scream and run away. As if sensing my hesitation, Chorda opened his arms wide, showing me that he was unarmed. He wore only thin black running pants. Despite his imperfect upper lip and downy striped fur, I could see the double image in his face, like an Escher drawing, the human beneath the tiger.

"Thank you for scaring them off." My words were little more than an exhale.

His auburn eyes traveled the length of me, slow and deliberate, which set my nervous system buzzing. I wanted to flee but I squashed the impulse. Everyone probably ran from him. I wouldn't be one more person making him feel bad about the way he looked. "What are you doing here?" I asked, wading out of the shallow water. I wouldn't run from him, but I would keep my distance.

"I should be asking you that." His voice was deep and rough. Mesmerizing. Yet unnerving too, like the rumbling of distant thunder. "I live here."

"In the woods?"

"No." He flashed a smile that revealed his disturbingly

large canine teeth. "In a house back that way." He waved a striped hand at the trees behind him. "I came to get water, and found this by the lake." He unslung my messenger bag from his shoulder, which he'd been carrying the whole time. I hadn't even noticed. "It's yours, isn't it?"

I sighed in relief. "Yes."

He nodded toward the cottage. "I was going to leave it on the porch."

I pushed through the reeds and stepped onto the grass. He held out the bag. I hesitated. There was something so odd about him. A strangeness I couldn't quite identify. Maybe it was the intense way he was watching me.

"I see," he said softly. "You're scared of me." His whole body seemed to sag a little. "I'll leave it here and go." He bent to put the messenger bag down.

"No, I'm sorry," I said quickly, feeling terrible. I hurried forward and he placed the bag gently into my outstretched hand. But when he lifted his fingers to my face, I stiffened. He traced a fingertip down the curve of my cheek. Had I imagined that he'd had claws when he was caught in Rafe's trap?

"You are the most human of humans," he said and dropped his hand to his side. "What are you doing here, Lane?"

I relaxed. After hearing about ferals from Rafe yesterday — how they drooled, growled, and tried to bite anyone who got close — I could tell that this man didn't have "animal brain." What was the harm in answering his question as long as I didn't get into specifics? "I have to go to Chicago."

His tail swished, whipping the bushes behind him. "Chicago is a dangerous place."

So I'd heard. "There's something there I need to get."

He tilted his head, considering me. "You're too young to have left something behind."

"I'm doing it for someone else."

"Ahh." He sounded pleased. "Because of your kind heart."

I smiled. Finally, someone who didn't see kindness as a flaw. "Not this time." I picked up my boots and glanced at the cottage, wondering if the guys would come looking for me. "I should get going. Thank you for bringing my bag."

"It was quite humane of me, yes?" he asked with a purr.

I smiled. "Yes."

"But not human." His expression hardened. "Not *yet*." And before I could react, his fist slammed into my forehead. A starburst of pain exploded behind my eyes and reality retreated, only this time there were no dreams to fill the void.

Consciousness returned with the fetid smell of blood. *Mine?* I wondered through the waves of pain crashing in my head. Slowly my eyes adjusted to the shadows. I was lying on my stomach on a hard surface. I tried to push myself up and found, first with annoyance, then fear, that my arms had gone numb from being pressed into the floor by my own body weight. Then a nerve path cleared in my brain, and I remembered how I'd gotten here. *Chorda.*

I struggled to get up, but my wrists were bound together. Again, I caught the scent of blood in the air . . . and death, sweet and rotten. I rolled onto my side and found a girl on the floor next to me, returning my stare with blank eyes. Dead eyes.

The cry that tore out of my throat was savage. Flailing, I tried to kick the corpse away but couldn't. I thrashed onto my back.

"Finally," a voice rumbled out of the dark. "I've been waiting for you to wake up."

Recognition hit like a lightning strike, searing my nerves, and then his face appeared above me, striped skin and gleaming fangs. *A beast that tears out people's hearts*, Rafe had said. I began to gag.

"Stop making that noise!" The tiger-man gripped my jaw in his large hand, forcing my mouth shut. "You sound like an animal."

Jerking my chin free, I flipped away — a mistake, for now I was face-to-face with the dead girl again. *Fabiola.* The girl who'd gone missing. Who'd known something was hunting her. I wanted to sob for the girl who'd been stuck in an abandoned building with only her sister for company. She looked like Alva, with her long, dark hair, gleaming necklaces, and lace-trimmed gown . . . which was torn open at the neckline, exposing the bloody, ragged hole in her chest.

Oh no, Rafe was right — Chorda *was* the rogue. He *had* been following me. I began to shake, hands and arms twitching uncontrollably. "You killed her. . . ."

"A waste," he said with a dismissive snuffle. "Her heart didn't work."

"Work?" *Breathe! Think.* But how could I with the stench of a corpse clogging my throat?

Gripping my arms, Chorda pulled me to a sitting position. "None of them worked." He peered at me with luminous eyes.

I looked past his face, unable to bear the jittery excitement in his expression. Beyond him was a vast and decaying parlor with its windows and French doors boarded up from the inside.

"They weren't human enough." A low rumble grew within him and he shifted on his haunches. "But *you* are. You saved me from that hunter, and now you will save me from this curse." He ran his hand through the fur on his chest, distaste twisting his features.

"The virus?" I shook my head in the face of his insanity. "I can't. I —"

"You will," he roared, spewing out foul breath.

What was wrong with me? Don't make the crazy man angry! "I'm sorry! I'll help you. I will. But I don't know anything about Ferae."

Letting go of my arms, he rose before me. "I don't need what's in your mind. . . ."

I inhaled deeply, fighting for clarity. He was a psycho with a virus messing up his thinking. I had no weapon. No way to defend myself. How was I going to get away from him? As if in answer, an engine rumbled in the distance. The jeep!

With a roar, Chorda flew from the room into the foyer where shafts of light slashed through the shadows. He extended his fingers and his claws appeared as he peered through the paneled-glass window beside the front door.

As he looked, I listened and held in my scream. The jeep was too far away for anyone to hear me, and yelling for help would just enrage Chorda. I exhaled slowly, suddenly calm. Calm in my decision that I would rather die trying to escape than be dissected alive. Calm enough to remember that Alva's father had insisted his daughters carry switchblades. Did Fabiola keep hers up her sleeve like Alva had?

I checked that the beast was still at the front door, and with my bound hands I reached for Fabiola's wrist, only to snap my fingers back after a single touch. Her skin was cold, and her arm, stiff. Closing my eyes, I forced myself to run my fingertips over her velvet sleeve. And there it was — a lump. Maybe, please, a switchblade. Wincing as I leaned over Fabiola, I attempted to nudge the lump out of the girl's sleeve. My head bobbed as I glanced up with every breath, terrified that Chorda had returned on silent, padded feet. Finally, a rounded metal edge poked out of Fabiola's cuff.

Sweat filmed over me like grease as I plucked up the knife and fumbled to open the blade with hobbled hands. A sob escaped me. The knife was tiny — only a few inches long. Unless I stabbed it directly into Chorda's jugular, the little blade wouldn't even slow him down. At least I could cut through the duct tape on my wrists. Then I'd be free to find another weapon. I shot a look around the room but felt swallowed up by the rotting furniture and swirling wallpaper.

Just then, Chorda stalked back into the room, hunched, feline, predatory. "Your friends are searching for you."

Stay calm. I drew up my knees so that my hands were out of view and sawed at the tape.

Slowly he closed in on me, claws tensed, tasting the kill — closer and closer he crept.

The knife sawing through the tape was too loud. I needed to cover the sounds. "Why will my heart break the curse?"

He sank until he was poised on all fours, his eyes burning me. "You are the most human of humans. . . . There is no trace of beast in you."

The knife cut through the tape, but it was too late. Chorda was going to pounce; I could feel his intention coming off him in hot waves. As desperately as I wanted to seem brave, tears spilled from my eyes. I didn't want to die like this or be left to rot in this killing house. I twisted away, trying to get a grip on my terror so that I could figure out how to escape. My wrists were free, but I wasn't.

"Look at me, Lane," he commanded, sounding more like the man that I'd first met.

Yet I stayed turned away, eyes clenched tight, not wanting the last thing I saw to be his gaping maw or his bloody claws. I fingered the knife in my hand.

"I think it would be quite something to know you when I'm human again," he said. "It's too bad I won't have that chance. . . ."

My breath caught at the finality in his voice, so close behind me. This was the last second of my life and I would not meet it with my eyes closed. I pried open my lids and saw, right beside me, what I hadn't before: a fireplace with iron tools propped beside it.

My hand gripped the rusty iron poker and I sprang up, turning and swinging high. Before Chorda could rise, I brought the heavy poker crashing down on his head. The vibration from the impact flew up my arm as the crouched tiger-man fell to his knees.

I watched him grab his head, his fingers splayed as if to keep his brains from spilling out. He didn't make a sound. Then my vision sharpened. *Run!* With the poker in hand, I took off, not even stumbling when his claws raked my calf.

I sprinted into the foyer, gasping as pain radiated up my leg. I reached the door, hand out, ready to yank on the handle — only it was wrapped in chains. But I still had the poker. I swung it into the diamond-paned window, but the glass didn't shatter as one and the poker caught. Even if I could wrench the tip free, it would take too long to smash away all of the panels.

I shot a glance back into the parlor where Chorda was still down on all fours, his face lowered and body swaying from side to side. Hurt? No — gathering his strength! I left the poker and ran through the house, dodging around corners, leaping over half-eaten animal carcasses, until I stumbled into the kitchen. But here too the door had been sealed. Not with chains but with boards hammered into place. I yanked open several drawers but they were all empty. No scissors, no knives.

The next room was long and narrow — a butler's pantry — with two doors at the far end. Somewhere in the front of the house, a piece of heavy furniture toppled. My legs melted into jelly, verging on collapse. I dashed forward and pried open one of the doors to find stairs leading up. I hated, hated this choice — trapped above ground level — but with no other option, I sprinted up the narrow staircase.

· TWENTY-TWO ·

I paused on the second floor landing to listen for the tiger-man, but the house had fallen silent. The smell of death coated the air like oil. A smear of blood stained the wallpaper. I hurried down the dark corridor past closed doors, too terrified to open any of them, afraid of what I'd find, until a blood-curdling roar shook the house.

I yanked open the closest door — an empty closet. I tried the door across the hall and blinked against the sudden flood of sunlight. A smell slammed into me, so foul that I had to clamp my hand over my nose and mouth. On the opposite wall, tree branches invaded the room through the broken windows. Like sturdy arms they reached out to me, promising to bear my weight. I stepped through the doorway, my eyes adjusting to the light, and caught sight of someone crumpled on the floor. My muscles went rigid.

No, not someone. A corpse. The room was filled with them. Dried out corpses with taut grins and shrunken eyes, they'd been flung into corners and on couches. All with their chests mutilated. All in various stages of decay. I felt something inside of me tearing and then breaking.

I backed out of the room so fast I bumped into the wall of the corridor. Something brushed my face and sent me spinning aside. A thin rope hung down from a hatch in the ceiling. I gave the rope a tug, pulling the hatch open just a few inches when I heard a strange rustling, like the sweep of dry leaves on concrete.

I knew that sound!

My fingers flew open and the hatch banged shut. I'd nearly pulled an attic full of weevlings down on myself. Creatures that were attracted to the glistening stuff dripping down the back of my calf where Chorda had clawed me. Chorda, who had to have heard the hatch bang shut.

Suddenly a plan formed in my mind. Insane. Dangerous. But I had no other ideas and someone was now pounding up the stairs.

I caught hold of the hatch rope again and backed into the narrow hall closet. With the door cracked and hatch rope in hand, I watched Chorda stagger onto the landing. Lowering his head, with his broad, striped back to me, he sniffed the first doorknob. Then, inhumanly fast, he swung around to stare at the cracked closet door, his pupils enormous in the dim light. As his muscles shifted, coiling for the pounce, I burst from the closet and yanked the rope as hard as I could.

The ceiling hatch dropped open and a skeleton tumbled out. I tugged harder and brought down the whole collapsible staircase. The dry rustle of featherless wings filled the air, followed by the deafening clicks of hundreds of weevlings. They poured from the hatch like black, billowing smoke. With the attic stairs now between us, I couldn't see Chorda, but I heard his scream — shockingly human — as I tore into the room with the corpses and hefted myself onto the largest tree branch poking through the broken window.

Outside, I perched in the tree and quickly scanned the area. Chorda's house was bound by an overgrown, tangled hedge with meadow beyond it. I saw no sign of the broken highway or the lake.

I climbed down a few branches, dropped out of the tree, and ran through the garden gone wild, wishing I had my father's machete. I had no idea if I was headed in the right direction to find Rafe and Everson, but no direction could be wrong so long as it led away from the death house. My ears pounded with the sound of my own feet hitting the ground. The cuts on my calf throbbed, and my lungs burned, but I didn't slow down, and I didn't look back.

As I barreled through the hedge, the branches caught my hair and scratched my face and arms. The evergreen scent was a welcome relief. On the other side, I tripped over something in the dirt and landed on my stomach. Inches from my nose, a human rib cage jutted out of the muddy ground. Too breathless to scream, I heaved myself up and raced through the meadow — a killing field — leaping over bones and tearing through the scrub until I reached a broken road. Was it the same one that we'd taken the day before?

I glanced back and saw the tiger-man lurching across the field, bloody and enraged. A cry burst from my throat.

How had he gotten away?

Something growled to my left. I spun to see the jeep skidding for me. It didn't even make a full stop, just swerved alongside me long enough for Rafe to lean out, grab my arm, and haul me into the backseat with him.

Chorda veered onto the road to cut us off. Everson laid

on the speed, heading right at the tiger-man. Blood streamed from the gashes that crosshatched his face and body. With foamy lips and glistening fangs, he locked eyes with me. Everson hunched over the wheel while Rafe braced us for impact. The jeep bore down on Chorda until — at the very last second — he vaulted aside and we flew past. I twisted around to see him throw back his head and bellow out his rage.

Rafe pulled me close and I pressed my forehead into his chest, trying to block out Chorda's roars. My muscles began to jerk and tremble. I dug my nails into my palms to give myself something to concentrate on, but it didn't work. Fabiola's vacant eyes kept floating into my mind, followed by the corpses. My stomach twisted, and with a groan, I pulled away from Rafe to lean out of the speeding jeep and vomit up the pineapple I'd eaten for breakfast. There wasn't much, but my body kept going until my throat burned raw. Rafe gripped my arm to keep me from falling out, and then he swore under his breath. "You could have mentioned you were bleeding to death." He guided me back onto the seat.

"He bit her?" Everson slowed the jeep and twisted to look at me.

"No," I croaked. "It's from his claws."

Rafe placed my leg across his lap and pushed up my torn pants leg. Blood coated my skin from the knee down. He grimaced, but a split second later, when he lifted his eyes to mine, he'd wiped the worry from his face. "Man, these will be some fierce scars," he said, as if that was something I would look forward to.

The jeep slammed to a stop and Everson leaned over the front seat. I knew the cuts were bad when he too steeled his expression. "That needs to be disinfected. Stitched."

"No kidding." Rafe pulled his T-shirt over his head. "Go! You don't want to know how fast a raging feral can run." As the jeep bucked and tore out, he wrapped the shirt around my lacerated calf. I closed my eyes and ground my teeth against the searing pain.

"Tell me when it's safe to stop," Everson said over the engine's roar. "I've got what I need in the med kit."

"You know how to stitch a wound?" Rafe asked skeptically.

"Yeah, and I won't leave her with a fierce scar."

I opened my eyes to see a fuzzy little gray face, peering at me over the front passenger seat. I sat up, legs still across Rafe's lap, and tried to smile. "Hi." Cosmo blinked back the tears that were rapidly filling his beautiful blue eyes. "I'm okay," I told him in a scratchy voice. "A-okay."

With a wet sniff, he popped up in his seat and thrust his ratty dish towel into my hands. I held it close to my heart and mouthed, "Thank you," knowing my voice would break if I said it aloud.

"You know, you scared the crap outta Cosmo," Rafe said and then cast me a sidelong look. Any other time I would have smiled at his reluctance to admit that I'd scared the crap out of *him*, but not now. Not when I was struggling to hold in a sob.

Everson glanced over his shoulder again, checking the T-shirt on my calf — now blood-soaked. "Wrap it tighter and apply pressure."

"I knew that," Rafe muttered. I gasped as he rearranged the makeshift bandage and cried when he clasped a hand to my calf. Pain blazed along each cut as if Chorda's claws were still embedded in my skin. I tried to wriggle free, but Rafe held on, and slowly, after several panting breaths, I realized that the firm pressure of his hand had taken the pain down by a degree.

I swiped the tears from my cheeks. "How did you find me?"

"I followed the tiger's trail, but lost you at the stream." He sounded apologetic.

"You got us close enough," Everson pointed out. "We found her."

"Yeah, we did." Rafe's voice sounded strained. Probably leftover worry. "There's a place about twenty miles from here. We can fix up your leg there."

My thoughts weren't on what lay ahead, but on the nightmare behind me. "You were right," I whispered. "He killed all those people."

Rafe stared at me, brow puckered. "Tiger-guy told you that?"

"I saw them." I could barely get the words out. "He eats their hearts. He thinks it'll turn him human again. If he eats the right one."

"Lemme guess, you have the right heart."

I nodded. "Because I stopped you from killing him."

"See what being nice gets you?"

"She doesn't need to hear that," Everson snapped.

But Rafe had been right and I'd nearly had my heart ripped out because I hadn't listened to him. "I'm so stupid. . . ." The memory of the tiger's claws threatened to pull me under. I focused on taking in air. Chorda was out there loose, because of me. If he killed someone else . . . it would be all my fault.

After thirty minutes of bumping over broken asphalt, Rafe pointed in the distance to what looked like a limestone fortress, complete with stockade walls, turrets, and towers.

Cosmo rose to his knees in the front seat. "What's that?"

"Home sweet home," Rafe said with a forced smile.

In no time we were cruising alongside a massive stone wall — the Titan in miniature. The place truly did look ready to withstand archers and battering rams. We rounded a corner and reached the front wall where my romantic notions were quickly dispelled by the windows — all iron barred.

Everson parked the jeep right next to a large sign near the entrance that read "Joliet State Penitentiary." "A prison?"

Rafe pulled a circle of keys from his knapsack and headed for the heavily fortified gate. "Doesn't get any safer than this." He unlocked a number of chains and used his weight to push open the gate. "We'll stay here tonight. And go into Chicago before dawn."

"But it can't even be noon yet," I said. "Let's go now."

Rafe gave me an odd look. "It's way past noon."

"Oh." How long had I been unconscious after Chorda's punch? "Still —"

"Let's see what time it is when Ev here is done stitching up your leg." He said it so firmly, I didn't bother to argue, just followed him through the gate.

With Everson's arm wrapped around me, half holding me up, I limped my way into a spacious courtyard where squawking chickens roamed freely. The afternoon sun lent a golden hue to the walls and parapets. But most striking were the solar-collecting panels. Almost the entire roof was taken up with slanting and shimmering panels that blazed in the sunlight. I had to admit the place wasn't horrible as we passed a vegetable garden. But still . . . "This is where you live?"

"I keep my stuff here. Mostly I'm out working for some compound, hunting ferals or path hacking."

Inside the main building, he led us through a series of barred doors, which had been electric at one time but now he just shoved open. "It'll be homier when I get the power on." He directed us down a caged-in stairway and along a hallway to a thick door with a small, round, wire-mesh porthole. Opening a panel, he found the circuit breakers labeled "Solar Generators." When he switched them on, the overhead lights flickered to life.

I felt a little better when we got to the infirmary. It was a large room, with old cots scattered haphazardly, but at least every corner was visible from every angle of the room. There were no closets in which a feral could hide; no doors to lurk behind. "Where's Cosmo?" Had we lost the little manimal in the halls?

"He's looking around the place," Rafe assured me. "How do you feel?"

"Stupid."

"No. Physically how do you feel?"

"My leg hurts."

He clapped a hand to my forehead and had me sit on the nearest cot. "How long since we picked her up?" he asked Everson, who was dousing a gauze pad with antiseptic.

Everson shrugged and wheeled over a table laid out with medical supplies. "She said she wasn't bitten."

"She's sitting right here!" I said irritably.

"Okay." Rafe propped a shoulder against the wall and crossed his arms. "Just tell me if you start feeling hot."

I nodded, which turned into a grimace when Everson pressed the gauze to my calf. As he cleaned my cuts, I squeezed my hands together to keep from yelling. Two of my nails were broken off below the quick and there was grit and dried blood under the others.

"This is going to hurt." Needle already in hand, Everson pulled up a stool, and sat, placing my foot between his thighs to brace it. He gave me a faint smile. "Do me a favor — don't kick."

I nodded, pretending like this was no big deal, though I'd never gotten stitches in my life. Even after he'd rubbed some kind of numbing cream around the cuts, I had to chew the inside of my cheek to keep from yelling every time he jabbed the needle into my torn flesh. But I didn't kick. If anything, the pain helped me keep certain images at bay — such as all the corpses, pale and cold on the floor.

When Everson finished, Rafe leaned over for a look. "Huh," he said with surprise. "Good stitches."

"I've had training as a field medic," Everson said.

But some cuts couldn't be sewn up. "Fabiola was there," I told Rafe as a wintery feeling filled my chest.

"Dead?"

I nodded. "You'll tell her father and Alva, so they'll know what happened to her?" I reached for my dial to see if I'd gotten an image of the dead girl, so they'd know for sure that it was her. But there was nothing around my neck. Chorda had taken my dial, along with my bag. I pressed my hands to my eyes, trying to block out the thought of Chorda patting me down while I was unconscious. "I'm so stupid. I shouldn't have gone near him. I should have run."

"Yeah," Rafe said evenly. "Why didn't you?"

I wanted to crawl under the cot, but I deserved their scorn. "I didn't want to hurt his feelings."

"No, seriously," Rafe said. "Why didn't you at least yell?"

Everson glanced up from bandaging my calf and took in my expression. "She is serious."

Rafe started to scoff but then turned a stunned look on me. "His feelings?" He choked on the words. "You were worried about a predator's feelings?"

"Cut her a break." Everson finished taping the bandage. "She didn't grow up over here."

"Right. 'Cause in the West you all just skip around and hug," Rafe said acidly. "You're all best friends and everyone gets a pony on their birthday."

Everson shoved the rolling table aside and rose. "Why don't you go check on your chickens?"

"You're not doing her any favors, silky." Rafe stepped forward to meet him. "Unless you're planning to stitch yourself to her side, you won't always be around. All she has are her instincts to keep her safe. And you want to tell her things are so different over here that she can't trust her gut? Gotta ask yourself why. Maybe because you like being the hero?"

Everson's fist moved so fast, I didn't even see the punch, only Rafe's backward stumble. He recovered fast, heading right for Everson. Tumbling off the cot, I threw myself between them. "Stop it!"

Both halted in their tracks. Each waited to see what the other would do.

"I'm done." Everson put up his hands though his voice was harsh with anger. "He's right."

"Then why'd you hit him?" I demanded.

"I didn't like the way he said it."

Something soft rubbed my arm. I glanced down to see Cosmo petting me with a threadbare stuffed animal — Curious George.

"No one said you could touch that." Rafe swiped the blood from his split lip and reached for the toy.

Cosmo clutched the stuffed animal to his chest. "Jasper's mine."

"Hand it over, ape-boy."

Hunching down, Cosmo curled back his lips and growled.

"Don't give me the get-back face," Rafe snapped. "I taught you that face."

Instantly Cosmo dropped the attitude, popped Curious George's head into his mouth, and took off running.

"Hey!" Rafe shouted after him. "Get back here."

"Oh for — Grow up," Everson growled while nursing his knuckles in one hand.

Obviously the toy had sentimental value for Rafe, but come on; Cosmo was eight. I limp-jogged after him, despite the burn shooting up my calf, but I lost him at the first inter-section of corridors. When the guys joined me, I turned on Rafe. "What's wrong with you?"

"Me? I don't go into people's homes and take their stuff." He paused. "Well, actually I do, but not while they're still living there!" He shouted the last part down the hall for Cosmo's benefit.

"Where did he take it from?"

When Rafe didn't reply, I glanced over to find him eye-ing me. "What?"

"Nothing." He shook off whatever it was he'd been thinking and led us to the cellblock, a three-story space with a gangway on each level. Rafe headed along the row of dingy stone cubicles that passed for cells. I trailed behind him with Everson's help and felt my heartbeat thumping in my calf with every step. I didn't want to think about what I had coming when the numbing cream wore off.

Rafe stopped abruptly and glanced back at me. "He got it out of that one." He pointed to the next cell in the row. "If he's in there, you should be the one to talk to him."

I nodded and limped into the cell. Everson started to fol-low but Rafe blocked him. "Let her do it."

Bunks hung off one wall and a crosshatch pattern cov-ered the opposite wall — ceiling to floor. Graffiti? I angled closer. Seven lines in a row, with a star after every three rows. It was a crude calendar, which reminded me of how little time I had left to get back to the tunnel before the bull-dozers filled it in. I turned and spotted Cosmo lying on his stomach on the top bunk with his chin propped on Curious George. He was looking at a picture book.

"Hey, buddy," Rafe called from the corridor. "You want to keep the monkey?"

Cosmo glanced back at him. I too shot Rafe a look, although mine was annoyed. I'd thought he was going to let me handle it.

"You can," Rafe went on, "but you have to do something for me."

Cosmo sat up, clutching the stuffed monkey to his chest. "What?"

"Come here and I'll tell you."

Whatever Rafe had in mind, it had better not be mean. And he'd better not even think about reneging. I held out my arms to Cosmo, but he leapt off the bed without my help and scrambled into the corridor where Rafe stood waiting.

Curious, I picked up the book that Cosmo had been reading — *The Runaway Bunny*. I remembered that one. Every place the little bunny ran off to, his mother found a way to follow him. I wished Cosmo's mother could follow him and keep him safe. I wished my father could find me as easily out in the world. I breathed for a moment, forcing down the sadness. Behind me, the cell door clanged shut.

"Very funny." I dropped the book on the cot and turned to see Rafe pocket the key.

"George is all yours," he told Cosmo.

"Jasper," Cosmo corrected and then cast a worried glance back at me.

"What are you doing?" Everson demanded. "She said she wasn't bitten."

Rafe pinned his gaze on me. "People lie."

TWENTY-THREE

Now I understood what those looks had been about. Rafe thought I might be infected.

"We're short on time," he said, sounding more serious than I thought he was capable of. "I know. But if you get fevered while we're out in the zone, it'll end bad. You'll run so far that by the time you cool down, you'll be completely lost."

I hurried to the bars, making my calf throb. "I'm not hot. Feel my forehead." I reached for his hand but he slid back, pulling Cosmo with him.

"It can take up to ten hours for the fever to show."

I looked to Everson for help. He shoved his hands into his pockets. "He's right. There's no way to know if you're infected this soon. Even a blood test couldn't tell us."

"But Chorda didn't bite me. I swear. I wouldn't lie about that."

"You said he knocked you unconscious," Rafe reminded me. "Maybe he chomped on you then." He slid down the wall to sit cross-legged on the floor, clearly settling in for a long stretch of time.

I pressed my forehead to the cold metal bars. "I can't waste ten hours stuck in here."

"It's been a while since we picked you up. We'll round down to eight," Rafe offered.

No, I wanted to yell, but it would probably come out sounding fevered. And what if Rafe was right? What if Chorda had bitten me while I was unconscious? No, that would have defeated his purpose. He wanted to eat the most purely human heart he could sink his fangs into. I tried explaining that to Rafe and Everson, but neither trusted Chorda to follow his own insane logic.

I couldn't spend the next eight hours worrying if I had Ferae. I'd go crazy. And even if I came out of it okay, we'd never get to Chicago and back by Thursday morning. I had to get out of this cell now. I had to prove to them that I hadn't been bitten. I lifted my arms. My skin was scratched from running through the hedge, and it was hard to tell what was a scab and what was just caked-on dirt, but nothing came close to looking like a tiger bite. I checked my stomach. Nothing. To see more, I'd need to take off my tank and pants, which were half shredded into ribbon. I opened my mouth to ask the guys to leave, but what would be the point? I couldn't see every inch of my body and even if I had a mirror, Rafe would still doubt whatever I said.

"I'll take off my clothes," I said before I could think about how that would play out. "And you guys check for a bite mark."

Well, I'd sure shocked the two of them. If I weren't so scared and desperate, I would have laughed at their twin expressions of wide-eyed surprise. Cosmo, on the other hand, screwed up his face and scampered from the cellblock.

Guess the idea of me naked was just too gross to stick around for. I pulled up my tank.

"Don't," Everson said hoarsely and I froze. "It won't be enough. Even without a bite mark, you could still be infected. Chorda's blood or saliva could have gotten in one of your cuts. We're going to have to wait it out."

"He's right." Rafe cast a sidelong look at Everson. "But you could have mentioned it after she took off her shirt."

"It crossed my mind," Everson admitted. He moved to stand within inches of the bars. "I'm sorry, Lane."

I swallowed against the ache in my throat and looked away. I'd just condemned my dad to a death sentence because I'd been stupid. I'd fallen for Chorda's act and gotten myself quarantined.

Rafe hefted a thin mattress out of the next cell and dropped it on the floor. "We'll split up the time, so that one of us is always with her. I'll take the first shift."

Everson watched me as if worried I'd start throwing myself against the bars. "Are you hungry?"

I shook my head. I wouldn't be able to eat until I knew for sure that I wasn't infected. I slid down the wall to sit on the floor.

He crouched by the bars. "You're probably fine."

I waved him away. "Go get something to eat so we can take off the minute eight hours is up."

"We're not hitting the road at midnight." Rafe pulled out a knife and started cleaning his nails. "Too many things hunt at night."

I leaned my head back against the wall. I might as well forget trying to do the fetch. I'd never get back to the tunnel in time.

"You've done this before," I said to Rafe after Everson headed back to the infirmary to refill his med kit. "You've locked someone up and waited to see if they were infected."

He shrugged and strode off. Guess he didn't want to talk about it. He was back a few minutes later with a sponge, soap, and a bowl of water. He pushed it through the opening at the bottom of the barred door. "It's not that goop you like, but it's better than a bucket of dirt."

I was too thrilled over the sight of soap and water to care if he teased me — too desperate to scrub away every trace of Chorda.

"The stiff would turn around now, wouldn't he?" Rafe asked and then gave an exaggerated sigh. "Of course, he would. I'm going to get some blankets." He set off down the row of cells, giving me his back in his own way. Despite everything, I smiled. Gallant might not come naturally for Rafe, but he was trying and I appreciated it.

I retreated to a corner of the cell where I washed my face and limbs thoroughly. By the time I finished, Rafe had returned with an armful of blankets. He dropped them in front of my cell.

"There are clean clothes in the metal trunk," he told me, without glancing my way.

I lifted the lid and found an assortment of prison-guard uniforms and bright orange jumpsuits. I opted for a uniform. Boring brown, but not too bad a fit. "You can turn around," I told him. "Thank you," I added, once he was facing me. "For everything. Well, except for locking me up."

"You should stay here tomorrow and let me and Ev do the fetch." Before I could protest, he went on. "If Chorda thinks your heart is the only one that'll cure him, he's not going to stop hunting you. And when a feral knows your scent, you're easy prey."

I wasn't going to fight with him about this now, especially since I might be so fevered tomorrow that I wouldn't be going anywhere. "The weird thing is," I said, "Chorda's not really feral. Not the way you've described it."

Rafe shrugged. "Some manimals go from sane to feral in a heartbeat. Others turn little by little. Sounds like cat-chow is halfway there."

I rubbed my forehead where Chorda had punched me. "So next time," I said, trying for a light tone, "I should skip the science lecture about why eating human hearts won't cure his disease."

"If you're going to try and talk a freak out of killing you, you gotta at least speak his language."

"I don't know tiger."

"How about crazy?"

I smiled faintly. "My school didn't offer that elective."

Just then, Cosmo loped into the cellblock, carrying an armful of picture books. He had Curious George stuffed down the front of his overalls with only the head peeking out. Guess the dish towel had been officially replaced. Cosmo set the stack on the floor by my cell and plopped down. I crouched by the bars. "Where'd you get those?"

"The room with the kids," he said while sorting through the books like a little pirate counting his gold.

"Kids?"

"On the wall."

The prison library, maybe? I leaned over to see a book he'd set aside. The title — *Where the Wild Things Are* — made me smile.

"That book makes no sense," Rafe said, getting to his feet. "Wouldn't you want to go where the wild things *aren't*?"

"Why would a prison library have kids books?" I asked him.

"Maybe the inmates couldn't read. How should I know?" He joined us and pointed to the stuffed monkey tucked into the front of Cosmo's overalls. "George."

Cosmo's bottom lip curled. "Jasper."

Rafe dropped to one knee and plucked a book off the top of the pile. *Curious George Visits the Zoo.* He tapped the cover. "George." He flipped to the first page and turned it toward Cosmo.

The little manimal shrieked and fell back against the cell's bars, clutching his toy monkey. I leaned over to see the illustration. Happy animals in a sweet little zoo. Rafe and I met eyes. "Forget this one," he said and sent the book sailing across the cell block. "You know what, buddy, none of these are as good as the stories this one guy used to tell me."

Cosmo perked up. "Stories?"

"Yeah, he made them up and they were great."

"My dad told you stories?" I asked in a low voice.

Ignoring me, Rafe settled on the mattress. "They were about this fierce girl who lives on the other side of the wall."

Cosmo crept onto the mattress beside him. "What wall?"

"The biggest wall you ever saw. As tall as the sky. And this girl, she lives over there in a glass tower."

"All glass?" Cosmo asked.

Rafe nodded. "Even the stairs. Pretty cool, right?"

Cosmo nodded, eyes wide.

"The stairs are not made of glass," I corrected. "The balconies are all caged in and it's far from cool. It's boring."

They both frowned at me. "I'm trying to tell a story here," Rafe scolded. "Why don't you go to bed?" I started to protest but he angled a finger at me. "I'm not taking you into Chicago tomorrow unless you're one hundred percent fine. That includes rested." He got up and pointed at the mattress. "Grab that end," he told Cosmo.

Together they dragged the mattress down the aisle and dropped it by the wall, facing the cells, where Rafe could keep an eye on me, but his voice was no more than a murmur to my ears.

Going by Cosmo's rapt expression, Rafe was a heck of a storyteller. Not surprising. He even seemed to be enjoying himself. Suddenly I was sorry that they'd moved out of earshot.

Rafe was right though. If I was going to be ready to head out at dawn, I needed to sleep. I was beyond weary. I just wished there was some way to keep corpses and insane tiger-men out of my dreams.

I jolted upright, confused and sweat soaked. In the gray pre-dawn light, I couldn't make sense of the bunk above me or the wall of bars. Where was I? Then the last two days crashed down on me in an icy wave and memories filled my mouth and nose until I was gasping for air. I hauled myself off the thin mattress.

A section of bars had been rolled aside — an open door. I tried to remember what Everson had said when he woke me during the night. He'd covered me with a blanket and told me that the eight hours were up. I'd been too exhausted to even register that he'd pronounced me Ferae-free.

I found Rafe asleep in the next cell and nudged his leg, He rolled over fast, pulling a knife from under his pillow. When he saw me — too stunned to move — he tucked the blade back under his pillow like it was nothing. "A precaution," he said.

I brought in a slow breath. "Have you ever cut yourself while you're asleep?"

"Did you wake me up to ask that?"

"No, I want to get on the road."

He groaned but threw his legs over the side of the cot. "Tell me you woke me up last."

"First," I admitted and he shot me a groggy glare.

I went looking for Cosmo next and got lucky on my first guess — the library. Shelves of dusty books lined three of the walls. A mural covered the last wall with vibrant colors and animals that stared out with knowing eyes. Three figures floated in the center, a man standing behind two children. What a weird picture to find inside a maximum-security prison.

Two little gray feet were propped up on the wall.

I circled the couch and found Cosmo on the floor, lying on his back with his Curious George clutched under one arm, looking at another picture book. The floating children in the mural were holding hands and Cosmo had his feet pressed on top of their entwined fingers. I didn't think it was a coincidence.

"Think that's Hansel and Gretel?" I asked Cosmo. "Maybe when they're being led into the woods by their father."

Cosmo tilted the book up and glanced at the mural. "They're my friends."

Okay, that was enough to break my heart. I sat on the floor beside him and noticed a series of grade-school textbooks on a bottom shelf. I hefted one up, thumbed through the pages, and found pictures of piled corpses and the evacuation. My fingers tingled as I paused at a photo of a city on fire.

This book had been published *after* the exodus.

I found Rafe in what was once the "Property Room," according to the sign outside the door. He had weapons stored in small cubicle shelves, like the stockroom of a shoe store.

I held up the textbook. "My dad gave you this, didn't he?"

Rafe gave me a sidelong look, clearly gauging my reaction. "He didn't want me to be illiterate."

"You don't just live here now, you *grew up* here," I said. Rafe shrugged, but my horror mounted. "You're the little boy who lives by himself in a castle! But it's not a castle. My dad left you all alone in an abandoned penitentiary."

"Why not? I had food, weapons, a library, a game room. I'd hook up the generator and watch old movies. It was a good time."

"You were *ten*."

"First you're mad that Mack spent time with me and now you're mad that he left me alone. Make up your mind."

I thought back to the hatch marks on the wall of his cell. That was how Rafe had kept track of the time until my dad returned from the West. Crossing days off the calendar had been one of my own painful routines. If I'd had the occasional pang, wondering if my father was ever coming back, that doubt must have consumed Rafe when he was younger.

"The mural in the library," I said. "You painted that."

"So what? It's my wall."

"It's you, me, and my dad, isn't it?"

"I was a bored little kid. I don't remember what it was supposed to be. Now, pick a weapon." He pointed to the assortment he'd laid out on the counter.

"He's like a father to you," I pressed.

Rafe sighed as though I was wasting precious time. "Mack would swing by for me on his way to Chicago so I could be his lookout. Afterward, he'd drop me off. Sometimes he'd stay for a while and sometimes he had to get home. That's all there was to it."

"You must have hated me," I said softly. "For taking him away from you."

"Look, I love the guy. I do. But like a mentor, not a dad," Rafe said firmly. "I didn't hate you."

I remembered the mural and realized it was true: He

hadn't hated me. He'd painted the children holding hands as if they were friends or . . . family?

"Actually, I kinda liked hearing about you," he admitted.

"Why didn't my dad bring you back with him so you could live in the West?"

"I wouldn't go. From what I hear, you don't *live* in the West."

I didn't think dealing with ferals was better, but he did have a point.

Before leaving the prison, the four of us gathered in the kitchen and spread out a map of Chicago on the table. Director Spurling's letter was long gone — lost with the messenger bag and my father's machete — but I remembered the address. We found her street and the Lincoln Park Zoo on the map. Before he ran away, Cosmo had worked in the farmyard at the zoo. He had friends there who could get a message to his mother in the castle. Best-case scenario, we would get out of Chicago with Cosmo's mother and the photo of Spurling's daughter. All of the possible worst-case scenarios, I shoved out of my mind.

Everson drove on the median strip between the rusted cars that lined the highway. Rafe slept in the front seat while Cosmo sat in back with me and told me stories about Chicago. Stories I probably could have done without hearing. Fog was a fragile web hanging in all directions, but eerier still was the silence, which was broken only by the occasional birdcall.

After over an hour, the landscape became more urban. Well, urban in the sense that there were more buildings;

however, there were also herds of deer munching lazily on the grass that now blanketed what had once been road. We wove through neighborhoods of three-flats and bungalows that had withstood eighteen years of neglect pretty well. The houses, stores, schools, and churches were still standing, though covered in creepers and ivy.

As we drew closer to downtown, Cosmo got quieter until he was saying nothing at all. We followed the Chicago River north and there it was: an obstacle even more intimidating than Moline's crushed-car wall. It had begun to rain, but even without sunlight, the fence around the Chicago Loop glinted like a heap of giant, deadly Slinkys — countless lethal coils of razor wire went on for what seemed like miles along the riverbank, cordoning off the skyscrapers. But the stretched coils weren't the horrifying part. That distinction belonged to the sharp wooden pikes lined along the west bank of the river. Each pole impaled a severed manimal head. Cosmo covered his face with his arms, and I pulled him closer.

"So this king of yours" — Rafe twisted in his seat to look back at us — "he sure has a thing about ferals, huh?"

"The king hates anyone who shows animal," Cosmo mumbled.

We passed the north end of the kingdom of Chicago, and kept driving until we reached the southern tip of Lincoln Park. Everson parked among the rusting remains of other vehicles, and we got out solemnly. We followed his lead as he gathered rusted bumpers and branches and artfully camouflaged the jeep. I focused hard on the task, but when it was over, there was nothing else to do but stare at the impaled heads lining the park with their milky white eyes and bulging tongues.

Rafe steered me across the weed-choked street. "It's easier if you don't think of them as human." A wince flashed over his face, and he glanced at Cosmo. "No offense."

I supposed that was progress. At least now he felt bad about hurting a manimal's feelings.

Now that it was time for us to split up, I felt a wild surge of fear. The fur on the back of Cosmo's neck and across his shoulders stood up, like a dog with its hackles raised. I wanted to assure him that everything would be fine, but how could I? This was where he grew up. He knew better than any of us what dangers lay ahead.

I hoisted Cosmo into my arms and hugged him tightly. When I put him down, he went to Everson and took his hand. My eyes moved from Cosmo's winter-blue gaze to Everson, who was scanning the abandoned buildings on this side of the street. What if I never saw either one of them again? Suddenly I wanted to put my arms around Everson too, and would have, even knowing that Rafe would smirk, but Everson seemed distant. His muscles were taut under his gray shirt and his expression impassive as he surveyed our surroundings. He was back in line-guard mode, fatigues and all, which was probably for the best given our circumstances. Still . . . He glanced over then and caught my worry.

"It's okay, Lane. You'll be safe with him." He tipped his head toward Rafe. "I'll see you later," he added, and I nodded. In his voice there was a certainty I clung to.

"That's it?" Rafe said. "I would've gone for the kiss."

Everson shot him an exasperated look. "Ever consider not talking?"

"Why?" Rafe scoffed. "Hey, Cosmo, try and keep the stiff out of trouble," he said, which got a big smile from Cosmo. "Ready?" he asked me.

No. But what choice did I have? I forced myself not to look back as we walked away.

We found Webster Avenue easily enough. It was just a block west of the park. However, locating Director Spurling's house was another matter.

"You're positive this was the address," Rafe asked me a second time.

I would have given anything to have been able to say no, but I was certain this was the address Director Spurling had given in her letter. I nodded because I didn't trust my voice.

The brick house before us had been gutted by fire so recently, the acrid smell of smoke still hung heavy in the air despite the rain.

· TWENTY-FOUR ·

We entered the brick shell of a house, which was missing much of its second floor. The rain streamed in, creating clouds of steam and smoke. Everything around us — the blackened remains of a couch, a charred desk — was one kick away from crumbling into ash. A metal picture frame lay face-down on the floor by the fireplace. I crouched, brushed away the grime, and lifted an edge, using my shirt to protect my fingers in case the metal was still hot. Under the cracked glass, colors bubbled and swirled. The photograph was so heat damaged, I couldn't even tell if it had been of a person.

Rafe toed through the wreckage as if there was anything left to find. I lifted my face to the cold pinpricks of rain and swallowed the tight feeling in my throat.

All this way. We'd come all this way for nothing.

Rafe drew his gun. All the color had drained from his face. "If this is a coincidence, I'll lick this place clean."

Coincidence? What did it matter? I'd failed my dad. I had nothing to offer Spurling in exchange for his life except broken dishes and clumps of melted plastic.

"Come on, we've got to get out of here." His hair was slick and darkened with rain. His soaked shirt stuck to his lean frame. "This place was torched."

Yeah, I could see that, despite the smoke that burned my eyes and chapped my throat with every breath.

"Lane," Rafe said as if trying to wake me. "Torched *on purpose.*" He pressed something cold into my hand. His knife.

My fingers curled around the handle even though I didn't want to go where his thoughts had carried him. "You said houses in the zone burn down all the time."

"You think this house — and only this house — just happened to catch fire last night? Even my luck doesn't suck that bad."

A cold snap cleared my brain. Chorda had my dad's messenger bag. And that meant he had Spurling's letter. I'd refused to give up my heart, so he had found another way to rip it from me — by making sure that I couldn't save my father.

"I like being the trap setter, not the settee." With a hand on my elbow, Rafe ushered me toward what was left of the doorway. "I guarantee cat-chow's around here somewhere, sharpening his claws."

I should have done it Everson's way back in Moline when he'd offered to help by having his mother use her clout. Why had I thought coming to Chicago was the better choice?

We stepped into the drizzle and Rafe pressed a finger to his lips. Something about his posture set my senses on high alert. He slowly withdrew his gun, motioning for me to stay put.

What did you hear? I wanted to ask. *Chorda?* I clenched my jaw shut as he moved into the street. Then I too heard the noise that had made him skittish — maniacal laughter. Somewhere close by people were trading *hee-hee-hee*s as if demented giggling were a language.

Rafe hauled me back into the gutted house. "Hyboars," he hissed.

Hyena-boars. My dad had woven them into stories and Cosmo had relayed facts. He'd told us that the handlers used hyboars to hunt down runaway manimals.

I followed Rafe through the burnt shell to the kitchen, where a section of the back wall had collapsed. We clambered through the hole and dashed across the overgrown yard. More braying laughter stopped us midsprint. A bristling creature scrabbled over a pile of debris that had once been a garage. The beast paused at the top to shift its powerful, sloping shoulders like a boxer priming for a fight.

I wheeled around to see more hyboars stampeding through the shadowy interior of the house. Panic bloomed in my stomach. Muscular and razor tusked, the cackling beasts leapt out the gap we'd just climbed through. I pressed into Rafe and felt him draw a shuddering breath. He followed them with the tip of his gun but there were too many.

Longhaired men stormed into the yard. They wore leather butcher aprons — just as Cosmo had described. Handlers. Other giveaways: the hunting rifles clutched in their meaty hands and the knob-topped batons and dog whips tucked into their apron pockets. They surrounded us, grabbed our weapons, and frisked us roughly without a word. When they turned back to the house, I went as still as a cornered animal.

A gruesome man stepped through the gap in the wall. Going by his face and scalp, I could tell he'd had a close encounter with some serious claws and teeth. A chunk of his nose was missing, along with one eye, a fact that he didn't hide under an eye patch — the sunken cavity and badly sewn eyelid were on full display. He strode toward us. Instead of an apron, he wore a leather coat with a fur collar. "Drop," he ordered. "Face down, hands behind your back."

"Fun as that sounds," Rafe replied evenly, "we're here on a job and we need to get going."

The man's brow lowered over his empty eye socket, and he made a sharp gesture.

The hyboars sprang. I screeched, flinging myself backward into Rafe. The beasts stopped just short of us and hunkered low, chuckling like maniacs. If I could've, I would've crawled down Rafe's shirt to hide.

"It's your choice. . . ." The one-eyed man bared his yellow teeth in some evil version of a smile. "Get down or the hyboars will take you down."

With a sigh, Rafe planted himself face-first on the wet ground. I remained frozen in place, mesmerized by a drop of drool suspended from a hyboar tusk.

"It's okay, Lane," Rafe said, his voice uncharacteristically gentle. "Come lie next to me."

Some fetch I was. I stretched out beside him, my cheek pressed into the soggy weeds, my eyes searching his desperately. His blue-green gaze was steady as always, and it reminded me that we might be on the ground surrounded by hyena-boars and crazy people, but that didn't mean we had given up. "Don't mention the silky," he whispered.

A handler straddled me and yanked my arms behind my back. I gasped as he tied my wrists together. Another handler bound Rafe's wrists, and then we were hauled to our feet. Rafe glanced at the handler gripping his arm. "Nice apron. You guys do a lot of baking?"

"No, manimal training," the handler snapped. "And none of us is looking to get bitten in the groin."

As Rafe grimaced at that image, the handlers wheeled us around to face the one-eyed man.

"I am Omar," the man said casually, "the king's overseer."

Omar — the man who had put Cosmo in the zoo for licking a spoon.

"You are in violation of the laws of Chicago Compound, which apply to the whole of the city and the surrounding areas. Trespassing," Omar ticked off, "possession of unauthorized weapons, and failure to display proof of your health. Therefore, your freedom is forfeit."

"By forfeit, do you mean —" Rafe's words cut off with a grunt as a handler's baton slammed into his ribs.

"The only time you'll speak is to answer my questions," Omar said. "Now, did you come here alone or with others?"

"It's just the two of us," I said. As hard as it was to look at his ravaged face, I didn't take my eyes from him. "We're here tracking a rogue feral. One that's killed a lot of people."

Omar's gaze sharpened on me. "*You* are a hunter?"

"If that's what a compound needs." I was certainly as dirty and bedraggled as the hunters and hacks I'd seen in Moline. I shrugged like I didn't care what he called me. "We lead scavenging trips too. Feed us, and we'll do practically anything."

"And you're certain it's just the two of you?" Omar asked again.

"I don't hunt in a pack." Rafe shot a scornful look at the gaggle of handlers surrounding Omar.

"Maybe not yet . . ." Omar smiled. "But we're good at getting beasts to obey."

I felt Rafe stiffen beside me. "Who are you calling a —" This time the handler slammed the baton into his gut.

"Stop talking," I hissed under my breath. How were we going to escape if he was a battered mess?

Omar jerked his chin and a handler gripped my arm and propelled me forward. Rafe's handler used the knobby end of his baton to get Rafe moving. What did they want with us?

"Keep going," my handler ordered as he directed me around the house. He was younger than the others. With his blond hair tied back, he didn't look nearly as cruel as the rest, even if his grip was cutting off my arm's circulation. He ushered me onto the weedy street where four rickshaws stood waiting, each pulled by a manimal of considerable size: three bull-men and one guy who might have been part rhino, going by his leathery skin and the fact that a sharp-tipped horn had sprouted along the bridge of his nose.

A hyboar thrashed on the ground behind the last rickshaw. A chain ran from the metal-link collar around the creature's neck to the wheel bar under the passenger bench. The handler who'd been prodding Rafe along snatched the dog whip from his apron pocket and lashed the animal. "Get up!"

As the creature slowly rose on its hind legs, my perceptions reeled and reconfigured. I wasn't looking at an animal, but a barrel-chested *man*. A man infected with hyena. Long, coarse fur covered every inch of his body. In fact — I looked away quickly, cheeks hot. The man was so hairy I hadn't realized that he was naked. He remained in a crouch, poised to spring at the handler who'd struck him. His claws and elongated jaws glistened with drool.

The handler grinned and lifted the whip in warning. "You want more?"

The feral launched himself at the handler with a snarl, only to be brought up short by the chain. I glimpsed his awful face, so inhuman and insane, I felt my own sanity slipping. Clawing at air, the slavering thing screeched at us. I stumbled back. There was no hint of the man this feral had once been. No humanity that I could see left in him at all. He had become an *it*. My whole being flinched at the idea and my control began to splinter. Suddenly I understood Rafe so much better. The callous distance he put between himself and manimals, his choice to live alone in a prison rather than in Moline — he was terrified of becoming a creature like this.

The blond handler gave Rafe a prod with his baton, leaving the other man to deal with the feral.

I needed to shut out the hyena-man's screams and focus on escape. But I still didn't understand how the handlers had known we were here. "What were you doing at the house back there?" I asked.

The handler shot me a suspicious look. I must have appeared harmless enough, though, because after a moment he shrugged. "The guys on watch reported the blaze last night, so we swung by to see what burned down."

A horned bull-man, brawny and impassive, set down the long poles attached to the rickshaw and knelt by my side. A heavy leather chest plate and harness encased his upper body and a collar encircled his thick neck.

"Get on up," the handler directed.

I looked back at him. With my hands tied, exactly how was I supposed to climb up to the padded bench? "I can't step up that high."

"There's your stool." He pointed to the bull-man's thigh. "Irving doesn't mind. Do you, Irv?"

The bull-man grunted in answer. Still, I hesitated. My boots were heavy and lug soled. Plus, I didn't exactly weigh nothing. Before the handler could bark at me, Rafe put a booted foot onto the bull-man's thigh and hefted himself up to the rickshaw's padded bench. The bull-man didn't so much as flinch. I shot Rafe an annoyed look. "Thanks for the demonstration."

Omar sat alone in the first rickshaw. When we were all in — me squeezed between Rafe and the blond handler on the bench — the bull-man lifted the poles from the mud. He then pulled our rickshaw along behind Omar's. The other two rickshaws, which were loaded up with handlers, fell into line behind us. The hideous, tusked hyboars loped alongside of us and kept me from even thinking about jumping out.

Our odd procession rolled through the dead city along a street that was bounded with piled cars. I kept my eyes on the buildings and side roads, noting every sign and distinct feature the way I had learned in orienteering. Most likely Rafe and I were going to have to find our way back to the jeep in the dark. Hopefully, Everson and Cosmo were there now, awaiting Cosmo's mother. If Rafe and I didn't make it back by midnight, they were supposed to leave without us. I wondered if Everson would stick to the plan. I hoped so. If they tried to rescue us from the compound, they'd just get "arrested" too. I glanced at Rafe, who'd settled into a corner of the padded bench as if he hadn't a care in the world. He caught my look. "Sweet ride."

"How is this sweet?" I demanded, not caring that the handler was listening. "There is a man in a harness breaking his back to pull us around." The manimal might be massive, but our combined weight had him huffing like a steam engine.

"You sure know how to suck the fun out of life," Rafe grouched.

As we traveled east, rain pattered on the roof of the rickshaw, and another sound rose on the air, a low, resonant moan that sent a cold wind over my skin. The sound grew louder as we turned south and rode along an iron fence, the area beyond it obscured by trees and brush. I caught flashes of stone buildings, clawed hands gripping iron bars.

"The zoo?" I asked the handler, who nodded.

"They do that every time we take a feral out of there," he said, sounding annoyed.

The lament intensified, turning ferocious. The infected people in their cages were keening. The hair on my arms stood on end. Rafe shifted uncomfortably next to me. There was something powerful and dangerous to the noise and it seeped into me like a threat.

The sound faded as we rolled farther south. The buildings sprouted to fifty stories and more and blocked out the light of the sky. The bull-man struggled to heave the rickshaw across the metal mesh surface of a bridge, overgrown with vines. I felt terrible for him, but my hands were literally tied and the stitches in my calf had reached an epic level of throb, which would make walking torturous. There was nothing I could do but stay put as the feeling of helplessness burned a hole in my gut.

On the other side of the river gleamed the razor-wire fence that encircled the Chicago compound. So much of this scene reminded me of Arsenal Island — the gate at the end of the bridge and guards standing by. Only instead of gray camouflage, these men wore leather aprons. The rain had stopped. In a way, I missed it. I liked having the sky cry, since I wouldn't let myself. My trip into the Feral Zone had yielded nothing but ash — a total failure by anyone's definition. Standing in Director Spurling's burned-out living room, I'd thought I'd hit bottom. Silly me.

I estimated we'd gone over three miles when we stopped at the perimeter of yet another fence, this one a tall briar hedge, thorns and all — trained to grow around coils of barbed wire. Beyond the brambles of metal and wood stood a pale limestone building that took up the entire city block. A section of the briar hedge swung in, and the rickshaw rolled through. We halted in the middle of a lush garden. An enormous caged enclosure took up one corner of the grounds. I jumped down from the rickshaw, gasping as pain ripped up my calf. I desperately hoped I hadn't torn open the stitches. I leaned against a life-sized bronze bull to steady myself and then noticed that, despite being green with age, the statue was uncomfortably similar in looks to Irving, the manimal standing beside it.

Rafe landed next to me and eyed the caged area. "This just keeps getting better," he muttered.

The building before us — the castle — could have been an armed fort. Handlers with guns stood on either side of the front door. Others ran to unhitch the feral who'd been trailing behind us. The hunched, shaggy man slowly pulled himself to full height with bared fangs like stalactites in his gaping mouth. "Get him primed," Omar ordered.

One of the handlers extended his baton and beat the hyena-man until he fell to his knees. I reminded myself that I was supposed to be a hunter — someone who saw ferals as a payday, nothing more. I grit my teeth as the handler forced the feral to crawl across the yard to a dog run, where a metal collar dangled from a high wire. It took three handlers to get the collar snapped around the feral's neck.

"What does that mean?" I asked our handler. "Get him primed?"

"They beat him to get him worked up," he replied. "Not enough to do real damage. We want a good fight."

"Someone is going to fight the feral?" I asked, trying to sound casual.

"Best way to know if a new handler is ready for the job."

Now that the feral was collared and chained, he couldn't escape their blows, and yet the handlers beat him until he was bellowing with rage and swiping his clawed hands at them. I couldn't look on any longer. I spun away to find Omar watching me.

A smirk spread over his wrecked face. "A hunter, are you?" He shifted his gaze onto our handler. "Keep them in the yard while I inform the queen of our visitors." He swept up the stairs and disappeared through the mammoth front door of the castle. Nearby, the handlers continued to hit the feral with their batons, making him roar. I stalked away. "Hey," the young handler called.

"Do you think I can climb a fence with my hands tied?" I snapped over my shoulder. That must have satisfied him because he stayed put as I headed over to the caged area.

Rafe caught up with me. "Getting a little feral yourself, aren't you?"

Now that I'd seen a real feral up close, I didn't ever want to joke about it. I ignored him and studied the enclosure. Not surprisingly, it was furnished for human occupants. A table and upholstered chairs had been dragged into a sunny patch while tents took up two corners of the caged area. Not weatherproof tarps like what I'd learned to set up in my survival skills class. These could have housed an Arabian prince.

A movement behind the crosshatched steel wire caught my eye. I angled closer and spotted a woman off to one side, sitting on her haunches on a pile of furs. She was a tawny creature — skin the color of burnt caramel glinting under a light dusting of gold fur. Her dark hair streamed down her back in wild waves. Infected with lion maybe? As I approached the enclosure, she stood — faster than any normal human could have moved — and I skittered back. She tilted her head, studying me with golden eyes.

"Um, hi," I said. Her brows quirked as if I amused her. "Can you understand me?"

"Of course." The corners of her split upper lip lifted. "English is my first language. But if you prefer to converse in French or German, I'm fluent in those as well."

"I-I'm sorry," I stammered. "I thought — Never mind."

"You're not feral." Rafe pressed closer, voicing what I had avoided saying.

"No, but the day we get loose" — she eyed the handlers with simmering rage — "feral won't even begin to describe us."

"We?" I asked, and as if on cue three more curvaceous forms slipped out of the shadows. At one point their gowns had been elegant but now the skirts hung in frayed strips.

"I am Mahari," the first lion-woman said and then cast a hand at the others. "Charmaine, Deepnita, and Neve."

They sauntered forward, elongated fangs protruding from their feline lips. The lion DNA had added muscle to their frames and a catlike grace to their movements, making them breathtakingly beautiful and utterly terrifying.

I cut a look at Rafe but his attention was wholly focused on Mahari's ample curves. Heat flashed through me. Because he was ogling her? Like I cared!

"And you are . . . ?" Mahari prompted.

"Lane and Rafe." My voice came out higher than usual.

"She would make a nice addition," Deepnita said, directing her amber gaze at me. With her dark, spiked hair and leonine features, she had a tough glamour to her.

"Think so?" Mahari laughed softly, her tongue lolling toward the back of her mouth. She leaned into the steel wire, her nostrils flaring as she took in my scent. "She seems more rabbit to me."

"What? No," I sputtered. Maybe when I'd first arrived in the Feral Zone. But not now.

Rafe guffawed and I glared him down to a smirk. Maybe I wasn't a lion, but rabbit? Not even a little.

"Handlers," hissed Charmaine, before retreating into the far corner. She crouched in the shadows with her wild curls curtaining her face. Only her luminous eyes and low, steady growl gave her away.

Two handlers approached the enclosure, dragging a fire hose. "Bath time, girls," one announced with a leer. He turned the nozzle and aimed the jet of water through the fencing so that it slammed Mahari across the cage.

Rafe and I scrambled back as the handler chortled and turned the hose on the other lion-women. Deepnita roared like an enraged jungle cat as the spray knocked them to the floor. Neve rolled onto her stomach and struggled to rise in her soaked gown, but the handlers pinned her to the concrete with the blasting water and laughed themselves sick.

I ground my teeth to keep from shrieking at the sadists. No matter how dangerous these lion-women were, in that moment I would have thrown open the cage door if I had the key.

Rafe stepped between me and the wire wall of their enclosure. "We can't help them."

Help them? I wanted to see them tear these men apart. "My hands are tied. I can't do anything."

"Yeah, but you're thinking it."

True. I knew now not to set free a trapped feral — or a murderous tiger-man. But these women were sane. They might have years left before turning feral. They shouldn't have to spend those years in a cage.

Rafe watched my face as if he could see the thoughts tumbling in my brain. "Figure out how to get us free and then worry about Cosmo and your silky."

He was right. I'd already failed my dad. I couldn't let them down too. My gaze fell on Neve, the youngest of the lionesses, wet and panting. My resolve faltered. Wasn't there a way to do both? Escape and help these women?

Handlers surrounded us. When one raised his knife, I panicked. But he simply used it to cut the ties that bound our wrists. "Queen Sindee demands your presence in the throne room," he announced.

Did he have any idea how absurd that sounded? Probably not, since he was too young to know what life was like before the country had divided.

The circle of handlers moved, and we had to move with them or be trampled.

We were marched through the brass doors and into the entry hall, which was three stories tall and dominated by an immense staircase. Despite the fact that I was a hostage, the castle's white marble interior took my breath away. I hardly noticed the handlers who stood at attention on the landing as we climbed the stairs. We were ushered through an archway and into a room topped with a dome made of iridescent glass. A mosaic. "What was this place?" I asked in an awed whisper.

"The Chicago Cultural Center," said a sultry voice from behind us.

We turned to face a woman tottering on impossibly high heels, swinging an ivory-headed cane. Her black hair had been teased into a stack — No, wait. . . . That wasn't hair; it was a fur turban, which really wasn't any stranger than her frayed evening gown and floor-length cape of blue leather. But even in odd clothes, she was very beautiful.

"So, you're hunters," she drawled, but within a heartbeat, her lowered lip plumped with displeasure. "Omar, they're not kneeling. Why aren't they kneeling, Omar?"

We stared at her, dumbfounded.

"Well, Queen Sindee," Omar said with feigned patience, "perhaps they don't realize —"

"I don't care what they realize. I won't be insulted in my own castle. Not by anyone." She jabbed her cane at us. "Feed them to the hyboars."

· TWENTY-FIVE ·

Rafe and I dropped in unison, wincing as our knees hit the hard marble. The queen sniffed. "Better." With a flip of her blue cape, she faced Omar. "I want them for the court."

It was like we'd dropped down Alice's rabbit hole. How were we going to get out of this place?

"We don't even know if they're healthy," Omar ground out.

She gave an impatient wave. "Then test them."

With deliberate slowness, Omar took a silver cigarette case from the inside pocket of his coat. He snapped open the case and extracted two plastic sticks. He then beckoned two handlers forward and handed each a white stick. "Open wide," he told us.

"Why?" Rafe looked as if he might throw a punch.

"It's a Ferae test," I told him. "He's going to rub it under your tongue."

The plastic stick was coated with a chemical biosensor. It wasn't nearly as accurate as a blood test, but a trace of the virus in saliva would turn the stick bloodred.

Reluctantly Rafe opened his mouth and allowed the handler to rub the stick under his tongue. I was more cooperative, and within a minute both of our sticks had brightened to electric blue — meaning we were virus-free.

I inhaled deeply. A saliva test wasn't infallible, but all the same, I felt lighter. I still couldn't believe that I'd escaped Chorda unscathed.

When the handlers held up our blue sticks, Omar turned smug. "Good thing we didn't let the hyboars have them, hm?"

The queen shot him an evil look as she fingered the blue stick that hung on a chain around her neck. I saw that Omar and the handlers wore their Ferae tests as well — like dog tags. The blond handler gave us each a thin cord to thread through the ends of our sticks. "Keep your health status on display at all times," he told us. "By the king's order."

Rafe snorted softly but he tied off the cord and dropped it over his head. "Can we get up now?"

The handler looked to Omar, who glanced at the queen, who waved us to our feet.

"You took the last interloper," she said to Omar. "These two are mine."

"How about a compromise? You take the girl." Omar eyed Rafe. "He has potential."

"You have enough handlers, and I am bored with every-one in court. They are all boooring." She stretched the word until it snapped. "Anyway, look at them." She jabbed a bejeweled finger at us. "They're a couple." She turned to us for confirmation. "Isn't that right?"

I gave a quick nod, slipped my hand into Rafe's, and felt his pounding pulse between his fingers. He was a good actor. Here, I'd been thinking that he was actually calm.

"They'll uncouple easily enough," Omar said dryly.

"You're wrong." Rafe met the man's one-eyed gaze head-on.

My heart slowed. What was he doing?

Omar snorted. "You'll forget her in a week."

"Not a chance. I've loved her since I was ten, long before we even met."

The queen angled closer. "You can't love someone you don't know."

"I did know her." All of his facile charm fell away, leaving Rafe sounding raw. "Through stories. Her dad likes to brag because he's so proud of her."

My vision blurred as my longing for my dad throbbed to life once more.

"I hung on every word," Rafe continued, without so much as a glance at me. "Because if there really was a little girl who went out every day, looking for stray animals to save, I figured that someday she would find me. And she did."

I nearly dropped his hand I was so shocked. Luckily, he tightened his hold on mine. "So if you try to take her from me," Rafe went on lightly, though his eyes had a dangerous gleam, "I will stick a steel knife in your happily-ever-after and gouge out its guts."

A stunned silence fell over the group.

"Well," said the queen, breaking the tension, "you're certainly not boring." She turned to Omar. "Don't even think about hauling him off to the zoo to live with handlers."

"Of course not," Omar said acidly. "That would leave the girl unattached. And why risk adding a single female to the court? Especially one so young. She might catch the king's eye. . . ."

A guttural noise burst from the queen's throat and her hands clenched as if they were around his neck. Omar pretended not to notice. "If you'll excuse me, I have an initiation test to oversee." He strode away with his handlers in tow. On their way out of the throne room, they passed a collared manimal pulling a drag sled piled with art and furniture.

The manimal, who had scaly green-gray skin, halted under the dome and bowed low. The queen lurched forward to pluck a painting off the top of the pile. "Hideous!" She struck the cringing manimal with the painting before flinging it across the floor. "Any *human* can see that's not art."

I bit my lip as the Jackson Pollock skidded to a stop against the far wall. My father would be having a heart attack about now.

"I'll take care of it, my queen." A servant appeared in the archway, wearing a spotless white suit and leather collar. When he bent low, his ears, which stuck out from the sides of his head, flopped forward. He picked up the painting with much more care than the queen had shown. His ginger hair failed to disguise the two thick horns that curled from the sides of his head.

"Burn it, Dromo," she ordered in a scratchy voice as if she were holding back a sob. "We don't need any more trash cluttering up the place."

"Of course." He beckoned the scaly servant to him and whispered quick instructions as he handed over the painting, meticulously touching only the frame.

I had a feeling that he hadn't told the servant to burn the Pollock. He might be part ram, but I'd be willing to bet he knew something about art.

Queen Sindee tore off the fur turban to reveal coiled auburn hair. She collapsed onto a chaise and pressed her fingers to her temples. "He wouldn't dare talk to me like that if the king was here."

Dromo clattered across the marble floor on hoofed feet and lowered himself to one knee beside her. "Omar is an old, ugly man inside and out. His handlers hate him."

She perked up at that. "Do they really?"

"I hate him," Rafe piped in.

Dromo took our inventory with one head-to-toe glance.

"They're joining the court," the queen told him. "They're all human."

From the slight curl of his lip, I guessed that it required more than a blue test stick to impress Dromo. "My queen," he said, "as impeccably human as they may be, they're filthy."

I resisted the urge to shove my filthy hands into my filthier pockets.

"So make them presentable," she said wearily and fell back on the chaise with an arm flung over her eyes.

"Of course." There was the barest lift to Dromo's brows. "Should I assign them rooms?"

"One room," she corrected without raising her arm.

The ram-man got to his feet and waved us toward the archway. I stole once last glance at the miserable queen. Just as I felt a stab of pity for her, she bolted upright. "Dromo," she called, her voice suddenly harsh.

The ram-man turned back. "Yes, my queen?"

"Not *too* presentable," she said, directing a red-tipped nail at me.

The room that Dromo assigned us was as beautiful as the rest of the building. The recessed panels in the ceiling were decorated with gilded suns, as was the huge four-poster canopy bed. As lovely as the room was, something terrible had happened in here. Dried blood splatter-painted the far wall, highlighting the bullet holes. I wondered just how long ago those bullet holes had been made. During the exodus or more recently?

"I'll be back in a minute with clothes for you," Dromo said. "Don't touch anything. In fact, don't move."

The moment the ram-man left the room, I heard a ferocious bellow down in the yard. I drew back the curtain and saw the feral stalking as far as his chain would allow. He threw his head back and howled. I recoiled at the sound and half expected him to pound his chest with his fists. At least the handlers had quit torturing him.

Right now, people in the West were having civilized conversations. They were ordering dinner and sending in their homework. No one was worrying about how to escape a king who kept severed manimal heads on spikes.

Rafe opened the bedroom door once he thought Dromo was out of earshot. Two handlers stood in the hall outside our room. "Where do you think you're going?" one demanded.

"We wanted to look around the castle," Rafe said. "Check out the —"

The handler jerked the door shut.

"How are we going to get out of here?" I whispered.

"I'm working on it," Rafe replied and flopped onto the bed.

I didn't want to make myself presentable, but when Dromo came back with a tux for Rafe, he laid out my options. "Either you bathe yourself or the queen will order the handlers to help you." Having seen how the handlers had "helped" the lion-women get clean, I slipped into the old-fashioned bathroom without another word.

I was surprised that the light switch worked. How had they kept the electricity on? I left the filthy brown uniform in a pile on the floor and turned on the shower full blast. The water shot out rusty orange. While I waited for it to run clear, I unwrapped the bandage on my calf. The three long wounds were crusted with blood and the skin enflamed but not infected, and Everson's stitches were intact. I eased my sore body under the spray, saving my calf for last. When I dug my fingers into my dirt-matted hair, a blade of pain stabbed my forehead where Chorda had punched me. I stopped all movement until it had ebbed to a manageable level, and then turned the water hotter.

How were we going to get out of this compound? And what was the point anyway? I'd failed Director Spurling, and now she'd execute my dad if he ever set foot in the West. So maybe Dad and I would stay in the East. Live in Moline. I'd sign up for work duty and live in terror of Chorda for the rest of my life. . . .

My skin was an angry red and steam had filled the bathroom but I continued to scrub my body, then rinse, then scrub some more, hard enough to make the scratches on my arms bleed. Too bad I couldn't peel off my flesh and sponge down to the bone. Maybe then I'd feel clean of Chorda's touch. I jumped back when the water turned icy. At least I'd rinsed off first.

After wrapping my hair in a towel, I eyed my lump of muddy, sweat-soaked clothes and couldn't even bring myself to pick them up. I put on the white robe that hung on the back of the door and stepped into the bedroom.

At Rafe's startled look, I realized just how short the robe was. Worse, the silk was clinging to my wet skin. I braced myself for the lewd remark that was sure to come.

"Oh, come on," he said, sounding dismayed, not lecherous. "Do not make my life this hard."

"What?"

He shot me an exasperated look. "You're Mack's daughter. You don't get to have a body."

For the first time since coming to Chicago, I felt a smile pulling at the corners of my mouth. "I don't?"

"No, you're a head. A floating head. And sometimes not even that. Unless you want me to be the jerk who's just after one thing."

"I can be a floating head," I said quickly. "But . . . you are the jerk who offered to take me to Moline if I shared your sleeping bag."

"That doesn't count," he sputtered. "I didn't know who you were. I —" He paused brow crinkling. "Hey, listen, could you maybe not mention that to Mack?"

I nodded. "So, what you said to Omar and the queen . . ." I wanted to ask how much of it had been true, but suddenly I felt exposed. And it had nothing to do with the skimpy robe.

"I didn't want them to split us up." He eyed me. "You know that was a lie, right? I'm not really in love with you."

"Of course," I said quickly.

"Good. 'Cause I'm not."

"I know."

"Glad we got that straight."

I'd known better than to believe that he was in love with me, but I did want to know about the rest of it. Had he actually thought of himself as a stray animal? And had he really hoped that I'd come find him?

"Dromo left this for you," he said gruffly, and scooped up a teal dress adorned with feathers from the bed. He tossed it to me and headed into the bathroom without another word.

I left my questions unasked. What would I do anyway if he said the rest was true? Hold him close and tell him that I would've come sooner if I'd known he was real? Oh, he'd just love that. Part of me did want to though — hold him close. And not just because he was the wild boy, my favorite character come to life, but for who he was now, and for the parts of him he tried to keep hidden. I held up the blue-green garment — a satin evening gown that was even skimpier than the robe. The material was a little moth-eaten in places, but it still gleamed. How was I supposed to make an escape in this?

Ten minutes later there was a soft knock on the door, and a girl with the flattened face of a Pekingese came into the room, her eyes lowered. Her white maid's cap sat over one ear and, as with Dromo, a thick leather collar encircled her neck. "I'm Penny and I'm here to — Oh, you're already dressed," she said, looking anxious. "Well, the fit is beautiful. Dromo always gets it right on the first try."

I smoothed down the bodice, which was embroidered with two peacocks whose tails cascaded over the flowing skirt in a shimmering mix of feathers and satin. "I didn't need help with the dress, but I do need a bandage."

Penny yipped when I showed her my lacerated calf. She darted from the room and then returned with everything she needed to disinfect my leg and wrap it up tight. After that, I settled on a leather ottoman while Penny pinned up my hair. I even let her dab lipstick on me.

"Is there a mirror somewhere?" I asked and then felt a pluck of guilt. I had two days to get back to the Titan wall before the line patrol blocked off the tunnel, and here I was curious to see myself all dressed up.

Fear sprang into Penny's smooshed face. She gave the barest shake of her head and hurried from the room on bowed legs.

O-kay. Were they extra superstitious here in the Chicago Compound?

Dromo entered without knocking just as Rafe stepped out of the bathroom. I'd seen my father in a tuxedo many times and had always marveled at how it magically transformed him into someone glamorous. Putting a tux on Rafe, however, just wasn't fair. With that face, that lean form, he was already the prettiest person in any given room. Did he really need a boost up to jaw-dropping?

He looked from me to Dromo, trying to gauge our expressions. "Go ahead, laugh. I know I look stupid."

Dromo lifted a brow. "You're not serious?"

"You look okay," I told him.

Dromo turned to me. "*You're* not serious?"

"What?" I asked, feigning ignorance. "It's nice to see him with combed hair for a change." Though his hair was still unruly, waving past his ears and along the nape of his neck.

Rafe scowled. "Forget it. I'm not going anywhere like this." He started to shrug off his jacket.

"No!" Dromo and I cried in unison.

"You look gorgeous, okay?" I added.

He broke into a slow grin. "Gorgeous?"

I directed a finger at him. "Don't be obnoxious about it. Is there a mirror anywhere in this castle?" I asked Dromo. After one glance at his reflection, Rafe's already healthy ego would probably grow as big as the Titan wall, but at least he'd keep the tux on.

"Mirrors aren't allowed in the castle," Dromo said flatly. "By the king's order."

"He's that ugly?" Rafe asked.

"No one's warned you about the king's appearance?" Dromo asked in a low voice.

That sounded ominous. We shook our heads.

He smoothed the sleeves of his white dinner jacket without meeting our eyes. "You've met Omar?"

"Is the king as messed up as Captain Half Nose?" Rafe asked, coming to stand beside me.

"They were outside the compound hunting when a feral attacked the king," Dromo said, speaking fast and low. "Omar saved the king's life, though both returned to the castle badly wounded. They don't hide their scars from that terrible day, but no one in Chicago ever dares to stare or bring up their deformities in any way."

"Of course not," I assured him . . . and then remembered that I was traveling with the rudest person alive. "We won't stare or comment on the king's appearance." I said it precisely, so that maybe it would stick in Rafe's brain. The grin he gave me wasn't reassuring.

Dromo strode over to Rafe and got within an inch of him, their noses almost touching. Now it was Rafe's turn to stiffen. "Here's a tidbit you might want to keep in mind," Dromo said so quietly that even though I was at Rafe's side, I could barely hear him. "The queen says she has eyes in the back of her head, but really she puts an ear to the door. So be very careful about what you say . . . even in private." He stepped back smoothly, lifting his hands to Rafe's tie as if he'd just straightened it.

"Thank you," I said, drawing his gaze to me.

He frowned as he looked me over and then clucked his tongue. "What was Penny thinking?"

I touched my hair, which Penny had pinned up in a loose knot. "She didn't do a good job?"

"She did too good a job." He began pulling pieces of my hair free of the pins. "She's going to end up in the zoo if she isn't careful."

"Hey, let me —"

Dromo pulled a handkerchief from the pocket of his suit coat and dragged it across my mouth, smearing rosy lipstick over the white cotton. "If the queen asks, say you declined Penny's help. That way she can't be blamed if the queen thinks you've upstaged her."

I pulled free of his hold and touched my now-raw lips. "I don't want to upstage her." I wasn't even sure what that meant, but it didn't sound good.

"No," he agreed. "You don't."

· TWENTY-SIX ·

Dromo led us up the stairs and to the roof. At the top, Rafe and I opened the door and stepped out into a lush garden just as the sun dropped past the horizon. We saw Omar smoking a cigar as handlers armed with rifles took up positions along the edge of the roof at various strategic points. The center area was crowded with freestanding cages, which held the oddest creatures that I'd ever seen — a snakelike dog, a bat-faced rabbit. . . . Chicken bones and dry pet food lay scattered across the cement floors of the enclosures. At least I hoped they were chicken bones. I wanted to run to each cage and see what was inside. Judging by his wrinkled nose, Rafe didn't share my curiosity.

"This is so wrong." He flung a hand at the nearest creature. "That mongrel has got at least five animals mixed in to it."

I peered inside the tall cage and saw what he meant. The long-necked creature had ermine fur and a body like a mini kangaroo. "They look like they belong in a dream." I turned in a slow circle, looking into all the cages.

"So you like my menagerie?" the queen asked. She stepped out from behind a blooming shrub, dressed in a semitransparent gown of yellowing lace with a white fur cape draped over one shoulder. Her auburn hair had been put up with dried bird claws. "They are fun, aren't they? I was in charge of infecting and breeding them even before I was queen. It's how I caught the king's eye. I impressed him with what I whipped up. Creatures with the softest fur, and leather in colors you wouldn't believe."

I murmured my amazement, while remembering the fate of the ugly offspring. On the jeep ride here, Cosmo had told us that the so-called failures were taken to the zoo and fed to the feral humans who were imprisoned there.

"You look pretty," the queen said to me while fingering her electric blue Ferae test. "Very pretty . . ."

Out of her mouth, it didn't sound like a compliment. It sounded ominous. "Um, thanks."

"You two are going to fit in just fine." She smiled at Rafe, but that smile tightened as her eyes moved back to me. If she'd only let us go, then she wouldn't have to worry about the king noticing me.

She bent toward the cage beside her. Inside sat a dejected little hedgehog-monkey thing. The queen waved a celery stalk in front of the bars, and the small creature reached out a hand to take it, but the queen jerked the celery back, out of the mongrel's reach, and laughed. "It's getting weaker and weaker," she said. "It hasn't eaten in days. It's an ugly one all right."

I had to turn away, or my hands would have found their way around her throat. But her attention span was short — big surprise — and soon she dropped the celery and headed for the edge of the roof. "Let's see who has arrived."

When her back was turned, I bent to get the celery, but Rafe had had the same idea. Our fingers touched and his closed on the stalk and he tossed it into the little mongrel's cage. Without a word about it, he strode toward the queen, while I stared after him in shock.

From the edge of the roof, we could not only see the guests arriving in their manimal-drawn rickshaws, we could also see the feral, still chained in the yard below. Eyes closed, he swung his head back and forth as if he was trying to shake loose a crick in his neck. Once the people climbed out of their rickshaws, they stopped to point and gape at him on their way into the castle. One man threw a rock at him, and the feral's eyes snapped open. He lunged for the man, but the chain pulled him up short. The group below broke into peals of laughter.

"Almost makes me ashamed to be human," Rafe muttered.

I glanced at him. "Almost?"

The queen waved to the stream of people arriving below. "Hurry up to the roof," she called down and then sighed, leaning against the low wall. "Can you believe it? That's just about everyone. All the humans left living inside the compound. Less than two hundred."

"Were there more at one time?" I asked.

"Yes, but they either took off or got infected at some point. Oh, and a lot died trying to overthrow my husband a few years back. Idiots. They just couldn't admit that we're safer now than we've ever been."

"Safer from what?" I asked.

She made a face as if I were too dumb to live. "Ferals. And then there's the servants. Given half a chance, they'd have us waiting on *them*. The king says we need more humans if we're to keep the manimals in their place. But not many people come to Chicago anymore."

"Where is the king?" Rafe asked.

"Off hunting, but he'll be back soon enough," Omar said as he joined us.

If the king bore even half the scars that Omar did from their encounter with a feral, then I was surprised he'd ever venture outside the compound again. "Were those the king's trophies on the spikes outside the fence?" I asked as if impressed.

"I hate those things," the queen groaned, and then gave a dismissive wave. "But the king says the heads keep the ferals away."

"Might also be why people don't come to Chicago anymore," Rafe said with a straight face.

The guests began trickling onto the roof in such elegant and elaborate clothing, they could have been attending a formal ball. Well, except for the fact that they all wore bright blue Ferae tests around their necks. But as the guests strolled closer, I saw that the fashions were from twenty years ago — pre-exodus — and that everything had a tattered, musty look. The men's tuxedos were faded and their cuffs frayed, while the women's gowns were discolored or disintegrating and some smelled of mildew. There had to be plenty of high-end stores in Chicago to raid, and even more closets inside the mansions, but the delicate materials weren't holding up nearly as well as a wool sweater might.

I let my eyes wander over what was left of Chicago. Towering shapes against the darkening sky, and beyond that, the dark expanse of Lake Michigan. There was something wrong with the view, but at first, I couldn't put a finger on what. . . . Right. There wasn't a single light on in any of the buildings beyond the fence.

Rafe joined me. "Figured out how we're getting out of here yet?" he asked.

I shook my head. "I'm sorry I dragged you into this."

He leaned back against the low wall and folded his arms. "I wouldn't have missed it for the world."

"You're trapped in the Chicago compound," I pointed out.

"Yeah, but I'm with the girl who's going to end the quarantine."

"What?" I stared at him.

He cut me a sly look. "The girl in Mack's stories always does."

"I'm not that girl."

"No," he agreed. "You're better. For one thing, you're real. And two, you fill out that dress better than a ten-year-old could."

I rolled my eyes.

"Give yourself some credit," he went on, "not a lot of silkies would have made it this far."

"I stopped you from killing Chorda," I reminded him and then felt sick, hearing myself say the name aloud. That demented animal didn't deserve a name. I shook off the memory of his twisted face. Thinking about the past would just shut me down and I couldn't afford to let that happen right now. Not if we were going to escape.

"Hey, come on," Rafe said. "It's your first time in the Feral Zone. Of course you made mistakes."

"Like falling for the wrong boy?" I'd said it to be funny,

since he was always teasing me about Everson, but Rafe grew still.

He returned his gaze to the dark skyline. "No, you didn't. He's a stiff, but he's a good guy. He won't crawl out your window after you fall asleep or come on to your sister."

"I don't have a sister."

"Missing the point."

"He's not you. Got it." I nudged his arm. "You know, for all your talk, you're kind of a good guy yourself."

"Wrong. I'm the guy that stays alive." He faced me, looking as serious as I'd ever seen him. "And the one you leave behind if you get the chance to escape. You understand?"

"What?" I frowned. "No. You got me this far. I'm not going to leave you."

"Yeah, you are," he said firmly. "I'll be all right. I'm always all right. Lane, promise me if you get the chance, you'll go and not look back."

"No!"

The queen strolled over just then, preventing him from saying more. Just as well. There wasn't any more to be said on that topic.

"What are you two talking about all by yourselves?" she asked in a sultry tone.

Rafe didn't miss a beat. "We're wondering what you have in mind for the feral down there."

"Oh, it's just a new handler's initiation test," she said with an airy wave. "To see if he can kill a feral armed with only a baton and knife. Omar is convinced this one is a natural. But he's been wrong before. I don't see how an initiate will be a match for the feral he's picked out. That thing has already maimed two men. Left one completely blind." She smiled suddenly. "Oh, this is going to be fun."

I felt a throb of loathing for her and the other members of the court, happily risking a new handler's life just so they could enjoy the show.

The handlers switched on the huge spotlights along the roof's edge that were aimed at the yard and outer fence, turning the castle into an eerie oasis of light in the dark city. With a howl, the feral covered his eyes and skittered back until he'd reached the end of his chain.

A door opened and the initiate stumbled into the yard as if shoved from behind. He eased back into the shadows along the castle wall as he surveyed the courtyard. Like the other handlers, he wore a long leather apron, but also some sort of burlap padding from his wrists to shoulders. The protective sleeves were so thick, he looked like his arms were in casts, although they seemed flexible enough as he reached for the weapons offered by a handler — a knob-topped baton and a knife. As the handler spoke to him, the initiate nodded and practiced extending the heavy steel baton.

"You know, it's strange, isn't it? Finding three strays outside our compound in one day," the queen mused. "Omar, where did the initiate say he was from?"

"He didn't. He refused to tell us anything, which is why he's down there." Omar's one eye sharpened on us. "He put up quite a fight," Omar went on. "Between that and his fatigues, I'm sure he's military, though I don't recognize the uniform."

After collapsing the baton, the initiate stepped out of the shadows and lifted his face. My heart stopped. In the yard three stories below stood Everson, dark haired, steel eyed, and fiercely defiant as he took in the crowded roof.

"Did not see that coming," Rafe murmured and then glanced at me. "Relax. He was trained to kill ferals."

"Why didn't you tell me he's a soldier?" the queen hissed at Omar. "What if he came to reestablish contact? What if he has orders for the king?"

"If the West wanted to reestablish contact with the quarantine compounds, they wouldn't send just one soldier." Omar's tone was so acid, the surrounding guests backed off as if afraid of getting splattered. "He's a runaway or criminal. Either way, he'll fit in here just fine."

"The king and I decide who fits in here. Not you."

Omar's lips twitched as he unclipped a key from his belt loop, tossed it into the air, and caught it like he was flipping a coin. "I believe Queen Mahari said that once. And Queen Charmaine, she also thought she had a say in things."

Mahari. Charmaine. The lionesses caged in the yard. They were the king's ex-wives! No wonder Queen Sindee was unbalanced and insanely jealous. She had no idea how much longer she would be queen. Or human, for that matter.

Omar tossed up the key again, caught it, and reclipped it to his belt loop with a pat. It had to be the key to the ex-queens' cage. If the current queen hadn't been wearing her Ferae test, I would have sworn that she was on the verge of going feral based on how she was glaring at Omar. I hoped the two of them would rip each other to shreds. I turned my attention back to the yard below.

With the bright lights aimed at him, I knew there was no way Everson could see exactly who was up here — didn't know that I was watching. As he took position where the handler indicated, I was tempted to call down to him. I wanted some sort of connection with him. Wanted him to know — What? What feeling was welling up in me? Fear, yes, of course. And worry. But something else too. Something I didn't have a name for. Then, when the handlers circled the snarling feral, I was suddenly glad that Everson wasn't paying attention to the audience on the roof. He'd need all of his focus to keep from being bitten by the slavering madman.

The feral lunged for the handlers, jaws snapping as he danced at the end of his chain. Two of the handlers backed away fast while the third lifted his gun and fired into the night sky. The sound echoed eerily through the dead city. The handler then unhooked the overhead chain and set the feral free.

· TWENTY-SEVEN ·

The handler who'd released the feral now escaped into the castle. The door closed with an ominous bang. The feral was a huge, hairy figure standing on two legs, with long, sharp claws that reflected the light from above. Instead of leaping on Everson like I'd expected, the feral pulled his chain free of the sagging wire, turned tail — literally — and raced around the building. Was he checking for a break in the fence? From this vantage point I could see that his search would be useless.

Everson headed the other way around the castle. The handlers on the roof followed him with the spotlights. We crossed the roof to watch him stalk along carefully. The crowd jeered and placed bets. Everson made it to the backside of the castle, but the feral wasn't there to greet him . . . or so he thought. At that instant the ivy erupted behind him. With an ear-splitting shriek the feral plunged from his hiding place.

I clapped my hands over my eyes. Suddenly there was silence. "Is he okay?" I hissed, and then dared to lower my fingers.

"Course he is," Rafe whispered. "Guy's no slouch."

The feral had his jaws clamped down on Everson's forearm, but the burlap padding protected his skin. Everson pulled his arm free and staggered back.

"He should have gutted it then," Omar growled. "He had the chance."

The feral bounded after Everson and, with a flying leap, took him down. Spinning and writhing together, they rolled over the grass. Everson cracked the feral in the face with the baton, which bought him enough time to spring to his feet.

Several people on the roof shouted their approval.

"Not bad," Rafe said.

I elbowed him in the ribs. "This isn't a wrestling match."

"It kinda is," he pointed out.

The feral bounced up and crouched, his yellow eyes catching the light. Everson launched forward and shoved the creature back against the wall. He lifted his arm and the feral instinctively clamped down. Again, the burlap padding protected Everson's flesh, but this time instead of pulling away, he wedged his arm in harder. The feral's eyes grew wide as Everson jerked the creature's head forward, only to slam it back into the wall.

Dazed, the feral couldn't get his jaws off Everson's padded forearm. Everson cracked the feral's head again and again against the stone, brutally, until the feral slumped forward unconscious. Everson ripped his arm out of the feral's slack jaws and stepped into the spotlight to look at the roof.

The guests clapped enthusiastically and a couple whistled their approval.

"He hasn't passed yet, Omar," the queen sneered.

Omar leaned over the low wall. "The test isn't over until the feral is dead. Gut it."

Everson threw down his baton. "I'm not killing an unconscious man."

"What man?" the queen asked, looking genuinely perplexed.

"The hairy guy on the ground," Rafe told her. "Human. Well, mostly." The queen shot him an annoyed look. He held up his hands. "You asked."

"Gut the feral," Omar shouted as he pulled a gun from inside his jacket. "Or I will —"

With a snarl, the feral leapt up and charged at Everson with flashing claws and snapping jaws.

Everson dug into his apron pocket, pulled the knife, and met the feral head on, driving the point of the knife into his opponent's gut. The feral roared, his fangs just inches from Everson's throat. Everson threw back his head and plunged the knife in again. The feral's claws caught Everson's face, digging savagely into his flesh. Blood streamed down his cheeks. He thrust with all his strength and buried the knife in the feral's stomach. They remained locked like that: Everson pressing the knife into the feral, the feral digging his claws into Everson's face. With a growl the feral's claws finally retracted and he sank to the ground — dead.

Everson collapsed by the feral's body and covered his face with his hand.

"Now that's more like it," the queen gushed. Clapping and cheers erupted across the roof. "Very entertaining!" she called down to Everson.

Hate for her burst in me like a geyser. Couldn't she see that he was devastated?

Omar holstered his gun. "He will take the test again every night until he guts the feral without hesitation."

The evil man couldn't have come up with a worse fate for Everson. To be forced into killing infected men night after night or get shot himself? We had to escape from this place before we all ended up insane or dead.

Dromo appeared before the queen and bowed low. "My queen —"

"What is it that can't wait?" she snapped.

"The king has returned."

The queen's face became masklike and her cheeks lost their rosy flush. "Oh. That's wonderful," she said in a flat tone.

The woman was clearly scared to death of her husband, and given what I knew now, she should be.

She faced the crowd on the roof. "Everyone, I have good news." The cheers and chatter cut out instantly. "The king has returned to the compound. You should all go to the ball-room on the second floor now. However, dinner will be delayed until the king joins us."

As people shuffled toward the stairwell, the queen snagged Dromo's sleeve. "What kind of mood —" She stopped herself, took a breath, and began again in a calmer tone. "Did he catch anything?"

"He must have. He's in a very good mood," Dromo said in a soothing voice.

The queen seemed to sag with relief. "I'll see if he wants to join us for dinner." She glanced at us. "Though he might be too tired."

I hoped that he was beyond exhausted. I had no desire to ever meet the king of Chicago. As soon as the queen hurried off with Dromo, I turned to one of the handlers. "Can we go down to talk to the new handler? We want to congratulate him."

"Absolutely not," Omar said from behind me. "For the next two months, the only people he will see are other handlers. And of course, the manimals he trains."

"Everson doesn't even know we're here," I whispered to Rafe as we followed the crowd down to the second floor. "There's no way he could have seen us with those floodlights in his eyes. We need to get him a message somehow."

"Cosmo," Rafe said.

"What? We don't even know where he is."

"I mean there's Cosmo." Rafe pointed down the hall.

Sure enough, our little friend was peering out at us from under a side table, his toy monkey clutched to his chest. As the guests headed into the ballroom, Rafe and I hurried over to him. I crouched in my gown. "Are you okay?"

"Yes," he said but then followed my gaze to his stranglehold on Jasper. He loosened his grip. "A-okay."

Rafe hunkered beside me. "What are you doing here?"

"The handlers took Everson."

"Cosmo, it's too dangerous for you here," I said. "If they catch you, they'll put you back in the zoo."

He put Jasper on top of his head as if to block out the image. "I have to get Everson out."

Rafe scoffed. "How?"

"Through the basement, where the servants live," Cosmo whispered. "The stairs by the pens go outside."

"Huh," Rafe said with surprise. "Good plan."

"Did you find your mom?" I asked.

Cosmo shook his head. "She doesn't live in the castle anymore. Nobody knows where she went."

I slid my arm across his shoulders and hugged him close. "I'll bet Dromo knows where she is. We'll ask him."

"Nothing much gets past that guy," Rafe agreed. "Hey, where do the handlers go after an initiation test?"

"The mess hall." Cosmo pointed to the floor. "By the kitchen."

"Then that's where Everson is."

"Cosmo, can you get to him and tell him we're here in the castle?" I asked. Rafe shot me a look but I kept my gaze on the little manimal. "You don't have to go if you don't want to. We won't be mad."

"I'll tell Everson," he said confidently.

"What are you doing?" a voice behind us snapped. We looked up to see the handler who'd been outside our bedroom earlier. "You're supposed to be in the ball-room." Then he noticed Cosmo hunkered under the table. "Get out from there. And where's your collar?" He grabbed a knob-topped baton from his apron pocket. "Next time you want a beat down, beast, just ask."

Rafe sprang up, primed for a fight. "He's with us."

I rose as well and tucked Cosmo behind me.

"What do you mean with you?" the handler sneered. "You think the king is going to let a filthy manimal sit at his table? If he sees your monkey, he'll slice its throat with a carving knife before you've even finished your curtsy."

"We're not taking him into dinner." With a hand behind my back, I waved Cosmo away. "He's going back to our room now."

Cosmo took off running down the hall.

"See? Problem solved." Rafe leveled the handler with a look that dared him to pursue it.

The man scowled. "Get to the ballroom."

Moonlight streamed in from a huge skylight above. Wavery light came from candles placed throughout the enormous room. Bare-chested manimal waiters, wearing collars, kilts, and Rollerblades, made whizzing hairpin turns between the tables. A fox-man stopped short, nipple rings gleaming, and held out a tray of long-stemmed glasses brimming with sparkling wine.

"No thank you," I said while batting Rafe's arm away from the tray. At his cranky look, I whispered, "We're trying to escape, remember? Not get impaired."

"Impaired," he scoffed. "That stuff won't even put me in a good mood."

The queen waved us over to where she was sitting on a raised chair, surrounded by candles. "So . . . have you thought about how you'll spend your time now that you'll be living with us?"

"You mean like on a work crew?" Rafe plopped down on the dais by her feet. The queen looked confused, by his question or his action or both. "You must have work crews.

Someone cleared all those cars off the streets between here and the zoo," he clarified.

"No, that's manimal work." She sized up Rafe from under lowered lashes. "I was thinking that since you're a hunter, you could track down new mongrels for my collection."

"Those things in cages on the roof?" Rafe asked.

"Those are just the small ones. It takes twenty of them to make a coat." She skimmed her fingers down her fur cape. "Wait till you see what I keep in the zoo."

Just as I was starting to feel sick, a small silver face peered in through the French doors that led to the balcony. When Cosmo spotted me, he held up a scrap of paper. I smiled. "Excuse me," I said to the queen. "I need to get some air." Which was absolutely true. Since she paid me no mind, I started for the balcony.

"If you already have a zoo full of mash-ups, what do you need more mongrels for?" I heard Rafe ask.

"I need new blood to infect animals with," she replied lightly. "I don't want to crossbreed the same old mongrels over and over. Where's the fun in that? I want new creatures in new colors with wilder markings."

I turned back so fast I tripped in my heels and had to grab on to a table to keep from falling. If the queen was giving Ferae to animals on purpose — and probably people too — then she kept infected blood on hand. She probably had a whole assortment of strains if she was playing around with new DNA combinations. . . . I bit my bottom lip to keep the hope rising in me from turning into a shout.

I tried to catch Rafe's eye. Did he realize what the queen's little pastime might mean for the whole country?

I hadn't been able to get Spurling's photograph, but if I could help Everson collect more strains of Ferae for Dr. Solis . . . If the doctor could find a cure . . . Everything I'd gone through in the Feral Zone — even being attacked by Chorda — would have been worth it.

Queen Sindee laughed at something Rafe was saying. If he didn't quit being charming, the queen would never take her eyes off him and then we'd never get the chance to find her treasure trove of infected blood and escape.

Escape. Right. With Everson and Cosmo, who was peering at me from the shadows on the balcony. I gave him the tiniest thumbs-up sign as I scooted for the glass doors. I glanced over my shoulder before stepping outside, only to find the queen watching me. I froze as she flung back her fur cape and stood.

"And what about you?" she asked as she strolled toward me.

I stood in the open door, using my skirt to hide Cosmo. "Me?"

She stopped inches from me. "Have you figured out how you're going to fit in here?"

"I, uh —"

A shriek erupted behind me. I turned to see Cosmo going crazy in the doorway, yowling and hitting himself in the head with his fists. I skittered back into the room. Oh no, he was turning feral right before my eyes! But Rafe had said that was impossible.

Omar shouted, "Get back!" as he shoved me aside and pulled his baton from its holster.

"No!" Rafe leapt to his feet.

I tried to block Cosmo from view. "Don't touch him." Whatever fit had gripped him, it seemed to be growing worse. His breath came in gasps and his cries became wails.

Omar turned on Rafe. "Is that thing yours?"

Suddenly Cosmo snarled with all the fury of a silverback and sprang at the queen, screeching as he clawed her. The first handler to reach them couldn't tear Cosmo off of her, he clung to her cape so tightly. Even as she careened around the room, squawking like a demented chicken, Cosmo held on.

It took three handlers plus Omar to finally throw Cosmo to the floor with the queen's cape still clutched in his hands. They surrounded him, hitting him with their batons.

"Stop it!" I caught one handler's upraised arm, hauled him off-balance, and dragged him to the floor.

Rafe threw another handler aside, drew the man's gun, and pressed it to the third man's temple. "Get away from him."

I crawled to Cosmo, but was afraid to touch him, afraid I'd make things worse. How many of his bones had they shattered? His mouth was a mess of broken teeth and blood. Yet still he clutched the queen's cape to his chest as he moaned. With a start, I realized that the noise was more than a pained whimper. It was a word. . . .

"Mom, Mom . . ."

The queen pushed Rafe away from the handler. "Is that

how you deal with a beast going feral? By fighting with the handlers?"

"He can't go feral." Rafe sounded as if *he'd* gone feral. "He's second generation."

"Your pet just turned," the queen huffed. "We all saw him."

"He didn't. You're wearing his mother." Rafe stabbed a finger toward the cape that Cosmo was clutching — the snow-white fur now soaked with blood.

The queen blinked. "Oh. Her." She sighed. "No matter what I bred her with, she never managed to produce off-spring with fur as lovely as hers. I finally gave up trying."

Cosmo gurgled blood. Rafe fell to his knees, his expression stricken. He laid the gun on the floor.

Even if there was a doctor in the castle, the queen would probably never let him or her treat a manimal. Maybe if we found Everson . . . Though how much could he do for Cosmo? He couldn't replace teeth or fix a smashed nose or . . .

As Rafe gathered the little manimal into his arms, Cosmo cried out in pain.

"Don't," I croaked. "You'll make it worse."

But Rafe ignored me and cradled him against his chest. Cosmo seemed to relax in Rafe's arms and he closed his beautiful blue eyes, only to open them again when Rafe's tears splashed on his face. "Don't worry. Ev will fix you up," Rafe said, his voice in shreds. "He's good at that, remember? You're going to be okay."

Cosmo touched his knuckles to Rafe's cheek. "A-okay," he whispered and then his hand dropped and he grew still.

"No." Rafe held him closer, but Cosmo's head lolled

back. His fingers uncurled, releasing the scrap of paper, which fluttered to the floor.

Dizziness swept over me and I swayed. I couldn't think. Thinking meant absorbing what had just happened. A handler snatched the gun from the floor. All around me, I saw stunned faces. And then I saw Rafe. His light brown hair fell across his cheekbones as he laid Cosmo's body on the floor, hiding his expression. I picked up the paper that had fallen from Cosmo's fingers and stuffed it down the front of my gown without reading it.

"All right, everyone, dinner is served. Take your seats," Omar commanded. The guests hurried to their places, while Rafe and I remained kneeling by Cosmo.

"Losing a pet is hard, I know," the queen said with feigned sympathy. "But you shouldn't let it ruin your evening."

Omar gestured to a handler to collect Cosmo. "It's easier if you don't think of them as human."

Rafe's jaw trembled as he lifted his gaze. I'd seen him angry but never like this — never so savage. He rose and closed in on Omar. "He was a little kid and you murdered him."

"That's funny, coming from a hunter," Omar sneered. "Or doesn't it count as murder when you're getting paid to kill them? Now, if you want to do what's best for you — and you strike me as someone who always does — you'll shut your mouth and sit down."

In a single movement, Rafe lifted a knife from a table, flipped it in his hand, and slashed Omar across the stomach. "Do I pass the test?" he asked coldly as the head handler staggered back. "I gutted the feral."

Omar stared down in shock as blood seeped through his shirt, spreading over the material like spilled wine.

The queen screamed and the other handlers surged forward. I gathered up Cosmo's body, not wanting anyone to step on him. I rose, and clutching him to me, I tore for the double doors on the far side of the room, hoping Rafe would follow. As I reached them, the doors flew open. I skidded to a halt to look up at the two manimals now blocking my path. The bull-man thrust me aside, while the rhino-man took several precise steps forward.

"All bend to the king," he announced formally.

The room echoed with a thud as everyone present dropped to one knee and bowed their heads. All except Rafe and me. Still holding Cosmo's limp body in my arms, I met eyes with Rafe across the room and with a single tilt of his head, we agreed upon a plan. With the knife in hand, he backed toward the French doors. I slipped along the edge of the room to meet him there. But when the bull-man said, "The king comes among you," I couldn't help but turn to look. And suddenly I knew, beyond any doubt, that this nightmare had only just begun.

The king who stepped into the ballroom wearing a green velvet robe and bejeweled crown was none other than the tiger-man who'd prowled through my nightmares and nearly every waking moment for the past two days.

Chorda.

· TWENTY-EIGHT ·

As everyone in the ballroom lowered their heads in deference to Chorda, I slid down the wall with Cosmo in my arms. Across the room, Chorda stood in the archway, his head bandaged under his crown. He surveyed his subjects like a dictator.

"My king!" The queen rushed to his side. "Omar has been murdered!"

My view was suddenly blocked as Dromo dropped to one knee before me and lifted Cosmo out of my arms. "No," I said hoarsely, grasping Cosmo's limp hand.

Chorda swept across the ballroom toward the handlers. They bent low before him. "Who did this?" he bellowed.

"Let me take him," Dromo whispered, "before they throw him on a trash heap." His eyes cut to the queen. "Let me bury him next to his mother's bones."

Around me, guests shifted nervously as the handlers spoke to Chorda in low voices.

I let go of Cosmo's hand. "Wait." I arranged Jasper so that the stuffed monkey poked out of Cosmo's overalls the way he liked. My lips brushed his fuzzy silver head one last time and then Dromo stood.

"Follow me," he whispered. He cut through the crowd, clasping Cosmo to him, as if carrying a sleepy child off to bed.

I rose unsteadily and searched among the glittering bodies for Rafe. Had he escaped through the French doors when the king was announced? I hoped so. But I couldn't do the same with Chorda blocking the way. I started after Dromo.

"Lane," a rough voice called out. "You got my invitation."

I glanced back to see the guests scuttle aside to give Chorda a direct view of me. A smile curved over his black lips.

"You know her?" The queen's words quivered like an over-tight harp string in the silence.

Bitterness filled my mouth. I hiked up my skirt and dashed for the archway. Shrieks erupted around me. I banged into a manimal servant and sent his tray flying. Plates loaded with food shattered across the floor. As I skipped over the mess, someone snagged my dress and hauled me backward. I screamed as Chorda spun me to face him, his expression triumphant. I thrashed against his hold, but he caught my wrists and pinned them together in one hand.

"Now what?" Rafe stepped through the open French door. "You can't rip out her heart here." He swung his arm wide. "Can't eat it with them watching. You only do that out in the zone when there's no one around. No one to see what you really are: a bloodthirsty beast."

Chorda bristled, and turned slowly.

"How many people have you killed, cat chow? Thirty? Forty?" The knife in Rafe's hand dripped with Omar's blood. "When are you going to notice that your cure — the cure your twisted animal brain came up with — it's not working."

With a roar, Chorda threw me aside and launched himself across the room. Rafe lifted his knife, ready for the fight, but Chorda's reach was longer. He slashed at Rafe, tearing through his shirt and leaving four bloody scratches across his chest. The knife clattered onto the floor.

I jumped up and snatched another from a place setting. A handler rushed for me. I dodged him and he stumbled aside. I ran for Chorda's back, but another handler tackled me from behind, bringing me down so hard, my chin hit the floor with a crack. He wrenched the knife from my fingers and kept me pinned down with his knee on my back.

With a laugh, Chorda retracted his claws and began to beat Rafe with his fists. Rafe defended himself as best he could against Chorda's superior speed and strength, but he lasted only moments before crumpling to his knees. He spit out a mouthful of blood and glared up at Chorda. "Time to face the facts, whiskers. You're a psycho with a disease and you aren't ever changing back, no matter how many human hearts you scarf down."

Chorda grabbed Rafe by the throat, lifted him into the air, and threw him against the wall. He extended his claws once more and moved in, his eyes glowing with hate and bloodlust.

"No!" I screamed.

It was enough. Chorda seemed to remember himself . . . and that he had a ballroom full of witnesses. Standing over Rafe, he pulled in his claws. "When you caught me in your snare, you were going to kill me without a thought. But now our places are reversed. You are at my mercy, yet I am choosing not to kill you. Tell me, hunter, who is the beast?"

He waved several handlers forward, including the one holding me down. I felt his knee lift and scrambled to my feet.

"Take him to the zoo," Chorda told the handlers, where he can live in his own filth like the animal he is."

I shoved through the guests to face him. "The only animal in this room is you."

The crowd gasped and I sensed them edging away. I whirled on them. "Oh right, you all can't see that he's part tiger." Not a single person would meet my eyes. "Cowards."

"Out!" bellowed Chorda. "All but Lane." He turned his red-brown glare on the handlers and pointed to Rafe. "Put the animal where he belongs or you will be joining him."

The handlers scrambled to do Chorda's bidding. I tried to block them, but the blond handler who'd ridden in the rickshaw with us shoved me aside. They hauled Rafe to his feet and three more handlers lifted Omar's body and carried him out of the ballroom. The guests and manimal servants stampeded out of the ballroom after the handlers.

Only the queen remained, her eyes pinned on me. "How do you know her?" she asked Chorda.

"I ordered *all* but Lane to leave." Chorda took a seat at the head of the table. Only then did I notice my dial hanging around his neck, as was an electric blue Ferae test. My father's machete was stuffed into the sash around his waist. I stared at the two of them: the tense, almost haggard queen, and the tiger-king with glittering eyes and twisted ideas.

"Leave!" Chorda snarled, and the queen flew from the room, though not without throwing me one last hate-filled look as she closed the door.

I was trapped.

"My bag . . . you found Director Spurling's letter. You burned down her house."

A smile crept over his black lips. "What else could I do? Once you got the photograph, you would have left the Feral Zone . . . without giving me what I need."

I couldn't bear the feverish excitement in his eyes. I looked past him. He seemed more horrifying than ever with his crown and his yellow-crusted bandages. He was going to rip out my heart. Right now, right here — with his handlers and wife in the next room. If Dromo was right, the queen was listening at the door — not that she'd stop him from killing me. All she cared about was making sure that I didn't replace her. I shuddered. *Speak his language*, Rafe had said. Talk crazy. But how could I talk, when I couldn't think?

Chorda ran a hairy hand down his velvet robe. "I will leave this room tonight in my human skin."

"Will you tell your subjects how you broke the curse? How many human hearts you had to eat to get the job done?"

"It's the beast that kills. When I'm human again, the beast's sins will not be mine." He took my dial from around his neck and laid it on the table in front of him. "And now I know the way into the human world. I will go to this tunnel" — he tapped the dial's screen — "and I will join it as a man."

And I'd shown him the way. He'd slip right past the quarantine line. He'd infect the West. All because of me.

Chorda watched me, enjoying my fear. Hate surged in me — hate for the evil thing that he was. Hate for his insanity. I was verging on crazy as well, so why not give in to it? Do the insane. The unthinkable. What did I have to lose?

I took a breath and then forced myself to do the absolute last thing I wanted to: I moved closer to Chorda. "It's a test, you know," I said in as steady a voice as I could manage.

The patches of whiskers above his eyes twitched.

"So far you've failed." I pulled the bobby pins from my hair and let it spill over my shoulder in a dark wave. "Are you going to fail again?"

His eyes narrowed. "What test?"

"Take my heart if you want, but you won't break the curse that way. Know why?"

He grew still, watching me with the luminous eyes of a predator. *Make him believe.* I leaned across the table. "Because I have to give it to you. Keep stealing hearts and you'll stay an animal forever." I ran my eyes down his body, letting my disgust show. "The beast has to win the girl's heart, that's how it works. How it's always worked." I tapped my chest just above the neckline of my dress.

He dragged in a breath, and time hung in the air between us.

"Make me love you," I said softly. "And my heart is yours for the taking."

"How?" The word was no more than a low growl.

I pushed aside a place setting, including the steak knife, which I so desperately wanted to snatch up. I leaned across the table. "Let Rafe go."

Chorda rocketed to his feet, the veins in his neck standing out like rope. I gaped at him. "No," he snarled as curved claws sprung from his nail beds. "The hunter stays."

The urge to flee buzzed through my veins like a drug, but I gripped the edge of the table and dug in. Run and the tiger would pounce. I waited until I could open my mouth without screaming. "Fine. Act like a beast; stay a beast."

His eyes were wild, and I knew that if I wasn't very, very careful, he'd break my neck on impulse. "Or find another way to win my heart," I added and held out my hand, but I couldn't stop it from shaking and I couldn't take back the gesture.

Chorda's mottled features relaxed. Bending, he turned my hand over and kissed my trembling wrist.

Suddenly, the door flew open and the queen stormed into the room. She paused, taking in the scene and yet clearly seeing it so wrong. "You don't need to win her heart, darling. You have mine!" she cried.

Chorda beckoned her to him. "You love me?" He cast me a sly glance as if we were sharing a joke. "With all of your heart?"

I wanted to warn her, to yell *Run!* But my vocal cords were frozen.

"Yes." The queen hurried over to us, thrusting a furious finger at me. "She's just after your crown. She doesn't love you. But I do."

Her voice edged on hysterical and I almost felt sorry for her. She was walking right into Chorda's trap. But I couldn't worry about her. I had to get as far away from Chorda as I could. And this was my chance. With his attention on her, I slipped my dial off the table and edged toward the open door. Not too fast. Not so he'd notice me.

"So your heart is mine for the taking?" Chorda purred, turning the queen in his arms so that he stood behind her.

She stiffened. She must have guessed the terrible double meaning of his words. "I just meant that I love you and —"

Chorda cupped her chin and tilted her face to his, as if to kiss her. Then he raised his other hand. His two-inch claws slipped forth.

"No, please!" The queen struggled in his hold. "I'll go to the feral house. Or put me with the lionesses. I'll —"

With one clawed hand, he tore open her throat. The queen thrashed in his arms, trying to get away as dark blood streamed down her neck. Her mouth opened but no sound came out. He'd sliced through her vocal cords. And then she sagged, though there was still life in her eyes. Chorda caught her flowing blood in the cup of his hand, brought it to his mouth, and lapped it up.

I skittered backward — unable to take my eyes from the scene, unwilling to turn my back to Chorda. He reached around the slumping queen and slashed her bloodstained chest once, twice.

I whirled and tore for the hall, leaving behind the sounds of bones cracking and a splatter of liquid. At the door I glanced back to see Chorda kiss his queen on the mouth and drop her to the floor. Crimson blood dripped from his fist. He was holding her heart in his hand! With her twitching body at his feet and his velvet robe flecked with red, Chorda lifted the heart to his lips.

I spun into the hall. So many doors, so many halls. Which would get me out of here? I couldn't open them all. I raced past a brass cage of an elevator and pivoted. Elevators and stairs went together, yes? I tugged at the nearest door and saw a spindly staircase that descended into darkness.

Down I went, into a darker, grimmer part of the castle. I ran through the rabbit warren of a basement — so like the chimpacabra tunnels — turning corners and skirting the entrances to darkened halls. The warren ended in a large, poorly lit room, and I skidded to a stop. Either Chorda himself or his handlers were going to come after me. I needed to find someplace to hide.

A stainless-steel worktable gleamed in the center of the room, laden with jars of chemicals and bolts of fabric. Mannequins lined the walls, some nude and some wearing colorful clothes of leather and fur in various stages of completion. . . .

I focused on the long zippered bag on the worktable — a body-sized bag — and my thoughts slowed until they crystallized into one chilling realization: This is where Cosmo's mother had been turned into clothing. And the same thing was now happening to other manimals.

Something clacked across the room. With a tap, I darkened my dial, tucked it into my dress, and darted among the mannequins. In the far corner, a seamstress sat hunched over an old-fashioned sewing machine, her wide back to me. She wore a dirty kimono and seemed completely focused on her work, which had to be unending. Torn clothes lay piled on the floor by her feet — maids' uniforms and white jackets like Dromo's.

There was nowhere in this room to hide, but maybe I could swap my silk gown for something less conspicuous. I crept as close as I dared, snagged the hem of a maid's dress, and dragged it to me. When the seamstress set the machine clacking once more, I snatched up the dress and stood. Again she paused, but only to fold the jacket that she'd been working on. I edged away from her, but then a collar with a glinting buckle fell from the folds of the maid's dress and hit the floor with a *ping*.

I froze.

The seamstress turned stiffly, as if her neck was fused to her shoulders. When she faced me, I had to bite off my gasp. Her nose ended in a mass of small pink tentacles, like a star-nosed mole's. We stared at each other for a moment, silent and gauging. Finally she spoke. Well, tried to speak. She could only manage garbled syllables. With a frustrated grunt, she hefted herself up and shuffled toward me.

Maybe she thought I was a servant? No. Not a chance. Not in a satin gown.

She pointed at the maid's uniform in my hands.

I tightened my grip. "I need it."

"Tra —" she wheezed. "Tra —" Her clawed toes jutted past the edge of her flip-flops as she hobbled forward, pointing at my chest. "Trade."

"Trade the gown for the maid's dress?" I plucked at my gown. She nodded. "Deal," I said and turned my back to her. "Please unzip me."

Despite having thick claws for fingernails, she had a delicate touch, and the gown fell away from my skin. As I shimmied out of it, the folded paper that had been in Cosmo's hand fell out. I snatched it up and read "21:00 on roof." The roof? What kind of escape plan was that?

I pulled on the ragged dress, fastened the collar around my neck, and then rubbed my hands on the basement wall until they were good and filthy. Without a second of hesitation, I smeared the damp grime over my face and down my arms. Finally I tore off my blue Ferae test and threw it into the corner. I had to get Rafe and be back here by nine, which was — I checked my dial — in an hour.

I glanced at the seamstress, who was brushing the satin across her cheek, and then she held the gown against her body. She swayed while making a rhythmic, chirping sound. Singing? Had the gown stirred up some long-buried memory?

She stopped abruptly and looked toward the corridor. A second later, I heard what she had: boot steps in the passage. The seamstress tugged off her head scarf and offered it to me. I took it gratefully and managed to pull it over my hair just as a five-man squad of handlers hustled into the room. Three of them hurried past, giving the seamstress and me the barest glance before moving on to search the hallways beyond. We stood silently among the mannequins as the two remaining handlers poked around the sewing room. After a moment, the seamstress slid my gown — now her gown — over a naked mannequin and thrust a pincushion into my shaking hands.

A handler strode over to us. "Did a young woman come through here?"

The seamstress shook her head while pinching in a side seam on the gown. I handed her a pin. The handler shifted his gaze onto me and I quickly shook my head. His look turned to one of disgust and he moved on, which meant — unbelievably — that I'd passed for a manimal!

I released my breath as the handlers left the sewing room. I'd bought myself a little time, but that was all. If I was going to escape from here and free Rafe, I had to get the handlers off my back. But how? Maybe if they had a bigger problem than me to occupy them. Something so bad or so dangerous that it would require all of the handlers' focus and energy . . .

Not *something*, I realized. Four very dangerous *some-ones* would do the trick. And to make it happen, all I needed was a key.

I turned to the seamstress. "Omar is dead." Her eyes widened at the news and then her lips pulled back. A smile? "Do you know where they would put his body?" I asked. With all the chaos, hopefully no one had thought to empty Omar's pockets.

The seamstress led me down yet another dark corridor and pointed to a walk-in freezer. "Thank you," I whispered, and with a nod, she was gone. I pried open the rusting door and stepped in, only to stumble. Omar had been dumped just over the threshold, limbs akimbo. I shoved him onto his back and unclipped the key from his belt loop — the very key that he'd used to taunt the queen. I clipped it into the neckline of my maid's uniform.

I was just about to step out when a thought hit me. The queen — her breeding program. I pivoted to look at the shelves that lined the walk-in. Where else would she store the infected blood but in a freezer?

And there they were — vials, on a shelf, tucked inside a metal box with a glass top. I unclasped the top, lifted a vial, and read the word scrawled on masking tape along the side: "cuscus." Was that a kind of animal? I didn't know. I pulled out another vial. This one read "colobus monkey." That was definitely a type of animal. I counted the rows. There were forty vials of blood in the box. A yelp of triumph escaped me. Thank goodness I was inside a freezer.

I quickly refastened the lid and put the box back on the shelf. I didn't have time to check if the vials were all different or if there were duplicates, and I couldn't take them to the zoo with me. The blood would spoil at room temperature. I'd have to leave the box here until just before Rafe and I met Everson on the roof.

I slipped out of the walk-in freezer only to hear the handlers' whispers down the hall. I hurried in the opposite direction and came to a large room lined with animal pens. The servants' quarters. This was where Cosmo had once lived with his mother. Thinking of him left me feeling shivery and close to collapse. I crouched in an empty pen with the heel of my palm pressed to my lips to trap a welling sob.

Cosmo . . . I buried my face in my arms. I could keep certain images pushed to the edge of my brain but not the sounds. Those kept playing in my mind, distorting and magnifying. The crunch of the handlers' batons battering Cosmo long after he'd crumpled to the ground. The wet noise of Chorda tearing out the queen's heart. His deep-throated growl. I curled onto my side in the hay, dizzy and on the brink of vomiting. But I couldn't afford to give in to my grief. Not if I was going to escape and free Rafe. I squeezed my calf, digging my fingers into the bandage. Pain blazed up my leg and sharpened my mind.

A creak outside my pen propelled me into a crouch. I peered over the rough wooden wall. Manimals wearing thick collars had emerged from their pens to stare at me with glowing eyes. I swallowed against the ache in my throat and wondered what explanation I could possibly give for invading their privacy. And then I saw the babies cradled in their mothers' arms and the children peeking out from behind their parents' legs.

Hate for Chorda and his handlers hardened in me like clay in a red-hot kiln. How evil did you have to be to force people — children even — to live in pens in a dark, dank basement? It wasn't their worst crime against these manimals, but after seeing so much mistreatment, it was one cruelty too many. Something inside of me snapped and suddenly I knew how it must feel to go feral.

A spiky-headed man straightened, his pointed ears erect. A badger-woman's nose twitched. And then they all scurried back into their pens, dragging their children with them. A moment later, three handlers stomped into the room.

· TWENTY-NINE ·

Flashlight beams crisscrossed the servant quarters. Hay snapped underfoot and gates were thrown open as the handlers searched the pens, breathing heavily under the weight of their leather aprons. I pulled my head scarf low over my eyes. The handlers kicked manimals awake, questioned them, and raked through their possessions.

A glaring flashlight sought me out and I lifted my face the way I thought they'd want. Someone gave a satisfied grunt. "Anything?" he asked over his shoulder.

"Only people who belong here," said a husky voice. A familiar voice. I peeked over the top of my pen and saw Everson in a leather apron. He had bandages on both cheeks from where the feral had scratched him.

"People," snorted the guard nearest to my pen. "That's funny. I'm done with this pigsty. I'm going back to the barracks."

The third handler followed him down the aisle, but before Everson could fall in line, I launched to my feet and blocked his path. "Stay," I whispered.

He blinked. "What?"

I moved closer, lifting my gaze to his. "Please stay here with me." If he'd just look at me . . . but no. He fixed his attention on the aisle beyond me as color crept into his cheeks.

"No offense, Miss," he said stiffly, "but I can't."

One of the handlers behind me broke into raucous laughter. "Sure, you can. The queen is dead and so is her little project. No one's gonna care if you get yourself a girlfriend."

The other handler groaned. "Don't listen to him, kid. And don't get fooled just 'cause she's not showing any animal now. If she's down here, she ain't human."

Everson tried to sidestep me, but I couldn't let him get away. Throwing my arms around his neck, I pressed him to the pen wall and put my mouth to his ear. "Ev, it's me."

He froze, then his bandaged cheek brushed my lips as he turned to look into my eyes and, finally, saw me. The *me* under the dirt and maid's dress. He pressed a hand to the small of my back and fisted the fabric, pulling my dress tight, holding on to me as if I might suddenly vanish.

A tremor ran through him. "Actually" — he cleared his throat and shot the handlers a wry look — "I think I will stay."

The first handler chortled. The other sighed. "Suit yourself," he said.

Everson waited for them to disappear up the stairs before pushing back my headscarf. My hair tumbled down and he stared. I understood his doubt. I barely recognized myself. "What happened?" His voice was heavy with dread. "Are you . . ." He couldn't finish the thought.

"No," I assured him. "I'm fine. I —"

My words ended up muffled against his chest. He'd pulled me to him so fast, my brain hadn't kept up. And now his breath stirred my hair. "I've been looking everywhere for you." His relief was so intense that something inside of me, which had been knotted tight, loosened a little.

There was so much I needed to tell him, and I would, but not yet. For just a moment, I wanted to be happy that we'd found each other and to feel sheltered against his chest. His hands lifted to cradle my face and suddenly, his lips were on mine. He kissed me softly at first, then turned ardent, and for the first time ever, I wanted more. My fingers curled against him as the warmth of his mouth sent electricity arcing through my body. When he leaned away to look at me, I was tempted to pull him back. To get lost in his kiss again, so that everything around us went away — the basement and the handlers and the things I had to tell him. . . . Sad things, I remembered with a start. Devastating things.

I stepped out of his arms and felt instantly cold. "What was that?" I asked in a breathless voice.

His expression turned rueful. "Back at the park, Rafe was right. I should've gone for the kiss."

"You just thought about that now?"

"No, from the second you walked away. And after the handlers grabbed me, I couldn't stop thinking about it. How I'd missed the moment. Missed it forever if I didn't pass their test or if I never found you . . . I —" He glanced away with a half shrug. "I wanted to make up for it."

"You did," I assured him with a shaky laugh. "And then some."

We stood awkwardly for a split second and then I reached for his hand. "Come on." I tugged him into my pen, where we settled down in the hay. I traced a finger over the bandage on his right cheek. "I saw the fight. I was on the roof."

He looked surprised. "And now you're down here. . . . A lot's happened, huh?" he asked gently.

I swallowed the ache in my throat and nodded. I wanted one more minute before I spilled it all and relived the horror. "Did you need stitches?" I asked, taking my hand from his face.

"Probably. The cuts feel deep." He touched the other bandage with a grimace. "A handler closed them with surgical tape. I wanted to do it but they said there are no mirrors in this insane place."

My minute was up. No more stalling. "Yes, by the king's order," I said, forcing out each word. "He doesn't want to see that he's turning into a tiger."

Everson's eyes flew to mine. "Chorda?" At my nod he sat back heavily against the pen wall. "That's why they're all scared of him. All except Omar."

"Omar is dead," I said and then softened my voice. "So is Cosmo."

"What? No. I just saw him. He . . ." Everson's words trailed off and for a moment we just stared at each other. "He's dead?"

My eyes felt dry and hot as I nodded. Everson seemed as if he was about to say something but then he bowed his head and laced his fingers behind his neck. "How?"

I told him all that had happened since we'd separated

outside the compound fence — what the queen did to Cosmo's mother and how the handlers beat the little boy to death. I had to pause, breathe deep, and swallow. The memory of him clutching the queen's cape, crying and moaning "Mom," cracked my heart all over again. I took satisfaction in describing how Rafe had knifed Omar — vicious satisfaction — which was lessened only by the wish that it had been me.

Everson glanced up as if surprised by my tone. "Where's Rafe now?"

"Chorda had him taken to the zoo. We have to get him out."

"The handlers' barracks are there in the zoo. And the hyboars have free run of the place." He met my gaze. "We'll get Rafe, but we don't have a lot of time. I used a ham radio in the barracks to call Arsenal. The captain agreed to send a 'copter to pick us up from the Cultural Center roof at nine. They'll drop a ladder, but they can't land."

I nodded, knowing the law.

He paused. "Did Chorda bite him?"

"No."

"Okay." He inhaled deeply. "We need to get the key from one of the handlers." Grasping the pen wall, he hauled himself up.

I rose as well and the ache in my calf surged, threatening to swallow me whole. We weren't exactly in great shape to run three miles to the zoo and back. "I already did." I lifted the key from my neckline to show him. "Cosmo said that Omar had the master key, so I took it off the body in the —"

I clapped a hand to my mouth. How could I have forgotten? "Follow me!"

I led Everson through the sewing room and into the walk-in freezer. Ignoring Omar's frozen corpse, I crossed to the back shelf and flipped open the metal box.

Everson grew very still. "Are those what I think?"

"I don't know how many different strains are in here or which ones, but there's more than eighteen. There should be some that you don't have."

"You're amazing." He swept me up in a hug and again brought his mouth to mine. His lips were as warm and as sweetly demanding as before, but the kiss wasn't nearly long enough. When he set me back on my feet, I suppressed a sigh.

"I can't believe you found blood samples," he said in a hushed voice. "In vials. Labeled." He touched the box as I refastened the glass lid. "You've saved us years of searching."

I set the box back on the shelf. "We'll leave it here until we get back from the zoo." When Everson didn't reply, I looked up. "What?"

He drew in a ragged breath. "I can't go to the zoo."

"But — you said you'd help me get Rafe."

"That was before you showed me this." He gestured to the metal box with a swipe of his hand. "If we don't make it back, no one will know these samples are here. I can't take the risk. I have to get them to Dr. Solis. Lane, I'm sorry. I —"

"You said you would!"

"And I meant it. I want to help Rafe. I do. But this is bigger than me and what I want. A cure would save everyone."

My anger ignited like a combustible gas. "Your captain will be so proud. You've put the population first — stopped seeing the people. People like Rafe."

The muscles in Everson's jaw shifted and clenched. "If that's what it takes to end a plague, then yes, fine, I'll act like a guard."

"Act? Don't kid yourself. You're a guard through and through. That's why you can't break the rules. Why you needed me to do it for you. Because, no matter what you think, you still do what you're told."

I'd taken him from mad to furious — his eyes blazed with it — but I didn't care. He'd hide it under his guard face soon enough. Not that I'd be here to see it. I shoved open the freezer door and stepped out.

Everson followed me into the corridor and caught my wrist. "You'll never make it to the zoo and back. There are handlers and hyena-things at every gate."

"Let. Go." I tugged on my wrist but he held tight.

"Lane, you can't go out there alone! It's too —"

I ducked and sank my teeth into his hand. Hard. He gasped and his fingers sprang open. Without so much as a glance at him, I bolted.

I took the stairs two at a time, heaved open a slanted storm door, and crept into the castle yard. Two handlers stood guard by the gate. I slipped through the shadows to the lionesses' enclosure, which was lit by a single overhead light. In the center of the cage, Mahari lounged on a couch piled with furs, her golden eyes hard and bright as she watched me make my way to a dark corner by the bramble fence. The others strolled forward, curious as well. I stopped within an inch of the cage, feeling as wild as the lionesses within.

Deepnita arched a brow at my maid's dress and leather collar. "You've come down in the world." Her voice was low and gravelly, much like a rock star's after a concert. "Did the queen decide you were too much of a threat?"

"The queen is dead."

Mahari stretched, arching her back like a cat. "Oh my, the girl's gone wild." She sauntered to the edge of the cage.

"Chorda killed her, not me." I unbuckled the leather collar around my neck and threw it aside.

Mahari's fangs flashed in the shadows — a smile. "And you were just beginning to impress me."

"I came to make a deal."

She stepped so close I could see the golden starbursts in her irises. "I'm all ears, little human."

"The handlers took Rafe to the zoo and I need to get him out."

Charmaine tossed back her curls with a chuff. "Good luck."

"They'll put him in the cage outside the feral house," Deepnita informed me. "Smack in the middle of the zoo."

"Which will be crawling with handlers," Neve added and dropped into a leather chair.

"Or they might put him in the small cage," Mahari said conversationally.

"The small cage?" I asked.

"It's not a real cage. It's the space between two exhibits in the feral house." Her voice turned so rough it was almost a growl. "One used to house a man infected with lion, the other, baboon. The space is so narrow that if you move more than a foot in either direction, one of the ferals will snag you and pull you to him."

"Is that what happened to you?" I swept my gaze over them. Had they all chosen to be bitten by a lion-feral over a baboon? That would have been my choice too.

"Infection is grounds for an instant divorce, by the king's law," Charmaine explained. "That way he can marry his next wife, the very next day."

"Whether she wants to or not," Mahari added dryly.

"If Rafe stays very still in the center of the small cage, then the ferals can't reach him, right?"

Mahari lifted a shoulder and let it drop. "The one who infected us was killed in an initiation test last year. I don't know what lives in that cage now. Maybe something with a longer reach."

I began to feel frantic. "I have to get Rafe out of there."

Deepnita snorted. "Even if you could get past the handlers, the cages are locked."

"And one key opens them all, right? The same key that unlocks your cage." I stepped back before unclipping the key from my maid's dress. Good thing, because when I held it up, three of the queens slammed against the wire fence. The cross-hatching wasn't wide enough for them to push their hands through, but their fingers strained for me with their claws extended. The hair on my arms stood on end, but I didn't back up any farther.

They yowled and hissed until a voice cut through their inhuman sounds. "Get back!" Mahari ordered, hauling one away from the fence and then flinging the other two aside as if they were sock puppets. No wonder she was the head lioness. For all her voluptuous beauty, she was stronger than three jumpsuits on steroids. She licked her palms and ran her hands quickly over her dark hair, smoothing it down. "So, about this deal . . . ?"

I knew that they weren't as tame as they looked and that if I let them out, there would be no way to re-cage them. I also knew that once released they'd unleash their fury on the handlers who'd tormented them. Mahari had made that very clear this afternoon. And I was counting on it. "I let you out and in return you get me past the gate." I pointed at the briar fence where the two handlers stood. "And then create a distraction at the zoo while I free Rafe."

Mahari's eyes smoldered and a smile crept over her lips. "Little human, you have a deal."

She looked so savage, I wondered if she'd rip out my throat once she was free. Maybe. But I was willing to take that chance because if anyone could clear my path to Rafe, it was the lionesses. I unlocked the cage and threw open the door. The women stalked out, grinning and stretching. Their muscles rippled under their dusting of gold fur.

I pulled my dial out of my maid's dress and pressed record. If I died tonight at least there would be a record of what happened, though I doubted anyone would ever see it.

"All right, girls," Mahari purred, tipping her head toward the handlers by the gate. "Let's get feral."

The other queens extended their claws and roared in answer. The sound sent an electric current down my spine. The handlers whipped around to peer at the enclosure. In the split second it took them to realize that the queens were free, the lion-women sprinted for them with long effortless strides. Deepnita flung one into the air. He landed on the coiled barbed wire on top of the fence, where he thrashed and screamed. Neve took the other down, laughing as she straddled his back, her blond hair spilling around his head. "He's a big one."

"Play later," Mahari ordered. She vaulted over Neve and threw open the gate.

With a quick twist, Neve snapped the handler's neck. She rose and dashed after the others. I ran after them as well, but they were too fast for me. I raced onto the street and nearly fell over when two figures stepped from the shadows. Dromo and the Pekingese-maid named Penny stared after the bounding lionesses.

"The queens . . ." Dromo gasped and dropped the shovel he'd been holding. "What have you done?"

"I set them free." I lifted my chin, daring him to berate me, but then I noticed the mound of freshly turned dirt behind them. My breath caught. "Cosmo?" When Dromo nodded, I flinched and very nearly bolted. But I wouldn't let myself run away from Cosmo. Couldn't. I dragged my wet palms down my dress and ventured closer to the small unmarked grave.

"The queens will . . . They'll" — Penny dropped her voice to a whisper — "go after the handlers. They'll kill them all."

"They'll try," Dromo agreed. "We have to tell the others."

I sank beside the mound of fresh earth, pulled down by

the heaviness in my chest, and began patting the loose soil into place.

"With the queens free, we have a chance," Dromo went on, his voice rising. "More than a chance." I glanced back to see him unbuckle his collar. "We serve no more," he declared and threw his collar to the ground. Penny dropped hers too, though with less fire.

I gave the dirt one last pat. "I'm so glad I got to know you," I whispered to the small mound. "Good-bye, Cosmo."

I rose and cut past the others. "Good luck."

"Where are you going?" Dromo asked.

"The zoo."

"You can't," he sputtered. "The queens have gone to free their followers — friends and family who were rounded up and infected after each divorce. No human will make it out of there alive."

I stared at him, aghast. "Rafe!" I took off running for the bridge.

"Wait!" Dromo shouted, but I didn't.

When I reached the bridge that crossed the Chicago River, I heard a clatter of wheels behind me. I turned to see the bull-man, Irving, trotting up with the rickshaw. "Dromo sent me," he said. "I can get you there faster."

"Thank you." I scrambled onto the padded seat and felt no guilt about being hauled around by a manimal this time. Nor did I feel guilty to see that the queens had taken down the guards who patrolled the gate.

When we arrived at the south entrance to the zoo, Irv stopped the rickshaw by an iron fence. I climbed down, feeling shaky. "Will you wait for me?"

"You can't go back to the castle."

"I have to. A hovercopter is going to pick us up off the roof."

He shook his immense head. "You'd never make it to the roof. Tonight we're declaring war on the handlers. The smartest thing a human can do is stay away from the castle. Better yet, get out of Chicago for good."

"But I have another friend who's still in the castle."

"Then you better pray for him." Irv dropped the rickshaw poles and strode back toward the compound.

I slipped past the freestanding cages inside the entrance, which contained mongrels, each stranger than the last. I slunk up the brightly lit path toward the stone animal houses in the main part of the zoo. It was all so quiet. Maybe Mahari and the other lion-women had run off and not caused the distraction as promised or even freed their followers as Dromo had predicted.

I arrived at a row of cages along the outside wall of the primate house. Each enclosure contained at least one person, all in advanced states of mutation. Some growled as I hurried past, others hunkered down, moaning and rocking. Most were wild-eyed and foamy-mouthed — well into stage three of Ferae. A girl with spines down her back gnawed on her fist and licked off the blood. A dark figure hurtled out of the shadows of the next enclosure to mash his bumpy face against the steel wires. "Taaassste." He grabbed for me. I whipped away, feeling hot claws drag over my back.

In the next cage, a ghostly woman crouched. She was completely hairless — nothing on her head, no eyebrows, no lashes. Her skin was so white, her veins showed through. She scratched her fingernails across the cement floor. "Why are you here?" she rasped.

She could talk. Good. "Which one of these buildings is the one they call the feral house?" I asked.

"Let me out and I'll take you." She rose on twisted legs, her eyes glinting.

"I'll find it myself." I moved on.

"The lion house," she called after me. "That's where the king keeps the most feral of us all."

I turned back. Did I believe her?

"De nada," she said with a flick of her forked tongue. I broke into a run.

The infected people paced alongside me as I passed their cages. They were so mutated and animalistic, they barely looked human. If Rafe had been shoved into a cage with one of them, given the battered state that he was in, he'd never be able to defend himself.

Voices came from around the bend. I ducked behind a tree, just as a group of handlers appeared, along with several hyboars. I scrambled up the back of the tree and perched on a thick branch, praying that the hyboars wouldn't pick out my scent from all the other smells in the zoo.

There was a sharp bark. I twisted on my branch but saw nothing. Then I heard another cry — an animal screech. I crept out farther on my branch and looked down to see Charmaine slinking between the bushes. She was stalking the handlers. More bushes rustled. The handlers jerked to a stop, turning in place as roars welled up around them. Branches cracked as the lion-women burst out of the brush, racing for the handlers.

The men shouted and the hyboars leapt at the lion-women. Mahari raked at a hyboar's face and sent it skittering back with a canine yelp. Two more lunged at her, squealing with rage. The handlers fired flares into the sky to call for backup. But it was too late. Growling lionesses took them down.

I should have felt sorry for the men, but all the pity had been wrung out of my heart when Cosmo died. The handlers had beaten him to death without a moment's hesitation. Who knew how many other manimals had suffered at their hands?

The ferals in the nearby cages grew frenzied. Shifting back and forth, they slammed the bars of their cages, scratched at their own flesh, and beat their chests. The lionesses roared and the caged ferals responded in kind. Mahari bent over the dead handlers, plucking keys from their aprons, which she threw to Charmaine and Neve. "Free them all!"

"No," I yelled, but the word was drowned in the bestial sounds thundering through the zoo. If the queens freed these ferals, Rafe and I would never make it out of the zoo alive.

The lion-women raced from cage to cage, unlocking them faster than I could follow with my eyes. The most savage ferals pounced from their enclosures while the timid hung back.

More handlers and hyboars ran up the path. They must have seen the flares. A wolf-man launched himself at the handler in the lead. The handler aimed his gun at the creature and pulled the trigger. The gun jumped in his hands, yet the wolf-man was upon him, ripping the gun away as his jaws closed on the man's face. He whipped him from side to side.

The handler went limp and the feral dropped him, threw back his head, and howled.

And then he noticed me.

He bounded for my tree and leapt into the air, trying to catch hold of my foot. I drew up into a crouch on my branch as the wolf-man jumped at me again, his eyes red with hate. But this time when he dropped, he collapsed on the ground in a heap. His clawed hand moved over his ribs and then stilled. Blood seeped under his fingers and his hand fell away, revealing the gunshot wound in his chest.

I dropped out of the tree and took a path that the lionesses hadn't. I ran in a mindless haze, ignoring the searing pain in my calf. I paused when I heard a shrill chittering. A hunchbacked, rodenty-looking man jumped down from an ancient carousel and ran at me. I screeched at him and he veered off.

I whirled to try another path but a large brick building loomed before me. Mosaic lions decorated either side of the arching glass door. The feral house! The queens had said that the handlers would put Rafe in the enclosure outside or the small cage inside.

I tried the outside first, rounding the corner to peer into the cage that ran the length of the building. I crept along the bars, searching for any sign of Rafe, but the enclosure had been landscaped with trees and rocky ledges. The streetlamps on the path cast strange shadows, making it hard to tell what lay beyond the bars. I brightened my dial, which was still recording.

Gunfire rattled somewhere close by, followed by men's screams. I'd reached the door of the cage, but had seen no sign of life inside . . . which didn't mean that something wasn't hiding within the greenery. And then I noticed the form huddled on the ground by a trickling waterfall. It was Rafe — eyes closed, his skin gleaming with moisture. Was it from the splashing waterfall or was he sweating out a fever? I pressed against the bars. "Rafe," I whispered as loud as I dared.

He didn't so much as twitch. *Oh no*, I thought. *No. Please don't let him be infected!* "Rafe, please wake up." He wouldn't lie to me. He'd tell me if he'd been bitten. "Rafe!"

The bushes across the path rustled as the branches were thrust aside. It was the blond handler, drenched in blood, his eyes wide and terrified. He staggered toward me but then something dark sprang from the bushes and brought him down with a snarl.

I jammed the key into the cage door, unlocked it, flew inside, and slammed the door behind me. I'd rather take my chances in here than out there. I hurried across the enclosure to where Rafe lay on his back by the man-made creek at the base of the waterfall. His tux jacket was gone, his silk tie undone, and his shirt, ripped and damp, clung to his body. All the color had drained out of his face. I could see that even in the dark. And worst of all, he was so still.

"Rafe," I said hoarsely. I dropped to my knees and touched his face. His skin was warm, but not on fire. I gave him a gentle shake. If he didn't wake up, how was I going to get him out of here? I could drag him through the cage door but then what? I'd never be able to carry him through the zoo without the ferals catching our scent. "Rafe, you have to wake up."

He swallowed and then whispered a single word: "Run."

He was conscious! "Where are you hurt?"

His eyes fluttered open. "Run," he croaked, more urgent.

"Not without —"

A clawed hand sliced through the waterfall and clamped on to my wrist. I screamed.

"I knew you wouldn't leave him behind." Chorda unfolded from the crevice behind the curtain of water, dragging me up with him. "Your humane heart wouldn't let you."

Reeling back, I twisted and scratched at his hand, but he pulled me closer still. I flew at his face and ripped the bandage from his head. With a roar, he released me. I staggered back with the bloody gauze in hand. His right ear was gone, eaten by weevlings, leaving only mangled skin and gristle. Bile burned my throat. Spinning, I ran for the cage door, but he got there first. I bit back a cry.

Chorda smiled, his long canines appearing yellow in the lamplight. "Look at us, together again."

"Is Rafe infected?" My words came out ragged. "Did you bite him?"

"Shouldn't you worry about what I'm going to do to you?"

· THIRTY ·

"It's time, Lane." Chorda smiled, bright and bitter. Long claws extended from his fingertips.

The memory of his claws tearing the queen's throat came back so clearly that I couldn't draw a breath. I looked into his burning eyes and saw his hunger. Terror shot through my veins and my legs shuddered. I ran from him, his laughter following me to the far end of the cage.

A pack of ferals loped around the corner of the building. One spotted me pressed against the bars and called to the others with a keening screech. They padded forward, sniffing and snuffling. One of them, a man infected with baboon, whipped around to look at the other end of the cage, his broad nostrils flaring. Suddenly, he sprinted the length of the enclosure and flew at the bars. Chorda sprang away from the door. The other ferals caught his scent too and went into a full uproar, shaking the bars and screaming — because of Chorda! They were straining against the bars trying to get at him.

Unconcerned, Chorda padded through the enclosure. He fingered the bright blue Ferae test hanging from a chain around his neck. "Once my handlers have this under control,

I'll walk out of here, a man once more. You, sweet Lane, will be in bloody pieces scattered across the floor, except for the chunks I throw to them." He cast a hand at the frenzied ferals. "Of course, your heart belongs to me."

I edged along the cage wall. "What happens when my heart doesn't work?"

"It will."

"It won't if I'm not human." I jammed my arm between the bars and the ferals came running. I whipped in my arm as the first one slammed against the cage. More piled against the bars behind me, thrusting their clawed hands through, scrabbling to snag me and drag me to them.

"One bite and I'm ruined," I said. "An infected heart won't do anything for you." I could feel the ferals' hot breath on the nape of my neck. All I had to do was tilt back a fraction and they'd have me.

A growl, low and quavering, came from deep in Chorda's throat and turned into the snarl of an infuriated animal. He leapt for me, his glistening jaws wide. At the last second I dove aside and Chorda slid into a wall of grasping hands. My chin smacked the ground, and I gasped. Pain spread through my palms and knees.

I dragged myself up to see Chorda thrashing against the bars, trying to back away, but too many clawed hands had gotten hold of him. The ferals, screeching with glee and fury, tried to pull Chorda between the bars to their snapping mouths while they ripped at his flesh.

The baboon-man tore at the scarf around Chorda's waist. My father's machete skittered out of the fray. I ran after it, but another hand gripped the hilt first. I looked up to see Rafe standing over me. My heart stopped. His chest was lacerated and his face, bloody and battered. His eyes had a wild look. Was he infected? Fevered?

He thrust the machete into my hands. "I told you to leave," he said hoarsely.

I rose, holding the machete so tightly my knuckles hurt. "I told you I wouldn't."

There was a strangled sound behind us, followed by a thin whistle of tortured breathing. Chorda had wrenched free of the ferals' hold. Drool unspooled from his lips, a piece of his scalp lay flopped over one ear, and his body was badly slashed. Time froze as I met his gaze, bloodshot and burning. And then, roaring in mindless rage, he charged for me.

Something flashed in my periphery.

Rafe slammed into Chorda with a savage snarl and they hit the ground, their limbs crashing together. Rolling on top, Chorda lifted Rafe's head and slammed it on the rocky ground. Rafe reached for the tiger-man's neck, snagged the Ferae test, and twisted the chain tight while jerking Chorda's head down. He slashed at Rafe's arm, shredding his flesh until Rafe loosened his hold on the chain.

The tiger-man sat back on his knees and lifted a hand to deliver a killing swipe. My vision narrowed to a single point and I swung. The blade hit Chorda's raised wrist and moved through it. One second the tiger-king had a clawed hand and the next, he didn't.

Chorda screamed and curled around the bloody stump that had been his hand.

I closed in on him, letting my terror guide my arm. I raised the blade, but he exploded upward, twisting to tower over me. Blood spurted from his wrist. I bounced off my toes into a sprint and drove the blade straight into Chorda's heart. He roared, flinging me away. I landed on my back, the air knocked from my lungs, but I pushed up to see him clawing at the machete with his one hand. The blade was stuck deep in his chest.

Chorda shuddered and blood welled around the blade and streamed down his striped ribs. The tiger-king fell to his knees and then onto his side. He stared at me, black lips working. He reached toward me as if still trying to take my heart. . . . Then his hand dropped and his eyes rolled back in his head.

"Rafe," I whispered. I crawled over to where he lay with his gashed arm flung out as if he couldn't look at it. The pool of blood around his forearm was spreading fast and wide. I grasped his hand and elevated his arm to slow the bleeding, but only a tourniquet would stop it.

"He's dead?" he rasped, trying to tug his hand from mine.

"Yes."

I cast about for something to use to bind his arm. His silk bowtie. With one hand, I pulled it from around his neck while the ever-growing pool of blood soaked my knees. I looked down and all at once I realized that it wasn't Rafe's blood. It was Chorda's, seeping from his body that lay nearby. Chorda's infected blood, which had puddled around Rafe's arm and drenched his open wounds. "Oh, no. No," I whispered.

Our eyes met, Rafe's searching mine, and then he twisted his face away.

Maybe Chorda's claws had torn only his sleeve. I lowered

his arm into my lap and peeled back the shredded, blood-stained material. My hair curtained my face and hid my horror at the gashes in his skin. I gathered up the folds of my dress and tried to wipe his wounds clean, gently at first, but then frantically as desperation set in.

A groan tore from his throat and I froze. My vision blurred and trembled with tears. "I'm sorry," I murmured and quickly bound his arm with the silk tie as best I could. When I'd finished, Rafe brought my hand to his cheek, which was warmer than before. He turned his face into my palm, resting there, eyes closed.

"It's my fault." The words broke apart as I spoke them. "I killed him and his blood got in your cuts."

"No." Sweat cut trails through the dirt on Rafe's face as he pushed himself up and got to his feet slowly. His breath came in gasps. "Chorda bit me an hour ago."

I rose on unsteady legs. "You're just saying that."

"He did. He — Look." He pointed past me but I didn't turn. I was searching for the truth in his face. "Lane, up there," he insisted, nudging me around.

A blinking light dominated the night sky, growing larger the closer it got, until we could hear the hum of rotary blades.

"It's Everson," I told him. "The patrol picked him up from the castle roof."

"Told you he'd get you back to Arsenal." Rafe was trying for smug, but all I could hear was the low vibration of fear in his voice.

The hovercopter swept the ground with a spotlight and sent the ferals scuttling and slinking into the shadows. Everson had come for us, but it was hopeless. We didn't dare leave the cage until the ferals cleared out of the zoo. I watched helplessly as the hovercopter veered south.

"You've got to get out there and signal them," Rafe said, pressing me toward the door.

I faced him. "If we get you to Arsenal, Dr. Solis can give you the inhibitor. Maybe it'll stop the virus from taking hold."

"People have tried that. It doesn't work." He glanced at the hovercopter, heading away. "Go," he growled.

"If you don't leave this cage, then neither will I, and Everson won't find either one of us."

He glared at me, but when I didn't relent, he exhaled sharply. "You are such a pain."

I took that for acquiescence and ducked under his undamaged arm, draping it over my shoulders. He let me help him to the cage door. But just as I opened it, a dark shape dashed past. I jerked back as more shapes leapt along the tops of the outside enclosures. My eyes skipped over the fleeing ferals, looking for a place out in the open, but where we wouldn't be attacked. Gunfire rattled on the other side of the building, giving me an idea.

"Come on!" I hurried out of the cage with him and down the path. He cursed under his breath and pressed his arm to his chest, but he kept up.

We rounded the building only to find ourselves in the middle of a nightmare. We backed up against the brick. The handlers had taken cover on the carousel. They popped up from behind the painted animals to shoot at the ferals. Blood sprayed as they managed to drop a few, but the ferals surged forward. More ferals came running up the path, sniffing out their prey. The handlers kept shooting until their clips were empty. There was a stunning moment of silence, and then the ferals attacked. They leapt over their dead, and the remaining humans scattered.

"Wait here," I told Rafe.

"Where're you —" he began, but I took off.

I ran for one of the dead handlers, stopping only long enough to pluck a flare gun from his apron, and headed for the carousel. As the ferals stormed the gates and swarmed over the zoo fence, I climbed onto the back of a carved elephant. I gripped the edge of the carousel's fiberglass canopy and swung up my leg.

The canopy was sturdy enough to stand on. From up there, I spotted Rafe limping along the path. "Stay where you are," I called.

Of course, he didn't listen. Bleeding and swearing, he clambered onto the canopy beside me.

"You are such a pain," I told him, and was rewarded with a strained smile that turned into a grimace as a shudder went through him.

"Shoot already." He jerked his chin at the gun in my hands.

I fired the flare gun into the sky. An instant later, the world around us felt like a hallucination as the flare exploded and illuminated the scattered bodies of ferals and handlers.

"They saw." Rafe pointed to the blinking light in the distance.

Sure enough, the light changed course.

As Rafe watched the hovercopter circle back, I saw that his aqua eyes now had a golden sheen, like sunlight reflecting off the surface of a lake. I couldn't move, couldn't breathe. "Your eyes . . ." I pressed my hand to his cheek before he could pull away. He'd grown so much warmer since we'd left the cage. "Please come back to Arsenal with me and let Dr. Solis look at you."

"They'd shoot me on sight." Rafe took my hand from his cheek, holding it curled in his own. "Can't blame them. I'd shoot me."

My heart lurched. "What does that mean? Rafe?"

"Nothing. Just promise me something. . . ." He looked down at my hand fisted in his and pushed his fingers into it, compelling me to entwine my fingers with his. A move that was perfectly him. He'd pushed himself into my heart much the same way. "Promise," he went on, "that if you hear about a grupped-up tiger gone feral, you'll hire a hunter to put me down."

"No," I gasped. "You'll have years before that happens and by then, Dr. Solis will have found a cure."

But the doctor could only find a cure if he had all the strains. Everson's words came back to me: "A cure would save everyone." He might be a guard through and through, but I was a hypocrite, because suddenly I was grateful that he'd made the choice that he had.

"Promise me, Lane," Rafe pleaded, letting me hear the depth of his anguish.

"Okay. I will," I said, hating the promise even as I made it. "But only if I hear about a feral infected with tiger, which I won't because I'll be on the other side of the wall."

A smile touched Rafe's lips, genuine this time. "You'll be back. A fierce girl like you belongs on the wild side."

I released his hand to move closer, not caring that he was fevered, and gently slipped my arms around his ribs. Rafe tensed at my touch, but then drew my face to him and brushed a ghost of a kiss on my forehead. The soft warmth of his lips sent a wave of longing through me and I tightened my hold on him as the hovercopter neared, its hum growing steadily louder.

"I won't go," I whispered against his shoulder. "I'm not leaving you when you're sick."

"You're not leaving me." He peeled out of my embrace and faced the edge of the canopy. "I'm leaving you."

"Wait," I gasped, reaching for him. I wasn't ready to lose him to the night and the chaos of the zoo. But when Rafe glanced back at me, my hand froze. His eyes were now as luminous as a predator's.

"In the bedroom . . . ," he said in a rough voice that I could barely hear over the approaching hovercopter. "Remember when I said I lied to Omar and the queen?"

I bobbed my head, unable to look away from his jewel-like eyes, shining in the darkness . . . so much like Chorda's.

"*That* was the lie. Good-bye, Lane," he said and then leapt into the darkness.

"No, wait!" A blinking red light caught my eye. My dial went black — out of power. Ignoring it, I scrambled down from the canopy to the carousel. When I hit the grass, I searched for some sign of him, but he'd vanished. I whirled to head for the entrance only to be brought up short by a firm grip on my arm.

"Why do girls always chase after the wild ones?" Mahari tsked.

The other lionesses slipped from the bushes as silent as shadows. "Same as us," Neve said, blood edging her smile. "She likes the hunt."

I struggled against Mahari's hold. Rafe's eyes had so distracted me — no, terrified me — I hadn't been following his words, couldn't piece together his meaning. "Let me go," I snarled at her. When she didn't, I slammed my heel down on her bare foot and she released me with a yowl.

The other lionesses closed in around me, their golden eyes gleaming. My breath caught at their ferocious beauty. With a slight shake of her head, Mahari stopped them in their tracks and their expressions relaxed.

"Told you she'd make a nice addition," Deepnita said, and licked a claw clean.

"Yes," Mahari agreed, eyeing me. "She's no rabbit."

"Get out of my way." I tried to push through their ranks.

"Don't waste your time looking for him," Charmaine said with a languid smirk. "He's long gone and you don't have any cat in you. You'll never catch him."

I slumped, realizing she was right.

"And why would you want to?" Deepnita asked in her rumbling purr of a voice. "Tigers are solitary creatures."

"But we're not," Neve said with a smile that might have come off as kittenish if it weren't for the accompanying growl.

Suddenly we were bathed in light. The whipping air stirred up the dust as the hovercopter slowed until it was above us. A hum filled the air and a rope ladder spilled out of the 'copter's open side. I looked up to see Everson leaning out, a gun in his hand, his expression determined. "No!" I shouted and waved to let him know that I was in no danger.

"You don't have to go," Mahari said, smoothing her tattered gown. She eyed me. "You could join us."

I stared at her, not quite sure what she was offering.

"You're a lioness. You know you are." She smiled, revealing her ivory fangs.

"You mean, let you infect me?"

"Let me *uncage* you," she corrected.

The temptation was there, all night. To be so strong . . . so fast . . . so terrifying. What would it feel like to move through the world so powerfully and with such confidence? "I want to be a lioness," I breathed. "I do. But I'm going to try doing it without the virus."

"Well, if you ever decide you want the trimmings" — Mahari extended her claws — "give me a roar." She waved the other lionesses onward. "Let's go, girls, we've got a castle to burn." And away they raced, roaring with fierce joy.

As the hovercopter glided over Chicago, I leaned out to see the ferals running through the abandoned streets, baying and howling, and I shivered. Chorda was dead, but now there were so many more ferals on the loose. Ferals who'd been abused by handlers and had good reason to hate humans. My eyes throbbed with the tears I held back. I wrapped my arms around myself. The ferals were free because of me and I didn't feel good about it.

"Did you get Rafe out?" Everson asked, sounding strained.

I felt a hundred fault lines spreading through me, invisible cracks that the slightest jostle would turn into fissures. "He's free. But he's infected."

Everson sucked in a sharp breath.

I turned back to the open door as the hovercopter swooped low over Chorda's castle. On the roof, manimal servants were throwing their collars and harnesses into the air while shouting in triumph. That much at least, I did feel good about. But where was Rafe in all of this chaos? I scanned the streets and shadows for him. His fever would be amping up now, and the thought of him suffering through it alone made *me* feel feverish.

"Chorda bit him?" Everson's hands were fisted in his lap.

I nodded, though I didn't believe it despite what Rafe had said. He'd gotten infected because of me. Yes, if I hadn't cut off Chorda's hand, he would have slashed Rafe's throat. And if I hadn't driven the machete into him, Chorda would have murdered us both. As Dr. Solis said, reason had its advantages. And yet knowing that I'd had no choice didn't comfort me in the slightest and it did even less for Rafe.

"Lane . . ." Everson faltered. "I'm sorry, I'm —"

"You don't have to apologize." I forced the words past the sob trapped in my throat. "You did the right thing, choosing that." I nodded to the box on his lap. "It wasn't my choice. I'd still pick Rafe. But I'm glad you put the samples first. And I'm sorry for the things I said, about you following orders. You weren't. You were following your conscience. I get that now. I do." Tears were streaming down my face now; I couldn't hold them in any longer.

"It's not about that. It's —" He took a breath and then began again. "When I got in the 'copter, Dr. Solis was on the radio."

I stiffened. He was using that consoling tone people took when they were about to break bad news.

"You remember the little girl at the gate, Jia, who brought in the mauled man?"

"The man who saved her from her own mother . . ."

"Yes. Dr. Solis says that he might not make it. He's lost too much blood."

Everson's voice seemed to be coming to me from far away. "Why are you telling me this?" I asked.

"Because it's Mack."

THIRTY-ONE

The moment we touched down on Arsenal, Everson took me to the infirmary, running interference on anyone who tried to question me. Two guards were stationed outside my father's room. Everson didn't follow me in.

I found Dr. Solis sitting by my dad's bed. My father was pale and sleeping, with his chest and leg encased in bandages. Dr. Solis rose and gestured for me to take his seat. "He's badly cut up, but he doesn't have Ferae."

"And he'll be okay?" I asked, touching my father's hand. He was so warm. Fevered?

Dr. Solis hesitated. "We're going to have to amputate his leg, Lane," he said gently. "I can't promise that he'll survive the operation."

"Amputate?" I echoed hollowly. "That's the only choice?"

Dr. Solis looked grim. "It's the only choice here, on Arsenal. In Iowa City the patrol has a surgery unit that might be able to repair the nerve damage. . . ."

"He's under arrest. They're not going to fly him over the wall."

"Actually, that's exactly what we're going to do," said a female voice from the doorway. I twisted to see a tall woman enter. At least I thought she was a woman. It was hard to tell through the transparent surgical mask that covered half of her face. It fit so snugly that it flattened her features like a stocking-faced thief's.

"Lane, this is Ms. Ilsa Prejean," Dr. Solis said.

Everson's mother!

Her hair was shaved as short as a line guard's and she wore latex gloves past her elbows. Guess the rumors about her germ phobia were true.

"Hello, Lane," she said.

I nodded in return, noticing she didn't offer me her hand. Didn't matter. It was her other offer that interested me. "You can get my dad back into the West?"

"Yes, I'll have you both flown to Iowa City in my private hovercopter."

I eyed her, trying to spot the catch. "Why would you do that?"

She waved a gloved hand at my father as if it were obvious. "Mack allowed us to test the inhibitor. The infected people in Moline wouldn't have touched it if a line guard had marched in and offered it to them. But they trust Mack. Not only did they take the inhibitor, they told him in detail how the medication was affecting them. The information he brought back is invaluable. The least Titan can do is fix up his leg. And you, Lane?" Her mouth widened under the stretchy surgical mask. A smile maybe, though smooshed. "Because of you, Everson brought in twenty-nine of the missing strains."

I gasped and looked to Dr. Solis for confirmation.

He nodded. "We just took a big leap forward toward finding a cure or at least a vaccine. Thanks to you, Lane."

"No," I said. "It was Everson. I only showed him where the blood samples were stored." He'd been right to make those samples his priority, even if they weren't mine. Those missing strains would go a lot further toward helping Rafe and millions of other people than anything I'd done.

"So," Ms. Prejean said, clasping her gloved hands. "I will get you and your father safely back into the West. Consider it payment for services rendered."

I slumped. "My dad can't go back. If he does, Director Spurling will have him executed."

"No, she won't." Ms. Prejean sounded pleased with herself. "Not if I say that Mack has been working for Titan all along on a classified assignment." Her eyes — pale gray like Everson's — crinkled over her transparent face mask. "Biohaz can't arrest him if he had authorization to enter the Feral Zone. And there is no higher authority than me when it comes to the quarantine line."

Within the hour, I accompanied the gurney bearing my father through the camp and across the shadowy bridge to the landing pad where Ms. Prejean's hovercopter waited. Along the way, guards stared at my dad, but none gave me a second look. And why would they? I was just a medic in green scrubs thanks to Dr. Solis.

Once the guards had gotten my father safely aboard the hovercopter, I headed for the edge of the landing pad where Everson stood in a pool of light talking with the pilot. We hadn't spoken since he brought me to my father in the infirmary. The pilot glanced from him to me and quickly excused herself.

"I wanted to thank you," I said, joining him by the lamppost.

He nodded, a line guard once more, ramrod posture and no hint of emotion on his face under the bandages.

There were several other guards on the landing pad and two more by the gate to the bridge. I knew why he was being so formal — they were watching — and I knew I should let it go. But we were standing so close to the dark, land-mine-strewn hill where we'd met just days ago and seeing him with the same cool expression as that night, appearing so unchanged, made it feel as if our trip to the Feral Zone had never happened. And that stung. But I didn't know how to draw out the boy underneath the military bearing. "Well, thanks and . . . good-bye."

He dropped his gaze to my medic shirt, eyeing it as though it was transparent. Long enough to make me uncomfortable.

"Um, what —"

He stepped closer and slid his hands under my hair. As his fingertips tickled the back of my neck, I grew still, sur-prised that he'd kiss me here. Not that I cared if the other guards watched. I wanted him to, in spite of the ache that had filled me since Rafe had disappeared into the darkness. As I tipped my face up to his, a small weight lifted from my chest and Everson drew back — no kiss.

He held up a gold chain in the sliver of space between us, letting my dial dangle. My cheeks grew hot. But then my embarrassment over mistaking his intention gave way to panic. I couldn't let him confiscate my dial. Those images were all that I had left of Rafe and Cosmo, and I needed to remember their faces. For them and for me.

"Put it in your pocket," Everson said quietly. "If a guard sees the chain, he'll know what it is even if you hide the dial under your shirt." He pressed it into my palm and curled my fingers around it.

A wash of gratitude warmed me and I stuffed the dial deep into the pocket of my scrubs. "Thank you," I whispered.

He gave the barest nod.

"Will you let me know when you're back in the West?" I asked.

"It won't be anytime soon," he said, relaxing a little. "Mack's fetching days are over, and not just because of his leg. But someone's got to take medicine to the manimals in Moline or they'll start mutating again."

"You would do that?"

"First, I have to get them to trust me." He smiled faintly. "I didn't make such a good impression last time."

The hovercopter's rotary blades started to hum behind me.

"Go to the mayor of Moline," I said in a rush of words, the solution clear in my mind. "Tell Hagen what happened to my dad. She'll want to know. And then tell the whole compound about Rafe — how he killed the rogue like he said he would. But that" — the ache in my chest intensified — "he paid a terrible price to keep them safe. And be sure to tell them that you're his friend."

A flush crept up Everson's neck. "Some friend. I would have left him in the zoo."

"He'd understand. He told me to leave him behind if I got the chance to escape."

"But you didn't," Everson said, his voice huskier than usual.

The wind from the hovercopter whipped my hair around my face. I turned to see a guard wave at me from the 'copter's open door. "I've got to go."

"Stay out of trouble," Everson said, only half joking. "And stay on your side of the wall."

As I nodded, the hill behind him caught my eye again. Only three days had passed since I'd come skittering down to the landing pad. Not much time at all, and yet I felt so different. More like the girl Everson thought I was — the one who did bold, unpredictable things. Who took action . . .

"You better —" He gestured *one moment* to the beckoning guard.

I leaned up, slipped my fingers into his cropped hair, and brought his mouth to mine. Everson froze, then his arms tightened around my waist, and so I deepened our kiss. This time when our lips parted, he was the one who looked slightly dazed. "What was that?"

"I didn't want to miss the moment," I said lightly. "See you around, Cruz." I would, too. I just didn't know where or when. As I headed for the hovercopter, I glanced back to see a very unguard-like smile on his face.

I sat by my father's gurney as the hovercopter lifted into the air. My dad twisted and muttered urgently as we flew toward the Titan wall, which was as imposing as ever. I touched my dial in my pocket. No one had patted me down or checked my bag when I came aboard. Maybe the guards thought that frisking a guest of the CEO would be overstepping their bounds. And so I was taking home hours of raw footage — enough to keep me busy, editing, for a long, long time. Because, as I'd learned, the fastest way to get people to care about neglected animals was to show them the animals. And I would — someday.

My dad stirred and then opened his eyes, but he was so pumped up with painkillers, he looked at me without recognition.

"Dad, it's me. I'm here."

His forehead shimmered with sweat. He was barely conscious. "Lane? You're not real."

"I am. See?" I gave his hand a gentle squeeze.

"Delaney?" His brows drew together. "Where are we?"

"In a patrol 'copter. Everything is going to be fine," I assured him.

"What's happened to you?" He struggled to sit up and winced. "Your face . . . are you hurt?" He was working to call up each word.

"It's just dirt, Dad. Nothing to worry about. Go back to sleep."

He blinked, fighting the drug coursing through him.

"Hey, want to hear a story?" I asked.

His expression softened and a corner of his mouth lifted. "About a brave little girl?"

"No, about a girl who's not so little and way too tame," I said. "But she did go on an adventure to find her father. She took the tunnel under the mountain and didn't get blown up by the harpy eggs. She made friends with a killer robot, who didn't like killing at all. And she found the wild boy who lives all alone in a castle."

Now, my father looked at me, completely present for the first time. "You found Rafe?"

My heart clenched as I nodded. "He helped me, looked out for me. We became friends." Or was it more than that? I shook off the thought, not wanting to pull apart my feelings for Rafe just yet. Not when picturing him fevered and alone made me want to sob myself sick.

"In the Feral Zone?" My dad's fingers tightened around mine. "Lane, I . . . I'm sorry."

"Don't be. I get it now — why you like coming here. Why you feel you have to."

"I should have told you."

"You did." I lifted our hands and rubbed my cheek over his knuckles. "Every night before bed."

His eyes drifted closed once more. "I just wanted you to be safe . . . and happy," he mumbled.

I stared out the window and didn't share the thought that had come into my mind: *Safe and happy don't always go together.*

With his eyes still closed, my dad began to murmur. His words were soft and blurred, but I recognized the way they rose and fell. It was the rhythm of a bedtime story. Gasping, he tried to finish a nearly inaudible thought. "And they . . . they loved . . ." And he fell into a deep sleep once more. But I knew how the story ended — how all of his stories had always ended — and so I finished it for him.

"And they loved happily ever after." Leaning down, I kissed his cheek. "I'll try, Dad. I will, but this story isn't finished yet." The hovercopter zoomed over the wall's ramparts and the line guards stopped marching to send up a salute. "Not even close."

· ACKNOWLEDGMENTS ·

With much gratitude, I would like to acknowledge the people who helped me take this story from a glimmer of a concept to a published book.

A huge thanks to my agent, Josh Adams, for championing my idea from the start and for his patience, perspective, and much-needed nudging along the way; and to my editor, Nick Eliopulos, who's been supportive beyond belief and whose keen story sense has made this book so much better.

Many thanks to everyone at Scholastic for their enthusiasm and faith and for all the amazing work they've done to bring my book into the world.

A special thank-you to the members of my writers group for reading my ugly drafts and giving me invaluable feedback: Molly Backes, Logan Turner, and especially Debbie Kraus, who's helped me through three books now with her insightful critiques. And to my dear friend Merle Reskin, for cheering me on and for providing me with the most charming writer's hideaway imaginable, Thatchitty Cottage. And my mother and father, avid readers both, who encouraged my love of stories.

And finally, extra-special thanks to my family, immediate and extended, for your love, encouragement, and infinite patience with me when I slipped away during vacations and holidays to write for an hour or two or three. . . .

Lane McEvoy has a promise to keep.
Even if it breaks her heart.
Even if it kills her.

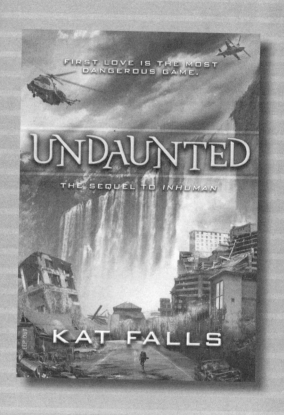

FIRST LOVE IS THE MOST
DANGEROUS GAME.

UNDAUNTED

THE SEQUEL TO INHUMAN

KAT FALLS

Don't miss the genre-bending,
pulse-pounding sequel to INHUMAN.

this is teen

Wan
lates
upda
YA b
and a
plus
chan
win g
book
mont...

Join the conversation
with This Is Teen!

**Visit thisisteen.com to find out how to reach us
using your favorite form of social media!**

SCHOLASTIC™
Scholastic Inc.

TE